# WHAT PEOPLE ARE SAYING
## ABOUT SUSAN MAY WARREN

*"In* Reclaiming Nick, *Susan May Warren once again delivers that perfect combination of heart-pumping suspense and heart-warming romance. In her trademark, fast-paced storytelling style, Susan keeps the reader enthralled and invested from page one to a very satisfying ending. I can't wait for book two in this fabulous new series!"*

TRACEY BATEMAN, AUTHOR OF THE CLAIRE EVERETT SERIES

*"Susan Warren writes with a fresh, new voice and creates characters that will delight her readers."*

KAREN KINGSBURY, AUTHOR OF THE BEST-SELLING
REDEMPTION SERIES AND THE FIRSTBORN SERIES

*"I'm proud of Susie; my friend gets better with every book."*

—DEE HENDERSON, AUTHOR OF *THE MARRIAGE WISH*

*"Susan May Warren is an extremely gifted storyteller, always keeping her readers in suspense to the end. . . . Susan's books are guaranteed to entertain, thrill, and inspire. Without question, they fall in the Can't-Put-Down category!"*

—D. M., AMAZON.COM READER

*"This author needs to write more books! I love her style."*

—C. T., AMAZON.COM READER

*"Susan Warren is a writer to watch! . . . Susan's characters are so real you can almost hear them breathe."*

—AMAZON.COM READER

# RECLAIMING NICK

# SUSAN MAY
# WARREN

## RECLAIMING NICK

Tyndale House Publishers, Inc., Carol Stream, Illinois

Visit Tyndale's exciting Web site at www.tyndale.com

*TYNDALE* and Tyndale's quill logo are registered trademarks of Tyndale House Publishers, Inc.

*Reclaiming Nick*

Designed by Jessie McGrath

Edited by Lorie Popp

**Library of Congress Cataloging-in-Publication Data**

Warren, Susan, date.
  Reclaiming Nick : noble legacy / Susan May Warren.
    p. cm.
  ISBN-13: 978-1-4143-1017-6 (pbk. : alk. paper)
  ISBN-10: 1-4143-1017-X (pbk. : alk. paper)
  I. Title.
  PS3623.A865R43 2006
  813′.6–dc22                                    2006017532

Printed in the United States of America

11  10  09  08  07  06
7   6   5   4   3   2   1

*For Your glory, Lord*

# ACKNOWLEDGMENTS

Our God is an amazing God. Not only did He put this story in my heart, but He gave me the resources to accomplish it. I saw 1 Thessalonians 5:24 worked out through the following people.

Dan and Julie Viren and their brother Bob, who took my interest in ranches to heart and arranged a visit out west. Thank you for your encouragement and enthusiasm!

Alan and Jan Lloyd—gracious ranchers who hosted two city slickers, patiently answered all my questions (including "What's the difference between a steer and a bull?"), and let me see inside the world of ranching under the big sky. Thank you for letting me fall in love with your world.

Curt and MaryAnn Lund, who took care of my boys while I disappeared into the Montana hills. Thank you for passing on the legacy of love and faith to your grandchildren.

Dannette Lund, legal whiz. Thank you for laboring with me to get the legal plot and jargon right. You're a gift to me. Any mistakes are entirely mine.

Sarah Warren, my traveling buddy, who flew into nowhere with me, navigated us to a ranch in a place not even on a map, and patiently followed me for three days, taking pictures and serving her mother. God gave me a precious gift when He gave me you.

Rachel Hauck, fellow author and all-around great plotter. The Frothy Monkey will always be one of my favorite memories. Your friendship makes my life rich.

Michele Nickolay, proofer extraordinaire. Thank you for your late nights! Your encouragement and insights are such a blessing to me.

Lorie Popp, my editor, who makes me sound good! Thank you for your hard work, your enthusiasm, and your attention to details!

Karen Watson, my new editor, who caught my vision for this series. Thank you for your wisdom and commitment to making this story exactly what I hoped.

Dave Kirchner, a modern-day hero. And his wife, Kim, who is a heroine in her own right. Thank you for inspiring us to think eternally and take to heart what it means to lay down your life for another.

Dan and Becky Schultz, who fought the good fight of faith. May the Lord bless you in this next season of faith and joy.

Finally, to Andrew. You show me every day what love means.

*I am certain that God, who began the good work within you, will continue his work until it is finally finished on the day when Christ Jesus returns.*

PHILIPPIANS 1:6

# CHAPTER 1

WHEN THE LANKY form of Saul Lovell walked into the Watering Hole Café, dragging with him the remnants of the late April chill, Nick Noble knew that his last hope of redemption had died.

Nick didn't have time to deal with the arrival of his father's lawyer. Not with one fist wrapped in the collar of Jake's duster and a forearm pinning his cohort Rusty to the wall.

"We were simply offering to buy her lunch," Rusty snarled.

"I'm not stupid. I know exactly what you were offering." Nick motioned for the girl to move away from the pair as he upped his pressure against Rusty's Adam's apple. "It's okay, honey. They're just fresh from riding fence. You go home now and say hi to your folks from me."

He didn't comment on her low-cut shirt or the way it seemed to have material missing at the waistline too. And a run into Miles City three hours south for looser-fitting pants might be in order. He'd have to swing by her parents' place after closing tonight to warn them of their daughter's recent bent toward trouble.

Only that wasn't his job anymore, was it? He had to stop thinking like a cop before it landed him in more hot water.

The girl glanced at Rusty, as if hurt, then turned on her boot heel and flounced toward the door, followed by her blonde best friend.

Nick didn't like the way Jake watched them leave. "If I see you within ten feet of them, I'll run you all the way back to the border."

Jake shoved him away, and Nick let go, not interested in swallowing one more whiff of day-old whiskey breath.

"You stay away from those two girls," Nick repeated as the door jangled shut behind the ladies. He noted the petite brunette who had entered during the tussle and now waited by the door. Tourist, waiting to be seated.

"I ain't interested in nuthin' she ain't already advertisin.'" Jake dusted himself off.

"Don't make me hurt you." Nick watched a flash of memory cross Jake's face.

Clearly it wasn't enough to deter his mouth. "There you go again, Noble. Jumpin' to conclusions. You've already got us tried and hung. Same as ole Jimmy."

Nick turned back toward the counter, quelling a flare of anger. "Take a seat. I'll get you boys a pile of beans."

Rusty, however, wasn't ready to move on. Nick saw the swing coming out of his peripheral vision and stepped back, letting the kid's fist breeze by. He rounded on Rusty, warning in his tone. "Don't start."

"You're not the law around here anymore, Noble."

"In here, I am. And if I need to follow you home to make sure you don't detour toward the girl's place, then I'll get my keys."

"A man can't even be friendly no more round you." Jake pushed past him and found a stool at the counter, a wolfish grin on his face.

Nick kept his stare pinned on Rusty. The cowpoke's off-kilter Stetson, his five o'clock shadow and padded jean jacket gave him the look of Billy the Kid. All he needed was a six-shooter and a wanted poster.

"Sit down, Rusty. I know all you've eaten for three days is oatmeal and coffee. There's a pot of chili and beans in the kitchen that'll make you forget all about high winds and Herefords."

Rusty gave him a tight glare and reached into his pocket for a pack of smokes.

Nick shook his head, pointed to the No Smoking sign, and headed behind the bar, calling in the order to the cook. His eyes flickered over to Saul. The attorney still wore the flat-topped black Stetson like Adam Cartwright out of *Bonanza* and had dressed for the drive out to nowhere in eastern Montana in a pair of boots and a wool-lined leather jacket. He met Nick's glance with a curt nod from his place at the end of the counter.

Yep, this was exactly the moment Nick had dreaded. He grabbed a cup, plunked it down in front of Saul, filled it, and walked away. They'd get around to the topic of his visit. Meanwhile, Nick had two surly cowboys at the counter, a rancher and his wife at table three, the hardware-store owner and his assistant hiding out at the table in back, the tourist waiting for a seat, and a redhead in a ten-gallon hat at the end of the bar, watching him with a frown.

He felt some solace in the fact that his father couldn't see him now. However, having Saul here seemed nearly as humiliating.

He took the rancher's and his wife's orders, served the redhead some water and a menu, gave the hardware-store owner his bill, and gestured toward a booth for the brunette.

Saul drank his coffee, eyes on Nick, saying nothing.

Outside, the wind chased paper along the cracked pavement of Main Street, a chill whistling through the cracks of the plate-glass windows. The etching from the Watering Hole Café now read Wclciino Hclc, but like everything in the tiny town of Welles-ley, Montana, signs were irrelevant. People either knew their way around town in their sleep or they were passing through. Quickly. Being right off U.S. Highway 2 on a straight shot between Minot and the Pacific Ocean helped some with the desperate economy. But over the last five years the harsh winters and drought had driven off all but the hardiest of cowmen and women. Even Nick would have left if he'd had anywhere else to go.

That anywhere had arrived on his doorstep today.

He served Jake and Rusty their beans and filled their coffees before heading to the redhead for her order.

"Steak and eggs," she said, closing her menu.

Filling a water glass, he stuck a menu under his arm and shook his head, watching the brunette at the booth clean the table with a wet wipe. He forced a smile as he approached her. Maybe she was one of those obsessive-compulsive types he'd read about in school. Or worse, one with a schizophrenic edge. He set down the glass quietly. "Would you like some disinfectant?"

When she glanced up, he saw a blush. "Oh no. There was some . . . ketchup." She took the menu. "What's good here?"

"The beef." He gave her a lazy smile, hoping she caught the joke. *Cattle country, honey, get it?*

She frowned. "Do you have a Caesar salad?"

He quirked an eyebrow that broadcast his answer.

She sighed, and he recognized fatigue around her blue eyes. "How about a house salad?"

"We're short on the lettuce and tomatoes right now. Can I interest you in a cheeseburger?" He glanced at Saul. The man watched him with a half smirk, probably remembering the time Nick had worked at Lolly's Diner. That had lasted all of one day and ended when his father had dragged him home by the scruff of his collar. The second time he'd left home, however, it took.

How he wished now he'd returned.

"All right then, I'll have . . . a bowl of chili beans." She closed the menu and smiled at him, tucking her dark hair behind her ear. For a second he wondered where she came from and if he should make sure she left town okay.

Especially after the article in last week's *Sheridan News* about Jimmy McPhee's release.

According to the newspaper, Jimmy was innocent. Nick didn't know what to believe. He hadn't exactly turned over every stone searching for Jenny Butler's killer. No, he'd bitten when they'd arrested Jimmy McPhee—hungover and smelling of guilt—for her murder. He'd bitten because Jimmy had pushed the law too far this time.

Nick should have listened to his gut, been the man his father had taught him to be, the one who protected the innocent and stood up for the truth. Clearly he'd left that man back at the Silver Buckle Ranch.

Thankfully, a drifter's testimony had exonerated Jimmy McPhee and set him free. Five years too late.

"Very good," Nick said to the woman as he took her menu. "You in town long?"

"Visiting family," she said. "Near Scobey."

"That's about thirty miles north of here. Roads are clear—you'll get there by bedtime." He resisted the urge to encourage her to stay the night in town. But the only beds open this time of year were the hunting cabins, and he wouldn't even send his sister there, even though Stefanie spent half her life camped out on the open trail. "Better leave before the sun hits the horizon," he said, surrendering to the ex-cop inside him as he turned away.

The cook had the steak and eggs under the heat rings, and Nick served them to the redhead. "You here for the rodeo camp?" he asked as he poured her a cup of coffee. Twice a year, a rodeo camp for barrel racers, bronc busters, and bareback riders was held right outside Wellesley.

Nick remembered his brother, Rafe, attending once—and coming home with more bruises than a truckload of apples. He'd figured out how to stay on a bronc by now.

"Nope. Just passin' through." The redhead covered her eggs with ketchup.

Jake and Rusty finished their meal, threw down a few bills, and left without a word.

Glancing at the rancher and his wife, still deep in conversation and not needing him, Nick knew he'd whittled his procrastination down to a nub. "Howdy, Saul," he said, a sigh at the end of his greeting as he faced his father's oldest friend and attorney.

"Good to see you, son."

Only Nick knew how well Saul delivered that lie. "You too, sir." Nick picked up the coffeepot and a cup and headed around the counter to an empty booth.

Saul followed him, sliding into the opposite bench. "I guess you're expecting me," he said, reaching for a toothpick. "No reason to pussyfoot."

Nick nodded, poured himself a cup of coffee. "How did it happen?"

"In his sleep. Your father went peacefully. Stefanie was there. And Rafe had been by not long before that."

Nick ran his thumb and forefinger along the handle of his mug. His mouth felt tinny. "When?"

Saul looked past Nick. "Near a month ago. We tried to find you, but the army still had you listed in Miles City. Newspaper in Sheridan had an article about that fella Jimmy McPhee last week. Tracked you down from there."

Something inside Nick had died when he'd seen that article. What was worse, however, was that he should have made it home years ago. He didn't exactly have anything in Wellesley holding him back.

Except shame, of course.

Saul chewed a toothpick.

"How's Stefanie?" *And Cole? And Maggie?* But he couldn't—no, *wouldn't*—ask about them.

"I can't lie to you, Nick. The Silver Buckle's in trouble. The drought has been bad. And one out of every three cows didn't conceive last year. The herd is dwindling, and Stefanie's only one woman. The Buckle is in debt over its head, and she's thinking of turning the ranch into a dude operation." Saul shook his head. "Your father would have my hide, but I can't stop her."

Nick stared into his coffee, cringing at the image of city slickers from Seattle or Denver or even California stomping on the silver sage and black-eyed Susans as they tried ranch life on for size. He closed his eyes. "I should have been there."

Saul said nothing.

Nick opened his eyes, taking a good look at his surroundings. From the kitchen the cook sang an old hymn. The rich smells of coffee, French fries, and baked apples filled the café. Late-afternoon shadows cast a somber glow across the dingy linoleum.

"There's something else, Nick." Saul drummed his fingers on the table for a moment, then reached inside his jacket pocket. "There's been an offer made on the ranch." He slid a packet of papers toward Nick.

Nick looked at the packet, uncomprehending. "An offer?"

"To buy you out."

Nick refused to touch it, feeling it a betrayal suddenly of everything his family had built. "I can't . . . I'm not . . . why would you bring this to me?" Surely Stefanie wasn't in on this. She loved the land.

Saul removed his toothpick and twirled it between two weathered fingers. Nick wondered if Saul still ran his own herd, falling back on his law degree as a sideline. Most people in their hometown of Phillips ranched first and fed their families with a second job.

"With the chunk of land your mother left you and your father's bequest, you own the biggest section of the remaining Noble property. Of course, you'll have to wait until the land officially becomes yours, but as your father's lawyer, I'm obliged to convey the offer to you. You can sign the purchase agreement today contingent on–"

"Wait–go back to the word *remaining*. I don't understand. Was some of it sold?" Nick pushed the folded papers back toward Saul.

Saul hesitated a moment. "It was divided into four sections."

Nick stared at him. "Last count I had, there are only three of us in the Noble family—Stefanie, Rafe, and me."

"Actually, you and your siblings are entitled to only half of the Silver Buckle land. Your father deeded the other half to Colton St. John."

*Half?* Nick stared at Saul, nearly choking on the word. "Half?" Nick felt something hot and heavy punch through his chest. "The Silver Buckle has been in the Noble family for three generations! How could my father—?" Words vanished, and Nick found himself on his feet, stalking back to the counter, coffeepot in hand.

"You need a refill?" Nick bit out the words to the redhead, filling her coffee before she answered. The order of beans sat baking under the heat lights; he grabbed the bowl without a tray, burning his hands. He plunked it down before the brunette, dropping a spoon on the table next to the bowl. It clattered and nearly fell on the floor. He noticed Saul watching him with pursed lips as he turned away.

Cole St. John. Nick still had a scar on his hand where they'd mixed blood so many years ago. Blood brothers, through thick and thin.

Cole St. John, wide receiver to his being quarterback, bulldogging partner, coconspirator in the case of the missing school mascot.

Cole St. John, son of the woman who'd stolen his father, Bishop Noble.

Nick swallowed as he sidled close to Saul's booth. He kept his voice low and tight. "What did he do to make my father deed him our land?"

Saul shook his head.

Nick looked out at the bullet gray sky and its refusal to grant a glimmer of cheer. This morning from his apartment above the café he'd seen a line of black clouds piled up against the far-off mountains. He'd hoped it meant rain, but apparently it only meant high winds and trouble.

"I may not have been the son I should have over the past ten years, Mr. Lovell, but I can promise my father this: I'll make sure that St. John never sets one foot onto Silver Buckle land."

It took Piper Sullivan about 2.3 seconds to confirm that everything she'd assumed about Nick Noble hit the mark. Underneath that six-foot-one-inch frame, dark eyes, and muscular alpha-male exterior lurked a bona fide bully. A man whose world revolved around one focal point—himself.

Case in point, his chest-thumping attack on the two tired cowboys making small talk with some pretty locals. What did he think would happen—that they'd buy the girls one too many milk shakes? maybe ask them to go for a stroll along the muddy street? She hadn't spotted even a hint of a saloon in this no-stoplight town, and they looked like two post–high school girls stuck in a one-horse smudge on the map. And Protector of the Weak had just eliminated two of their very few options for escape.

And if his barroom-bouncer act didn't confirm her reporter's instincts, his low-toned vow to the lanky man at the booth said it all.

Nick Noble was trouble.

"I'll leave first thing tomorrow," Noble growled as he moved away from the booth. Clearly the man had delivered some dark news, because Noble's expression went from sizzling to downright hostile. And the way he poured her coffee made her want to don protective gear.

"Thank you," she mumbled, not wanting to add to his mood. Thanks to her father she knew how quickly a bad mood accelerated to danger, pain, and sirens. And this time, thanks to Noble, Jimmy wasn't here to protect her.

"You okay, miss?"

The voice, full of more concern than she expected, jerked her from her thoughts. She looked up, frowning. Noble stood over her, coffeepot in his hand.

"You're hurt." He gestured to her bandaged wrist.

She realized she'd been rubbing it again. Even bandaged, the scar still felt funny, nearly numb. Wouldn't it be nice if all wounds eventually went numb?

She found a different voice. Not that he would recognize her, but she hoped to smear beyond recognition any associations for the next time they met. "It's healing. I'll be fine."

She watched as Noble filled the other woman's coffee, then dug out her guest check. The redhead at the counter paid him, and he didn't even look as she slipped out the door, obviously hoping for his attention. Apparently he didn't bend easily to feminine wiles. Perfect. Piper didn't want him assuming anything the next time she showed up with an innocent smile.

She could do this. She could. They didn't award her the Silver Pen for investigative journalism two years running for buckling under pressure. After going undercover at a stockyard to expose a ring of mad-cow beef smugglers and wheedling her way into a lumber company to confirm illegal clear-cutting of a national forest, she could easily fake her way onto the Silver Buckle Ranch. And hopefully into Nick Noble's confidence.

She owed it to Jimmy. To her mother. To herself.

She ate slowly, gathering information, listening, plotting. Piper remembered the headline she'd read on the Internet: "Convicted Murderer Exonerated." She wondered where Jimmy had spent his first night out of jail. By the time she'd read the news, it had been too late to travel down to Colorado to greet him. She didn't know what to say, anyway. Especially after she hadn't visited him even once during his five-year prison term. She felt sick that she'd actually been *relieved* when he'd bargained for a lesser sentence and she didn't have to appear in court. She'd been able to hide from all of it while her half brother lived his nightmare out in the open.

*I'm sorry I didn't believe you, Jimmy. I'm sorry I failed you.*

Her way would be better for both of them—proving that Noble had lied, had purposely framed her brother for murder. And proving that her brother could have never been a killer would be a thousand times better than any apology, regardless of how heartfelt. Payback. Justice. Healing.

If Piper played her cards right, her ploy would net them both a new future.

Noble slipped her a guest check, and she peeled off the bills and left the café. For now she knew enough.

Noble was guilty. And she planned not only to prove it but to destroy his life. Just like he had Jimmy's.

❧

There were times when Maggy St. John felt like the land might consume her whole. It poured over her senses—all of them. The sharp smell of sagebrush, the squeak of prairie dogs in the warm afternoon sun, and the wind, tasting of spring and new life, throwing tumbleweeds from one horizon to the next. The sight of the morning sun rising over the east, gold like syrup running over the bluffs and draws, and in the afternoon, kissing her face with warmth. She loved this land. And she hoped it loved her back.

She tugged her beaten hat over her auburn braids, tightened the string under her chin, and gauged the clouds for rain. Cumulus had been gathering in the east, over Silver Buckle land all day, but they refused to unload their burden on any of their lands, greedy for the western mountains. *Please, Lord, let it be a fertile summer.* Growing up on the range, Maggy had seen many a drought but none like the last five years. The ground seemed dead, and the billows of dust in the wake of passing vehicles this early in the season set her jaw tight.

"Ma, should I catch Suds for you?" CJ closed the door to the house behind him and met her at the edge of the porch. "Or do you want to ride my horse this afternoon?"

Maggy smiled down at her ten-year-old, reaching out to wipe a smear of ketchup from his mouth.

He jerked away. "Mom!"

"I can't believe you can even move after four hot dogs."

CJ laughed as he buckled the straps to his leather chaps. Thankfully, he had the energy of ten cowhands because she and her husband, Cole, counted on their son more than they ought. Especially now.

Tugging on his hat, CJ stared out at the sky with the wisdom of a seasoned cowhand. His reddish brown hair stuck out the bottom of the hat, curling around his ears. Sometimes CJ looked more like Cole than she'd ever imagined he would.

"We gotta get those heifers into the barn before the storm hits or they'll panic and drop their babies out in the field." He glanced at her as he tugged on his worn work gloves. "I'll take Suds if you want."

"No, I'll ride him. He's just mad because I didn't put him in with his girlfriend last night. They have a little thing going. He won't buck me off again." Her hip still hurt from the animal's last temper tantrum.

"What about riding Pecos?" CJ glanced at the paint that stood in the corral. The horse lifted his nose to smell the wind, as if longing for home.

"Not yet." *Maybe never.* She still couldn't believe that Bishop Noble had gifted her the horse. Trying to repair the broken bridges. But they weren't his bridges to repair, and well, sometimes things were better left broken.

Maggy zipped her jacket tight against her chin, feeling the chill seep into her body. Today she wore her long johns under her jeans and three layers—a thermal shirt, a flannel shirt, and her wool-lined jacket. Sometimes she felt ninety instead of twenty-eight. And stiff and crabby to boot. But thirty minutes on the back of her horse would have her limber and sweating, and the cool air would revive her youth as she hunted down the heifers—soon-to-be new mothers—hidden in the draws of the winter pasture.

For an unchecked second, she wished for the days when Cole rode Suds. How many times had she watched him from this porch, riding in from the range, with their collie at his heels? With his wide shoulders, a white smile against his tanned face, hat-tousled dusty brown hair, and lazy dark brown eyes, Cole conjured up every image of an Old West hero. His patience and strength had drawn her in, and every minute beside him had made her a grateful woman. If only she could somehow still make him believe that.

They'd made a good team back then, when the alfalfa rippled like waves under the wind and their love felt young and forever. When their dreams felt within their grasp.

Those easy days had slipped away from them right before their eyes. And Maggy hadn't the first clue how to keep from losing them completely.

But now everything would change. With Bishop's death, regardless of the grief, they'd find a new season of forevers. A new season of hope. *Please, Lord.*

Maggy followed CJ to the barn and watched while her son roped her horse, then his horse, Coyote. He had a natural throw, so like another man she'd once admired.

"Where do we start?" CJ asked after he'd saddled his horse.

Maggy kneed Suds in the gut. He let out his air, and she quickly cinched the saddle tight. "Your father said he saw the heifers bunching up near the south draw. He went out to see if he could locate Old Nellie. She still thinks she's some sort of midwife."

Maggy had learned, first by watching her father poke cows as a cowboy for hire and then by working shoulder to shoulder with Cole, that cows weren't unlike human mothers. The first baby scared them and usually threw them off. More often than not it took an experienced mother to come alongside and show them the ropes. Old Nellie mothered the first timers like a grandmother, earning her keep every year for nearly a decade.

Maggy wished her own mother had done the same for her. But they'd been too busy trying to start over. After watching her parents pack up their lives and move to Arizona hoping for an easier life,

Maggy swore to herself that by the time she got too old to run a ranch, she'd have land, a home, and enough cash to hire the help she'd need. And someday CJ would own his father's land.

*His father's land.* Bishop Noble had kept his word. She could hardly believe that the land might be theirs. She'd said more than one prayer over the past month that Saul Lovell wouldn't be able to track down Nick Noble. Or rather that Nick's anger had cooled, and he might be willing to forgive for all their sakes. Now *that* would be a miracle from the Lord.

CJ led the horses through the gate before Maggy closed it, then swung into the saddle. She had thought that by now she'd have at least one more son to help with the work. If Cole's health didn't improve, they might have to take on a hand come summer.

The clouds shadowed the trampled grass. Only the creak of the saddle and the occasional lowing of cattle passed for conversation as they climbed the ridge that overlooked the winter pasture. They brought the cattle in close during the cold months to keep an eye on them and make it easier to distribute the hay. Sometimes Maggy hiked out here to stand at the ridge and check on the herd, heavy with calves, their black bodies huddled nose to nose for warmth. She loved the sight of a contented Angus.

Today, however, the herd seemed loud and agitated. Maggy and CJ reined their horses, scanning the horizon.

"What is it, Mom?"

"I don't know. I don't see your dad. And something has the cows spooked."

"Is it a wolf?"

Maggy shook her head, not sure. It drove her to fury when the government had kept the predator on the endangered-species list.

Ranchers had little protection against wolves stalking and destroying thousands of dollars of precious beef. She'd called her senator's office so many times, she practically had his telephone number imprinted on her fingers.

"Maybe it's a coyote. Or the weather." Although large animals, cows were easily spooked, and the looming storm might have them on edge. She urged her horse forward, watching for prairie-dog holes as they descended into the valley.

The sound of nervous mooing came from a tangle of cottonwoods that sheltered the still-frozen creek.

"C'mon," CJ said to Coyote, breaking out in front of Maggy.

For a second, she heard Cole's words: *"CJ's cowboy enough to handle a .22. It's men who kill, not weapons."* Still, Maggy couldn't help wanting to hold CJ close, especially now. He'd have to fill Cole's shoes soon enough.

She urged her horse to a canter. Overhead, a hawk screamed, slicing through the brisk air, right into her soul.

CJ disappeared over the edge of the wash.

Spotting Maggy's horse, a cow ran from her path, its eyes bulging in fear.

"Mom! Come quick!" CJ's voice carried the edge of panic she'd come to fear. A tone that drove their hopes and dreams one more step out of reach.

*No, Lord, please–*

Maggy topped the ridge and her heart caught.

Along the shore of the creek, in a pocket of mud and trampled cheat grass, his hat lost and his leg crumpled beneath him at an ugly angle, Cole St. John lay unmoving, bleeding into the earth.

# ~ CHAPTER 2

NICK TAPPED HIS BRAKES to take his pickup off cruise and turned off Highway 59, heading west toward Phillips and the Silver Buckle Ranch. The low sun glimmered through the shaggy protective bluffs of Custer National Forest that rimmed the small town.

Nick decided that a decade hadn't diminished the charm of Phillips, Montana, population 1,847. The town still resembled an Old West Hollywood mock-up, with the false fronts and a wooden boardwalk separating the now-paved street. Part of some John Wayne Western had even been shot here—which had given the town enough funds to add the streetlights, spruce up the old community center, build the football stands, and install a stoplight at the main intersection.

He drove past the dime store and noticed an updated carved wooden sign for Claire's Gifts and Books. Beside it, the Red Rooster grocery store had updated its coin-operated rides with a truck and a race car. Across the street, on the corner by the light, Big John's pickup still sat in the shade in front of Lolly's Diner, an old dining car she'd picked up from the Northern Railroad and turned into a novelty establishment. In high school, Nick had spent nearly every Friday night at Lolly's, dropping quarters into the jukebox and hanging out with Maggy and Cole. He wondered if Big John had popped the question to Lolly yet and if Lolly still served coffee that could curl a person's hair.

Across from Lolly's, a few cars were parked in the dirt lot beside the Buffalo Saloon. The false front had been repainted, along with the plate-glass window that for too long had been covered by plywood after an unnamed someone had driven his truck through the front window. Thankfully, Nick had been able to wheedle his brother, Rafe, out of that trouble before their father caught wind. Nick bet that Rafe still owed the saloon owner money. He smiled at the memory. Rafe had since become the local hero. How far they'd both wandered from their roots.

Next to the Buffalo, the appearance of spring garden supplies—rakes, hoses, fertilizer—advertised a sale at Phillips's redbrick hardware store. Nick well remembered the smell of dust and the creak of the floor as he had searched through bins for nuts and bolts to match machinery parts. The building next to the hardware store advertised Custer Travel on one side and Hal's Barbershop on the other. The barbershop's candy-cane light, long since defunct, collected dust, but Nick spotted old Hal in the window, doctoring a patron in an old-fashioned shave.

Nick felt suddenly eighteen again, sucked back in time. He couldn't help but glance at the school—all twelve grades housed in a one-story brick building—situated north of Main Street across from the small neighborhood of modular homes. Behind the school, the afternoon sun glinted off the goalposts of the football field. Despite Phillips's meager population, summers spent on the range lifting hay bales and punching cows made for the best defensive line in the county. One that had cut off the blitz and allowed Nick to bring their team to a triple-A victory two seasons running.

A momentary smile and the image of Cole meeting him in the air with a victory clap sent a shard of pain through him. Evidently some things had lost their charm. Soured, even.

Nick turned south on County Road 73 right by the auction barn, a steel gray building with pens out back. Glancing at the cattle prices, Nick shook his head. Feed and gas costs rose with the economy, but the price of beef never seemed to keep up. Especially with the mad-cow scares.

Beyond the auction barn, the rodeo ring looked hard and barren. Still, he could hear the roar of the crowd in the back of his mind, smell the animal sweat, taste his own fear. Football had only been a pastime—rodeo had been his breath and his blood.

Nick drove past the rodeo stands, where the landscape turned to tract housing and mobile homes, the occasional shiny truck parked outside. Remnants of black snow edged the dirt roads snaking off to each side. Nick lifted his hand to Egger, the town salvage collector, who stopped and watched him drive by. His hound dogs lit out after the truck. Egger didn't bother to call them back.

Nick wondered if Stefanie knew of his return. If Saul hadn't already told her, the news would follow Nick like a prairie gust. Nick didn't know if his little sister would load her Winchester or put out the yellow ribbon. After his behavior, he didn't expect any favors from God, but deep in his heart he hoped for the ribbon.

"I'll leave first thing tomorrow," he'd told Saul, but it had taken nearly a week to pack his gear, quit his job, and summon the courage to head south and back to his mistakes.

*"Nick! Come back!"* His father's voice, which had dogged him nearly every day since that night over a decade ago, seemed to mock him now. How he longed to turn back time and utter the words that burned in his throat: *I'm sorry.*

Time had gradually allowed him to face the truth. In spite of his father's betrayal, Nick should have shown him the respect he deserved. Bishop Noble had raised him, had molded him to be a man, had wanted to give him everything.

And Nick had blindly, arrogantly spat in his face.

His hands tightened on the steering wheel as he drove past the massive Kincaid spread, the Big K. He wondered if Big John Kincaid had taken over for his father, running the place. Brock-faced, half-black, half-white Angus/Hereford lounged in the pasture, along with a smattering of purebreds. Bishop had always been a purist—only Black Angus ran on Silver Buckle land. Nick fleetingly wondered if Maggy's father still ran the herd as the Big K's cow boss.

Maggy. He should probably keep his thoughts clear of his high school sweetheart. Most likely she hadn't thought of him in years.

But wouldn't it be nice if–?

No. He'd walked out on her too.

He noticed a new sign for the Breckenridge Bulls as he drove by the ranch, aptly named the Double B, toward Silver Buckle land. While Nick surveyed their property on either side of the road, he found himself looking for signs of trouble—prairie-dog cities, broken windmills that had stopped pumping water, an errant cow. The habit tightened his jaw, and he forced his eyes back on the road. Maybe he had no right to think about ranching anymore. . . .

But he was returning, the prodigal son aware of his sins, ready to make restitution.

He turned into the Silver Buckle drive, passing under the swinging oval sign, freshly painted in green and white, and memory nearly engulfed him. *"Someday, Son, you'll run the Silver Buckle."*

*Then why did you hand it off to Cole, Dad? To punish me?*

Nick tasted the answer in the back of his throat. Memories crested over him as he drove into the yard—swinging on the main gates, eating apples on the front steps, practicing his roping on Pecos in the corral, or feeding the orphaned calves, the bums—in one of the other corrals. He wondered if time had yet worn off his grandfather's initials from the foundation of the main house or if the weather had collapsed his great-grandfather's 1900-era homestead in the pasture over the hill. Nick had helped build the dining hall—expanding the bunkhouse during the height of the Silver Buckle's prosperity, etching his own initials into that foundation.

On the far side of the yard, three barns held the livestock—one for heifers, the other for the calves or bums, and a third for horses. Beyond those, the late-afternoon sun glinted off the tin machinery shed and the airplane hangar. Farther up the road the modular home owned by their foreman, Dutch Johnson, boasted a new roof. And overlooking the entire affair from the top of the hill, a log hunting lodge brought to mind raucous wrestling matches with Rafe and Cole.

Admittedly, Nick couldn't pinpoint exactly how he felt about returning home.

His father's cherry red '68 Ford Ranger pickup sat in the shadow of the garage, its windows permanently half open, the tailgate crooked, the license plate missing. He remembered the smells of dust and oil and his father at the wheel, his hat shading his eyes as he manhandled the truck over the pastures.

Nick pulled up in front of the house, right behind a newer model black pickup. As he got out and slammed the door, four horses in the nearby corral lifted their heads, one pushing his nose between the crossbars.

He stopped to pet the animal, get his bearings, and take in the smells—the musty sharpness of sagebrush, the occasional whiff of fertilizer. He recognized the roan as his father's old cutting horse, but the two new horses—a paint and a sorrel—he couldn't place. And Pecos's absence gave him a moment's pause.

A door slammed behind him.

Nick stood quietly, rubbing the quarter horse's nose, listening, suddenly unable to move, feeling as if he were a thief or an interloper. Maybe he should leave now before . . .

"I s'pose you got lost, huh? Sorry, I tried to give you good directions. Anyway, welcome to the Silver Buckle Ranch."

When Nick looked over his shoulder, words left him. Stefanie had been thirteen the last time he saw her, with long, stringy, black hair; gangly legs; and freckles.

Clearly some things had aged over the decade, starting with his little—er, not so little anymore—sister. Although she'd written to him over the years, especially during his stint in the army, sending him news clippings of Rafe's bull-riding exploits and occasional tidbits from town, she'd neglected to mention that she'd, well . . . grown up.

Stefanie still wore her favorite battered brown Stetson, but the freckles had vanished along with the stringy hair and any sense of awkwardness. She strode toward him, pulling on her work gloves, wearing a fur-lined coat, jeans, and boots. In her bearing he saw grace and strength that bespoke the responsibility of eighty thousand acres and three thousand head of cattle.

It was a good thing he'd come home, because from his big-brother vantage point, the ranch wasn't the only thing that needed protecting.

"Stef?"

She stopped, frowned, gaped at him. "Nick?"

He shrugged, finding a half smile.

"Oh, Nick!" Stefanie launched herself into his arms, knocking off her hat, no holds barred in her welcome. "I can't believe it's you!"

Nick crushed her to his chest, giving over to the feelings he'd stuffed away for way too long. He held her tight, closing his eyes. "Hey, Stef."

He heard his own emotion in her voice when she said, "Thank God He finally brought you home."

⁂

*Please, God, let me live long enough to see CJ win.* Cole barely listened to Maggy as she spoke in low tones with his doctor. She had her back to him, her hand over the mouthpiece, as if he couldn't figure out what she might be talking about.

"When do you think the tests will be in?"

He didn't need any more tests to tell him what he already knew. His body had given up. Simply worn out. Just like his mother's. He remembered her symptoms—low white-cell blood count, her soft bones that seemed so easily broken. The tremors in her hands and arms. The feeling she had that she would die.

That, more than anything, told Cole the truth. They hadn't found a cure then ... and he felt sure they wouldn't now. Regardless of how many tests they did.

Cole readjusted his cast, turning in the old recliner to watch CJ circle the corral, riding round and round on his roping horse, chasing a bum. *Shift your weight more, CJ.* CJ had beautiful form, not sloppy like his. Cole had preferred steer wrestling to roping–it had less finesse, more muscle power. He'd only been wrangled into roping because of his friendship with Nick.

Nick had been the one with pizzazz and style. And the fact that CJ possessed the same easy throw rankled Cole more than he could ever voice. A constant reminder that he would always be second best.

Maggy hung up, and Cole heard her sigh. He didn't look at her. She was still so beautiful that sometimes it took his breath away. He loved the way she took care of the bums and the times she'd met him in the pasture in the truck, his lunch in a box on the seat. He watched her at night as the hours stretched long, her reddish hair turning to copper in the moonlight, the soft lines around her eyes relaxing. He loved her eyes, loved that once upon a time they shone with hope and desire.

Now only worry filled her expression when she was awake.

She deserved so much better than this.

Maggy's hand squeezed his shoulder. "Dr. Lowe asked us to go down to Sheridan. He wants to do some more tests."

Cole stared out at CJ. "The horse is breaking too early. CJ has to teach him to wait. And he's not catching the right horn."

Maggy said nothing.

"I should be out there." He hated the desperation in his tone, that he'd let his frustration trickle out. She had enough on her, with running the ranch and taking care of him. Maybe it would be better if he went quickly. He prayed for that sometimes. Especially on his bad days.

"CJ's amazing, and when he comes in you'll tell him how to fix his errors. He listens to you."

Cole gripped his wife's hand on his shoulder, disturbed by how cold and calloused hers felt. A woman's hands shouldn't be that toughened. "I don't want any more doctors poking at me."

He glanced at her, saw her purse her lips, anger flare in her pretty green eyes. "Are you saying you're not cowboy enough for another round, Cole? Because I am."

Cole refused to rise to her tactics. Instead, he smiled, shook his head, and took hold of her wrist, pulling her into his lap. She braced herself on the arm of the chair as she landed, and that irked him. He wouldn't break. Well, probably not.

Cole put his arm around her, ran his other hand through her hair, then cupped her cheek. It was wet, but he said nothing as he brushed it dry. She leaned her head softly against his neck. She always fit so perfectly in his arms. Or perhaps he'd only wanted her to.

He pushed a lock of her auburn hair behind her ear. "We have a ranch to run and no time to be going down to Sheridan on a wild-goose chase. We've done this four times, and they still can't figure out what's wrong."

She met his eyes with such pain that the back of his throat ached.

"I'm not getting better, and we both know it." He left unmentioned the sorry state of their finances. She as well as he knew what the trips cost them. And he'd had to let their health insurance lapse the second year of the drought. But he didn't want to argue and cast a further shadow on this day. He had so few left; he simply wanted to cherish them.

She closed her eyes and pushed up from the chair.

*Don't go, Mags.*

She folded her arms across her chest. "I'm not giving up."

Of course she wouldn't. That probably scared him the most. She'd spend every last dime, sacrifice everything. And when it didn't work, she'd have nothing left to start over with.

He was about to reach out for her when she stepped away from his grasp. She picked up the phone book and put it back in its slot on her kitchen desk. Then she opened the freezer and dug out a pound of ground venison. She didn't look at him as she put the venison in a pot in the sink. "We need to hire a hand. Roundup is just around the corner, and we'll need help."

"What about Stefanie and her outfit?"

"We can't count on the Silver Buckle every time we need help." Maggy wiped her hands on a towel, turned, and rested her hip against the counter. Still, she wouldn't look at him. "I'm going into town later today to put ads up around town."

Cole's jaw turned hard, and he turned away from her, staring back at CJ's roping practice.

The drip into the sink fractured the silence, the sound of their impasse. Finally, he heard Maggy sigh. "I have heifers birthing in the barn. Please just . . . stay here. If you need something, call me on the two-way." She headed into the entryway.

He wanted to throw the two-way against the wall.

He should have taken the family away from here years ago when Maggy's parents moved to Arizona. They'd offered to let them live in their two-bedroom home until Cole found a job. But what was a born-and-bred cowboy supposed to do for a living? He knew how to ride broncs and herd cattle, fix a baler or a broken windmill, but he couldn't make a decent living in the city. Besides, Maggy had practically begged him to stay.

*Yeah, sure, blame it on Maggy.*

If he were to assign blame, that would go to his pride. And wanting to see Nick Noble's face when he made something of himself.

*I can't believe I ever called you my friend.*

Nick hadn't been back in a decade—probably wouldn't ever set foot on the Silver Buckle again. And Cole had two hundred sorry-looking head of cattle on rented land.

Yeah, he'd really made a name for the St. Johns in eastern Montana.

*Please, God, provide for my family.* He couldn't count how many times he'd sat on his horse, praying that very prayer.

Probably he'd go to his grave with the plea on his lips.

But maybe Bishop's bequest was God's provision. If so, Cole aimed to make sure that Maggy and CJ used it to start over. They could sell the cattle and the land Bishop had left them—hopefully back to the Silver Buckle—for a tidy sum. Then Maggy and CJ could have a life free of praying over the weather, wrestling stubborn cows, living from hand to mouth, and hoping they had enough to pay the rent.

In the meantime, he had to keep Maggy from mortgaging the land and spending it in vain trying to make him well.

Cole watched Maggy cross the yard, wearing her overalls, a wool cap, and gloves. Birthing could be messy business. He remembered too well the late nights during the early years. Maggy had insisted on sleeping in the barn when the heifers delivered.

How she cried when they lost a newborn or a mother. Back then it felt like they'd taken on the world. Now it was Maggy and CJ wrestling with the land for their future.

Maggy and CJ and a soon-to-be hired hand. While Cole sat in the warm house and quietly faded away.

His leg itched, and he refused the impulse to stick a hanger or a pencil or even a butter knife down the cast and give it a good scratch. His bones had turned to twigs over the past couple of years. First his ankle, then his wrist, and now his leg. It had taken his wrist nearly six months to heal, and his ankle still ached, despite Maggy's prayers for healing.

These days he prayed only to live long enough to see CJ win the Custer County roping championships. And then that the Lord would take him quickly.

Most of all he prayed that he was right and that Nick wouldn't show up and steal everything he loved out of his hands.

❧

"Do you even know where you're going?"

Piper clicked the cell phone into its dashboard cradle, yanked out the map, and unfolded it across the steering wheel. Tapping her brakes, she swallowed a retort as a cattle truck pulled out of a dirt road and lumbered up to speed ahead of her. Didn't he ever hear of right-of-way?

"Piper?"

"Yes, I'm here, Carter. Of course I know where I am. I wrote down everything you said. It's just that . . . well, your landmarks weren't great."

"I told you to MapQuest it!"

"MapQuest gave me a big red star in the middle of Montana."

In her mind's eye she could see Carter shaking his head. "I told you this is a bad idea. You're gonna get yourself in trouble. Starting with getting lost out in the middle of nowhere. I'll find your carcass in July, being eaten by coyotes."

The thought of her skinny friend and colleague Carter Eaton, in his pressed khaki Dockers and Doc Martens, flying halfway across Montana to Billings from their office in Kalispell, then driving another two hundred miles to search for her corpse put a smile into her long and torturous day. If three hours in a plane the size of a station wagon didn't give her the willies, winding through the back roads of Custer National Forest in a rented Jeep after taking a wrong turn off the highway had plopped her back into the center of her nightmares. Or rather her memories. Last time she'd been in cattle country she'd been running with her mother for their lives as they escaped the rage of Russell McPhee.

She'd forgotten the barren land, the feeling that it could swallow a person whole.

After an hour of following the two-lane pavement cutting through rolling hills and limestone that rose like sentinels to her journey, she'd spotted a highway sign. She'd been so relieved that she didn't care when she emerged a mere thirty miles from where she'd entered. So much for a shortcut.

That brief tour through her dark memories only left her more determined to make Nick Noble pay for his sins. She owed it to Jimmy—the one person who had made sure she'd escaped that world.

"I'm not going to be eaten by coyotes, Carter. Don't forget you're talking to the woman who snuck across the border not once but twice to expose the porous Montana borders."

"You nearly got shot, if I recall."

"*And won an award.* You need a memory course."

"No, you're the one with the memory lapse—I distinctly remember the word *probation* being used by your boss after your second arrest at the border."

That wasn't all. *"Piper, your work is good but jaded,"* her editor at the *Kalispell Gazette* had said as she paced her small office. *"Someday you're going to go too far and fabricate what isn't there. And then this paper is going to pay the price."* The words had stung, even though Piper shrugged them away. "She wasn't serious—especially after the publicity I got for the paper—"

"And the legal bills—"

"I won't need the paper after I send in my audition tape to *Wanted: Justice.*"

The cable show had contacted her twice after she'd won her second award and again last week after she'd returned from Welles-ley, saying she had just the "spunk" they were hunting for in their *Wanted: Justice* series. Living in Seattle would put her about as far as she could get from her childhood, short of going overseas. And dedicating her career to helping people find justice struck at the very core of her life goals.

Even if she did wonder at times if she weren't in three leagues over her head.

If she was honest, yes, there were moments when she didn't exactly like the person she had to be in order to enact that justice.

It seemed Carter, as usual, had ESP. For a restaurant critic, he had uncanny psychic abilities. "Piper, are you sure this is what you want? Ever since your mother's death and then Jimmy's arr—"

"This is *exactly* what I want—a chance to strike back at all those bullies in the world who think they can run over people without a thought. Who use people for their own gain." *Who take out their anger on women and small children.* She loosened her grip around the steering wheel. Oh no, her stomach had started to burn. She fished around in her purse for an antacid.

"As long as you don't end up one of them."

Carter's words had the effect of a jab to the ribs. "No chance of that," she said, keeping the pain from her voice and hating how close to her fears he'd struck.

"I'm holding you to that promise. But I'm a little worried you're going to starve. I'll bet they don't have Thai food and a Starbucks in Cow Land."

She popped the antacid into her mouth, crunching and washing it down with a gulp of bottled water. "I'm the queen of adaptation. I can live without my tofu and chai. For a week or two."

"Do you seriously think it'll take only a week?"

"I'm hoping less. If anyone knows how to cut to the truth—"

"Piper, are you sure this is a good idea? Because if you're right, then this guy is a murderer."

Piper tried to ignore the churning Carter's words started inside her. According to the police report—and collaborated by witnesses—Noble had an argument with the victim outside a bar only two hours before her time of death. It felt so convenient that Jenny had gone inside and hooked up with Piper's brother. And even more convenient that Noble had been the one to pry from Jimmy a so-called confession. Which Jimmy later recanted. She'd bet every award she'd earned that Noble had some hand in Jenny's death even if it wasn't directly, making this little excursion dangerous indeed.

But she'd vowed long ago to stand up for the innocents, to expose the bullies of this world. She wasn't the same girl who had hidden under her bed, hoping to be invisible. Her half brother had his faults, but she could be dead right now if it hadn't been for his courage and the way he had stood up for her to their father. She felt partly to blame for the mess Jimmy's life had become. If only he'd escaped with her and her mother, maybe his life would have turned out better. This was the only way she could think of to apologize. To show that she believed in him. To put things right and free Jimmy to move on. "I don't know if Noble actually *killed* her, Carter . . . but he didn't even try to find her killer. Simply pointed the finger at my brother and pulled the trigger."

"Well, he's not going to be exactly thrilled with someone sneaking around his past, digging up dirt."

"Yeah, my brother wasn't *exactly thrilled* with losing five years of his life either." Five years. She'd just gotten out of graduate school when he'd been arrested. She'd been ashamed. And a part of her wondered . . . even believed . . .

"Be careful, Piper. You yourself said this guy had bully written all over him. And I don't want you to go through—"

"I'll be fine. I've got three years of Kempo karate under my belt, and I've got you watching my back."

"Not from a thousand miles away. You call me every—"

His voice died and with it the reception. Great. She'd just been disarmed of her secret weapon for this assignment—Carter and his culinary skills. How was she supposed to pull off filling the post of cookie of the Silver Buckle when she could barely scramble eggs? "Carter!"

She tossed her cell phone onto the passenger seat. At least she still had her copy of *Joy of Cooking* and the memory of her mother feeding the masses at the school cafeteria. If she had to learn to stir a pot of biscuits and gravy in order to nail Nick for his crimes, it seemed doable. She hoped Carter hadn't oversold her. When he'd called, acting as the director of Bon Appétit, a cooking school in Kalispell looking to place their students in summer jobs, Stefanie Noble hadn't been even slightly suspicious about someone answering her ad so soon. And Piper's list of "qualifications" had eliminated every other candidate.

But what if they discovered her dismal cooking abilities? She hoped that the cowboys' years in the middle of nowhere had hardened their taste buds. Besides, how picky could a bunch of cowpokes be?

She maneuvered her Jeep Liberty to the middle of the road, gauging her passing options, and nearly lost an inch of paint from an oncoming Chevy Silverado.

So, she wouldn't pass for a while.

She retrieved the map and traced her route. Although she'd exited on the wrong side of Custer National Forest, if she read her map right, thirty more miles would land her in Phillips. Then she simply had to "veer left at Lolly's, go past the Bumblebee, and when she got to a dead-end T, take a right." No problem.

Despite the feeling that she'd landed on the back side of nowhere,

Piper had to admit that in the daylight and with plenty of population around her, eastern Montana had a beauty all its own. The sky stretched across the horizon, turning magenta in the west as it fell into the grasp of the hazy Bighorn Mountains. The first blooms of color filled the draws and gullies—blue-and-white wildflowers amid lime-tinted grass. Now and again a bluff rose from the prairie, the earth rough and dark along the exposed edge.

Barbed wire fringed the highway, dissecting the fields into manageable plots, and in many she saw black or red cattle, some grazing at piles of hay, others staring at her with white faces and dark beady eyes. Jack pine and black spruce spired from hillsides amid tumbles of rock, and an occasional red or brown barn trimmed in white reminded her of the old spaghetti westerns.

It all brought to mind her childhood cowgirl fantasies of being Calamity Jane, living by the Old West code of honor and independence. Of justice.

Maybe in this part of the world God would help her find a small piece of that justice. And maybe, finally, she'd also find a measure of peace. Piper glanced briefly at the heavens . . . wondering, hoping.

In spite of her mother's prayers for Piper's so-called salvation, she'd never had God's attention. She didn't know why she looked for it now—she'd figured out her own path to redemption.

Turning off Highway 59, Piper passed a weathered Welcome to Phillips sign. At first glance, she decided the town needed an *Extreme Makeover* episode and a Starbucks at the very least. She located Lolly's—an old railroad dining car that might have been novel in a big city but here looked like it had been left for scrap—and hung a left, passing a service station and empty rodeo stands. She'd attended a few rodeos while doing an investigative piece about the dangers of bull riding. Even met a few of the cowboys.

She wasn't impressed. Although she'd had a plethora of offers from gentlemanly to seedy, she hadn't entertained even the barest of rodeo-romance fantasies. The last thing she wanted in her life was a man who loved his horse more than his woman. Cowboys might come with muscles and Western charisma, but she'd as soon cuddle up with a cactus than a man with arrogance where his brains should be.

That assessment had nothing to do with the fact that her last boyfriend—during college—had nearly gotten her killed running his International Scout pickup into a tree after lying to her about the number of beers he'd consumed.

Men—especially cowboys—came packin' trouble. And she'd had her share of that, thanks.

She drove past a neighborhood of tract homes and watched the eyes of a local follow her as his dogs lit out after her pint-sized SUV. Clearly the town of Phillips also needed a video-rental store, if not a theater. Dust plumed behind her, evidence of the dry, cold winter. She'd read something about a drought in the area and guessed that the lack of snowfall and plummeting temperatures had to hurt cattle country.

Not that she worried about America's beef supply. After her stint at the stockyards she'd vowed never to eat another piece of meat again—*particularly* beef. But Kalispell hadn't exactly embraced the vegetarian lifestyle, so she'd been existing on Caesar salads and Thai vegetable stir-fry for the past year. Not knowing what to expect at the ranch, she'd packed a goody bag of fruit, nuts, and ramen noodles.

Piper motored past a spread that advertised bulls on its sign and felt a surge of hope when she saw two *B*s. *Oh. Double B, not bumblebee.* She needed her ears checked.

She slowed as she came to the T, then turned right. The Silver Buckle sign, an oval "buckle" with a green carved *S* in the middle, swung in the slight breeze between two peeled cottonwoods. The driveway held no splendor, no giant pines like she'd imagined, no split-rail fences to line the path to the house. Then again, this wasn't an Old West television show, and the glistening pool of water to her left wasn't a sparkling lake but a cattle watering tank.

To her surprise, however, the main house looked pure Old West romance—two stories of logs, a window dormer off the side, an overhanging porch, a stone chimney, and even a stack of firewood by the side-door entrance. Beyond that, she saw more outbuildings, corrals, even a bunkhouse. Horses hung their heads over the tall corral, nickering to her in welcome. For an uneasy moment, Piper felt charmed.

She pulled up, stopped the Jeep. What. Was. She. Doing?

Justice. This was about justice.

But what if Noble recognized her? She'd been so careful last week in Wellesley—wearing a brunette wig and her city clothes—and she'd changed her name years ago. Noble couldn't possibly link her to Jimmy, couldn't possibly suspect her agenda.

She found her smile, the one that had disarmed a ringleader of a sweatshop importing illegal aliens, and stepped out of the SUV, slamming the door. The smell of cow manure and hay caught her nose.

A young woman came out of the house, pulling on a coat. Smiling, she appeared not much younger than Piper, with long black hair in two braids and deep brown eyes. She came down the stairs. And right behind her, wariness in his expression, a coatless Nick Noble.

So he'd beat her here. He looked exactly as she remembered—tall, with flannel shirtsleeves rolled up over strong forearms, and wearing accusation in his dark eyes. He shoved his hands into his back pockets and didn't smile.

*Don't look at him.* All the same, she felt his stare boring into her, peeling away her confidence. "Hello," Piper said, extending her hand to the woman, "my name's Piper. Piper Sullivan."

"Stefanie Noble." The young woman met her handshake with only a moment's pause. "I'm sorry. I thought—"

"You thought I was a man."

"Well, I wasn't sure. I guess when I said the job was a trail job, I assumed . . ." Stefanie frowned, looking at Nick. "I had planned on putting you in the bunkhouse, but, ah . . . that won't work."

Noble's suspicious look never wavered, and a chill brushed through Piper.

Stefanie regained her smile. "No worries. We're glad you're here, Piper. With our new operation, we need to class up our menu a bit. Your teacher spoke highly of you."

Of course he did. Piper had taken Carter out for dinner, left him her entire DVD collection, and filled up his Starbucks card. "Thank you."

"The first group doesn't come for a few weeks so you'll have plenty of time to get your supplies and settle in."

"That sounds great." Piper didn't mention that by then she hoped to have enough dirt on Nick to bury him. No way did she intend to stick around and cook over a campfire. Not unless they were content with roasted marshmallows for every meal. "I can't wait to get started." She kept her smile, glancing at Nick, who came off the porch to join Stefanie, his eyes still pinned to Piper.

"This is my brother Nick," Stefanie said. "Nick, this is our new cookie."

When Nick held out his hand, Piper forced herself to take it, hating the feel of his skin. She barely met his perusal, forcing from her expression the derision that filled her throat.

As his dark eyes lingered on her, he cocked his head and frowned. "Have we possibly . . . met before?"

# CHAPTER 3

"ARE YOU SURE we haven't met before?" Nick had been a cop for three years before he'd turned in his shield, unable to face the man in the mirror. And in that time, he'd learned to listen to his instincts. Something about the petite woman's smile, those blue eyes, and the lift of her chin nudged a memory inside him. But it wasn't enough to spit out a name or a place.

She frowned, pushing her shoulder-length straw blonde hair from her face. "I don't think so." Then she shrugged. "Are you in the restaurant industry?"

"Only recently," he answered. She didn't look much like a chef— weren't they supposed to be slightly padded? This woman hid any discernible curves under a new leather jacket and a fisherman's sweater, and in her clingy low-rise jeans, she looked like she spent more time running from food than tasting it. If she did cook, it would be at an upscale B and B, not down on the ranch, frying in cast iron over an open fire.

His scrutiny took in not only her attire but the way she held herself—jaw tight, hands balled in her jacket pockets, her body half turned in a slightly defensive posture. He could have sworn that he saw a flash of fear in her eyes as he'd come off the porch.

He flicked a glance at Stefanie, one eyebrow up, hoping for an explanation. "I s'pose this is who you were expecting earlier?"

"Miss Sullivan is going to cook for the groups, Nick. We need a little high class to entice the tourists." Stefanie turned to him, hope in her eyes. "Ah . . . I know you just arrived, but I think we need to put her in your room."

"What?" He'd been in the kitchen pouring himself a fresh cup of coffee and asking about Rafe when they'd heard the Jeep pull up. Hadn't even dragged in his duffel bags, hadn't strolled through the house, smelling the memories, hadn't heard a whisper from the ghosts. He didn't hanker to playing catch-up. "She's staying here?"

"Well, I can't rightly put her in the bunkhouse," Stef continued, apparently ignoring his dark look. She turned back to Piper. "Your teacher says you're nearly ready to graduate?"

Piper nodded. "This will give me great experience and help me launch the next phase of my career. I appreciate the opportunity."

Stefanie nearly glowed.

"If you'll excuse me," Nick said to Piper, "I need a word with my sister." He caught Stefanie by the elbow, dragging her toward the house.

Stefanie twisted out of his grip the second they reached the porch. "What?"

"We have to talk about this. Tourists? Stef, c'mon—" Although he hadn't seen her for a decade and had been back less than thirty minutes, he knew instinctively to brace himself.

Stefanie's dark Noble eyes flashed. "Stop, Nick. I don't recall inviting you here. You haven't set foot on Silver Buckle property for ten years. You haven't shown one iota of interest in keeping this place alive, and even when we needed you, you couldn't be bothered to cross your shadow and head home. I'm glad to see you—" she took a deep breath—"I'm *so* glad to see you. But I have a ranch to run. And the only way we're going to keep it running is to figure out another source of income—"

"But city slickers? What, a dude ranch? I remember that movie, Stef. Jack Palance wasn't having any fun."

"It's not a dude ranch. It's a chance to spend a week on a *working* ranch. It's a family vacation with purpose. The first family is already registered, and they're from Chicago, looking for a Western adventure for their kids. We'll take them on a roundup, have a minirodeo, go on a few trail rides as well as incorporate them into our daily life."

"So we're babysitting city folks all summer long?"

"I'd prefer to call it *educating*."

Nick glanced at Piper, dropping his voice. "That lady looks like a stiff wind could knock her clear to South Dakota. Do you seriously think she'll be able to cook over an open fire?"

"She comes highly recommended."

"So does a weekend retreat at a spa—it doesn't mean that it fits my lifestyle. She doesn't belong out here. Besides, what happened to Chet?"

"Chet died. Right before Dad." She folded her arms across her chest and looked away, as if holding back a wave of ache.

He winced. "Sorry."

"Stay out of it, Nick. Daddy left me to run this ranch, and we need the cash. The hunting lodge has always brought in enough to tide us over—I'm simply ramping it up a notch. I'm not going to lose the ranch—"

"No, you're not. Because I'm going to make sure Cole St. John doesn't get any of it!"

Stefanie stilled, her mouth slightly agape, blinking at him. "What does Cole have to do with this?"

Nick shot another look at Piper, who was studying the horses, a slight smile on her face, as if she might be in a romantic Hollywood Western. He had a sick feeling that he might have to get used to that sort of look once they opened the Buckle to cowboy wannabes.

He lowered his voice. "Dad's will. I know St. John has half our property—land we need to feed our cattle. And I know that he swindled Dad into leaving it to him."

For a moment Stefanie seemed to lose the power of speech, her mouth moving but no sound emerging.

He filled in the words for her. "This isn't the place or time."

She stared at him and even pressed her fingertips to her forehead as if checking her head for a fever.

*Oh, sure, act bewildered.* As if she hadn't a clue why he might be back, guns blazing. He shook his head. Apparently time had blinded her.

As if to reinforce that truth, she said, "I can't believe this! You didn't come back to help. You came back out of revenge." Stefanie's voice shook. "How long are you planning on staying? Long enough to wreck Cole's life again?"

*Hey, exactly whose life had been wrecked that night?* Apparently she wasn't only blind but brainwashed. "When did you become his pit bull? Because last time we talked, you were helping me pack."

Her expression tightened, along with her fists. "Things change, Nick. And if you'd been around at all, you'd know. Suffice it to say that Cole is a part of this family–"

"Part of–have you lost your mind? Cole St. John wants to take everything away from this family, just like his mother!"

Stefanie looked like she wanted to strangle him. "If you're not interested in helping, then go back to whatever corner of the world you slunk out of. I don't know what happened to you. This ranch used to be in your blood. You lived for the day when Daddy turned it over to you."

He remembered that too, those days when he'd sit on Pecos, surveying the land, dreaming of working it with Rafe and Stef. Seeing pride in Bishop's eyes. The sharp edge of grief caught him, cut off his words.

Stefanie put her hands on her hips, staring at the porch floor, as if trying to school her emotions. "I don't know what kind of man you've become, where you've been, or what you've done. But I would have thought that by now you'd learned to forgive. I guess I was wrong." She looked up, and right behind her anger he saw the faintest edging of tears. "I have a ranch to run, and I'm not going to let you destroy more lives."

He studied her, stymied, and not a little shaken at her words. Destroy more lives? What did she mean by that? He'd returned for atonement, to *protect*. To be the Noble he should have been. According to his recollection, only *his* life had derailed that horrible night ten years ago.

"I have to believe God brought you back for more than this," Stefanie said, taking one parting shot before she shook her head, turned, and nearly leaped off the porch steps toward their new chef.

God had brought him back? Hardly. Nick had drifted so far from God's plans that he hadn't a clue what God wanted from him. No, he'd simply followed the feeling in his gut. The one that wanted to finish this business between him and Cole once and for all.

Piper's words to Stefanie brought him back to the moment. "How about if I get a hotel room? Really, I don't want to put you out." The woman smiled, but Nick noticed how she clutched her cell phone in both hands, like a Taser, watching the two of them as if they might break out into a fistfight right in the yard.

Nick came off the porch. "No, you can have my ro—"

"How about the hunting lodge?" Stef asked suddenly. "It's clean, even if we're not finished with the updates. Will that work?"

Nick watched relief pass over Piper, as if staying in their house had been her worst nightmare. Then again, he wasn't thrilled to have her stay with them—at least not until he took the Daisy Duke posters down from his walls.

"I'll take you to the hunting lodge," Stefanie started.

"No, I will," Nick said, one step behind her. He wanted his own interview and perhaps to instill in this woman the harsh realities of life out on the range. If that didn't work, he'd rekindle his assault on Stefanie's lunacy. Clearly he'd also returned to the Silver Buckle to be the voice of reason. He forced his nicest smile and zeroed in on the new chef.

Stefanie pursed her lips. "I have this under control, Nick." She looked at Piper. "You can follow me."

"I'll show her," Nick growled.

Stefanie glared at him, wariness in those eyes that used to hold such admiration.

He turned away, watching the horses ponder him over the corral fence, pitching his voice low. "Let me help, Stef."

"I could find the lodge myself. I mean, I made it here, right?" Piper gave the slightest laugh.

Nick glanced at her and couldn't decide if she looked nervous or was trying to help cut the tension. Obviously he and Stef would have to work on their welcome reception if they hoped to run a dude operation.

The thought make his stomach turn. Yes, the hunting lodge had always brought in enough to tide them over during the lean months, but full-time tourists? If the Buckle could keep the land Cole hoped to steal, they could grow extra hay and start a side business. That seemed a thousand times better than kowtowing to cowboy wannabes. He envisioned screaming and injury. And lawsuits.

He'd have to be on his last pot of beans before he'd open the ranch to a bunch of tenderfeet.

"Well, ah . . . thanks, then." Piper smiled. It was a pretty smile, and for a second Nick wondered how he'd turned into such a jerk.

"I need to make sure you have some firewood tonight too. In case it gets cold."

"Would you like a tour of the ranch tomorrow?" Stefanie asked.

"If she wants a tour, I'll take her," Nick blurted. He could hardly believe the words emerged from his mouth. Especially when Stefanie blatantly gaped at him. He shrugged and offered a smile as if to say, *See, I'm on your side.*

Apparently he still possessed his Noble charm, because Stefanie's posture went from attack to wary and she returned a soft smile.

Tomorrow, right after the tour, Nick would help Piper move to a nice B and B. Or better yet, fill up her tank and send her back to her cream puffs and tiramisu.

Stefanie's glare softened. "I've got to check on the heifers. Two are due to drop their calves soon. Thanks, Nick."

Something warm and painfully familiar filled him, and he turned away from his sister before it swept over him. "Follow me," he said to Piper.

She scanned the two of them before she nodded and climbed back into her vehicle.

He found the keys in the ignition of his father's pickup and fired it up. Glancing once into the rearview mirror, he watched their new cookie follow in her chick Jeep. More importantly, he saw the look of tenderness that colored Stefanie's face.

*No, Stef, don't look at me that way.* It only made his chest hurt.

The bell above the door of Lolly's Diner dinged as Maggy closed it behind her. Big John Kincaid sat at the counter, chatting with two locals. A couple of teenagers wearing Custer County letter jackets drank milk shakes at one of the end booths that lined the dining car, and a young mother fed French fries to her toddler at the other.

Apparently she'd hit the four o'clock siesta. "Hey, guys."

John touched the brow of his hat, while his friends nodded. Lolly stood behind the long Formica counter, dressed in jeans and a Hard Rock Cafe T-shirt, her long blonde hair swept up into a messy bun. She'd never come to grips with the fact that her twenties had left her long ago. Then again, if Maggy had kept the figure Lolly still possessed, she might wear a tight T-shirt and low-cut jeans too.

Would Cole even notice? Sadness brushed through her at the

thought, and she forced a smile. "I'd like to put up an ad if that's okay."

Maggy had made three ads for a hired man, who could live in their empty bunkhouse and help them run their cattle. She had already posted one at the Red Rooster grocery store and another at the Buffalo.

It felt like a surrender of sorts. A concession to the truth. She could still see Cole staring at her from his kingdom on the recliner, his eyes hard as she drove away.

"Sure, honey." Lolly gestured with her coffeepot toward the town bulletin board. "Can I get you something?"

Maggy shook her head. She pinned the ad next to one advertising a litter of kittens.

"Looking for a hired man, huh?" Lolly had come up behind her.

Maggy stepped back, emotions knotting her voice. She managed a nod.

Lolly glanced her, her hazel eyes kind. "C'mon, coffee is free today."

Maggy felt fatigue rush through her as her legs moved toward the counter without command. She slumped onto a stool and peeled off her gloves.

Lolly took down a cup from the shelf behind her. "Heard some wolves howling last night. John said he saw some on his property. Had to chase them off." She glanced at Big John as if to confirm it.

Maggy cupped her hands around her mug as John grunted. She often wondered what Lolly and John saw in each other. Fifteen years seemed too long to wait for a commitment, but their daily banter might be enough for them. In fact, maybe Lolly and John talked more than Maggy and Cole did.

Was that what their marriage had been reduced to? Occasional grunts of conversation? She couldn't remember the last time Cole had rolled over to her side of the bed and wrapped his arms around her.

His tenderness today had made her nearly weep with longing. If only he hadn't been trying to sweet-talk her out of going back to the doctor. If only he could believe that she ached for his embrace, for his presence beside her to help battle away the cloud of fear that closed in more each day. But as always, doubt hung between them like a barbed fence. His fragile health only widened the space.

"Have you seen any sign of wolves, Maggy?" Lolly asked, clearly trying to reel her back from her despairing thoughts. For all her mystery, Lolly understood people. She'd appeared nearly sixteen years ago with a wad of cash, landing in Phillips seemingly by accident. It didn't take her long to decide to stay, especially after she met Big John. She rescued the dining car from the Burlington yard and set up the café within months. No one had ever pried from Lolly a smidgen about her past.

And she was still waiting for the ring.

She made delicious key lime pie, however. And offered free chili fries whenever the Custer County Buffaloes won a football game. Maggy and Nick and Cole had spent too many nights here, slurping chocolate shakes, fighting over fries, dreaming of their futures.

Back then she'd dreamed of being the queen of the Silver Buckle. The woman at Nick Noble's side.

"Maggy?"

Maggy looked up. Lolly had her eyebrows raised in quiet humor. "Uh, no . . . no wolves. Not yet, thank God."

"You let us know, okay?" John said. He didn't look at her.

She didn't look at him either but nodded. Clearly, John Kincaid still felt guilty, even after all these years, about firing her father after his many years of service on the Big K.

"How's CJ?" John's friend asked. "Going to enter the Custer rodeo this year?"

Maggy grinned. "Of course. He's hoping to go to junior nationals."

"I remember when Cole and Nick swept the team-roping championships. Those two could have been brothers the way they worked together. I thought for sure they'd go to Vegas for the nationals—"

"CJ's a star," Lolly said, glancing at the man. Maggy saw disapproval in her look. "He comes by his talent naturally. I'm sure he'll win."

"I hear Rafe took first this year in the national finals in Reno."

"He's riding in the PBA now." Maggy shook her head. Why Rafe Noble wanted to throw his life away taking on a two-thousand-pound bull made her want to scream in frustration. Then again, Nick's actions had affected them all in ways no one would have imagined.

There were times when she wanted to track Nick down and tell him exactly what his temper tantrum had cost his family. Or rather rewind time to the day he rode to the Big K on Pecos and charmed his way into her heart. She would have turned and run to her parents' trailer instead of joining him for roundup. But although Nick Noble—rodeo star, football captain, and homecoming king—had left scars, the name still had the power to stop her in her tracks.

Nick . . . and Maggy Noble. Old habits caused her to fill in her name next to his. It didn't help that it had been carved into too many cottonwoods on the Silver Buckle range.

And soon . . . St. John land.

*Please, Lord, don't let Nick come back.*

"The forecast out of Sheridan says rain," said John's friend.

John grunted. Maggy sighed.

Lolly handed her a piece of pie and a fork. "How are your folks doing in Arizona, Maggy?"

"Mom got on full-time at the hospital. And Dad's still doing maintenance at their trailer park. He likes it." Maggy scooped a piece of pie into her mouth, hating the feel of Big John's silence. She'd long forgiven him. These days, they all had their own set of problems. Still, old sins took an eternity to die in a small town. She thanked God every day that hers had never been discovered.

"You tell them hi from me," Lolly said. She handed Maggy a Styrofoam container. "That's for Cole."

The door opened and Lolly said, "Howdy, Egger. What's new?"

Egger Dugan sat down next to Maggy and plopped his dirty feed cap on the counter. Lolly set a cup of coffee in front of him and filled it.

He sipped it, then looked over at Maggy. She smiled in greeting. Egger had scared her as a teenager, and he still made her uncomfortable. Something about the way the chaw stuck in the crevasses of his teeth. Or those two hound dogs of his that chased everyone in and out of town.

Something entered the old man's eyes. Then he nodded, as if part of some internal conversation, turned back to his coffee, and took another sip. "Funny thing happened today," he said to no one in particular.

Maggy ate her pie in silence.

"Thought I saw Nick Noble drive through town."

If Piper could have asked fate for anything, it would be to *not* let Nick Noble accompany her into the middle of nowhere with the sun beginning to dip into the horizon and a lone bellow drifting from some forlorn place between the bluffs. She felt like she should be in the audience of a movie theater, her arms waving in warning as the victim drives away with the serial killer.

But at least this was better than sleeping in his bedroom. Talk about creepy.

What if Nick *did* recognize her? Not as Jimmy's sister, but if he knew she'd staked him out in Wellesley only to appear here, that might start his detective wheels turning. Thankfully the little go-around with his sister had thrown him off. And good thing too, because just seeing those dark eyes had nearly stripped Piper's thin veneer of courage.

Destroyed lives, huh? Apparently Jimmy's life hadn't been the first on the list of Nick Noble's casualties.

And if she wasn't very, very careful, Noble might have a chance at her. Not only did he exude a presence that unsettled her, but the way he watched her made her mouth turn to dust. As if he could see right through her, past her agenda, past her anger, and right to her scars and fear that lurked so deep she barely noticed them anymore.

Until, that is, she got around arrogant, bossy men.

Unlike Nick's sister, Piper didn't fall for his let-me-help plea for a nanosecond. So he used a voice that might make every woman within fifty miles want to believe him. Piper knew better—way better. She knew too much about men to believe a bully like Nick Noble might have a tender, even chivalrous, place inside him.

Okay, yes, something about the look of shame that crossed his face when his sister accused him of destroying lives had rattled her. As if . . . inside that intimidating exterior lived a man of honor.

In that moment Piper had felt like a snake. But she had only to remember that even her father had had his moments of tenderness to snap her back to her senses. She wouldn't let her guard slip again. She could do this. Next time she got a glimpse of that shame, she'd turn it into an admittance of guilt, even a confession.

And she'd finally publicly brand Nick Noble an outlaw.

The pickup bumped at a slug's pace as she followed along the rutted road to the lodge. The setting sun cast low shadows across the hills, and she felt a hint of chill creep into her Jeep and under her cable-knit sweater.

The hunting lodge sat in a hover of jack pines and a large honey locust. She felt an idiotic spurt of delight when she noticed its front porch, complete with a rocking chair overlooking a view of the Bighorn Mountains. Part of her apparently thought she might be on vacation instead of on a covert operation involving spatulas and cookpots.

But if she got near either, the jig would be up. She could barely make toast, and her oven in her two-bedroom condo hadn't been used since the last tenant vacated two years ago. But she needed only a few hours alone with Nick to wheedle the truth from him. If he was a true cowboy, she'd simply bat her eyes and give him a c'mere smile, and he'd be running over himself to write her poetry and sing her a ballad. Two days, tops. No cooking needed.

She could fast for two days if she had to.

She pulled up behind Nick and got out of her Jeep. Nick appeared beside her to wrestle her duffel bag out of the hatchback and carry it into the house.

A light turned on, spilling out of the cabin windows in a welcome-home glow. Piper stood on the porch, debating her options. The last thing she wanted was to be in close quarters with this man, especially if any of his foul mood lingered. Still, she didn't have a prayer of coaxing the truth out of him if she acted like a nervous puppy every time she got near him. *I am Lois Lane.* No, today she was Wolfgang Puck. She painted on a smile, hiked her backpack over her shoulder, and went inside.

The place smelled freshly scrubbed, with the faintest hint of lemon lingering in the air, as she entered the ancient great room. The log walls gleamed with age and polish. On one side of the room, in front of a copper-toned, ledgestone fireplace, a braided rug was anchored by a worn leather sofa and two burnt red, overstuffed chairs. On the other end of the room, a small kitchen, complete with fifties-era appliances and a microwave, suggested low expectations for the culinary abilities of the guests.

Of course, that was where she came in.

She dropped her backpack onto the table.

Noble appeared from one of the two bedrooms that exited off the main room, as if he'd been scouring for bandits. "I'll start a fire in the hearth and load the wood burner out back. The place should be toasty in an hour or so."

"Thanks," she said to his back as he began to assemble the fire. She stood there watching him arrange the wood, tuck in a wad of newspaper, and light the fire. He had strong arms and wide shoulders that filled out his navy thermal shirt. His black hair had grown out enough to hint at curls.

He wasn't good-looking. Not at all. Just tall, dark . . . and despicable.

The fire started to spark and pop, the smell of smoke filling her nose, reviving her memories. She spiraled back in time and felt the cold rush of wind whipping through her polyester nightgown. . . .

*"Piper, stay back! You'll get burned!"*

She heard Jimmy's voice, felt his hands on her as he yanked her from the mesmerizing blaze. How fast the pillow had burned, flames gobbling the synthetic insides, pungent black smoke drowning the small room. Jimmy had grabbed her by the arm and nearly dragged her from the trailer.

She felt again how her bare feet had stung in the soupy, half-frozen grass. She remembered hugging herself as she watched the smoke billow out of the trailer door in the early morning mist.

"Stay here! I'll get Mom!"

She'd watched Jimmy run back inside, watched the black fog swallow him, felt a sickness so thick in her stomach that she thought she might throw up. She sank to her knees shaking. Jimmy would get Mommy. Jimmy always protected them. She was safe with Jimmy near.

But Jimmy wasn't there when she heard the crunch of tires on gravel. She turned, and her fear found her bones as she saw the headlights slice through the predawn gray.

Daddy was home.

"Ms. Sullivan?"

Piper didn't realize she'd wrapped her right hand around her left wrist, her thumb rubbing the place where her jacket hid her scar, until Nick Noble touched her arm. She nearly leaped right out of her new cowboy boots. She jerked away from him, at a loss for words, her mouth open. The memory seemed so alive, so bru-tal—she felt that if she didn't close her mouth, it might climb right up her throat in a howl.

One hour in Nick's presence and already she had turned into a mess of nerves.

"Are you okay?" he asked.

She forced a smile and nodded. "Thank you."

"You sure? You look a little—"

"I'm fine."

He stared at her a second longer, then slapped the bits of wood off his hands. "The cabin is a bit rustic. I checked the plumbing, and it seems to be working. You'll have to hold the handle down on the toilet to make it run, and the water is hard, but the well is good." A shadow crossed his face. "Or it was . . . I guess I'll have to check on that."

Piper nodded, glad she'd added bottled water to her supplies. "I'll be fine."

"So . . . have you ever worked on a ranch before?" He stood there, his eyes boring into her.

She summoned her smile. "Nope. I'm sure I'll have a lot to learn."

"You know you'll have to cook out on the trail and that the guests will want authentic trail food."

"Sure, granola bars and s'mores. Got it."

Apparently he'd been in the wrong line when they handed out a sense of humor. His mouth didn't even twitch.

"I know a little about Dutch-oven cooking. I'll be all right," Piper said, keeping her voice solemn, wishing she had invested in a few more books but thankful she'd watched *Campfire Cooking* at least once.

"I guess we'll see," Nick said. "I'll leave the two-way radio. Call if you need anything. Although the road seemed to take its time winding back here, the main house is only down the hill, through the winter pasture. There's a trail."

"I'll be fine, Mr. Noble."

"Nick. Please call me Nick." He smiled at her, but it didn't reach his eyes, which continued to look clear through her, nosing about to find her secrets.

She swallowed. "Nick." Her voice sounded like a grunt.

"Tomorrow, if you really want, I'll take you on that tour around the ranch, show you the lay of the land."

She rubbed her hands over her arms, nodded.

He was turning to go when she heard a low, mournful wail that lifted from the purple hills and drifted in with the drafts.

"What's that?" she asked without thinking. She hated to sound so . . . unnerved, but the noise had raised every hair on her arms. Somehow it sounded painfully familiar.

"Wolves," Nick answered as he reached the door. "But don't worry; they won't come after you. They're lonely or lost and trying to find their way home."

No wonder she recognized the sound. Her heart made the exact same wail.

❧

It had taken him nearly all day to find this spot overlooking the homestead. He'd followed an old cow trail, then hid his truck in a draw and climbed a ridge that overlooked the valley. Now, lying in the sodden grass, moisture crept into the elbows of his jacket as he held the binoculars to his eyes.

He'd watched them as they drove up the trail toward the cabin. The slim blonde and tall, righteous Noble. Now they moved in and out of the light of the windows.

A muscle pulsed in his jaw. He never thought it would come to this. Or that he'd finally get a chance at revenge after all these years.

He simply needed to wait. Nick would make a mistake again. And this time he would pay.

He was a patient man. After all this time, he was a very, very patient man.

# CHAPTER 4

STEFANIE MET NICK in the living room right after he'd returned from the lodge. If he thought she'd be appeased by his willingness to show their new guest her digs, he'd guessed wrong.

She sat on the leather sofa, her legs crossed. She'd shed her work clothes, showered, and changed into a long-sleeve shirt and track pants. She looked about thirteen without her makeup, her dark hair slicked to her head, and she had the explosive, teenage emotions to match.

And while his little sister still couldn't cook, she served up guilt like an iron chef. "You have no right to come in here and start telling me how to run the ranch!"

"Howdy to you too. She's fine. I started a fire and tucked her in." He didn't mention that Miss Piper Sullivan had looked rattled by the lonely mourn of the wolves that carried across the prairie. If she knew, Stefanie would head out to the pasture to sleep with the cows, her shotgun over her knees.

Stefanie had also started a fire, and it crackled in the hearth, sending a cheery glow into the room. The sound conjured up memories of snowy Sundays and Monopoly around the stone coffee table, the smell of chocolate-chip cookies drifting from the kitchen.

Obviously Stefanie didn't share that cozy memory at the moment. "You have no idea the trouble we're in, Nick."

He sighed, used the bootjack to work off his boots, then settled into the leather easy chair opposite her. "Saul told me a little when he found me in Wellesley. The herd's numbers are down, and the drought–"

"The drought is killing us. We haven't had a decent alfalfa crop for two years, and I had to take a loan out to buy feed. Add to that the loan we have for Tiny–"

"Tiny?"

"Dad bought a new bull last year, and he hasn't earned his keep. Or at least the cows aren't producing." She ran her hands through her wet hair, rolling it up in back and holding it in place. "Not only that, but a couple days ago, Dutch and I found two of the younger bulls, the ones we kept in Hatcher's Table, dead."

"What?" Two dead bulls out of the ten or so they kept dug a hole in their abilities to produce a new herd.

"Vet checked them for mad cow disease. They're not infected. But they died of dehydration."

"Hatcher's Table is watered by Cripple Creek. Did it run dry?"

Stefanie shook her head. "I don't love the idea of a dude ranch any more than you do, Nick. But until we figure out how to turn this ranch around, we have to do something."

Nick said nothing but let his attention roam the room. The elk head still hung over the door, and in the corner his father's reading chair and stack of books seemed ready for his evening occupancy. On the far wall, the aerial shot taken of their ranch showed the glory days when their bunkhouse overran with eager cowboys, when the alfalfa grew as high as his chin. When he and Cole spent every waking hour on the range.

"How's Rafe?" Nick asked, without looking at her.

"Making money hand over fist. He's got a couple endorsement deals."

Nick could see his little brother hawking just about anything with his bad-boy smile and cutting good looks from the Scottish side of the family.

His focus fell on their family picture taken his senior year in high school, still hanging opposite the fireplace. Rafe and Stefanie seemed so young–gangly twelve-year-olds with buckteeth. Their mother, Elizabeth, stood beside their father, leaning into his embrace. Nick always wondered if she knew even then that it would be their last family picture. That the cancer would soon consume her. Nick's perusal passed Bishop, the larger-than-life patriarch in the middle of the picture, and stopped on himself. Dark wavy hair past his ears, darker eyes, a wry smile as if he might be too busy to stop and take a picture with his family. He recognized his best snap-button shirt and the shiny team-roping belt buckle he'd won at nationals that year.

He thought then that he'd spend his entire life on the Silver Buckle. And that someday Maggy would join the picture as his wife.

The thought of her still sent a twist of regret through him. He'd hurt her too.

"I thought you wanted to be a horse trainer," Nick said suddenly to Stefanie. She had spent all her teenage years helping Maggy and her father train horses at the Big K. "What happened to your dream of raising and training quarter horses?"

"I don't have time. Between Dutch, Old Pete, and me, we barely get the cattle fed and watered. We've got roundup coming up, the rest of the calves to birth, three new two-year-olds to saddle break, a windmill to fix, and once again the tractor won't start despite Dutch's magic. . . ." She leaned her head back on the sofa and closed her eyes.

Nick had noticed Dutch's pickup outside the modular house Bishop had built for him, and it didn't surprise Nick in the least that the old foreman had stuck around after his father's death, especially with Stefanie's to-do list. Besides, he and Bishop always seemed to have a unique bond. Then he thought of the Silver Buckle's old chef. "I'll miss Chet's biscuits. Remember when we used them as ammo?"

Stefanie let her hair drop, drew up her knees, and hugged them to her chest, smiling weakly. "They're not so bad out on the trail, soaked in gravy."

Nick let himself hear the longing in her voice. He hadn't considered how hard it might be for Stefanie to run the ranch on her own. "I told Ms. Sullivan that I'd show her around the property tomorrow." He still wasn't sure how he felt about her being here—at the very least he hoped to instill in her some good old-fashioned respect for the land. At best, he'd convince her that now was the time for her to tuck tail and run. But he didn't mention that to Stef.

"I'm hoping she'll cook for roundup this Saturday. Let her earn her spurs."

"You're really hoping this will work, aren't you?" Nick couldn't look at his sister, feeling suddenly like a traitor.

"I'm really hoping we don't lose this ranch."

"When you open a place to the public, you're asking for trouble."

"She'll be fine. *We'll* be fine. No one is going to cause any trouble."

Nick sighed and ran his hands over the smooth leather chair. "Stefanie, do you have any idea why Dad would leave half our land to St. John? What did Cole do for him?"

Stefanie looked away, into the fire. "I don't know. But Cole and Maggy have helped us a lot over the past ten years. Please, please leave it alone."

"Maggy?" Nick felt a slow squeeze of dread inside. "Did she hire on?"

Stefanie glanced at him. "No, she . . . oh, boy." She blew out a breath. "I thought you knew. I thought I told you. . . ."

*Told me what?* He didn't like the look on her face. Nick swallowed. Shook his head. "Nope."

Stefanie didn't meet his eyes. "Nick . . . Maggy is Cole's wife."

❦

A little leg cast wouldn't keep Cole from driving his Ford. He waited until Maggy and CJ left to check the heifers this morning, then pried himself out of bed, wrestled on his sweatpants and an old flannel shirt, wedged his hat over his unruly hair, brushed his teeth, left the week-old growth of beard, and shoved his free foot into his boot.

Just that activity caused him to nearly collapse in the entryway, breathing hard. A sheen of perspiration blanketed his brow. He tugged on his jacket. *Please, Saul, be home.* He hadn't called the attorney, but with his office attached to his house, Saul Lovell kept casual round-the-clock hours.

Besides, if Maggy caught him using the phone, she would think he was canceling the doctor's appointment she'd made for him in Sheridan. The woman clearly didn't trust him, the way she watched his every move, as if he were a heifer about to drop a calf.

Then again, it wouldn't be the first time he'd foiled her plans. Like the ones to grow old together, passing the ranch on to a passel of kids. By marrying him, she'd sacrificed so much.

Not anymore. He grabbed his crutches, wincing as pain shot through him. The door squeaked as he opened it, but he closed it behind him quietly and hobbled out to the truck. Glancing at the barn, he opened the door, tossed the crutches in the cab, then levered himself onto the bench seat. The truck smelled of dust, the residue of working in the field all day. He fired up the engine and threw the truck into reverse as Maggy came out of the barn. She stood there, hands on her hips, eyes blazing. He drove away without acknowledging her.

Good thing they had only one vehicle. But with his luck, she'd probably saddle her horse and follow him into town.

Or Pecos. Nick's roping horse was faster. Sturdier. Better than Cole's tired stock horses. Cole shook his head. Another reminder of the harsh truth. And Maggy's sacrifices.

He drove toward town, past the Silver Buckle and the Big K, cutting south at the Breckenridge place. Saul Lovell owned a section to the east, on which he'd run a fancy French breed of cattle called Salers. Although fewer head, their high birth rates and fatty, beefy bodies brought in more money per pound. Over the years, it had kept Saul's ranch in the black. But with Saul's sons now in

Sheridan and Denver pursuing their own lives, Saul had sold off most of his herd. At least he had his attorney shingle to hang on to. Not for the first time, Cole wished he'd gone to college and earned a degree to go along with his vet skills.

He'd make sure CJ had that option if he wanted it. He'd put it in his will. Cole knew very little about the probate process—but even a rancher with a mere high school diploma knew that unless he had things spelled out, all his hopes for Maggy and CJ might get tied up in court. He wanted a clean start for her. He'd written everything down on the notebook paper in his pocket, outlining how she was to sell the land quickly and move to Arizona with her parents. CJ could attend a public school instead of doing his lessons on the kitchen table, and Maggy could finally join a big church, one that played all those praise songs she sang to the cows.

Cole pulled into the yard, a little envious of Saul's two-story home. He'd had the house trucked out from Sheridan and assembled on the property right after his boys graduated college, finally abandoning the family's log cabin handed down from his wife's parents. Cole remembered how Maggy's eyes had shone as she described Loretta's new house.

*Someday, Mags, someday.*

He parked behind a black Silverado and maneuvered himself out of the truck.

A collie rose from the porch to meet him.

He patted the dog and opened the door. "Saul?"

"In here." The voice came from the study, where Saul conducted his business.

The house smelled of polish and cinnamon. Saul's wife, Loretta, hummed from the kitchen as she whipped up cinnamon rolls. The oak door to Saul's office stood half closed, and for a second Cole wondered if he should knock. Instead, he pushed the door open with his crutch.

Saul sat at his oak desk behind his computer, talking to a man seated in a leather side chair, his back to Cole.

"Excuse me, Saul. I didn't know you had—"

Cole's words died in his throat as Nick Noble turned and glared at his former best friend.

Nick should have listened to his sister.

"Nick, please don't do this." Stefanie's plea this morning as he'd informed her of his plans shot through Nick's mind as he stared at Cole. He'd filled out, his face harder, his shoulders wider. He watched Cole's fists close on his crutch handles, saw the clenched unshaven jaw, noted the familiar glint of anger in his brown eyes.

*"You're achin' to blame someone, aren't you?"* Cole's voice rushed at him in memory, and he shook it away.

"What's he doing here?" Nick growled, mostly to Saul, but if Cole heard, he didn't care.

"I could ask the same about you," Cole growled back.

Nick saw him inch forward. Closer, he looked pale and gaunt. For a second, worry sluiced through Nick. He ignored it and turned back to Saul. "We're done here anyway."

Saul shook his head, defeat in his eyes.

Nick didn't care that the man had spent the last hour trying to convince him that Bishop Noble had been genuine in his desire to give the land to St. John. So what that Saul had questioned Bishop to ascertain his ability to make sound decisions?

Nick knew that Cole had coerced Bishop to lie even to his best friend.

But the truth would find Cole out. Nick planned on filing the petition today and would spend every millisecond between now and the date of the hearing proving what he knew with ever fiber of his soul—that Cole St. John was a thief.

After what Stefanie had told him last night, Nick labeled Cole even more of a thief than he had before.

Nick stood and snatched his hat from the desk. "This isn't over." He turned and waited for Cole to clear the door before brushing past him without another word.

He felt Cole's eyes on him as he left. Cole had always given off a holier-than-thou vibe and used it with precision when he wanted to bring Nick to task. Dudley Do-Right, Nick had called him.

In high school Nick had blamed the do-gooder niceness on the fact that Cole didn't have a father to teach him backbone, and he and his mother were at church every time the doors opened and then some. No wonder Maggy always considered Cole a gentleman. Nick couldn't believe he had actually felt sorry for the guy. Wanted to make him part of his family, begged his father to hire him on during the summer. Too late he'd discovered Cole's games.

Thankfully he wasn't fooled any longer.

Marching out to his Silverado, Nick got inside, noticing St. John's battered Ford behind him. He couldn't believe that thing still ran.

Pulling out, he spit gravel as he drove back to the Silver Buckle. *Maggy is Cole's wife.*

Cole had stolen everything from him—his land, his woman. Not that Nick deserved her—it had taken him about two years to figure that out—but he hadn't found a woman since he left who laughed at his wry humor, who put up with his bullheadedness, who listened until he unraveled the thoughts that knotted his brain.

Someone who might fit into his life.

Then again, what kind of life did he want? Since he'd turned in his badge, he'd been waiting tables, occasionally throwing flapjacks.

He'd sacrificed everything because of his temper, and even now his sins seemed to haunt him. According to Saul, Nick couldn't do a thing to contest Bishop's will. Not unless he found evidence that the will had been signed under duress—that Cole or some other benefactor had been in the room putting unseen pressure on his father during the signing. But Saul said they'd been alone in Bishop's bedroom during that critical hour. Unless Nick unearthed a miracle—in Bishop's journals or an untapped vein in Stefanie's memory—he'd lose his past and his future to Cole the Thief. It felt like yet another punishment from God.

*When, God? Everyone else seems to have forged on. When will I get to pick up the pieces? Will I ever feel Your forgiveness?*

He drove into the Silver Buckle yard and parked right behind his father's old pickup. He'd driven the truck yesterday out of some errant desire to reconnect, to belong to the ranch again. He strode past the pickup and headed into the house, bracing himself for another go-round with Stef.

Only the old Maytag fridge met him as it kicked on and hummed in greeting. He tossed his keys on the counter, listening to his heart thump. He'd been ready, even eager, for a verbal sparring. Instead, Stef had left him a note in her bubbly handwriting.

*Dear Nick,*

*Went to town. Dutch is in the barn, working with the heifers. Please check on our new chef. I'll be back for supper.*

*S.*

Peering out the window over the sink, he saw Dutch's hulking frame exit the cow barn. The old boss, ten years his father's junior, had been like an uncle to him. Nick had always been a little afraid of Dutch's stern expression and huge hands. He wasn't foolish enough to ask for—or expect—Dutch's forgiveness.

Pouring himself a cup of coffee, Nick leaned against the counter and drank it black, his mind churning. Dutch might know what Cole had on his father—Dutch had always seemed to take an extra interest in Cole and, in particular, his shapely widowed mother, Irene. Spent a lot of Sunday afternoons on her porch. For a long time Nick thought he might marry Irene. Cole had even called him Uncle Dutch.

Nick finished his coffee, pocketed a granola bar, and headed outside. The smells of early yarrow and Wyoming kittentail hung in the warm air. The late-morning sun had begun to cut the chill from the cool air.

Rounding the house, he shot a glance toward the hunting cabin. He'd have to figure out a way to talk their new chef into hitting the road. After he figured out how to get their land back, they wouldn't need Ms. Sullivan anyway, and she'd be out of a job. He was doing her a favor.

He stood there, remembering her troubled look as she watched him build the fire last night. Vulnerable, even afraid. He had the strangest sense that she might be lost or running from something.

Then again, weren't they all?

He hoped Stefanie checked her references. He turned, heading for the corral.

Pecos was gone—had probably died—but the old bay lifted his head in greeting and nickered. Nick took down a lead rope and easily caught the horse, bringing him into the barn to be saddled.

It wouldn't be the first time he got on a horse to escape his problems.

Nick would be a hard nut to crack. Even though he'd showed a glimmer of his true side after Piper's arrival yesterday, since then he'd played the part of a perfect gentleman—searching the cabin and building her a cozy fire. He played his game like a gambler. But she aimed to earn his trust. By the time she finished with him, he'd spill his secrets like a drunken sailor, and she'd have it all on her digital tape recorder.

She'd spent the night curled inside the quilt in the center of the double bed, listening to the wolves howl. The last time she'd heard howling like that, she'd been five, and her brother had heard her whimpering in fear. She remembered how he'd crawled into her bed and let her fall asleep next to him.

Piper pressed her hand against her empty stomach, feeling it burn. She'd eaten a bag of dried fruit and an antacid earlier in the morning, but she'd need more than that if she hoped to fortify herself to face Nick Noble. He'd offered to take her riding today, which meant that if she showed up in the yard, hoping to cash in on the offer, he wouldn't be suspicious.

She pulled on a pair of jeans, boots, a long-sleeve shirt, and a lined leather coat. She slipped the recorder into her jacket pocket. She'd outfitted herself at a Western apparel store before leaving town, hoping she might fit in, and she hadn't appreciated Noble's condescending look yesterday.

The air felt fresh and the sun warm as she stepped out of the cabin and stood on the porch. The vista swept her breath away. The cabin looked out onto rangeland, and for as far as the eye could see, greening prairie rolled over bluffs and washes, gullied by brown streams and occasional patches of wildflowers. Clouds brushed the periwinkle sky in the lightest of strokes, and down in the valley the hulking bodies of black cows completed the pastoral frame. Big-sky country, indeed. It made her want to sing or spread her arms and run through the grass in a sort of *Sound of Music* emotional outburst.

Evidently she'd played one too many parts. Piper had never been the sentimental kind, and she was no Julie Andrews do-gooder nun. As long as she got to the truth, she didn't mind getting her hands a little dirty, telling a few white lies.

Most of the time she slept just fine.

But this view nudged a place inside her, something she hadn't felt since childhood when hope felt easier to grasp. When she believed that God looked down upon her, saw her, loved her.

But only dreamers and five-year-olds believed in that fairy tale. God, like the big sky, was simply too far away. Untouchable. And unconcerned with righting the wrongs in the world.

Leaving people like Piper to fill in the gaps.

Nick had told her to follow the path through the winter pasture to return to the main house. She only briefly considered her Jeep. She probably needed the exercise, and with her SUV close by, she couldn't beg Nick for a ride back to the lodge, could she? She stepped off the porch and walked to the barbed-wire fence. Not seeing an opening, she held it apart and gingerly climbed through.

The slight sound of bellowing drifted in the air. She'd heard that sound yesterday, and it had surprised her. She thought cows mooed . . . not bellowed. As she descended the hill, she noticed that another fence stood between her and the homestead. She'd entered one pasture too soon.

As she hiked down the hill, one cow raised its black head, then got to its feet. A windmill creaked, and another animal looked up from the round metal water tank and stared at her, water dripping from its jowls.

"Hi, cow," she said. Such a big cow, such a petite face. She wondered where its calf was—didn't they all have calves?

She stopped halfway down the hill between her cabin and the homestead, staring at the animal, her heart doing a slow spiral to her knees.

The beast stared back at her, switching its tail.

She liked cows, didn't she? They gave milk and were mostly afraid of humans.

The animal turned as she passed, and in her peripheral vision she watched it shift toward her. Then it let out a bellow that raised every hair on the back of her neck.

She picked up her pace.

The animal continued to follow her.

"Shoo!" She broke into a jog.

The bellow came again and nearly lifted her from the earth.

"Go find your baby!" Piper started running, and her heart nearly broke from her chest when the animal behind her followed suit.

Its hooves thumped the ground, and it blew out of its nose as it chased her.

"Go away!" Piper stumbled, fell hard, scrubbing her knees and skidding the heels of her hands into the mud. Scrambling back to her feet, she looked over her shoulder to see the cow nearly upon her.

The scream that was building in her felt as if it might have the power to send her airborne and hurl her to safety. She let it rip, then rolled into a ball, covering her head with her hands.

# CHAPTER 5

"PLEASE, OH COW, DON'T PUSH," Maggy pleaded as the laboring cow's eyes bulged with effort.

Next to Maggy, dressed in insulated Carhartt overalls and a feed cap on backward, CJ looked worried. "She's going to kill her calf."

The sunlight had begun to soak the day, but the chill that invaded Maggy's bones wouldn't dissipate. Not with another heifer on the verge of dying. Last night they'd found two stillborn calves and a heifer dead next to her struggling calf in the field by Rattlesnake Creek. Maggy had rounded up the few heifers ready to drop their calves and sent them into the barn along with this laboring cow, one of their oldest, who'd had a difficult birth last year. She'd watched them through the night, catching a few winks in the wee hours of the morning. Now it looked like that precious sleep would cost her another life. During her absence, the cow had gone into labor, pushing her uterus out in front of her calf.

"We've got to get her to stop pushing, so we can push her

membranes back inside." Blood covered Maggy's armpit-high plastic gloves.

"Should I call the vet?" CJ asked, his voice tremulous.

Maggy said nothing, blinking back a film of exhausted tears. No. They didn't have money for a vet. But they couldn't afford to lose this calf either.

*Please, God.*

If only Cole were here. Where he'd gone this morning she didn't know, but it nagged at her, especially with this cow dying. Cole would know what to do. He had a way with animals, a sixth sense about what they needed, and he'd have some home remedy.

"CJ, see if your father has any whiskey in the toolshed."

He frowned. "Why would Dad have–?"

"Just go check for me." She found a syringe, cleaned it, glancing out to the yard, praying that Cole might return. *Please.*

CJ returned with a dirt-crusted half-full bottle of Everclear.

Relief filled her. In her darkest hours, she'd feared that . . . well . . . maybe Cole's forgetfulness of late had other origins. But her husband–Dudley Do-Right, as Nick had so often called him–wasn't a man who turned to drink to solve his problems. However, he didn't turn to her either.

Maggy took the bottle and filled the syringe. Then, feeling for the place between the sixth and seventh vertebrae along the cow's back, she injected the alcohol into the spine. "Please work."

CJ stared at his mother in fascination.

The wind hit the tin barn, whistled through the cracks, and rustled the feed sacks shoved into the larger holes.

The cow moaned, but when the next contraction hit, she didn't bear down upon it, the alcohol relaxing her enough to keep her from killing herself and her baby. Maggy began working the cow's prolapsed uterus back inside her body.

After a moment a small black hoof appeared.

"Get the calf puller, CJ."

Wordlessly, he handed her the contraption—a long metal bar that fitted over the cow's rear. She attached one end of the chains to the small black hoof that protruded from the cow's body, then attached the other end to the bar. Once upon a time, Cole had been strong enough to heave a baby calf free from the womb. Now Maggy would have to ratchet it out herself.

Perspiration beaded on her greasy hair as the cow bellowed. CJ caught another hoof as it appeared, bloody and sticky with birth. Together they delivered the baby, lowered it onto the hay, and wiped it with a towel.

The calf opened its eyes and let out a high-pitched cry.

Hot tears burned Maggy's eyes.

"Wow, Mom, that was cool."

"Sure was." The familiar voice echoed through the tin barn.

Maggy startled. "Cole. You're back."

He looked tired from his excursion, leaning on his crutches, his hat pushed back. But she saw pride in his eyes. "I can't believe you remembered the whiskey trick."

Maggy let a tear drip from her cheek. She was just tired. So tired. Overwhelmed, really. Yet as Cole hobbled farther into the barn, his smile reminded her of those late nights and early mornings when they had watched new life come into the world together.

"Where were you?" she asked, hating the edge of accusation in her voice.

His smile dimmed. "To see a feller. I'll tell you later." He glanced at CJ. "How's your ropin'?"

CJ clapped his gloved hands together to clean them. "Thought I'd head over to the Buckle this afternoon. Dutch said he'd work with me on timing."

Cole said nothing, and it was right then that Maggy realized that Egger Dugan had spoken the truth yesterday in the café. Nick had returned. And with him the old rivalries, the old hurts. They showed on Cole's face like war scars. Cole shot a look at Maggy, then turned away, walking out of the barn.

Maggy closed her eyes.

"Dad—" CJ ran after him—"how about you coming with me?"

"No."

Maggy winced at Cole's curt tone, and something inside her snapped. This feud had eaten away at Cole long enough. So what that Nick had returned? They all knew he would someday. And after all these years, certainly Nick had gotten over the past.

Most importantly, CJ deserved his father's attention. "Cole St. John, don't you walk out on me!" She followed Cole, catching CJ first. "Go back to the barn. Keep an eye on the cow."

Cole had reached the front porch by the time she caught up with him. She slammed her foot against the door before he could open it, snapping off her surgical gloves. "What is your problem?"

"You know what my problem is." Cole kept his voice low, glancing once toward the barn, a signal that usually meant go away.

Well, she was sick of his silence, this cloud of doom that hovered over him. After ten years he should figure out that she planned on sticking around.

"Just because Nick Noble is a selfish jerk doesn't mean you can't be the father CJ needs. Dutch is only offering to help him because you won't. CJ needs you—he wants you there."

"*Can't*—not won't—help him. And I'm not going to Noble's property. Not with him there. Every cell inside him still wants to get his hands around my neck. Probably even more now."

She swallowed her reaction, kept her voice sober. "You saw Nick?"

He nodded, not looking at her.

"What did he say?"

Cole met her gaze, and for a second fear flashed through his eyes—something naked and so vivid that every word in her mouth crumbled. Then he looked away, leaving only the residue of his doubts. "Why don't you ride over and talk to him yourself, Mags? I'm sure you have lots to catch up on."

She slapped him. Hard.

He simply closed one eye, absorbing the pain.

She stood there, trembling.

"Just say it," he said in a low voice. "Say it."

Her words emerged on a breath. "Say what?"

"That you wish you'd waited for him to come back. That you wish you'd never married me."

⊱⋆⊰

"Tiny, get out of here!" The voice came from behind Piper, accompanied by hooves thundering across the ground. "Shoo!"

She opened her eyes just in time to see a cowboy on a horse, waving his coil of rope and running his horse right at the animal that rushed her.

At the last moment, the animal turned, shaking its head and snorting as it ran off.

Piper lay on the ground, breathing in tremulous gasps, precariously close to tears. *Get a grip!* She'd handled being shot at better than this. Gritting her teeth, she climbed to her feet, feeling light-headed.

The cowboy chased the beast off, then turned and trotted back toward her, shaking his head, a smirk on his face. Of all the rotten luck . . . of *course* it had to be Nick Noble coming to her rescue. And he looked straight out of some updated Western flick—dark leather chaps, cowboy boots, an open leather jacket, a day's worth of black whiskers gracing his chin, and an arrogance in his demeanor that made her want to shoot him between the eyes.

"A pretty gal shouldn't be walking through the bull pasture if she doesn't want to attract attention."

*The bull field?* Piper opened her mouth but couldn't conjure words.

Nick leaned forward in his saddle, pushing up the brim of his hat with one long finger. "Tiny wouldn't have hurt you. He just hasn't seen a cute gal in a while." He held out his hand and took his foot out of the stirrup, indicating she should climb up behind him.

If it weren't for the absence of a charming smile, she'd think he was delivering her a pick-up line. But he didn't smile, and the edge of sarcasm told her he meant every word. And not in a good way.

Whatever she did to turn him prickly side out, Piper intended to fix it. She took his hand, slipped her foot into the stirrup, and, ignoring the heartbeat filling her throat, swung up behind him. "He needs to find someone more his type," she quipped.

Nick didn't laugh.

The man had a serious glitch in his funny bone. Piper sat there a moment before she realized that this mode of transportation didn't come with a seat belt or even handles. Exactly where was she supposed to put her hands? The back of the saddle? Noble's belt loops? The horns growing from his head?

"Hang on to my jacket," Nick said, as if reading her mind.

She dug her fingers into the soft leather as he urged the horse forward. He smelled good—rebelliously good—like leather and a hint of soap. And he was tall, with broad shoulders and a straight posture. Strong, in a natural build sort of way.

Yeah, strong enough to wring her stupid neck.

"Thanks for . . . the rescue." She heard the tremor of fear still rattling her voice.

Nick urged his horse toward a gate in the fence. Behind her the bull stared at her with glassy black eyes.

"How did you get in this pasture?" Nick's voice still sounded peeved. She had angry beasts on all sides apparently.

"You told me to go through this pasture," she said, trying to keep accusation from her voice.

"There's a gate down the road from the cabin." He shook his head. "Stay out of the bull field."

"Are you sure? Because it's great exercise."

Silence.

For the first time, she wondered if she would be able to chink his armor. She was reaching deep, tapping into her best stuff. "Sorry," she added.

He angled toward a gate in the field dissecting the barbed-wire fence. "I don't suppose you want to rethink this job opportunity?"

"Not on your life."

"Well, out on the trail all day surrounded by cattle ... you're bound to make a boyfriend or two."

Was that humor? "Very funny. I didn't know this was the bull field. Next time be more clear in your instructions. Unless, of course, you're *trying* to get me killed."

Oops, her tone held way too much accusation. And she didn't want this skittish horse to run for the hills. She added laughter, so he might know she was kidding. Really.

Okay, so that wasn't a funny quip to either of them.

He reached the fence. "I have to dismount to open the gate."

"I'll do it." Piper held his arm as she slid off, opened the gate, then waited for him to pass through. "What were *you* doing in the bull field?" she asked as she closed it.

"Looking for tracks from the wolves we heard last night." He held out his hand, and she swung back up behind him.

She held on to the back of his coat, putting as much space as possible between them. "Do you really think there are wolves out here?"

"It's been a brutal winter. I wouldn't be surprised if we found dead stock in one of the outlying pastures."

"Will you shoot the wolves?" She replayed the lonely sound of the howls again, felt them sink into her bones.

"We can't. They're endangered. We have to call DNR and ask them to remove them."

"That's good."

"When a wolf takes down a cow, it not only costs the life of the cow but all the future lives the cow would have produced. Other cows panic, and it can cause a stampede, more deaths, and even stillbirths. Wolves aren't the cute animals you see on National

Geographic specials. They're serious predators and a threat to every range rancher."

"Oh." Yep, they'd be fast friends in no time at this rate.

The saddle creaked in the silence that followed.

"How long has your family owned the Silver Buckle?"

He seemed to appreciate her change of subject. "My great-great-grandfather came out here in the early 1900s as a homesteader. He ran the ranch with his three sons, and it's been in the family since then. My sister, brother, and I are the only remaining heirs." His sentence ended in a curious sharpness that edged on anger.

"Your ranch is beautiful," she said. "This morning I saw an antelope." She hummed the tail end of "Home on the Range."

He cut her off. "You should probably know that we have about three thousand head of cattle and eighty thousand acres." He turned south, where the line of Bighorns ridged the horizon. "Our property goes from here down to the Wyoming state line, so if you get lost . . . keep going and you'll end up in Sheridan."

"I won't get lost." She planned to stick like Velcro on Nick. And somehow dodge the pricklers he sent out. For pete's sake, who didn't like to sing along to "Home on the Range"?

"And then there're rattlesnakes. Stay away from the prairie-dog towns and sagebrush."

"Are you trying to scare me?"

That silenced him.

*Great.* Piper spotted black cattle lounging with babies standing nearby. They watched her, some chewing hay that dangled from their mouths. "What kind of cows do you have?"

"Black Angus. My father liked to run a pure breed, and Angus cattle have a lot of fat along with their muscle. They make a good cut of meat."

It looked like now wasn't the time to mention that she was a vegetarian. "Do you have any other cowboys working the ranch?"

"My sister runs the place, and our cow boss, Dutch Johnson, runs the hired hands. Right now, we only have Old Pete, who has been with us since I was a kid. But we'll bring in some day laborers for the roundup and keep a full bunkhouse on for the summer."

"What do you do? Shoe the horses?" She chuckled, hiding the fact that she knew he hadn't been near a cow in a decade. She wanted to see how well he lied.

"No. I've been . . . gone."

"What brought you back?"

He urged the horse into a canter. "Curious, aren't you, George?"

*Oh, I'm just getting started.*

Cole peered into the refrigerator, wondering what Maggy planned to make for supper. He knew how to cook steaks—he should probably take a couple out to thaw. How many times had he come in from a long day to be greeted by Maggy's smile and a hot meal?

He so didn't deserve her love. His sore cheek from her stinging slap only reminded him of that.

In fact, she hadn't been meant for him at all. Perhaps this was simply God's way of reminding him of the grace he'd been given—ten years of a life that didn't belong to him.

He closed the fridge, remembering Nick's expression this morning and how everything inside him had raged between trying to take the guy down and pummeling him and running home to pull CJ and Maggy close.

Nick Noble was back in town. This could mean only one thing. Trouble.

Cole filled a glass with water and collapsed on the old orange sofa in the living room. He'd worn himself out with his jaunt to Saul's. In the end, the lawyer had warned him that if Nick could find a reason for the will to be set aside, it probably would be. Especially given the rumors after Nick's mother had passed on. Even Cole wondered why Bishop had left him the property.

Cole closed his eyes, letting exhaustion overtake him. He should have known that Nick would return. And with him the old feelings, the old rivalries.

The memories . . .

The beat of a country-western tune across the green field grass signaled young Nick's appearance long before his truck came into view. Cole looked up from where he was reburying the water hose. So Bishop had come through with his promise to his older son.

A brand-new midnight black Ford 150 with a 4.9 liter engine, a V-6, with five on the floor, plus overdrive and rack-and-pinion steering came into view. Nick was behind the wheel, one hand out the window waving wildly as he drove off the road, over the cattle gate, and into the field.

Cole's mother would shoot him. Because Cole could never say no to Nick, and he had a hunch that Nick had plans to take his new wheels off-road to work out the kinks.

A smile followed that thought. Hopefully Nick's shenanigans would include a stopover at the Big K to pick up their friend Maggy.

Cole finished covering the hose, then pushed his hat back on his head and watched Nick bump over the field toward him. As usual, Nick drove way too fast for the vehicle's good, but then again he never had to pay for anything. Ever.

All hail the prince of the Silver Buckle.

But Nick's laughter and charisma were too infectious for Cole to be jealous. Nick swept everyone up with his smile and went down with his friends when trouble sucked them in. Of course, Nick had Bishop to pull him out.

"Hey, amigo, wanna ride?" Nick leaned across the bench and yelled out the passenger window.

Cole hiked the shovel over his shoulder. "Can't. Gotta fix the water line. Dutch said he wants to move the herd over to this pasture tomorrow, and there's a leak."

"C'mon, Cole—they can drink from Rattlesnake Creek. I only have three more days before I leave for school. You don't want your best buddy to leave with his new truck without trying it on for size, do you?"

"You're going to let me drive?"

Nick cocked a grin. "We'll pick up Maggy, go out to Cutter's Rock."

Oh, sure, and he'd be there watching the moon and freezing his backside while Nick and Maggy kept warm. "No, thanks, Nick. You go."

A shadow crossed Nick's face. "I need a hazer. Please?"

A hazer? "You're not thinking of going after Breckenridge's bulls again, are you? He'll hang you from the nearest cottonwood, and I'll bet your dad would help!"

Nick snorted. "No, of course not. C'mon; I promise we'll have fun, and your mom won't care."

Cole knew his mother way better than that. But when Nick gunned all 150 horses and cranked the radio, Cole felt a smile creep up his face.

After all, they had only three days left, right? Then Nick would be off to Montana State University, and Cole would stay here, working as a hand on Nick's father's land and trying to put together his own herd of Angus.

His life would dead-end, while Nick's soared into the future.

But for now, this blink of time, they weren't the rich man's son and the town joke. No, they were the dynamic duo. Nick and Cole, blood brothers, partners in crime.

They drove to the Big K and rounded up Maggy. She was in the corral working a new crop of stock horses. She had a way with horses, knew which ones made the best roping and cow horses and which ones would never ride right. She shouted orders at a gangly, dark-haired cowboy.

"Rafe's working with Maggy now?" Cole asked as they parked.

"Just trying to get some horse sense. I think he's figured out that the key to staying on a horse's back is getting inside the horse's head."

Thirteen-year-old Stefanie sat on the fence, freckle-faced, her long black hair in two braids. She shook her head when Nick honked, and Maggy bounded over.

"Heya, beautiful, wanna go for a ride with your cowboy?" Nick leaned one arm out the window, pushing his hat up with his thumb.

Cole rolled his eyes.

Maggy looked at Nick, then at Cole and grinned. "Where to?"

"Cutter's Rock?"

Maggy gave him a sly look, and Cole's heart twisted. Did Nick have even an inkling of how lucky he was?

Maggy ran back to the corral, her long red ponytail flipping behind her. "Rafe, that's enough for today. Brush down the horse and make sure you put away the tack." She unbuckled her chinks and hung them over the fence. "See you later, Stef."

Stef gave Nick a dark look as Maggy climbed in between Nick and Cole and they peeled away.

"So Bishop came through," Maggy said, pulling out her ponytail. She ran her hands through her hair to work out the tangles.

Cole looked away before his feelings showed on his face. How many times had he wanted to do that? But Maggy had always been Nick's girl . . . and always would be.

Cole hung his arm out the passenger window, looking past the fields as the pickup sped down the gravel road.

"Yeah," Nick said, curling his arm around Maggy. "Dad promised me that if I got into MSU, he'd make sure I could make it back to my girl every weekend."

Maggy giggled. "I think Bozeman's a little far to travel every weekend, Nick."

Nick glanced at her. "I don't want you sitting home alone on Friday nights. People might think you're available."

Maggy slid her hand through Cole's arm, patting his shoulder. "Cole will watch out for me, won't you?"

Cole couldn't pry words past the boulder in his throat, so he nodded. Wasn't that just Jim Dandy?

The sun had begun a slow slide down, but it would be nine o'clock before it hit the horizon. They cut off into a pasture south of the Buckle and wove through the coulees and bluffs all the way back to the border of the neighboring land. As they bumped along, cows and their calves lifted their heads, watching them.

Nick stopped the truck. "Okay, Cole, you get the wheel." He got out.

"What are you doing?" Cole asked as he rounded the back of the truck.

Nick had climbed onto the bed, unearthed a coil of rope, and was beginning to form a loop. "Ropin' practice."

Cole shook his head, but a smile broke across his face. "After you, it's my turn."

They chased the poor calves around the field for two hours, first Nick, then Cole, balancing on the back of the truck bed. Cole knew that if Bishop or any of the hands caught them, Nick could kiss his new truck good-bye, not to mention the hours of work Cole would owe the rancher.

But the sound of country music booming from the radio, the satisfaction of a well-thrown lasso, and the grin of amazement on Maggy's pretty face made it worth the risk.

Being with Maggy always made it worth the risk. Worth even hiking up to Cutter's Rock and sitting opposite the couple as the campfire glowed and flickered across their faces. Maggy stirred the coals with a stick, contemplative. The fire sizzled, and sparks shot into the blackness. Out here, the stars felt so close a man could touch them. Cole lay back on the grass, wishing this moment could last forever.

The door slammed, and Cole's eyes opened. He'd fallen asleep on the orange sofa. What was wrong with him? He pushed himself into a sitting position, feeling mortified.

The late-afternoon shadows darkened the house, and he barely made out Maggy's form as she entered the kitchen. She stood in front of the fridge, the light from the door illuminating her face and her auburn hair, now cut an inch above her shoulders. She seemed so young in the dim light, so unscathed by her life. She'd had everything and surrendered it for him.

Maggy broke the spell by sighing. She reached into the fridge and retrieved a Tupperware container of leftovers. Cole watched her as she dumped the contents into a casserole dish, turned on the electric oven, and shoved it inside.

She left without a word, without a glance in his direction—if she even knew he was here at all. Had she really ever seen him? Or had he simply been the one whose arms she fell into when her dreams had died?

Nick's stand-in.

Cole took a deep breath, hating the feelings that roiled inside him. His eyes burned, and for a sickening second, he thought he might cry. He battled the urge to surrender. To do as the old dogs did . . . disappear into the fields and die.

*Oh, Lord, please help me.* He flicked on the table lamp, and there, in the glow, sat his Bible. How long had it been since he'd read the Bible, found the sustenance he'd needed from God's Word? He opened it to his bookmarked chapter in Philippians and read: "I am certain that God, who began the good work within you, will continue his work until it is finally finished."

The words found Cole's broken places. He had so many dreams, so many hopes. . . .

*Please, O Lord, finish the good work You started in me. Whatever that is, finish it for the good of Maggy and CJ. I don't know why this is happening to me, but I beg You for enough time to do right by them. Please fix this, Lord.*

He closed the Bible, rubbed the leather with his palm. Nick Noble might be back, but he wasn't going to take the ranch from Cole. And Cole wasn't going to leave this world until he knew that his wife and son had a future.

Which meant he had to keep Nick from taking them to court.

The sound of a door closing turned his attention out the window toward a beat-up blue Ford pickup. He watched as a man, dressed in a pair of work trousers, a flannel shirt, a canvas jacket, and a dirty feed cap approached the front door. Cole eyed the barn, but Maggy didn't appear.

Cole struggled to his feet, leaning on the crutches.

The doorbell chimed.

"I'm coming!"

As he opened the door, the man stepped back. He wore the grizzled look of someone who'd spent a few nights in his truck.

"Can I help you?" Cole asked, reserving a welcoming smile.

The man met his eyes, and in them, Cole recognized himself, a spirit broken, a man near desperation. "I hope so. I come about the ad. For a hand. You still lookin' to hire on help?"

# ᵀ CHAPTER 6

"So, what do you think of the Silver Buckle?" Stefanie Noble looked every inch a cow woman in her brown-felt Stetson with her black hair tumbling down her back, a brown work jacket, and worn jeans over a pair of boots. She manned the wheel of her pickup with gloved and capable hands, undaunted by the fact that it nearly swallowed her.

Sitting beside Stefanie in the passenger seat, Piper stored the image in her thoughts for later retrieval—a metaphor about a woman facing the vast, overwhelming task of running a ranch.

After this morning's excursion, Piper knew the vastness of their land. As Nick had given her a tour of the ranch, explaining the operation, pointing out cows, fields, dangers, and history, she'd drifted back through the layers of time—to a time when men and women battled the harsh elements to carve out a life. She wondered if this life got lonely for Stefanie. Wondered at the resolute expression on her face and how often she smiled.

In a way, Stefanie Noble reminded Piper of her mother—the

mother who'd emerged after they escaped Russell McPhee. The mother who worked from six to six at a school cafeteria, then waited tables to put a roof over her and her daughter's head. The mother who had taught Piper to be strong, to hope, to have courage, and who had died too young.

"I like your land," Piper said in response to Stefanie's question, surprised a little that the words flowed from an honest place inside her. "It's beautiful, all those bluffs and valleys. I can smell the flowers in the wind, along with a little manure—"

"*A lot* of manure." Stefanie looked over at her and grinned. "We can admit it. That's how we make a living."

Piper laughed, and it felt good, even freeing. "Okay, a lot of manure. But I also like the whisper of the breeze across the grass, the squeak of the prairie dogs. I can understand why they call it Big Sky Country. The sky seems to touch the ends of the earth."

"It is beautiful. I hope we get some rain, though, or we're in for another dry year. And that won't be good for anyone."

"Nick said you lost some cattle recently."

The little lines around Stefanie's mouth tightened. "Yep."

"Is that why Nick returned? To help with the ranch?" Piper hoped that Stefanie might be a tad more revealing than her brother had been this afternoon. To hear Nick speak, he'd simply erased from his mind his stint as a cop. And along with it any thoughts of her brother.

Well, she hadn't. Wouldn't.

Stefanie shook her head. "I don't really know why God brought Nick back. But I hope he stays." Sadness touched her eyes as she glanced at Piper. "I hope he treated you better today than yesterday."

Well, since that first rough meeting he'd started a fire for her, helped her settle into her cabin, and saved her from a raging bull, so Piper wasn't sure how to respond. "It sounds like you and he have different agendas for the ranch."

"With the drought, all the ranchers are looking for creative ways to keep afloat. The Breckenridge raises bulls, the Big K is hosting a fancy celebrity roundup, and Lovell's turned to coal-bed mining for methane, trying to eke the last little bit of resource out of his land. Nick's simply upset because he hasn't been here to rule his kingdom. He's always fancied himself as the prince of the Silver Buckle."

"Why did he leave?"

Stefanie didn't look at her as she shrugged, but Piper recognized family secrets buried inside her gesture. Something had driven Nick away, and it only ignited her investigator's instincts. Piper stared out the window, as if not interested in the subject.

The first time through this stretch of ranch country, Piper had noticed only the collection of tract houses and mobile homes on the outskirts of town, but driving in through the sweeps and curves of the land now, she spotted homes tucked into valleys or sitting on top of bluffs, grand houses built for leisure and vacation. It seemed an odd contrast to the one-horse town of Phillips. She pointed one home out to Stefanie.

"That's owned by someone in Sheridan. Most of these nice places are. They're vacation homes or hunting cabins. Some of the Phillips folks live out here, but mostly those who don't own ranches live in town. Even the day hands who work on the big ranches live in town with their families." Stefanie slowed for the stoplight, then turned right into the parking lot of the Watering Hole Café.

"How big is Phillips?"

"'Bout eighteen hundred. But they keep expanding the town borders." Stefanie climbed out of the truck.

Piper slid out of her side. She felt as if she were in a Louis L'Amour novel, with the false-front buildings, the saloon, the rain barrel at the end of the roof of the feed store, the barbershop with the candy-cane pole. "Do you have a newspaper here?"

Stefanie came around the truck. "A weekly." She pointed across the street to a small stand-alone building wedged between a bookstore and the Red Rooster grocery store. *The Phillips Journal.*"

Piper wondered if she should drop in and see if she could nose around the paper's microfiche—if they had any—for mention of Nick. Some history would add color to her report.

"I want to introduce you to Lolly. You'll do all your ordering through her." Stefanie climbed the steps to the dining-car café.

Piper forced a smile, donned her chef's aura, and followed her. She entered the dining car to find it surprisingly homey and larger than she expected. Orange booths lined the wall against the windows, and a few Formica tables gave it a fifties-era feel. Behind a long counter with wooden stools, a woman who could have stepped out of the seventies, with her blonde hair falling out of a high bun, wearing tight jeans and a tighter shirt, held a coffeepot and flashed them a smile.

Stefanie motioned Piper to a stool and took one beside her. "Lolly, this is Piper—our new cook. Could you fix her up with your food distributor, like you did Chet?"

Lolly set two white ceramic coffee cups on the counter. "Yep. I'll get you that order list." She poured Piper a cup of coffee. "Glad to meet you, Piper."

Piper gave her a vague smile, hoping the woman didn't see right through her. Lolly looked street savvy, with years of experience in her eyes, something she couldn't have picked up in this small town. If anyone would see through Piper's facade, it would be this woman.

Piper blew on the coffee before taking a sip. Even so, when she sipped, the liquid seared her throat. She forced it down and gasped. "That's hot. And strong."

"Sorry. Around here we like it with some bite." Stefanie looked at her over the rim of her own cup.

Piper wiped her mouth with a napkin, searching for the sweetener, the creamer, wishing she could order a chai.

Lolly set a book on the counter in front of Piper and beside it a piece of key lime pie. "Order goes in every Thursday—delivered on Mondays."

Piper picked up the book, saw that it contained food lists.

"We have an account with the company, so the bill will come to me," Stefanie said. "I trust you, but I'd like to see your menus before you order anything, okay?"

Piper nodded, her eye on the pie, her stomach nearly leaping. She'd had a package of cheese crackers for lunch after Nick had dropped her off at the cabin, and her stomach felt on fire.

"So, where're you from, Piper?" Lolly asked, serving Stefanie a piece of pie.

Piper had a bite in her mouth, so Stefanie answered for her. "Kalispell. Bon Appétit Culinary School."

Piper washed the pie down with the coffee, more careful this time. "I'm nearly finished. This is just a summer internship." She felt the lie lodge in her mouth as she took another forkful of pie.

What was her problem? She'd lied to drug dealers, smugglers, and even to a man connected to the mafia—so why did her mouth feel like glue now?

"Ever worked on a ranch before?"

She shook her head in unison with Stefanie, who flashed her a warm grin. The fact that Stefanie Noble had given her a chance— a chef who had no experience, even if she wasn't a chef—made Piper wish she could cook just a little.

"So, what's your specialty?" Lolly asked.

Piper scrambled for an answer. Her mother had loved . . . ah, tuna casserole. "Seafood," she answered quickly.

Lolly raised a penciled eyebrow, smirked at Stefanie, who shrugged. "Do you also fish?" she asked.

Piper heard a jest in her tone. She smiled and took another fork- ful of pie. "Oh yes," she said easily, "I love to fish."

Nick found the grave easily, without asking Stef. Why he'd avoided it until this evening—well, he knew it had something to do with shame, but until today, when he'd tromped his old trails, he hadn't wanted to admit it.

Bishop was gone. And with his passing vanished any hope for reconciliation. Now his father had a power over him he'd never escape. Nick dismounted and draped the reins of the horse over the wrought-iron gate that ringed the tiny cemetery. Every Noble had been buried here since old Benedict Noble had homesteaded the place. Twelve graves in all. Twelve stones—some at angles and worn, others solid and engraved—marked the legacy that went before him.

Nick felt a sickness welling inside him, heard the disappointment of his ancestors in the chilly wind. To the west the bruised sky seemed to sense his wounds, and a breeze scurried across the fields, pushing brittle yellow tumbleweed.

Bishop lay in the northeast corner, his name added to the stone that already read *Elizabeth Noble, beloved wife and mother.* Stefanie and Rafe had done their father right by burying him beside their mother, despite his behavior after her death. Nick remembered the days after her passing, the pain that nearly suffocated him. The few times he'd wandered out here he found himself sitting in quiet sorrow, wishing he could see her one last time—her long dark hair like Stef's, her solemn eyes that could surface his secrets, his fears. His mother had believed in him, and she had loved her older son with a fierce mix of confidence and unconditional love.

For a long time he'd felt as if the cancer had eaten through him also. Had left him hollow.

Nick's choices since then had filled up that hollow space with fury. His eyes burned now, hoping that she couldn't look upon him from heaven to see the mess he'd made.

The dirt over Bishop's grave had begun to prickle with new grass. Nick took off his hat, then closed his eyes. He heard a sigh, troubled and deep, and realized it was his own.

It wasn't supposed to be this way.

He cleared his throat, and his voice came out weak and stupid in the vastness of the landscape of all that had been. "Hey, Dad. I'm back."

Last time they'd been here together, his father had pulled him into a rare embrace. Nick could still remember feeling like a little boy, needing to know that his world wasn't over. Now, seeing Bishop's grave, the old fears surfaced. How he longed to see Bishop's smile, the dark eyes that knew him so well, his wide work-worn hands curling the brim of his Stetson or slapping him on the back.

"I know I let you down. I know that I should have come home sooner, said I was sorry. I . . . don't know why you did what you did, but I should have given you the benefit of the doubt. I was angry and hurting . . . and wrong." Nick curled the felt of his hat into his fists. "I know Cole has something on you." He shook his head, emotion filling his throat. "I should have been here to make sure he stayed away."

The image of Cole, the fury on his face that night Nick had left only made Nick's voice stronger, the anger spiking through. "But I'm here now. And I promise, Noble land will stay our land. Stef and I will get the Buckle running again. We'll carry on what you started."

He ran a thumb under his eyes, catching the moisture there, wiping it on his jeans. Then he knelt before the grave and pressed his hand against the etching in the stone. *Bishop Nicholas Noble. Psalm 103.* "I'm sorry, Dad. I'm really sorry."

The sun had completely vanished, leaving only a burn in its wake by the time Nick returned to the ranch house. Stefanie's truck sat parked in the yard. From the lodge on the hill, dim lights from the windows pushed into the shadows. He stifled the impulse to pay Piper a visit and build her another fire. He didn't know quite what to think about their new cook. Something still nagged him, a feeling that the math didn't add up. Yet Piper seemed . . . friendly, if not naive to the life here. Curious George—she had more questions than a CIA interrogator, and his answers only encouraged more questions.

Still, after a while he'd realized he enjoyed talking to her. Enjoyed putting to words things he'd known his entire life, feelings and impressions of ranch life he hadn't let himself consider for a long time. Eventually he'd abandoned his hope of talking her off the ranch and surrendered to the fact that they'd hired on a romantic, someone enthralled with the cowboy way, the big skies, the open range.

Someone frighteningly like himself.

If he had to, he'd admit the morning hadn't been sheer torture. Not at all.

He rode to the barn, unbuckled his horse's saddle, and swung it over the sawhorse, then loosened the bit and bridle. Working that free, he grabbed a curry brush.

He could smell Piper, as if she still sat behind him, the scent of wildflowers and the sound of her laughter trickling into his senses, lingering there. He couldn't remember the last time a woman had gotten close enough to leave an impression.

Then again he'd been dodging women with 100 percent accuracy since Jenny Butler's death. Not that he and the rodeo instructor had particularly hit it off, but in the end, if he hadn't been in the picture, maybe she would still be alive. If the prosecution was to be believed, McPhee had been looking for payback when he went after Jenny. The last thing Nick wanted was to have anyone else hurt because of him.

The old barn smelled of hay and horse sweat, and the scents felt so familiar that a new wave of regret rushed over him. What would his life have been like if he had never left home?

At the least, Cole wouldn't have his name listed in Bishop's last will and testament.

Nick finished rubbing down the horse and freed him into the

corral. He whinnied to the other horses, shaking free of the feel of the saddle. Nick poured out the feed before he sauntered toward the house. The cicadas were out, buzzing in the sunset hours, and the smell of bacon drifted from the house.

"Stef?" Nick called as he entered, hooked his boots into the bootjack, and worked them off. His stocking feet felt cool against the stone floor of their entryway, ledgestone polished to jewel tones under years of Noble feet. He shucked off his jacket and hung it and his hat on the hook before entering the kitchen.

Stefanie stood in her wool socks, sweatpants, and sleeves of her chamois shirt rolled up past the elbows, stirring a pot of baked beans on the stove.

"When did you learn how to cook?" He came up behind her and laid a hand on her shoulder.

She leaned into his half hug. "Never. I just open a can and pour it in a pot. Chet spoiled us all." She blew on her spoon and gave the beans a taste. "But I know when a pot of beans needs some liquid smoke." She added the liquid, along with a few drops of Tabasco.

Nick took out the brown sugar, pinched some in. "Maybe you should let me do the cooking."

"Are you disrespecting my beans?" Stef gave him a slight push to match her mock smile.

"No." Nick held up his hands in surrender. "Just trying to keep you from burning a hole through my gut." He tugged on one of her braids, an old gesture from their childhood, then sat down at the table.

"Well, in a few days Piper will cook for us. And I'll bet you won't run from her cooking."

Nick poured himself a glass of lemonade from the pitcher sitting on the table. "Are you sure we can afford her? I was looking over the books—"

Stef turned, wooden spoon in hand. A blob of beans dripped onto the floor. For a moment, Nick expected their old sheepdog to appear and gobble it up. A pang went through him when he didn't. "She's practically working for free, Nick. It's part of the school program she's in. She has to have one quarter of hands-on experience—"

"And cooking out on the trail is going to give her the training she needs?" He reached for the newspaper and angled it toward him, scanning the headlines.

"Her boss said she makes a mean stew. Trust me; hiring Piper is a good investment. This is what we need to really put the Silver Buckle on the map with the tourists. "

Nick pushed the paper away. "It already is on the map. We have one of the largest spreads in eastern Montana. We don't need a dude ranch to make our mark. The Buckle brand has always been known for quality beef in every stockyard from here to Nebraska. We'll be the laughingstock of the cattlemen's association."

Stef turned back to the stove. "I don't go to those meetings anymore."

It had to be difficult for the men of the cattlemen's club to take his sister seriously. Not only was she a woman—and very few women besides legendary Libby Collins had made it in the cattlemen's world—but Stef was also young and beautiful, and he had a feeling that she'd heard one too many remarks to that end. Cattlemen were nothing more than cowboys who owned a few or many head of cattle. It didn't necessarily tame the maverick in them and make them gentlemen.

"Piper knows nearly nothing about ranching, Stef. I spent the morning with her, showing her around, trying to explain why this job is over her head. The more I talked, the more she ate it up." Perhaps that's what bothered him. She seemed too . . . idealistic. Too taken by the life he lived.

Then again, once upon a time, he'd been idealistic too.

"Then she'll do fine. I took her into town today to meet Lolly. Did you know Piper's a connoisseur of fish?"

"I'll head right out and catch her a trout."

Stef threw a washrag at him. "Where she comes from there are plenty of trout streams. And maybe we should all have more fish—"

"We raise beef—"

"My point is that she'll bring flair to our down-home Western hospitality." She grabbed the chili pepper and began to shake it into the beans.

Nick stood, taking the pepper from her. "It's just that in my gut—"

"Please, Nick, I don't want to hear about your gut feelings ever again!"

The sudden explosion from Stefanie stopped him cold. He braced himself as she rounded on him like the bull after Piper. "Your gut feelings have caused this family—and others—enough pain!"

Her words found the shame inside, the churn of regret that had been dogging him all afternoon, and twisted. He wanted to turn away from her, to let it go, to start over. But, as if he'd reverted into the rebellious teenager from the past, his mouth wouldn't obey. "I was right, wasn't I?"

Stefanie stood there, mouth agape, then threw her spoon back into the pot. "Ten years and you still haven't figured it out," she said before storming from the room.

Figured what out? That he shouldn't follow his instincts? shouldn't stand up to secrets and betrayal and lies?

He stirred the beans, then turned off the flame. He heard Stef upstairs in her room, stomping about. Apparently that aspect of her anger hadn't changed.

Well, she could have a point about not trusting the rumblings inside him. He'd spent the morning with Piper Sullivan, thinking she didn't have the stuffin' for life on a ranch. Instead, he'd found her pleasant, interested in their life, and undemanding. Even . . . spunky.

Nick hadn't found a woman like that since Maggy. Piper had spent the whole ranch tour drinking in his words. It had been ages since a woman listened to him, really let him talk without filling in the end of his sentences. Not that he'd told her much—mostly he'd rambled on about the difference between silver sage and black sage, how to tell when a cow was about to drop her calf, how to read the weather, and how to sing a soft song to the herd while on a trail ride. Things he'd once done as naturally as breathing. Things he'd locked inside that she'd unwittingly pried free.

What if his uneasy feelings had nothing to do with suspicion but rather the fact that Piper had gotten under his skin just a little?

⌘

He sat on the bluff and watched Nick Noble ride back across Noble land, knowing Nick had brought this on himself. Darkness crept over him, and he felt like a criminal. If he hadn't let her go, he wouldn't have lost everything he'd ever wanted. Lost his dreams, lost the woman he thought he loved . . . lost his future.

He could hardly believe he'd found Noble or even that the man had returned to his hometown. He wasn't sure exactly what to do about this turn of events . . . at the least it meant trouble. At worst, well, Noble had a history of mangling people's lives. He'd have to watch him, wait, and hope that Nick left her alone and rode back into the sunset without hurting anyone else.

He hunkered down along the ridge, saw how his shadow bunched up, turned dark and thick. Ominous in the fading light.

He never thought he'd become that kind of man. Ominous. Dark. But sometimes circumstances drove people to do things they'd never imagined they'd do. Things they couldn't control.

Things they would always regret.

# CHAPTER 7

THEY WERE ALL going to starve. Because if Piper didn't get creative, she'd never wheedle the truth out of Nick, and then she'd have to attempt to cook.

That wouldn't be pretty. For any of them.

Piper had finally dragged herself to the dining hall. If Stefanie Noble really intended to open a dude ranch, she had the right vibe going. The log cabin dining hall housed a twelve-foot, rough-hewn table etched with names and symbols from past cowpokes. Piper even found the words *Maggy + Nick* on one end and stored that in her mental files to explore later. Rustic wagon-wheel chandeliers hung over the table, and someone had recently cleaned the milkglass wall lamps that bracketed the door.

Beyond the eating area, a kitchen graced with an ancient four-burner stove, a standing freezer, an old green Frigidaire, a two-bin-deep well sink, and a stainless-steel work area evidenced a bygone era of a full bunkhouse and hungry cowboys. Piper concluded that the chuck wagon she'd seen parked outside probably wasn't for decoration.

Boy, was she in trouble. She'd better start working her Piper
Sullivan magic because three hours of moseying about the ranch
yesterday morning to get her "bearings" with Nick and a trip into
Phillips with Stefanie had netted her a new appreciation for the
term *saddle sore*, two exceptional pieces of pie, and a caffeine rush
but exactly nil about why Nick arrested and framed Jimmy McPhee
for murder.

She'd spent last night listening to their dreary conversation on
her digital recorder, hoping to find a scrap of information she might
latch on to and follow to a lead. Her long, dark evening had ended
with her falling asleep on the very comfortable patchwork quilt to
the sounds of a fire crackling in the fireplace and another lonely
sonata from the neighborhood wolves.

Hearing Nick's voice in the recorder and the way he'd called her
Curious George more than once—well, she'd also fallen asleep with
his face in her mind.

A face that was way too handsome for her own good. He reminded her a little of that country singer Tim McGraw, without
the mustache. An all-around grade-A cowboy. Piper's pulse leaped
to attention every time she thought of Nick riding across the range,
sitting tall in the saddle, reins held loosely in his hands. His deep
voice and sturdy confidence had invaded her pores.

Muddled her focus.

Or maybe she should blame that on the soul-filling beauty of
the Silver Buckle Ranch. The land rolled out over bluffs and down
riverbeds, a palate of yellow green cheatgrass, wild irises, white yarrow, yellow bells, and purple pasqueflowers. Even the pincushion
cactus bore its own beauty.

Nick had shown her prairie-dog cities, and they had waited

until one poked his gopher face out of a hole. She'd listened to the squeaking, much like a city of rats, and it raised gooseflesh on her skin. She'd seen a red fox and an antelope and watched a killdeer straggle off, protecting its nest. At a bird's song, Nick had stopped and pointed out the red-and-black body of the meadowlark.

Cicadas chirruped as the morning wore long, and by the time Nick had brought her home in time for her to head to town with Stefanie, she had to reluctantly admit that he'd been a gentleman, even if he hadn't unveiled a hint about his feelings.

It made her even angrier, more determined to ferret out the truth. Not because she had hoped he'd be a cad, but if he was, she might be able to keep a firmer grip on her righteous indignation.

From all outward appearances, Nick Noble was just that . . . Mr. Noble. Sincere, capable, and trustworthy.

Piper didn't trust the conniving, handsome liar from here to the front door.

Her father had been handsome—at least in the early years. But she'd learned well from her mother's mistakes. She wasn't going to let a pair of sizzling dark eyes and range muscles, let alone this romance-novel setting, make her forget why she'd concocted this lie.

Piper stood in the kitchen, taking in the cast-iron Dutch ovens that hung from hooks over the work area, the huge griddle that lay atop the stove, and the stockpots under the counter and wished she had cell-phone reception.

Maybe she should cut and run before the Nobles discovered that she could turn even a frozen pizza into a pile of ash.

The place smelled of cleanser and the faintest odor of grease. She found the pantry. Someone had labeled the containers of flour and sugar, the bins of potatoes, the onions and carrots, and even the rutabagas. Good thing too, because she had been about to identify the purple roots as cabbage. On the second shelf, she found an impressive display of hot sauces, from Tabasco to Tiger to triple-X barbecue. Maybe she could fry up hamburgers for every meal.

Yuck. Even if she hadn't turned all-out vegetarian, she'd eliminated beef and chicken from her diet. According to her trail recipe book she had few other choices. Tofu and beans. Yeah, Dutch and Grumpy Pete would go for that.

Piper crossed her arms, leaning against the pantry door, staring at the row of canned pork and beans. "Carter, I wish you were here."

"Boyfriend?"

The voice startled her. "Mr. Noble, you scared me."

"Again, call me Nick. I see you found your way to the kitchen."

He looked very cowboy this morning in a pair of jeans, boots, and an untucked corduroy shirt. He'd shaved, but his eyes seemed tired. And he gave off a distinct freshly showered aura.

She cut her gaze away from him, pushing the feel of those strong shoulders out of her mind, and walked over to the freezer. "I'm trying to take an inventory."

"Stef said she'd take your list into town today if you wanted."

"Swell." Piper let the cool air from the freezer whisk the sweat from her brow. She found a half-eaten carton of ice cream and some frozen snap beans.

At least she knew what she was having for breakfast.

"Everything okay, Piper?"

She closed the freezer door, turned, but didn't look at him.

"So, who's Carter?"

"He's my cooking teacher." Her voice didn't even change inflection at the lie. Well, it wasn't really a lie—Carter *had* taught her the meager little she knew about cooking.

"Stef was hoping you'd cook the roundup meal on Saturday. We usually invite a few other ranch hands over to help with branding."

Piper glanced at him, at the way he smiled at her, at his hands shoved in his back pockets. She shrugged. "No problem. How many will there be?"

"'Bout thirty."

*Thirty!* Thirty people to witness her humiliation. She had until Saturday to work her magic on Nick and hightail it back to Kalispell with her story.

"Perfect," she said smoothly. Piper had found the former chef's desk earlier—a beat-up table that held ancient cookbooks, stained recipe cards, and reams of invoices. Now she turned to the desk and dug through the books and unearthed one of Chet's cookbooks called *Range Cooking*. She flipped to the index, her attention turned to the recipes, and tried to swallow the dread that crept up her throat. *Beef Bourguignon, Stew, Peasant's Pie.* A carnivore's paradise. She closed the book, letting out a sigh.

"You seem flustered," Nick said.

He was still here? She pasted on a smile, then shook her head. "Just thinking about menu options."

"Chet used to make a delicious batch of chicken and dumplings. That and a blueberry dump cake and some homemade vanilla ice cream and—"

"I'm not Chet, okay?"

He stared at her, eyes wide.

She winced, making a face. So maybe she needed more sleep.

"Sorry. I just don't want you to expect the same kind of food Chet made." *As in edible.* "My food probably has its own . . . um, flair."

"I'm sure it does." He smiled at her—Mr. Magnanimous—and she tried to keep the glare from her eyes. *Please be a jerk.* "You're right. You're the cookie. You can make what you want." He backed away. "By the way, Stef mentioned that the pots haven't been cleaned since last fall, so you might want to clean them up."

Of course she would clean the pots before she used them. Dismay shot through Piper. Did he see through her so easily? "I'll do that, thanks." She forced a smile, scrambling for footing back on solid ground. "Did you help Chet much in the kitchen?"

His grin, wide and sweet, accompanied by a gentle laugh, made her heart skip just for a second. "No. Chet wouldn't let us ten feet near his cook fire. But I did some time out on the range, me and Co—I mean, me and some of the hands. So I learned the basics."

*Great.* She walked past him, desperate to move him from the kitchen—her own personal quicksand—and outside. "Thank you for the ride yesterday. It was gorgeous."

"No problem." An enigmatic smile played on his face and sent a shot of warmth through her. *Stop looking at me.*

*Stop smiling.*

*And smelling good.*

She stepped outside, aware that all relevant thoughts had escaped her brain again. Some reporter she was. They should rescind every award she'd won and put her back in obits. She'd write hers first because it was becoming clear that being around Nick Noble could indeed be lethal. To her career *and* her good sense . . .

"You said yesterday that you'd only recently returned. . . ." She faced Nick. "Why did you leave?"

A shadow crossed his face, and he gazed toward the horizon. "I . . . I . . . found out something about someone I loved. And it hurt me. It was a poor decision made in my youth." He pursed his lips, studying his boots suddenly, as if he'd let out more with that veiled confession than he intended.

"We often make poor decisions when we're young," Piper said softly. "I know I've made my share. I find that the ones who love you will forgive you." At least she hoped that was the case.

Nick didn't smile. "There are some things a person can never be forgiven for."

Piper didn't know why, but his words, accompanied by those sad eyes, seemed to zero into her soul. She looked away before she cringed.

Silence passed between them, filled with the sounds of the wind combing the grass and the occasional low of a contented cow.

"I didn't show you everything yesterday," Nick said quietly. "Would you . . . could I show you something else?"

⋘⋙

The truck turned into the Silver Buckle drive as if it might be connected to her thoughts and knew her questions. Maggy simply held on to the steering wheel, eyes focused on the house, dissecting every detail for evidence of Nick's return. She hadn't been here since Bishop's burial and hadn't planned on returning. Not that she didn't miss Stefanie—they'd been best friends, nearly sisters for her entire life. But she didn't have time or reason since the funeral. Until now. Until Nick Noble returned like the Prodigal Son, hoping for his father's forgiveness not to mention his inheritance.

Sorry, but according to that parable, the son had already spent his inheritance. He had nothing to claim. The reward would go to the son who had stayed by his father's side. The allegory wasn't completely accurate, but it felt that way as she parked next to Bishop's old Ford.

Maggy sat there, her emotions tumbling over each other. She'd spent the night propped up on one elbow, staring at her husband, watching him groan in his sleep, favoring his injured leg even as he shifted. Cole had been her real hero. The man who showed her what real love looked like.

Nick had simply been a teenage fantasy. A fairy-tale prince. She should have known better than to trust in Cinderella dreams.

She got out of the truck, climbed onto the porch, and stood outside the door for a long time, wondering whether to knock. She hadn't knocked in years—and in the end the Nobles had needed her to be someone who simply walked into their lives to help, to care.

Maggy often wondered if leaving Cole that land had been Bishop's way of making up for all Nick had rejected, all the hopes he'd destroyed. She missed the old man. Missed hearing him spin CJ yarns about the Old West, the frontier days, the outlaws and mavericks who flavored the Noble history. She'd seen stars in CJ's eyes—especially when Bishop had shown him his roping medals.

She probably had Bishop—not CJ's father—to blame for CJ's rodeo addiction. Her ten-year-old breathed rodeo, slept with his lasso, wallpapered his room with posters of roping champions. He already had his Custer County junior rodeo registration filled out and tacked to his bulletin board. As if they might forget.

Maggy decided to forego knocking and eased the door open. "Stefanie?" She wouldn't call out Nick's name, but her stomach fluttered all the same when she heard a creak. She stilled, listening. Nothing—not even the sheepdog who used to greet her with a yawn and a nudge from his black nose. She missed digging her hands into his shaggy fur. He'd disappeared a week after Bishop's death.

Sunlight slanted into the kitchen and across the floor, turning the linoleum to gold. Elizabeth Noble had updated the place back in the midnineties, and the paisley wallpaper and dark-oak cabinets attested to her good taste. Maggy could still remember sitting with her, paging through magazines while Nick and Cole ran a poor steer around the corral, working on their timing. What Elizabeth hadn't known was that Maggy had dreamed up her own design plan for this kitchen.

Maggy passed through the quiet kitchen to the living room, her steps light, her heart heavy. She still couldn't define why she'd returned, why she might be skulking through the house like a bandit. Maybe she only wanted to see Nick. See his face and search it for shame or guilt. He hadn't called. Hadn't even written. As if she—and the note she left him the night he'd left—had meant *nothing* to him.

She lingered in the living room, staring at the last Noble family picture. In her memories, Nick would always be eighteen, always smiling, always ready to charm her into his arms.

In some way, all the whole Noble family had that charm in different measures. And with different effects.

The smell of last evening's fire lingered in the hearth. Upstairs, she'd find Bishop's darkened room where she'd served him herbal teas and read him his favorite psalms. Nick would like to know that, know what his father had said about him in his last days. Know the secrets the old man had hidden for so long.

Anger flared inside her, fresh and vibrant, releasing in a cry. No, Nick didn't deserve to know. After all, he'd turned his back on her when she needed him the most.

Maggy pressed a hand against her mouth, her throat suddenly tight. She turned and stole back through the kitchen. What was she doing here?

Through the kitchen window, she saw him.

Maggy froze, watching Nick stride out of the barn, leading a bay quarter horse. Her breath caught. He wasn't eighteen anymore. This Nick had broad shoulders and a confidence to his gait that bespoke experience, not cockiness. He'd found his old black Stetson, and his dark curly hair barely showed from beneath the rim. He hadn't shaved in a day or two. And in a corduroy shirt and jeans he looked every inch the outlaw she'd branded him after he'd stolen her heart.

She watched with captured breath as a petite blonde followed him out of the barn.

Maggy turned away, fresh heat burning her chest. No, there were some things Nick Noble didn't deserve to know. Some secrets she would never betray. Because if she did, it might cost Cole everything he loved.

Everything that now belonged to Cole.

❦

Nick remembered clearly the last time he'd been to Cutter's Rock—three days before he'd left for college. He'd run his new pickup around the neighbor's field, scaring the cows, acting like a hotshot in front of Maggy. Occasionally over the past ten years, he returned to that day and the memory of sitting around the campfire under the stars,

Maggy under his arm, Cole trying not to glare at him from across the flames. There had been times in high school when he'd felt the jealousy radiate off Cole like heat. Not often, but sometimes when the three of them were together, it felt palpable. Never, however, did it seem dangerous. Because Nick also remembered the day he and Cole had sat on Cutter's Rock, had drawn their knives across their palms and crossed hands, letting their blood become one.

The Cole who had been his blood brother would have never taken his girl.

Nick let that thought rake through him as he'd saddled his horse and an old gentle mare and led them out of the barn. Nick didn't know why he had the urge to show her this place that had once been his alone. Maybe he needed to see it through new eyes, like yesterday when he'd shown her around their land.

Or perhaps he simply couldn't return alone.

Nick held the stirrup as Piper gripped the pommel and swung into the saddle, then gave her the reins. "Ever been on a horse?"

She nodded. "Trail ride through Glacier National Park once."

He mounted his horse, then urged him out ahead. "Would you rather ride behind me on my horse?" He wasn't sure why he asked . . . yes, he was—he'd liked the feeling of her arms holding on to him, needing him for protection.

Apparently he'd forgotten what happened when he let a woman close to him. Someone usually got hurt. In fact, he had accumulated a short but vivid list. Maggy. Maybe even his friend Jenny.

"No, this is good," Piper said as she urged the mare forward with her knees and a click of her tongue.

They rode up the road, cutting south through the winter pasture, then down across Rattlesnake Creek. He'd pointed out most of their property yesterday, how the creek meandered across their land from north to south. He'd left out the part about Cole now inheriting the creek on the southwestern side of the property. Piper's mare followed Nick's horse easily over the wooden bridge, and he urged the horses into a canter as they dropped into a coulee. Boulders and pincushion cacti prickled the prairie, along with a showing of pink steerhead. Azure blue stained the sky in every direction.

"Were you born on the ranch, Nick?"

*More questions.* Nick looked over his shoulder, saw Piper nearly abreast of him. She was bouncing in her saddle, one hand on the pommel, the thin decorative scarf that roped her neck flapping behind her. He slowed his horse to a walk, caught her reins, and slowed her also.

"Thanks," she said. She looked flushed, but the color seemed pretty on her, a distinct contrast to her leather jacket and black pullover. He hadn't been able to study her much yesterday . . . well, not her features as much as the way she seemed to follow his moods as she'd ridden behind him. But looking at her now, he'd easily label her as pretty. Shoulder-length blonde hair tangled into waves, the slightest hint of freckles over her nose. She had shapely lips and blue eyes that glanced at him and away, as if afraid she might be asking too many questions.

He felt his guard lowering, especially when she looked down, as if blushing. "No, actually, my mother had a difficult pregnancy," he said in answer to Piper's question. "She was hospitalized the last few months and nearly died delivering me. It was hard on my father to see her suffering . . . especially since he had to run the ranch alone. My mother didn't have another child for five years.

. . . I think they were afraid. Ironically, she had twins—my sister, Stefanie, and brother, Rafe."

"I like your sister. I saw her earlier today, going out in her pickup with a load of hay."

"Probably to check on the bulls. We had a couple bulls die recently in another field."

"What did they die from?"

"Vet says dehydration, but there's plenty of water there. Dunno. But we moved the rest of the cattle off Hatcher's Table and the surrounding fields. Hopefully it wasn't locoweed."

"What's that?"

"When cows eat too much black sage, their brains can poison and they lose their minds and die."

"They OD on sagebrush?"

He shrugged and gave her a deserved chuckle.

"How do you come up with the names of your fields?" When she moved ahead of him slightly, he mentally traced the shape of her jaw, her neck. He noticed her delicate hands.

"We name them after their former owners. The Buckle has bought out a number of struggling ranchers over the years."

"It's a hard life from what I can tell. I saw a big man with blond hair working in the barn this morning. He didn't look like a relation."

"That's Dutch—I'll introduce you later. The only other Noble is my brother, Rafe. Rides bulls in the PBA. Has won a couple national championships."

"A bull rider. That's dangerous."

She had no idea. But they had all dealt with Mom's death in their own way. Sometimes he wished he'd had the guts to do it like Rafe did—head-on, attacking the pain with his teeth clenched.

"So, your sister runs the ranch, and your brother rides bulls. What do you do?" She looked back at him and smiled.

*Sweet. Naive.* The kind of naive that could get a girl in trouble, just like Jenny. "Right now I'm trying to right an old wrong. Before that I was in the army."

Piper's smile dimmed slightly, briefly. "Wow, a soldier. How long were you in?"

"Six years. National Guard and then a four-year stint in the army. Used it to help pay for college." No, that wasn't exactly true. He'd used it more as a get-even-with-Dad strategy. Like Rafe's bull riding, it had also helped him work out some of his anger after their mother's death.

Some.

"What was your specialty?"

"I was an MP." He urged his horse up a hill, watching for prairie-dog holes. "Stay on my tail."

"Okay, boss." She moved her mount behind him. The horses huffed as they walked.

"So you were a cop?"

That woman could talk. Or maybe he was the talker. He frowned as he nodded.

Overhead a hawk circled, and he wondered if it was on the lookout for mice. "There's another redtail," he said, pointing. He glanced over his shoulder.

She shaded her eyes and looked up. He'd need to get her a hat. "Beautiful." She didn't pursue her question but remained quiet.

The silence settled a sweetness in him. *Yes, very beautiful.*

Cutter's Rock overlooked nearly their entire spread, from the field to the southwest to Hatcher's in the east, the winter pasture, and the bluffs and draws beyond. Below the ridge, boulders scattered across the mint-tinged prairie grass.

Reining in his horse at the top, Nick dismounted, then held Piper's mare as she followed him.

"This is gorgeous, Nick. I feel like I'm at the top of the world."

He looked at her, smiling. "Actually, there's something else." He nearly reached out his hand but caught himself. Then reconsidered. To his astonishment, she slipped her hand into his.

He led her to the edge of the ridge and down, picking their way through the tumble of rock and sage and yucca plants until he reached a large rounded boulder. "We have one of the best collections of petrified wood in the county."

He watched her eyes widen. "This is a piece of petrified wood?" She placed her hand on a tree stump as big as a kitchen table.

"It's all petrified wood." He dropped her hand and opened his arms in an arc, gesturing toward the valley, dotted with other stumps, now turned to rock.

"But they're huge." Piper crouched before the stone. "I can see the texture of the bark and the rings!" She picked off a loose piece to examine it closely, and he was caught by the look of wonder on her face. She scanned the valley, her mouth open at the geological treasure. "This is amazing. It's like a giant ax went through and took the trees out with one swipe. And they're all petrified? How?"

"We don't know. But I used to love coming here to examine the stones, ponder their fragility as well as their strength. It amazed me, and I wondered what elements took these trees down and what's happened since then to turn a living plant to stone." He pried off a piece of the tree, held it in his hand, and then ground it to dust with his thumb. "Even more interesting is how easily this rock, this ancient living thing, is turned to dust by the right force."

Piper stared at him a moment, her smile gone, her eyes troubled. "I guess all things have their breaking point." She turned away, taking her piece of petrified tree with her, and sat on the ground, studying it.

There it was again—that uneasy feeling that blew through Nick, making him wonder what had really brought Piper Sullivan to the Silver Buckle Ranch.

# CHAPTER 8

"Give it to me straight, Doc. How long do I have?" Cole sat with his plastered leg propped up on the ottoman in his doctor's office, enjoying the contours of the sofa after being poked and prodded for two days, every known fact about his existence pried out of him by eager medical students.

Doc Lowe closed the office door behind him.

By the look on his lean face, Cole knew his words weren't far off the mark. Clearly he'd put too much stock in the hope that his jest would be countered with "You're just tired. You'll be back on your feet in no time."

Instead, Dr. Wilson Lowe, a longtime friend of the family, rounded the desk and sat in his leather chair. He wore the years in his face and now looked every inch like a man who'd known Cole from the beginning. And apparently to the end.

Lowe sighed, then looked at his folded hands.

Cole stared out the window at the outline of the mountains ringed with clouds.

"Your liver is failing, Cole. That accounts for the lethargy, the trouble sleeping, the itching, even your depression. We still don't know why, but without a liver transplant–" he sighed again–"your son will need to be checked for a possible match."

"No, absolutely not." The last thing Cole wanted was to have CJ subjected to dozens of tests, to pain and infection, only to discover that he couldn't help his father. "Even if he was a match, which he isn't, I'm not letting you cut his liver out of him. He could die."

"*You* will die if we don't find a match."

"We're all going to die someday." Cole watched a small plane fly in over the mountains.

Dr. Lowe leaned back, folding his arms. He shook his head, but Cole ignored him. Finally the doctor said, "Fine. We'll put you on the transplant list and pray."

In the silence, Cole heard the ringing telephones and the intercom system of the Sheridan hospital. He could smell the antiseptics still lingering on his skin. For a moment he wished he'd let Maggy accompany him. She'd practically thrown herself in front of the truck as he'd left, furious when she'd discovered he was going alone. But he wasn't interested in two days of her fawning over him, making him feel like an invalid. And he wanted the facts, not Dr. Lowe's soft words meant to ease Maggy's pain.

Yes, this was much, much better. Cole pressed his hand against his roiling stomach, feeling fatigue wash over him. How would he tell her? He'd called her last night, and she'd limited their conversation to a ranch report–an overview of the day, total calves birthed, details about the upcoming roundup at the Silver Buckle. He could hardly believe that she was planning on attending. He stopped just short of forbidding her.

But he couldn't stop his frosty tone and the way he didn't respond to her "I love you" before he hung up.

Cole clenched his fists on his lap, suddenly wishing he had Maggy's hand to hold. "How long, Doc?"

Lowe swallowed. "I don't know. Could be as long as the end of the summer. Or sooner. "

Cole nodded, but he was only half listening. Instead, his mind cataloged his to-do list—the things he'd have to accomplish before he left this world.

Like helping CJ win the junior nationals. He'd settle for watching him take first place in the Custer County Rodeo.

Buying Maggy a house in the city, one that didn't shudder when the snow piled against it.

Or even facing his so-called blood brother and telling him what he thought of his betrayal.

"I have to make it to the end of this month, Doc," Cole said without looking at him. "CJ has his roping event . . . and I promised him I'd be there."

"We'll do everything we can to make sure that happens."

❧

"You sound exhausted. Are the nightmares back?" Carter's voice, her connection to civilization, felt surreal as Piper stood on the highest point near the lodge, faced north, and didn't move an inch. In this exact position, she had one bar on her reception, and she needed to tap into Carter's expertise if she hoped to pull off another week—no, another *day*—of this charade. After returning from the petrified forest two days ago, she'd searched Chet's recipe books for something—*anything*—she might be able to make.

So far her only hope was stew, and even that could turn into paste if she wasn't careful.

Piper rubbed her eyes. "Yeah," she said in answer to Carter's question.

"I thought so. I can tell when you've had a rough night. You get crabby."

"I'm not crabby. Just in over my head. And desperate. I need some cooking tips and pronto. The Nobles want me to cook for the roundup this Saturday."

Stefanie had cornered her yesterday to confirm that Nick had relayed the message. It was all Piper could do to look at the woman, see the hope in her dark brown eyes, and lie. Oh yes, she'd be delighted to put on a bash for the entire county.

"You're kidding. How many people?" Carter asked.

"Thirty." She'd spent yesterday scouring the cookware. Amazing the layers of dirt caked on the cast-iron pots. "We're going to go out on the range. Please tell me you know something about campfire cooking."

"No, but I'll bet Google does."

She could hear Carter at the computer and longed for the insanity of the newsroom, the arguments, the smell of coffee, and most importantly the fact that having a buzz constantly in her ears kept her from thinking. Out here, only silence met her mornings, and memories too easily camped out to torment the nights. Last night had been the worst—she'd woken up in a sweat, feeling as if her father, Russell, had actually been in the room hovering over her.

"Says here on this Web site that campfire cooking is easy and fun," Carter's voice cut through her thoughts.

"Does it? What a relief. And here I was worried."

"You cook in big cast-iron pots over an open flame. And the fire has to be a certain temperature to cook the food through. Or you can use charcoal briquettes. It's a matter of math—you put a certain amount of briquettes on the pot in order to get the right temperature."

"You're making my head hurt."

"First you have to have the right pots. You have to season them. Most likely yours are already seasoned, having been used for years. Says here to look for rust—"

"I washed them yesterday. They're fine."

"Washed them how?"

"I dunked them in the river a few times—how do you think? With dish soap and hot water."

"Bad, bad, Chef Piper. You needed to only *rinse* them out. Soap and cast iron don't mix, sorta like you and a juicy porterhouse."

"Oh, swell. Now what?"

"You'll have to season them. Says here that you need to rub oil on them, then put them into the oven, upside down or over a campfire, for four hours."

Piper shook her head in frustration, and Carter momentarily cut out. "Are you there?"

". . . text you these recipes, if that will help?"

Piper blew out a breath, keeping herself still. "I have these recipe books, but really, I just wish you were here."

"What happened to the world famous Piper Sullivan, purveyor of truth? Remember, *feel* the story, *be* the story."

"Stop. And get on a plane. I need you."

"You don't need me. Wash and cut up some vegetables, throw in a hunk of meat—I'm sure you can find that somewhere around there—and add a bit of water and salt. You'll make what my mother made every Sunday afternoon—beef roast."

"What I wouldn't give for a bowl of Pad Thai noodles."

"What *are* you eating?"

This morning she'd had an apple, a bottle of water, and a package of crackers. She was saving her antacids for a midafternoon snack. "Not much."

"You know, antacids aren't a food group."

Sometimes she seriously thought he could read her mind. "I'm fine, Carter."

His voice turned soft. "Piper, this is the part where I ask you again—are you sure about this? This isn't a news story, not really. This is personal. And you could get into big trouble and not just with the Nobles. I know you want to get to the truth—"

"Carter, I know Noble set up my brother for Jenny's murder. And this is the only way I can find the truth."

"I just don't want you getting hurt. Especially if he is the kind of man who could kill someone."

Piper said nothing, watching as Nick Noble stepped out of his house and walked across the yard toward the barn. Could he kill someone? *"Even more interesting is how easily this rock, this ancient living thing, is turned to dust by the right force."* Was that some sort of killer's foreshadowing? Yet his words had felt personal, as if directed toward himself.

All the same, they had stung her and hung around her thoughts the entire quiet ride home. Petrified trees. Living things turned to stone.

"Have you gotten anything on Noble yet?" Carter pressed.

"Other than that his family started the ranch at the dawn of time and that he's a real-life cowboy?" And that she'd really liked it when he helped her on and off her horse.

"Starting with the basics, huh?"

"I don't know, Carter. I need more than this."

"You know, if you plan on airing your dirt on Noble, you don't need an ironclad case. Find some circumstantial evidence, even simply a tendency toward violence. Journalism is all about perspective these days."

"Where did you go to journalism school, anyway?"

"Cable News University. Listen, a history of duplicity will be enough to convict him in the media. It's all in how you craft the story. That will probably be enough for the DA to open an investigation. And isn't that what you're after?"

Piper didn't answer.

"Piper?"

"I guess so." She cringed at her mealymouthed tone. "Yes, of course. You've got a good idea there, Carter. Nick's been tight-lipped about why he left the ranch—and why he returned. But the townspeople might have a few insights." Her mind went to Lolly . . . and the editor at *The Phillips Journal*.

"That's my girl. Thinking like a pro."

"I wonder if our cop keeps any pictures of Miss Jenny Butler. . . ." She shot a look toward the house.

"Be careful, Piper."

"Careful is my middle name."

"No, I don't think it is—"

"Stop acting like my mother and tell me what to make for the shindig this Saturday."

"Sweetheart, I'm better than your mother. How about I call Joe's

BBQ and ship you eighty pounds of their special-order ribs, twenty-five pounds of potato salad, and enough homemade biscuits to feed a hundred?"

"Did I ever tell you how much I love you?"

"Don't get my hopes up. I'll call you later."

Piper closed her phone as she watched Nick disappear into the barn.

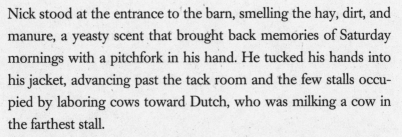

Nick stood at the entrance to the barn, smelling the hay, dirt, and manure, a yeasty scent that brought back memories of Saturday mornings with a pitchfork in his hand. He tucked his hands into his jacket, advancing past the tack room and the few stalls occupied by laboring cows toward Dutch, who was milking a cow in the farthest stall.

The big man's hands worked the udder with practiced grace, white milk streaming into the bucket. The fact that Dutch had been relegated to hand work told Nick how far the Buckle had fallen from grace. Years past it had been Nick's job, then Rafe's and Stef's, and finally the local teenage hands they hired to milk the cows and feed the bums. But on a ranch, especially one in financial straits, they all pulled their own weight.

He couldn't remember a time when Dutch hadn't run the place, hadn't been the eyes and ears for Nick's father. Dutch had taught Nick how to rope, wrestle steers, wrangle horses, and fix balers, and he occasionally dished out straight shots of cowboy wisdom. Nick felt ten years old as he stood watching Dutch, hoping the man didn't squeeze the life out of him with his huge gloved hands.

Dutch didn't acknowledge him as Nick leaned against the post separating the stalls, but Nick knew Dutch sensed his arrival. He'd been avoiding Dutch for nearly four days now, instead going over the ranch's finances or running scenarios of Cole's shenanigans through his head.

Eventually most of his thoughts drifted back to Piper. And the way she'd withdrawn like a prairie dog back into her hole, only her big eyes showing, after he'd shown her the petrified forest. As if she were suddenly scared of him.

She'd spent every hour since then in the kitchen. For some reason, Nick felt as if he'd driven her there, although he didn't know why.

"Saw your truck outside. When did you start driving Chevys?" Dutch didn't turn as he spoke, and the cow's tail hit him occasionally across the back.

Nick shrugged. "Got a deal at an auction."

"Your father left his keys in his Ford. Said that someday you'd be back for it."

Nick reached to pick up a kitten that twined around his legs. "I can't believe it still runs."

Dutch backed off the milk stool, took the bucket, and poured some of the milk into two saucers. Two gray kittens and a mama appeared from the shadows of a neighboring stall. Meanwhile, Dutch poured milk into two bottles, capped them with nipples, and handed one to Nick. "Your father took care of things, even when it seemed they were on their last legs. Took that Ford engine apart twice last year. Thing purrs like a kitten now."

Nick followed Dutch out to the corral, where a handful of bums frolicked in the yard. They saw Dutch and came toward him expectantly. He caught one between its legs, holding out the bottle. The calf latched on, sucking greedily. Nick caught his own bum and began to feed it.

"I can't get these to take a different mother. The mama in the barn lost her baby two nights ago, and the rest of these bums seem to like her okay. But these two are particular. They know they're alone, I guess." Dutch stroked the animal's neck as it drank. "Remember that bum you raised your senior year?"

Nick chuckled.

"As I recall, you slept with that animal a few nights."

Nick also remembered someone creeping into the barn and covering him with a blanket. He'd spent all his time watching over that sick calf, hoping that if God deigned to save him, He might also save his mother. In the end, only one had lived.

"You made a good rancher even then, Nick." Dutch pulled the now-empty bottle from the calf's mouth. "It's good to see you back."

Nick let his calf go play, watched it romp with the other orphans. It struck him that he'd become a bum too. "Dutch, do you know anything about my father's will?"

Dutch opened the gate, waited silently for Nick to pass through. Then he set the empty bottle in the pail to be washed. "Why?"

"Saul Lovell told me that Dad left half the Silver Buckle, the four pastures on the southwest end, to Cole St. John. I . . . can't figure out why."

Dutch stared at him a moment, his wide face betraying nothing, his eyes hard on Nick's. Then he slowly shook his head. "If you haven't figured that out yet, then nothing I say is going to help." He picked up the pail. "Your father was a good man. You soak on that for a while, and you'll get it."

Dutch walked out of the barn toward the washhouse.

# CHAPTER 9

PIPER PAUSED ON THE PORCH of the house, holding her breath, one hand on the doorknob. She watched Dutch exit the barn, carrying a pail while Nick stood in the shadows of the barn watching him go, looking troubled. She'd seen Stefanie leave earlier in the morning in her pickup, and a brief survey of the road revealed the all clear.

Improvisation. It's what she did best. And for the first time in four days, she felt as if she might be finding her old footing. Opening the door, she slipped inside.

The silence in the house felt thick as she tiptoed across the kitchen, through the living room, and up the stairs. She'd start with Nick's belongings. She knew that he'd moved out of his apartment above the diner in Wellesley, and unless he had a storage unit somewhere, he had his personal possessions with him, probably in his bedroom.

When she opened the first door, she immediately recognized a feminine touch in the room. From candles on the bedside table, to the bed neatly made with a pink-and-blue patchwork quilt, to pictures of family on the bureau, it spoke of Stefanie Noble.

Piper closed the door and went to the next one. The floorboard creaked just outside the door and she stopped, her breath catching in her throat. Silently, she listened for reaction.

Nothing except her heart drumming in her ears. She cracked open the door. The bull-riding posters layering one wall, blue ribbons, and a framed silver buckle over the bed told her that once upon a time some little boy had dreamed of rodeo. The other side of the room revealed tangled bedsheets and an open suitcase stacked with rumpled jeans and hastily folded shirts. It even smelled like Nick—leather and soap and a hint of cologne. Ridiculous how quickly his smell had crept into her awareness.

The morning sun slanted through the windows, dust swirling in the rays. The old-fashioned digital clock next to his bed clicked as the time changed. The room wasn't large and didn't even contain a closet. But she saw mementos of time etched on one of the walls—a picture of Nick and a younger kid, probably Rafe, posing in front of a handsome buck, their guns lifted like some old-time rustlers. Nick's dusty high school diploma was propped on his bureau. A rolled-up poster stood in the corner.

She pushed aside a pair of jeans crumpled on the floor and went straight to the suitcase. All indications said that he hadn't unpacked, and she dug her hands into the spaces between his clothes, pushing aside the spurs of guilt. She was doing this for Jimmy, for justice. Nick Noble had framed him. She wouldn't be fooled by the Old West–gentleman charade.

She unearthed a ratty book—Louis L'Amour's one about the Sackett brothers. Of course. She tucked it back under his sweater and felt around the pockets on the edges. Her fingers landed on a wallet, and she wiggled it out. No, not a wallet. His badge. She stared at it only a second before putting it back.

It galvanized her, however. How she hated hypocrisy. Hated people who hid behind titles, behind the justice system. She closed the suitcase, feeling inside the top pocket.

Something hard . . . she pulled it out. A manila folder. And inside a printed copy of a Web page entitled "The Probate Process."

Wasn't that interesting? She flipped through the other pages, found highlighted sentences, in particular those concerning beneficiaries.

That fit with what she'd overheard in Wellesley. The conversation replayed in her head and stopped on one name: Cole St. John. She'd even written it down in her reporter's notebook.

After closing the manila folder, she slipped it back inside the suitcase. She'd wanted to find some connection to Jenny Butler, but what if she was going about this all wrong? Maybe it wasn't about exonerating Jimmy as much as about making Nick suffer.

"I'm not going to let you destroy more lives," Stefanie had said. Maybe Piper couldn't nail Nick for hurting Jimmy, but she could certainly stop him from hurting someone else. In fact, the thought centered her. She'd discover the truth about Nick and Cole St. John and use it to ensure that St. John received every penny of his inheritance.

She was turning to leave when she heard a creak outside the bedroom door.

She stilled, conjuring up explanations.

Footsteps moved farther down the hall.

Holding her breath, she eased Nick's door open. At the end of the hall, a third doorway stood half open. Wasn't this interesting? Stepping past the squeaky floorboard, Piper snuck toward the open door and looked in.

She observed Nick Noble sitting on a double bed, a book in his hand, leafing through the pages.

Piper started to leave when she heard a voice in the yard.

"Dutch, are you here?" Downstairs, the kitchen door squealed open. "Dutch?"

Nick jerked, as if branded by the voice.

Piper ducked behind the door.

Apparently she also wasn't the only snoop in this house.

*

"Dutch, are you here?" The voice lifted through the quiet house, echoing against the stinging silence.

Nick shoved the journal he'd been reading into his jacket pocket and crossed the room in three long strides, closing the door behind him softly.

It wasn't as if he had found anything, anyway. His father's journals held nothing but the Scripture passages he'd read over the years and the thoughts he applied to the readings. Nick wouldn't learn anything revealing or life-changing from them.

"Dutch?"

Nick thundered down the stairs and entered the kitchen. A kid stood by the door, wearing a grin on his dusty face. It vanished when he spotted Nick.

"Hey there, kid. Dutch isn't here. He took the pickup out to the pasture."

The kid looked all of ten or twelve, poised on the cusp of

adolescence, with wide shoulders and a defiant swagger about him. Reddish brown hair poked from his tan felt cowboy hat, and Nick noticed a hint of color on his forearms where he'd pushed his thermal shirt up to the elbows.

The young boy looked at Nick, curiosity on his face. "Who are you?"

"I live here," Nick said, glancing out the window, wishing he saw Dutch or Pete around. Since when did they start taking on kids? Maybe it was Pete's kid—hadn't he heard something about Pete getting hitched shortly after Nick had left town?

"Ms. Noble lives here. Alone." The kid folded his arms over his chest, wariness in his eyes.

For a second Nick felt like the time he'd been caught picking tomatoes from his mother's kitchen garden. He'd had to pull weeds for a week. "Uh . . . well, I'm her brother. I just moved home."

The kid stared at him as if trying to read the truth.

*Oh, brother.* "Listen, kid, I really live here. My name is Nick, and I should be the one asking questions. Who are you?"

The kid raised his chin. "CJ."

"Okay, CJ, what are you doing here?"

CJ's bravado appeared to slip. "Dutch is supposed to help me with my roping."

*Yes, he must be Pete's kid.* Pete had the rope throw of a blindfolded mule. "Well, like I said, Dutch isn't here."

CJ's face twitched, and he betrayed his disappointment in a sigh. "Okay. Thanks, mister."

Watching the boy's shoulders slump turned a shard of pity inside Nick. He didn't have a kid, but if he did he hoped to teach him to rope. "What event are you in?"

"Breakaway roping."

Nick couldn't help a grin. "One of my favorite events. I won the Custer County Rodeo three years in a row during my junior years."

CJ's face brightened, and with his expression, excitement lit in Nick. "I had a great roping horse. He knew when to stop, as if he could read my mind."

"My horse, Coyote, does that! But sometimes he gets excited and breaks the barrier too soon."

Nick grinned at his enthusiasm, the spray of freckles over his nose, and eyes that held a like passion for throwing a rope. "That'll fix easily enough. Probably need to put more score in him—make him sit there as you let the calf out, only letting him free when you say."

CJ nodded, but his face fell. "He's not the biggest problem. It's me. I do fine on the dummy. But when I'm on Coyote, half the time I catch only air. I don't know what's wrong. My dad says that I need to make my loop travel outside my elbow, but I'm doing that, and I still keep missing."

As Nick listened, he played the kid's throw in his mind. "I have an idea. C'mon."

CJ followed him out to the barn, where Nick took a lasso off the wall. The coils felt tight and rough in his hand, and he remembered the blisters and the heat marks the hours of practice had etched. He'd eventually learned to rope with a glove, but those early years he had to feel the rope, had to make it an extension of his arm.

On their way back out to the yard they detoured to the shed, where a sawhorse with a dummy steer head lay in silent anticipation. Nick dragged them out.

The sun had eaten the clouds, and a perfect blue sky blanketed the greening bluffs. The occasional loll of a cow carried on the spring breeze.

CJ stood a few feet away, smiling at him.

"You might need to change your pitch . . . only about five degrees. Otherwise you'll throw it like a Frisbee and completely miss your calf. Angle the tip of your rope down across the calf's head at least one swing before you deliver. Two swings would be even better. The loop wants to follow the same trajectory as the couple swings before it." Nick made the loop and swung it around his head, showing the difference in the angles. He roped the dummy steer perfectly around both horns, yanking back on the rope to tighten it in a smooth, practiced flow.

When the rope snapped, Nick felt a surge of that old pride. He could nearly feel Pecos moving beneath him.

"Cool," CJ said.

Nick loosened the rope, wound it back up. "Secondly, watch your targeting. You know you start from the heeling box on the right side of the chute. When you're catching up to the calf, your weight should be in your left stirrup, and Coyote's nose should be angled about at the calf's left hip. When you throw, shift your weight to the right stirrup. If you teach Coyote that your weight shifting is his cue to plant his back end and stop, you'll get the fastest times."

Again Nick demonstrated, shifting his weight.

Clearly thinking over Nick's words, CJ's gaze fixed on the rope.

"You try."

CJ stepped up, threw a perfect loop. But the boy used muscle to compensate for rhythm. Cole had once had the same problem. The guy had always used brute force instead of timing and finesse.

Nick gestured for the rope. "Good job. But again, it's about timing and angle. Power your loop forward as you turn it over, but let the tip lead and give it a full release." He held CJ's arm, moving it to the right timing.

When Nick stepped back, CJ threw two beautiful loops.

"That's right." Nick climbed on the corral fence, sitting on the top rung to watch CJ. He remembered too well his own hours of practice catching that renegade steer dummy. But watching a lasso land around a calf's head, seeing it jerk to a stop, listening to the crowd roar, and landing the silver-buckle first prize—well, that was worth the blisters and sunburn and hours of frustration.

"If you want, I'll help you and Coyote with your timing sometime."

CJ landed another throw, then worked off the lasso and walked over to Nick. Beads of dirty sweat ran down his face, off his chin. "Really? Because Dutch is so busy, and his event is bronc bustin'. He's just helping me 'cause my dad can't."

Nick jumped off the fence, laughing. "Yeah, well, Old Pete is better at steer wrestling than throwing a rope." He clamped a hand on the kid's shoulder in sympathy. "You keep practicing. Old Pete will be back soon." He turned toward the house.

"Old Pete?" CJ ran to catch up to Nick. "He's not my dad."

Nick stopped, turned. "Who is your dad, then?"

"Cole St. John."

Nick stared at the boy, taking in the dark brown eyes, the cocky demeanor, the reddish brown hair, the build. He felt like an idiot. CJ . . . Cole Junior . . . Maggy's kid. Stef had said that she'd helped out on the ranch a lot over the past ten years. Of course the kid would know Dutch. And if he remembered correctly, Cole was wearing a cast when Nick saw him at the lawyer's–a hindrance to helping his son learn roping tricks. He blew out a breath.

"You okay, Mr. Noble?"

He turned back to CJ, saw concern on the boy's face. "Yeah, kid, I'm okay. I . . . well, I know your dad. And your mom, I guess. Her name is Maggy?"

"You and them friends?"

Nick snorted. "Once upon a time. Yeah. Your dad and I actually roped together."

CJ's mouth opened. "Really? So you're the one in the picture? the one from the paper?"

Nick had to scroll through his memory. He remembered a few pictures. The year they'd won state in football, the photos of the school prom, but Cole had probably kept the one of them with their buckle prizes raised high, hands clasped over each other's shoulders at the zenith of their friendship. "The national high school rodeo finals. We won the team roping event."

The boy's brown eyes widened, and in them Nick saw no hint that Cole had been filling his son with lurid stories about his former best friend.

Then again, Maggy was this kid's mother. Cole didn't have to trample over Nick's reputation to inflict pain. He'd married Maggy. That did the trick. "So, do you have any brothers and sisters?"

CJ shook his head. "Ma always wanted another baby, but . . ." He shrugged. "It's just me. Ma and I run the ranch. Someday I will probably."

He saw himself in CJ's eyes, in his smile. *Someday I will.* He'd said that too many times to the ranch hands and to his younger brother. He would be the king of the Silver Buckle.

No, apparently that honor would go to Cole. Or at least half of it. Saul Lovell hadn't given him much hope in getting the will set aside. Not unless Nick could find a reason Cole would coerce Bishop. He'd done some online sleuthing. If Nick could prove that Cole had been in the room the day the will was signed, it would be enough for the judge to set the will aside and divide property the way it should be . . . among the Noble children.

However . . . he hadn't found a shadow of suspicion, the barest hint of coercion, even with his casual, probing questions and his inspection of the family finances. According to Stef, only Saul, Bishop, and Big John Kincaid had witnessed the signing of the will.

But now this little buckaroo seemed willing to chatter. . . .

Nick stared at CJ and smiled. "CJ, would you like a drink of lemonade?"

Maggy knew CJ had left the moment she stepped into the barn. His horse was gone as well as his lariat.

He'd gone to the Silver Buckle; she knew it. *No, CJ, please don't. . . .*

She stood on the porch and shivered in the wind, even though the sun's heat lingered, despite its downward slide behind the ragged horizon. She felt grimy and old, having spent the morning checking the new calves and wrestling one out of a tangle of chaparral with their new hired man, Jay. She found him to be capable and quiet with horse sense and the cowboy manners to let her lead.

The fact that Cole had hired him without asking her permission had rankled her, but she let it go.

Just Cole's meager interest in the ranch seemed like a good sign, even if he'd insisted on making the trip to Sheridan alone. *Please, Lord, help them figure out what is wrong with him.*

Jay came out of the barn, a sack of feed over his shoulder. If she'd been alone, she would have had to load it in the wheelbarrow to take to the corral. The relief at seeing someone stronger than she on their property . . . well, the emotions pushed tears into her eyes. She turned away from his wide back, his strong arms, realizing how fragile she felt inside and out.

And CJ was at the Silver Buckle. Most likely meeting Nick.

Maggy sat on the porch swing, let the creaking rock her. She closed her eyes and remembered. . . .

"Hey, Mags, check out my new rig!" The voice, even in memory, always had the power to start a tingle inside her, and with Nick's approaching departure for college, she had savored every moment with him. It had taken only his maverick smile and the sizzle in his dark eyes for her to abandon her chores and climb in beside him and Cole.

Her mother had been waiting on their small front porch when she returned. Sometimes she could still smell that night. Could still see her mother's silhouette. The redolence of summer and campfire smoke clung to her hair, and she refused to let fear destroy the feeling of Nick's arms around her.

"It's nearly midnight, Maggy." Her mother's voice stayed low, and she pulled her sweater tight around her body. Her mother never looked anything but old to Maggy. Maggy blamed it on her job at the Big K, at the hours in the kitchen and the smell of cleanser on her chapped skin.

"Sorry, Ma." She stepped into the dim light. "Nick got a new truck."

"I saw that."

Her mother's tone betrayed her feelings and ignited all Maggy's defenses. Didn't Ma know that Nick loved her? that he was one of the wealthiest boys in the county? that someday Nick would ask her to marry him? that Maggy could give her parents a real home instead of the trailer they lived in? that her parents wouldn't have to work from sunup to sunset and go to bed smelling of Ben-Gay? She shook her head, moved to go inside their two-bedroom trailer.

Her mother caught her arm.

Maggy turned, annoyance in her pose.

"Maggy, I know you love Nick. But he's leaving Phillips. And, sweetheart, you're staying."

"He's coming back, Mom. He loves me."

Her mother's eyes glistened in the dark. "Don't do anything foolish, Maggy. Nick's a wild one, and he's hurtin' from his mama's passing. He's headed for ruination if he doesn't get his head on straight."

Maggy couldn't believe her ears. Nick Noble happened to be the best catch in eastern Montana. Not only was he take-her-breath-away handsome, but he hailed from a good family, had led their football team to a state championship in their division, and just a month ago won the top roping prize in the nation. He was funny and fun, and her mother should be on the sidelines hurrahing. "What is your problem? Nick's a great guy. He's cute and rich–"

"And doesn't have a heart for the Lord."

Maggy stood there, openmouthed, her eyes adjusting to her mother's sad expression. "He goes to church."

"When the mood suits him."

"He *works*."

"He makes a choice." Her mother sighed, patting the place beside her.

Maggy ignored it and stared out toward the Silver Buckle. Inside, however, her mother's words stirred a place that had her afraid.

Nick *was* wild. And she feared that someday he'd go too far. That even his charm wouldn't be able to wiggle him out of trouble. More than that, sometimes she wondered if he really, truly loved her. She'd been his girl for three years, but sometimes she felt closer to Cole.

Or maybe she could just *depend* on Cole. Cole felt safe, the calm to Nick's storm. Cole listened before he spoke and measured his words.

On those occasional times when Nick had made her cry, Cole had been the one to gather her into his strong arms without comment. Cole didn't have Nick's devastating good looks, but his generosity of spirit never let her down.

Her mother spoke through the darkness and voiced Maggy's fears. "Nick has the ability to be a great man. But until he begins to follow his brand, he'll always be a maverick. He's going to hurt himself–or someone else–someday. And I don't want you caught in the middle."

In the end, her mother had been right. Nick had hurt them all.

Maggy rubbed her arms and stared past the bluffs and draws toward the Buckle, praying that her son wasn't next on Nick's list of casualties.

# CHAPTER 10

SHE COULD RIDE THIS PONY. Piper stood in the pool of light outside Lolly's Diner, watching the shimmer of orange glaze the dusty horizon. She had her collar turned up and her hands shoved into her pockets as she waited for the deliveryman to load the last of the dinner into the back end of her Jeep. Spare ribs, potato salad, biscuits, and beans–the perfect roundup dinner. She would have to give Carter a hug and probably her entire collection of *Monk* DVDs for this favor.

This meal bought her time. It meant that for at least a few more days Stefanie and Nick Noble would buy her alias as a chef and let her pry deeper into their secrets.

Who exactly was CJ? She'd watched from Nick's window as he taught the kid to throw a lasso. His patient voice and his gentleness with the boy weren't lost on her–something that only irked her as the lesson lingered. She'd expected Nick to send the kid packing, not have a rodeo clinic. Then he'd served CJ some lemonade. Listening to Nick ask the boy about his family and his life didn't compute—until she remembered that he'd been a detective and had coerced her brother into a confession. Nick was clearly on a fishing expedition. So why was he plying CJ for information?

Just one more question in her notebook, along with the bigger ones: What was Nick searching for in the room at the end of the hall? What had caused the bad blood between Nick and Cole St. John?

And how could she use the information to serve up justice?

Most importantly, how was she going to get this food back home and into the chuck wagon without detection?

Piper tipped the driver, closed the hatchback, and drove to the Buckle, hoping she'd make it before Dutch or Pete or Nick emerged for morning chores. They all rose before the sun. Good thing her nightmares sometimes drove her to sit huddled in a blanket on the porch, watching the sunrise, or she'd have never known how early to rise to pull off her ruse.

Sure enough, the compound hadn't yet stirred as she drove past the house, the barns, Dutch's place, and the bunkhouse to the dining hall. She parked around back, then unloaded the potato salad into the plastic storage bins in the pantry, storing them in the fridge. The ribs arrived tangy and hot, surrounded by the magic of Styrofoam. According to Carter's written directions, all she had to do was transfer them to the pots and bake them over the fire. She had spent all yesterday reseasoning the cast-iron pots—and nearly dying of asphyxiation.

She'd also nearly burned down the kitchen—well, not really, but from the smoke that heralded from the two ovens, it seemed that she'd created a small inferno. She had to smile at the memory of Nick charging up the path just as she'd been carrying the steaming cast-iron pot outside.

He had run up, wild eyed. "Are you all right? Is the kitchen on fire?"

Not sure what question to address first, she set the pot on the grass and bent over, coughing. Tears streaked her face. "I . . . was . . ." Coughing overtook her body.

"For pete's sake!" Nick ran into the kitchen. Moments later, he burst through the door carrying another pot. "The room is filled with smoke!"

Oh, that Nick, he was quick. "Yeah, I know," she'd said, covering her mouth as she coughed again. "I was seasoning the pots–"

Nick gave her a look of disbelief, then spun and returned inside. She watched him open the windows and disappear again. He emerged from the dragon's mouth a few moments later with a glass of water. He handed it to her. "Drink."

"Is it hemlock?" She gave him a small smirk.

He narrowed his eyes at her.

"I'm kidding." Piper drank, then wiped her mouth. "I'm sorry about the smoke."

"I suppose they didn't teach you in cooking school not to season pots inside the kitchen? That's why we have a grill–or even an open fire. And why are you seasoning them, anyway? They've been oiled and seasoned for years."

*Of course.* Piper scrambled for a response. Because she'd wrecked the seasoning by washing them with soap? Because she hadn't yet found the answers she needed, and she had to keep up her charade? Because she didn't want Nick to grab her by the scruff of her neck and throw her off the Silver Buckle without getting the answers to the questions that nagged at her? She stared at him, her eyes burning. "Sorry, Nick. I wasn't sure how Chet had seasoned them in the past. I wanted to make sure they were ready for roundup."

Staring at his furious expression, she fleetingly felt the slightest tingle of fear. She lifted her chin, but in the back of her mind she called herself silly.

For a second, Nick had seemed genuinely concerned for her well-being.

As if to confirm that thought, he said, "Are you all right?" His voice softened this time, and he yanked the handkerchief from his neck and wiped her sooty cheeks. "Let me fire up the grill, and we'll get these things seasoned properly."

It didn't help that he smiled, his eyes kind, his touch gentle. He packed a powerful punch with his dark curly hair, the slightest dusting of whiskers, a dusty blue work shirt, and a pair of Wrangler jeans. "I'll bet this is different than what you're used to working with."

Words deserted Piper for a moment. "Uh . . . yeah . . ." Could he see through her? that she didn't know the difference between baking soda and baking powder? that she had been fired from her only attempt at cooking—helping her mother make cookies for the school play?

"But I'll bet you make a mean crème brûlée."

Oh yeah, like nothing he'd ever tasted before, she felt sure. She found her smile. Nodded.

The sound of a truck gunning toward the dining hall made Nick turn.

"Piper! Are you okay?" Stefanie stopped her pickup ten feet short of them. "I saw smoke!"

"We're getting the pots ready for roundup," Nick said, shooting a look at Piper.

At his words, his smile, she'd felt something inside her shift, something she'd been holding on to for support: her steadfast belief that Nick Noble was an outlaw.

Now, as Piper dumped the ribs into huge kettles and found the serving bowls for the potato salad, she still felt her world sliding. She simply couldn't get a fix on Nick—one minute he was showing her around the ranch and coming to her rescue, the next he was helping a neighbor kid rope a steer, and the next he was snooping into said kid's life.

Apparently Nick could play games as well as she.

However, as long as she didn't let his charm affect her heart, she'd be fine.

The sun had cleared the bluffs and shortened the shadows by the time Piper had the chuck wagon loaded. The Silver Buckle, along with three other ranches, participated in an old-time roundup at each ranch every May. According to Nick, they'd spend the day branding the new steers, and then partake of the meals furnished by the host ranch. Last week, they'd worked at one of the other ranches.

It made her think of the day her mother had dragged her to church for their potluck lunch. Although she'd attended Grace Bible Church for the better part of her childhood, she hadn't darkened its door since the day she graduated from high school.

She simply didn't see God's intervention in her life the way her mother did. And she had the scars to prove it.

That day back then . . . it reminded her of the hope she'd fool- ishly harbored that someday she might have a family, sisters, her brother back, a father who loved her.

She'd walked out of the potluck right after the banana pudding and had never returned to church. Childhood dreams were for children, not adults who knew better.

Still, today could be fun. A new experience and yet another opportunity to get underneath that Nick Noble guard.

She was loading the last of her supplies into the five-by-ten wagon outfitted with coolers and utensils and campfire cooking extras when the subject of her investigation appeared. She only momentarily lost her focus at his cowboy attire—a pair of leather chaps over jeans, a brown corduroy shirt, and a Stetson drawn low over his eyes. He was leading two horses.

"Howdy," he drawled in his cowboy tenor.

"Right back atchya," she drawled back.

His dark eyes sparkled, but he said nothing as he hitched the horses to the wagon. He mounted, then offered her his hand to join him on the seat. She took it, disgusted at how it sent tingles up her arm. So he looked like every cowgirl's dream. She wasn't a cowgirl, and she didn't have dreams anymore. At least not the romantic kind.

He took the reins, holding them loosely between his fingers. "Ready to get this done?"

Piper nodded, then held on as the horses eased the wagon forward. They rode along the driveway before turning off onto the road.

She felt as if she might be riding back into time. She just hoped she might also be riding into Nick's past and that today would be the day for some answers.

⤬

Every nerve in Cole's body felt as if it had been branded. On fire, burning, he could barely stop himself from shouting as he watched

Maggy dress for the roundup. As if she might be dressing for the prom.

Although she'd said nothing, he knew she'd been waiting for this day for a decade. And everything inside him wanted to cry.

As usual, she took his breath away. She'd always been pretty—in high school he could barely keep his eyes off her. But as his wife, knowing her like he did, she'd become breathtaking to him. He loved to watch the way her beautiful green eyes took in every situation, how her hands deftly plaited her hair into two braids. Those same hands had held his when he'd returned home last night, her eyes searching his face for answers.

He hadn't been able to tell her of his failing liver. Not all of it. He'd simply told her that Dr. Lowe had given him medicine, and that he'd probably be well soon.

He'd omitted the part that said he'd be well in heaven. Relief washed her expression as she'd hugged him, and he'd held on longer than a man who'd lied to his wife had a right to. When she drew away, she kissed him, and he felt pity in her touch.

He hated pity.

Most of all he hated the pity. Because of all the emotions that tied her to him, pity was the one he most feared. Pity would turn to disgust . . . then hatred. Then again, she'd once accused him of pitying her, and he'd loved her more each day.

The night ten years ago when he'd found Maggy sitting on the back steps of their church, the stars had spilled across the February sky like frost glistening against a black windowpane. She had had her hands cupped to her face, her shoulders wringing out her pain even as she muffled it. He would have missed her completely if he hadn't returned to vacuum the sanctuary in his mother's stead after Sunday evening services.

The winter wreath over the back door hung, stiff and green, its blue-and-gold velvet bow laced with a dusting of snow. The chilled air bit at his ears as he squatted before Maggy, touching her softly on the arm. "Mags, what's the matter?"

Somehow he had known, as she lifted her face, as he traced the tracks of tears, that Nick was to blame. Deep inside, he'd expected this moment.

Maggy shook her head, wiped her tears with her knitted mittens. "I can't–"

"Whatever it is, you can tell me." He sat beside her, put his arm around her, drawing her close. "Remember, I'm supposed to look after you." He alone knew how those words twisted his chest.

She sighed. "You can't fix this."

He brushed her tear away with his thumb, wrestling the sudden desire to kiss her. Softly, just enough to make her forget Nick and how he hurt her. Her auburn hair tumbled out of her knit cap in soft curls, and when she shivered slightly, he tightened her against him. "Let me try."

She leaned her head against his chest, relaxing into him.

Cole closed his eyes, wrapped his other arm around her. If this was all he could have of Maggy, then he'd be happy.

A shard of fury divided his thoughts. Nick didn't deserve her, had dallied with her for years, taking her love for granted. Cole knew all about Nick's exploits at college–Nick wasn't the only one of his classmates who attended Montana State.

Yet Nick had returned home for Christmas break, showing up at Maggy's place and trotting her out on his arm for the annual pie social and New Year's Eve dance. Cole had watched them from across the community center social room, watched Maggy laugh, nearly glowing, and tried to feel happy for them. They seemed even closer than before. Apparently Prince Noble had her completely snowed.

"Is it about Nick?" Cole asked, hating the tremor, even the hope in his voice. Had she found out about Nick's shenanigans with other girls on campus? Even if she had, well, Nick was still his best friend. Despite Nick's deceptions, Cole believed in the cowboy code—a cowboy never goes back on his word. He'd never actually promised not to woo Maggy, but it had been implied in his word to watch over her for Nick. And a cowboy never takes unfair advantage, especially of his best friend's gal. Cole blew out a long breath and loosened his hold on her.

Maggy nodded, and her sobs started again.

What was he supposed to do? Cole held her, soothing. "Don't cry, Mags."

She sniffed, wiped her eyes again. "I'm sorry, Cole. I just don't know what to do."

He ran his thumb across her wet cheek, wishing he had words for her. But Nick would always be Nick, a charming cowboy, a conqueror of hearts. "I know," he said feebly.

She looked up at him, her mouth opened slightly. "You do? Can you tell? How?"

"Nick hasn't ever been very discreet."

He watched as Maggy's face drained of color. "He told you."

Cole held very still. "No . . . I just heard it."

She gasped and her face crumpled, a low moan issuing from her body.

"Mags, I'm sorry." Her tears turned him inside out, and for a moment, all he wanted to do was bury his fist in Nick's face.

She broke free of Cole's embrace, stood, and stalked out into the icy parking lot, shaking her head as if engaged in some inner argument. Then she whirled, and her expression scared him with its ferocity. "I suppose you think I'm some sort of tramp."

*What?*

"I wasn't planning . . . I mean, we . . . it just happened." She covered her face with her hands. "Don't look at me like that. It wasn't supposed to be this way."

Her words froze him. Oh no. *Oh no.* He felt as if he'd been belly punched, all the wind sucked out of him. "What do you mean?"

She didn't look at him. "My mother is going to kill me."

Although he hadn't gone to college, Cole had been at the top of his class, and it didn't take a genius to connect the dots. "Mags . . . are you pregnant?"

She lifted her head, and the tortured look on her face made his throat tight.

Somehow he found his feet. "Oh, Mags." He took a step toward her.

She held out her hands, stopping him. "If I tell him, he'll hate me. He'll think I planned it or something."

Cole ignored her gesture and gripped her shoulders.

She hung her hands on his arms, as if for support. "You can't tell him, Cole. Okay? Please don't tell him."

He ground his teeth, wanting with everything inside him to track down Nick and . . . and . . . but what good would it do? Nick would come home, marry Maggy, and they'd live happily ever after. Just as fate had planned.

"No, I won't tell, Mags."

He'd been silent then and for all the years that followed.

Even now, as Cole watched his wife standing barefoot in her worn jeans and one of his old flannel shirts, dolling herself up for the prince of the Silver Buckle, he knew he had to stay silent again.

Nick Noble had finally returned. And if Cole cared for Maggy at all, he couldn't stand in her way. Nick might be able to give her the future she deserved. At the least, his rekindled feelings for Maggy would keep him from contesting Bishop's bequest until the land became theirs.

And if . . . if Nick still loved Maggy . . . then at least Maggy and CJ would be provided for, wouldn't they? And CJ would have a father.

Cole actually thought he might stop breathing.

Maggy finished the second braid and turned to him. "I'll be back by suppertime."

He forced a smile. He loved her more than this, more than his insecure dreams, more than his fears and broken heart. "No, I'll be fine. Stay for supper. Stay as long as you want."

❧❧❧

Nick couldn't believe how much he enjoyed spending time with their new cook. As he sat beside Piper on the bench seat of the chuck wagon, feeling her arm brush against his now and again, he began to relax. Something about sitting next to her, listening to her hum, as if she might be looking forward to the blistering work of roundup, made the tensions inside him loosen.

"The ribs look good, George. You must have been baking them all night."

Piper glanced at him, a slight smile on her pretty face. She wore her blonde hair pulled back and up, and it only accentuated her high cheekbones, her perfectly shaped lips, those big blue eyes. The wind stole the wisps from her hair clip and played them around her face. It was all he could do not to push the errant strands back. She didn't seem to mind the interference and kept her hands folded between her knees, looking about seventeen in her black T-shirt with a buffalo-head imprint and slim-fitting, low-cut jeans.

Nick tore his attention away from her, disturbed at how often she filled his mind these days. It didn't help that every time he turned around, he seemed to be rescuing her—from stopping the bull from turning her to mincemeat to the near fire in the dining hall yesterday. It had taken him half the night to dislodge her image—shapely in a charcoal-stained apron and a hint of mascara staining her cheeks—from his thoughts. And her grateful smile only made her seem sweet.

Yes, somehow Piper had gotten under his skin, enough to keep him awake and relish the idea of helping her cook today's meal.

The barbeque sauce on those ribs smelled like heaven. He couldn't wait to taste them. Apparently, despite her fiasco with the cast-iron pots, the woman could cook.

"Do you do roundup every year, or is this for my benefit?" Piper asked.

Give her silence and the woman would fill it with questions. Curious George. "We've done it every year I can remember. Ages ago, before the ranches had fences dissecting the land, cowhands rounded up the cattle, divided them by brands, and worked on the cattle together. Now it's a way to bear one another's burdens."

He couldn't help but think of all the roundups he'd missed over the past decade. Yeah, he'd been great about bearing his family's burdens. Guilt tasted fresh and acrid in his throat.

"Who else will be there?"

"The hands from the two other ranches and a few day hands Stef hired from town yesterday. And of course Dutch and Old Pete."

"I met those two hands Stefanie hired. Quint and Andy? They're cowboys in every sense of the word."

Nick nodded. Tall and lanky, the pair looked as if they'd been dragged a hundred miles behind a mustang. But they were willing and cheap and knew how to throw a rope. Right now, the Silver Buckle couldn't afford better. "Yeah, I saw their gear. And their truck. They're probably fresh from the amateur rodeo circuit, looking for some solid work for the summer."

"The one looks rough around the edges. He's got a barbed-wire tattoo." Piper clamped her upper arm to indicate where.

Nick had seen it too, and it had all his instincts firing. Not that he judged Quint based on a tattoo—good people the world over wore tattoos these days. No, it was his demeanor, his swagger, the way he'd studied Piper as she walked to the lodge last night. Nick had sat on the porch, watching, and made a mental note to keep one eye on blond and shifty Quint Fadden. "If he gives you any trouble, let me know."

When Piper glanced at him, he couldn't read her eyes. "Okay. But I can take care of myself. I know self-defense."

The way she said it, like Tweety rolling up her sleeves, made him smirk.

Her expression darkened. "I can. I'm working on my purple belt." She looked away from him, apparently piqued.

He tried to stifle a chuckle, but it burst through his teeth.

Piper glared at him.

He forced the smile from his face. "Sorry, George. I can't imagine you going toe to toe—or rather chin to forehead—with Quint, regardless of what color belt you're wearing."

Her glare didn't ease.

"Fine. If they get in your way, I'll be looking forward to your roundhouse kick," Nick said.

That earned him the smallest of smiles. "Good."

"But seriously, Piper, don't be a hero."

"Because you'll be one for me?"

Her accusation startled him. "No . . . I mean . . . well, if you need one—"

This time she laughed. "I promise, Nick, after I flatten him, I'll come running straight to you for help."

"Deal." He held out his hand and grinned as she shook it.

She stared off at the horizon. "I wish all cowboys thought like you."

The comment made him pause. He looked at her and wondered if she'd actually said it.

Especially when she turned as if they hadn't had that segue in their conversation and asked, "Where are we having this roundup?"

"Uh . . . a central pasture between the winter pasture and one of the fields. Stefanie hopes to get a few hundred head branded and tagged today. They'll also vaccinate them and castrate the steers."

"But don't you have three thousand head?"

"Yeah. Pete, Quint, and Andy will spend the next couple of weeks rounding up and branding the rest of the cattle." He'd probably be out there helping too. When he wasn't helping CJ throw a rope. He'd been surprised at how much he'd enjoyed getting to know the kid yesterday and had hated himself a little for his agenda. But he'd discovered some interesting information.

Like CJ was ten years old. If Nick did the math right, he would have been conceived right about the time Nick left. Cole had certainly wasted no time moving in on Nick's girl.

But the gem of information—the one he'd been plowing for—had surfaced just as CJ was leaving. He'd stopped in the living room, staring at the picture of Bishop. "I miss him," he said softly.

Nick knelt beside him. "You knew my father?"

"Uh-huh." CJ started again for the door, picking up his hat from the hook. "He let me call him Pops. Probably 'cause my mom was here all the time, taking care of him."

Nick watched him go, but the questions burned at him until Stefanie returned home. He probably hadn't picked the best time to pounce on his sister—he should have waited until she'd showered and cleaned off the dirt of the day. But his emotions had played havoc with his thoughts, and he'd followed her upstairs, nearly into her room, asking questions.

Wearily, she'd told him only that Maggy had worked for them, cleaning and cooking and taking care of Bishop until the end.

That didn't answer the question of why she'd married Cole only two months after they broke up—and according to his recollection, they hadn't broken up, not officially.

He guessed that now it could be deemed official.

Nick glanced at Piper beside him, watched her scanning the scenery, and remembered the days when Maggy would ride beside him or on her mare while he rode Pecos. Maggy had worn the same look of appreciation for the land under the big sky as Piper did now. Maggy loved the life—training her horses, working alongside her father at the Kincaid ranch, riding fence with Nick. She belonged here, as if she made up the very breath that caressed the bluffs and draws.

Cole had also loved the land.

Perhaps that was what drew Cole and Maggy together. That and their common hatred for Nick.

The thought stabbed at him. Although he hadn't had a real girlfriend since Maggy, he thought that wound had scarred over. Evidently not. With Piper sitting beside him, however, it suddenly seemed easier to bear.

"I can't imagine growing up out here so far from the city and pop culture. Was it lonely?" Piper turned, a slight smile playing on her face. "Or did you spend every moment with your cattle?"

"I was a regular kid. Played football, went to prom, hung out at the local diner on the weekends. But I loved ranch life. Loved roundup and branding and working alongside my father's ranch hands. I even dabbled in the rodeo circuit for a while—won a roping championship."

Her eyebrows raised at that. "I saw you roping with a kid yesterday. You looked like you knew what you were doing."

He shrugged but liked the shine in her eyes. He had to wonder if she saw in him a shade of the old cowboys, the heroes of the Old West.

After all the years of being an outlaw, he didn't mind that idea at all.

# CHAPTER 11

ROUNDUP WASN'T ANYTHING like the glamorous events on television. Acrid smoke and the smell of burning hide hung in the air, and the sound of calves bawling for their mamas made Piper want to cry. She'd finally tied a handkerchief around her nose, not only to keep out the smells but to keep herself from coughing at the smoke that watered her eyes as she prepared lunch–or dinner, as they called it in cow country–for the thirty or so workers who'd shown up.

Everywhere she looked there were cowboys in chaps and hats swinging ropes. If it weren't for Nick's focus on helping her prepare the food, her journalistic instincts would have taken hold and she'd have been swept up in fascination, dictating into the recorder tucked into her pocket.

It took her about fifteen seconds to figure out that the skills cowboys displayed on the rodeo circuit were honed out here on the range. First, they separated the cows from the babies, moving the calves into a separate pen. Their cries sounded so much like children hollering for their mothers, it pricked the latent nurturer inside Piper. Then some cowpoke would free a calf, and a header would rope the head while a heeler netted the two hind legs. The calf would fall, and a third cowboy would twist its head into a submissive position while another hand took an iron from the furnace and applied the Silver Buckle brand, an oval with one line passing through it. Piper stood too close the first few times—so close she heard the skin sizzle. That turned her stomach enough to make her back away and watch from afar. After branding, yet another hand would pop the poor animal with a vaccination.

Then, to her horror, came the worst part. Castration. Piper forced herself to watch the first time, her face surely betraying her emotions as a cowboy's hand turned the bull into a steer. The poor animal struggled to its feet and ran to its mother, crying.

Piper sorta felt like doing the same thing. The entire process took less than five minutes. Stefanie Noble presided over the entire event, separating the cowboys into teams, even pitching in to wrestle a calf into the dirt. Piper would bet that cowboys like Quint didn't give Stefanie any sass.

"Rocky Mountain oysters," Nick said, coming up beside Piper as she turned away from the bawling, hot, bloody mess. "Yum."

Nick looked so tall beside her. With a red handkerchief tied at his neck and wearing gloves and a hat, he looked pure cowboy. Especially with the two-day-old dark beard growth and those look-through-her eyes. Earlier, sitting next to him on the chuck wagon, she'd felt . . . well . . . safe. Like he *would* step between her and Quint or whoever tried to harass her, regardless of her roundhouse kick.

It had felt so much like Jimmy that she'd had a hard time speaking.

It didn't help that Nick had spent the last hour helping her build the giant cook fire and hanging the kettles of ribs over the flames.

"I'm sorry. I'm not sure what you're talking about," she said. "Oysters?"

Nick gestured toward the growing pile in the pot near the branding center. He couldn't mean . . .

"That is so disgusting!" Piper put her hand over her mouth, then made a face. "Yuck!"

Nick grinned, clearly enjoying her revulsion. "I guess I'm in charge of that entrée."

She gaped at him. "Gross. We are *not* making that!"

He raised one eyebrow in amusement. "Yes we are. It's a tradition."

"Not over my fire." Piper shook her head for emphasis.

"Yes, over your fire." He stared at her a long time, frowning as if not believing that she'd hold her ground. "All right, fine. I'll build a new fire." He shook his head, but his grin didn't vanish. "But trust me, you'll like them."

She made a gagging noise and gripped her throat as if she were choking.

Behind her, a truck pulled up towing a horse trailer and parked next to the assembly of other trucks and trailers. As Piper watched, CJ climbed out of the cab and lifted a hand to Nick.

Nick's smile vanished. He swallowed and returned the wave. "Guess I'll go get that fire going," he said more to himself than to Piper.

She watched him nearly run from CJ and the shapely redhead who were now opening their trailer to free their horses.

Who was this woman and what power did she have over Nick? Another question to add to the collection. This one also ignited an annoying quiver of discomfort in Piper's belly.

The roundup continued over the noon hour and into the afternoon, calves bawling, fire spitting, the sounds of cowboys whooping as they separated the cattle or drove the calves into pens. They broke in early afternoon for dinner. Piper served the ribs and brown biscuits, keeping an eye on the redhead. She hoped for a moment to draw her aside, casually ask her name, maybe even her history with Nick that so clearly bristled him. He'd been pensive all day, frying up the . . . ah, oysters, helping Piper stoke the campfire, and avoiding the redhead as if she had the Ebola virus.

Yes, Piper definitely needed to track down the history on these two.

After dinner the cowboys resumed their terror on the cows. Long shadows filled the gullies and draws by the time they called it quits for the day and rode in for round two of the ribs—supper. Piper served the leftover ribs, beans, potato salad, and biscuits to the exhausted workers.

Stefanie leaned against the retractable shelf at the end of the chuck wagon, balancing her plate while she ate a rib. "Nicely done, Piper. This is an awesome recipe, and you made enough for two meals. That's the way to think ahead."

Piper felt a blush creeping into her cheeks, hating the twinge of guilt that hung on her like a burr. Hey, she'd done a decent job of tracking down a meal, and it had cost her that bonus she'd been saving for Cancun—for that she deserved an honest thank-you.

"Delicious potato salad, Cookie," Quint drawled from his spot nearby.

Piper spied Nick at the other campfire, at the end of a short line of cowpokes dishing themselves up the gourmet range treat he'd prepared. Now and again he gave Piper a reassuring smile.

For a second, she saw herself working here all summer, stoking the fire, actually baking the ribs, enjoying Nick's attention.

*Enjoying Nick's attention?* Clearly her good sense had run off into the horizon, probably with her righteous vendetta at its side.

Someone should remind her that she didn't want or need a sweet-talking cowboy in her life. She had a career. A future uncovering injustice. A life that included chai and bok choy.

Piper no more fit on the Silver Buckle than Nick fit in a gourmet kitchen, baking scones.

The redhead and her son sat cross-legged on the other side of the fire, talking with Dutch, the big blond cow boss of the Silver Buckle. Piper and he hadn't exchanged more than ten words, but he seemed nice, if quiet. He wore a white ten-gallon hat, and his shadow took up nearly an acre. He smiled at the boy like a proud uncle.

Nearby the cows and calves, now reunited, grazed happily, the day's terrors at an end. Horses tethered to their trailers ate a well-deserved meal.

"I hope we have leftovers for tomorrow," Stefanie said.

Piper scraped the last of the potato salad into a container. "What do you mean?"

"We didn't get done today. There's another small herd that needs to be rounded up. We'll head down to that field first thing in the morning and finish up with this section."

"All of us?" Piper watched a big man, the owner of the Big K, rise and deposit his plate and tin cup in her dishwater. He nodded in her direction, showing a white smile on his tanned face.

"No, just the Buckle crew."

"You mean, we're going to spend the night out here?" Piper grimaced at the tremor in her voice. She'd been camping before plenty of times. But being out here, with the cows and wolves . . . and men . . .

Stefanie laughed. "You can sleep in the chuck wagon if you want."

"How about I head back to the ranch?"

Stefanie sopped up the last of her sauce with her biscuit. "I can ask Nick to take you back. But you'll have to get up early in order to meet us out at the field." She didn't sound in the least like she might be pulling Piper's leg.

"How early?"

"Fourish." Stefanie deposited her plate in the dishwater. "That coffee done?"

"Uh . . . I dunno," Piper answered. Nick had started the coffee brewing over the fire; she hadn't the faintest idea when it might be ready. But *4 a.m.*?

She'd slept in a culvert, a cattle trailer, and even her Jeep a few times. But never next to manure . . . and in the same airspace as Nick Noble. Even if it was wide-open airspace.

But with the stars scattered above, Nick might offer to take her for a walk or a ride. It wasn't a good sign that the thought of being alone with him sent tingles through Piper that had nothing to do with fear.

⁂

Nick had changed and not only in his appearance. That much Maggy could tell from observing him all day. He had stretched out, become a man. His laughter sounded deeper, his face more solemn when he listened. So much different from the renegade she knew in high school.

The renegade who had stolen a huge chunk of her heart.

And said outlaw knew she was here—by the way he practically ran circles around her, as if she wore an electric fence around her body.

However, he had no problem high-fiving CJ and even showing him a few more roping pointers before supper. CJ simply glowed with the attention. Maggy's dread burned inside her.

She'd come to the roundup today prepared for all the old emotions to rise from the grave and ravage her, like they had the first time she saw Nick outside his barn. She didn't exactly expect that she'd swoon at his feet, but she did worry that Nick would send her one smoldering look and she'd feel afresh the wounds he'd left her with.

Instead, as she watched Nick dodge her, she felt a sense of satisfaction. Nick no longer had power over her. The strings that held his memory to her heart had finally, quietly been severed.

In fact, Nick was the one who looked wounded. Instead of leading the teams, he'd stepped aside and let Stefanie take over—or rather, resume her place. She'd been leading roundup for the last three years, since Bishop had gotten too sick to work.

Stefanie had given Maggy a hug, then assigned her to help with roping. Maggy worked as a heeler, then took her turn heating the irons.

All the time, the new cookie watched her as if she might be Calamity Jane come back from the grave. Maggy gave her a small smile when she served her a plate of ribs and received a once-over, along with the obligatory smile.

Maggy finished her supper, listening to Dutch spin a yarn to CJ about the outlaws who used to hide in these hills while watching Nick out of the corner of her eye.

"Mom, Dutch says that their new hand Andy is gonna play his guitar. S'pose we can stay for a bit?"

Maggy sighed, torn by the eagerness on CJ's face and her desire to return to Cole. She'd come to the roundup against Cole's wishes, even if he'd said the opposite. *"Stay as long as you'd like."* Yeah, sure. He was probably sitting by the window with his binoculars, holding his breath for their return. She knew he'd refused to come because of Nick and not because of his broken leg. Cole didn't exactly loaf around the house, even with his cast. Yesterday she'd caught him overhauling the carburetor in the truck.

She wasn't stupid. Something had changed after his doctor's appointment. Something that put desperation in Cole's eyes, and it frightened her.

*Lord, please, I can't lose him.*

"Please, Mom?" CJ pleaded, bringing her thoughts back to his request.

"For a while, I guess," Maggy said. He ran off to join a circle of other cowpokes as she leaned back on the grass. The sun had dipped beyond the ragged Bighorns, leaving only splashes of reddish orange along the horizon. The scent of the campfire and the lull of contented Angus soothed her tired bones. This was her life. She never felt more whole and content than when she spent a day on the range.

"How's Cole?" Dutch asked, gathering their plates.

"Sore. But not complaining. He'll pry off that cast in a week or two, I'll bet."

Dutch gave a wry chuckle. "You call me if you need something."

Maggy nodded. "We hired a man. Quiet. Gets his work done.

He went to check on the herd today. I expected him to show up here, but I guess he got tied up."

"That happens. We 'bout got 'em licked."

Maggy gestured toward the blonde, the one with barbeque sauce staining her apron. "Where did Stefanie find her?" She'd noticed how Nick had helped her stoke her fire, stir her food. And he'd been in charge of frying the oysters.

"Some school in Kalispell. Going to cook for the city-slicker tourists this summer."

Maggy watched as the woman began to wash the dishes. Even as she did it, however, she seemed to study people, hear conversations. "Stef is going through with that idea, huh?"

"She's got a full schedule of folks heading here for the 'ultimate family adventure.'" He inflected a British accent into his words.

Maggy laughed.

Dutch's voice fell. "You know, Nick's kicking around trouble about Bishop's will. He's been asking questions, hunting up reasons why Bishop mighta left that land to Cole."

Maggy said nothing. She knew little of estate law, but it seemed to her that if Bishop wanted to give them his land, Nick couldn't stop him.

"He thinks he can find a reason to get the will set aside."

Maggy turned to Dutch. He'd been a good friend to Cole and his mother, Irene, over the years, helping them out with their motley crew of cattle. The years wore hard on Dutch's face, turning his skin leathery, his pale eyes wizened. She always wondered why he'd never married.

She used to think that Dutch and Irene would have made a wonderful couple. But then again, some things just weren't meant

to be, regardless of how good they looked in dreams. And now, of course, she knew why.

"What kind of reasons?" she asked.

"I don't know. Like something Cole might have had over Bishop's head. Or someone coercing Bishop. He asked me if Cole was around when the will was signed."

Maggy glanced at him. "Why would that matter?"

"Well, because Cole got the land. And Nick says if any of the beneficiaries are in the room when a will is signed, then it can be contested."

A coldness started in Maggy's belly and spread through her. "He wasn't there."

"'Course not. But just so as you know. Nick's a'huntin' trouble."

"Thanks, Dutch."

While he carried their plates to the dish bin, Maggy's eyes settled on Nick. So that's why he returned. To make sure Cole didn't get a blade of Noble range. And she had a sinking feeling she knew why.

Perhaps the old emotions weren't as dormant as she thought. In fact, she found herself crossing the fire pit before she could stop herself. She stood above Nick as he crouched by the fire, cooking.

He glanced up at her. Good. He actually looked a little pale.

"I want to talk to you."

"Hi, Maggy." Nick stood, but she didn't care that he towered over her. "How are you?"

"Don't 'how are you' me! I can't believe that you came back to take away Cole's land."

He gaped and glanced past her.

Maggy followed his line of vision and saw Stefanie freeze, her mouth drawn in a dark line.

"It's Noble land. But, Maggy, this isn't about you."

Not about her? "This is completely about me, Nick. I know that! I'm not an idiot."

His voice dropped. "Of course you're not. It's just that . . . this is between me and Cole."

She wanted to pull back her fist and sink it squarely in his arrogant jaw. "You think I don't know why you left? why you haven't come back for ten years?"

He stared at her, at a loss for words.

"You're really a piece of work, Noble. Well, for your information, Cole is twice the man you are. He's kind and honorable and patient, and he keeps his promises. He deserves that land your father gave him. And you, of all people, should know that." She turned and realized that the entire camp had stopped speaking. Motioning to CJ, she stalked toward her pickup.

She didn't make it. A hand caught her, spun her around, and in a second, she saw the old Nick, the one she'd loved, the passionate boy she'd given herself to thinking it would last forever. He wore hurt and not a little anger in his piercing dark eyes. "I don't know what you're talking about, Maggy, but you got this all wrong."

She couldn't hold back any longer. She slapped him—hard.

As if he were made of stone, he didn't even blink.

"You turned out exactly as my mother predicted," she said in a lethal voice. "I'm so sorry I didn't listen to her sooner."

∞∞∞

What had Nick done to her?

After not seeing Maggy for nearly a decade, and most importantly, after the way he left, he didn't expect her to leap into his arms. But slap him?

He stared at her, feeling her eyes needle him, not sure how to respond. First of all, he thought her mother had always liked him. But secondly, what was this business about Cole being twice the man he was?

"Mags, calm down."

"I'm Mrs. St. John to you. And I'll have you know we've done just fine for the last ten years without you. We didn't need you then, and we don't need you now." Her eyes flashed, and he braced himself for another slap. She snorted in disgust. "It's a good thing you didn't return before Bishop died. He would have been devastated."

She could have picked anything else in the world to say, and it wouldn't have phased him. But the way she stood there, smug and sneering, speaking the truth, Nick felt as if she'd blown a hole clear through him with a deer rifle.

"C'mon, CJ."

He watched as she loaded Suds—yes, he recognized Cole's horse—into the trailer and drove off.

He couldn't meet Stefanie's angry expression as he turned back to camp.

What did Maggy have to do with this? He stalked away from the prying eyes toward the campfire. He remembered that explosive night too well, in vivid dime-store-novel detail, and according to that recollection Maggy had only been around for the tragic ending. Why would she think his anger at Cole had anything to do with her?

Unless, of course, he'd been right that night when he'd accused them of having an affair.

He crouched beside the fire and stirred the coals, hating the fact that after ten years Maggy still hadn't forgiven him, still despised him. Hating that once upon a time she'd been someone who understood him without his having to speak words.

Maggy alone knew how his mother's cancer had turned him inside out. She'd been by his side as his mother's disease slowly took her. Had comforted him with more than her words that first Christmas without his mother. He'd held her, knowing he'd broken every rule his mother had instilled in him and didn't care. Maggy had been his best girl, and at the time he thought he loved her. Told her that, convinced her.

But even a grieving kid knew that love didn't manipulate, it didn't connive, and it didn't use emotions to seduce a person who trusted him.

He deserved that slap and more.

He got up, walked away from the glow of the flames into the coming darkness, where no one could see his grief.

He owed Maggy an apology and had been trying to form one ever since that fateful spring break when he'd returned home, a proposal on his mind. But as he watched her truck lights disappear into the horizon, he knew he didn't deserve her—not now, not then.

But neither did Cole. At least not if he was anything like his mother.

"Nick, are you okay?"

The voice—soft, sweet, gentle, and consoling—behind him made him breathe out, uncoiling the knot in his chest. He felt Piper's hand on his arm and looked down at her. "Yeah."

"That was quite a show back there. She hit you hard?"

He gave a wry grin. "She could probably match that roundhouse kick you're so proud of."

Piper didn't smile. "I'm sorry. I don't know what happened between you two, but it seemed that you were trying to apologize—"

"I should have apologized years ago." He looked toward the setting sun and Cole's ranch. "There's a lot I have to apologize for."

"It can't possibly be that awful." She sat on a boulder, her fingers laced on her lap. The sun set her gold hair on fire, and she smelled like barbeque sauce. He could trace the outline of her smile, and it made him want to let go, to confess it all regardless of the pain, much like the lancing of a wound.

After checking around for prickly pear cactus, Nick sat on the ground near her feet, facing her. "I don't know. Ten years is a long time to go without apologizing."

She reached out and touched his shoulder. The contact felt warm and reassuring. "I agree."

He glanced up at her, again touched by how well she seemed to understand.

Her smile was kind, unaccusing.

"Did you like your first roundup?"

She wrinkled her nose, shook her head slightly. "Sorry. I was happier living in ignorance."

That made him smile. "My first roundup I was five years old. My mother had just given birth to my sister and brother, and she didn't want me underfoot, so she sent me out with my dad. I cried the first time I saw them brand the calves. But by the end of the day, I was helping them, pulling the lassos off the steers, keeping the branding irons hot. I loved the chaos, the smells, the men treating me like I was one of them. Old Pete gave me a chaw of chewing tobacco, and I threw up all over the grass. My dad nearly killed him."

Piper laughed.

Nick looked at her, grinning, his chest expanding. "My dad used to tell me that one day I'd run the ranch. I used to ride this land watching my own shadow, seeing myself tall and bold and strong. The king of the Silver Buckle."

He picked a nearby yellow bell, turning it between his fingers. "I really thought I was something. Then my mom got sick. She had cancer my senior year of high school. Died in the spring, right before graduation."

Piper's eyes glistened. "I'm sorry."

"Yeah, well, I didn't handle it well. Thought I was fine, but I was torn up inside. Maggy was my girlfriend in high school, and her husband, Cole St. John, was my best friend. Without them I think I might have driven myself right off a cliff. As it was, I lived pretty wild that first quarter of college. I don't know what my dad heard back home, but by Christmas I was ashamed of myself."

"You were grieving."

Nick began to pull the petals off the flower, flick them into the wind. "So was my dad." He tossed the whole flower out into the sunset. "We had a fight over Christmas, and I came home drunk on New Year's Eve. I knew I'd shamed the Noble name. I came home for spring break, sorta hoping to set things right—tell my dad how sorry I was for my wild behavior. But he wasn't home. I had this . . . eerie feeling. I still don't know why, but I went to Cole's house." He huffed, weaving his hands together.

From the camp, the soft sounds of laughter and the tones of a guitar drifted in the breeze. Piper didn't move or even breathe, it seemed. But she frowned, a hint at her confusion.

Nick gazed at the slight sprinkling of stars. "My dad and Cole's mom. They were . . . well, I didn't exactly find them in the back bedroom, but what was going on in the kitchen was certainly rated PG."

"Oh, Nick."

"It wasn't pretty. Cole came to the door just as I spun to leave, and all my anger erupted. I hit him, maybe even broke his jaw. My dad yelled at me to leave him alone, and I couldn't believe that he was taking Cole's side after he'd betrayed my mother's memory so I ran out. Maggy was in the yard—evidently she and Cole were coming in from working some place, but I thought they were up to something, even though she nearly leaped into my arms."

His throat tightened at his remembered words: *"Get away from me, Maggy! What, are you having an affair too?"*

"My dad came out and things got worse. Cole was furious and tackled me right there in the yard—I'd never seen him so mad—and we rolled around beating on each other and getting bloody. Then my dad separated us and told Cole to go in the house. But Cole stood there as my dad shoved me against the truck and told me that it wasn't what I thought."

"What did he mean by that?"

Even now, Nick tasted the moment, stinging, acrid in his mouth. "He told me that he wanted to marry Irene, that he loved her, and I told him that he'd do that over my dead body." He closed his eyes, seeing again his father's face, the hurt, the disbelief.

"Then I told him that I wanted nothing to do with him or the

Silver Buckle–with any of them–and I made a point of looking at Maggy when I said it. I finished by telling them all where they could go, hopped in my truck, and drove back to the ranch."

Piper drew a small breath. "That sounds horrible. But you were young and hurting."

"It gets worse." Nick could still hear the yelling, watched himself go after his father like a man possessed. His voice began to tremble. "My dad followed me back to the ranch, and when he came into the kitchen I was so angry, I tackled him."

Piper had gone silent and still.

"I forgot everything I'd been taught about respect and even self-control and attacked him. Hit him as hard as I could." He flinched, remembering his father's broken expression. "And he didn't even fight back. Just tried to push me away or grab my hands. I know that if he wanted to he could have sent me flying through the wall. But he didn't. He just let me spend my energy on him."

He lifted his gaze. Her face twitched, and she looked as if she was trying not to cry. "I finally came to my senses, cursed him, and . . . left."

"You left?"

Nick scanned the land that had once been part of his soul. "I left. I didn't write. I didn't call. I hated him and what I thought he'd done to our family. I fell off the end of the earth."

It took her a moment to respond. "For how long?"

"Until about thirty minutes before you arrived."

Her mouth opened, and in her expression he felt his own grief. Then, to his frustration, his eyes began to burn. He turned away, losing to the sweep of his emotions. "It took me about two years to figure out how much I'd hurt everyone. I joined the reserves and finally upped for a four-year stint in the army. I threw away every letter from home–my sister's, my dad's. Stefanie finally tracked me down through some college friends at Montana State and left a message for me at my base. She told me that my dad had had a heart attack and asked me to come home."

"You didn't."

He shook his head. "I was still angry and ashamed of myself. I blamed them all for the pain I felt when really I was just furious that I couldn't make it go away. I hated the person I had been that night. Hated the feeling of being out of control, of letting every evil thought take possession of me. I vowed that I'd never be that way again. The army taught me a lot about self-control, even in the worst of moments, and being a cop helped me see what happened when things went south. But I could never face that night, couldn't return home to the consequences. And now, because I was a coward, it's even worse."

"I don't understand."

"My dad would have never fallen for Irene St. John. Yes, she was beautiful, but he loved my mother. Irene was lonely, and a man is entitled to a mistake or two. I know his affair with Irene would have disintegrated in time. But she seduced him–she and Cole had been hanging around the Silver Buckle for years, and I finally saw why. Cole's father had run off before he was born, and Irene was fixing to get herself hitched ... to the richest man in Custer County. But she didn't get a chance to get her claws into him because she collapsed that same night. She died about six weeks later."

Nick wound a blade of grass around his forefinger. "Cole

used my dad's guilt to make him leave half our property to him in his will. Dad would have never let Noble land outside the family."

"Why would Cole force your father to give him your land?"

"He wanted this land since he was a kid. We used to ride fence together, and he'd stare out across our property and say, 'Someday I'll own a ranch. Have my own cattle.' I never dreamed he meant Silver Buckle land."

"Can you prove this?" Piper asked quietly.

He shook his head. "Not yet. But I will."

She sighed and folded her hands in her lap. "I'm sorry, Nick."

He met her eyes, saw in them compassion, which gave him the courage to dig deeper, feeling a catharsis somehow in the emptying of the tangle of his emotions. "My sister said that God brought me back here. I don't know about that, but I do think I'm here for a reason. I grew up learning about faith in God, but I never really applied it. Especially after that night."

"Maybe she's right." Piper's voice was so soft he barely heard it. "Maybe you're here to make things right."

He studied the way the twilight played on her features, her hair tossed by the wind, the slight smile she gave him, assuring him. Somehow being around her made him see himself, this land, with new eyes.

As if he might not be the outlaw, the renegade he'd branded himself for so long.

"It's taken me ten years to regain the footing I lost that night. Ten years to get a glimpse at the man my father wanted me to be."

"What kind of man is that?"

"A man who fights for justice. A man who protects his family."

Nick reached up and took her hand, lacing her fingers with his own. "Can you understand that?"

Piper slid off the boulder to sit beside him in the darkness. Her presence felt warm. And when he found his arm moving around her, as natural as the sun setting behind the far mountains, she leaned into him. "Yeah, Nick, I think I can."

# CHAPTER 12

NICK NOBLE HAD TO DIE.

He'd come to the conclusion—somewhat reluctantly, if truth be told—but he couldn't see it any other way. Nick simply had stirred up too much trouble, caused too much pain. Someone had to stop him.

He flattened himself on the rocky bluff, feeling satisfaction sluice through him that he'd gotten up here behind the herd unnoticed.

He'd be the last person they'd suspect should things go south tonight. Should something rile the herd . . .

He watched as Nick rose, left the woman, and walked back to the camp. The man seemed to carry the weight of a broken spirit in his gait—something he himself knew too well. But unlike Nick, he'd found a way out, a way to put his life back together.

And he wouldn't let Nick get away with stealing his future from him. The life he deserved.

His thoughts spiraled out and turned dark as he hunkered down in the precious cover of night. If only he hadn't let her go, if only he'd fought harder for her . . . then everything would be different.

But just because he'd had a run of hard luck didn't mean that he couldn't draw out. And if the dealer was on his side, he'd also win back all that belonged to him—and more.

But first, one way or another, Nick Noble had to die.

⁓⁕⁓

"You did a great job tonight. Thank you, Piper." Stefanie wiped the last of the dishes, stacking the tin plates on the chuck-wagon tailgate.

Piper rinsed her washtub with hot water a final time. "Thank you for your help. I'm pretty sure the boss isn't supposed to help the chef with cleanup."

Stefanie wiped her hands, then hung the towel on one of the many hooks along the back of the wagon. "Around here, we all have to pitch in. Besides, I didn't want to overwhelm you—yet. By the time we have guests, you'll be an old pro." She winked.

Piper returned a faltering smile. If Stefanie only knew. Piper felt a little sick. After what Nick revealed tonight, she had enough to smear his reputation from one side of the state to the next. At best, he had a propensity toward snap judgments and blaming others. At worst, a tendency toward violence. She could slant her article toward suspicion over Irene's death and even the violence against his father and use that to shadow the circumstances of Jenny Butler's murder.

But Nick had sounded shattered when he'd unraveled his story. His pain had found the unguarded places in her heart, and in that moment their friendship was no longer a game but became something real and alive.

That same something made Piper want to jump into Stefanie's pickup and head back to the Silver Buckle, pack her bags, and run home. Seeing Nick on the edge of his emotions, as if barely roping them in, vowing to never hurt someone again . . . she believed him.

And that made it even worse. Hadn't she learned anything from her mother's horrific experience? Apparently not.

Think of Jimmy. No, think of *Russell*. Of the nightmares and scars he'd left on her life. She still ran from him in a way, still dodged his blows.

Still cried out in pain.

She—more than anyone—knew better than to get close to a dangerously charming and utterly unpredictable man like Nick Noble.

Piper carried the dirty water out of the ring of campfire light and threw it out. She wished all sins and debris in a person's life might be as easy to discard.

Stefanie was pouring herself a last cup of coffee when she returned. "Saw you talking to Nick. He doin' okay?"

Piper considered the woman, saw the tinge of worry on her face. "Yeah. He told me everything."

Stefanie appeared surprised. "He did?"

"How he'd hurt everyone, how sorry he was."

Stefanie stared at Piper a long time, wordless. Then finally, "That's good. He needs to get it out." She took another sip. "Tomorrow we'll leave at first light. We need to drive this cattle to the other field, then round up the herd over in the pass. I'll ask Nick to help you close up the wagon and drive it over."

"No need to ask," Nick said, approaching them. He took a cup and poured coffee for himself. "I'll be glad to help her." He glanced at Piper with a soft smile. "Right, George?"

Piper felt something warm and terrifying course through her at the nickname. She put away the last of the utensils, untied her apron, and joined the pair by the fire, sitting next to Stefanie. The campfire sparked into the blackened sky. Stars spilled out in brilliance, an immense canopy that took her breath away. She heard a harmonica in the distance, backdropped by the sounds of restless cattle.

She could get used to this. Get used to the sound of the wind stirring the black spruce, the smells of the open range and the campfire, the taste of beans and biscuits.

Get used to breathing deeply, without worrying about deadlines or depending on duplicity to get a story. She hadn't realized how tightly coiled she felt most of the time until she came out here and let it go . . . little by little.

"I put up a tent for you," Stefanie said, gesturing into the darkness toward the neighborhood of green two-man nylon structures. "Inside is a sleeping bag."

"Thanks," Piper said, leaning back on her hands to gaze at the sky.

Stefanie got up, brushing off her backside. "I'm headed in."

"Good night, Stef," Nick said, catching her hand as she passed by.

Piper saw a tender smile pass between them. Her eyes pricked and she looked away.

"It's beautiful out tonight," Nick said, picking up another log and settling it into the fire. "I never get tired of sleeping on the range. I used to dream of being out here, singing to the cows with my own son or cuddling up around a fire with my wife."

Piper had a feeling that imaginary wife had been Maggy St. John. She said nothing, trying to ignore the abrupt twist of pain inside. So what that he'd once dated Maggy? Clearly whatever had been between them had died. Moreover, it didn't matter to Piper who Nick pined for, who might someday be the wife that snuggled under his arm before a romantic prairie campfire. Didn't matter in the least.

She gasped, seeing a star loosen and drop from the sky. "Did you see that?"

"Yep." Nick chuckled, a low rumble in his throat.

Sitting here quietly with him felt easy. Too easy.

"What made you want to be a chef?"

Nick probably intended the question to be friendly, but Piper winced, feeling a sting. "I . . . ah . . . my mother was a chef. And I like to . . . investigate the . . . flavors of . . . life." She felt some satisfaction about her version of the truth.

"I like to cook too. I used to help Chet, and when I was a teen, I worked at Lolly's a total of one day. But most recently, I worked at a café, filling in wherever they needed me. I make great blueberry pancakes."

"Yum."

"My sister says you're a whiz at cooking trout. Funny, you don't strike me as a girl who likes to fish."

"You'd be surprised at what I like to do."

"Really?" A slight smile played on his face. "Like what?"

Suddenly Piper wanted to give him a piece of truth, something genuine and . . . her. "I like to read. And . . . write. I write stories sometimes."

"Like novels?"

She shrugged. "I haven't tried a novel since college, but yes, at one time I thought about writing a novel. Something epic and literary and life-changing. Something that reveals human nature and gives hope."

"Why hope? I thought all novels were about love."

"Hardly. But maybe hope is a part of love. Maybe loving someone means that you're hoping in something better for them. Giving them the encouragement to be more and believing in more for them."

Nick fell silent, his eyes on her, searching her face, his expression unreadable.

Piper shifted beneath his scrutiny, wondering if she'd given up too much.

"It sounds like a best seller. I think you should write it."

Piper grinned, tucked her hands between her knees. "Someday."

"After culinary school, huh?"

She gave a wry, sad laugh. "Yeah."

The fire crackled and spit, and Nick picked up a poker, stirring the coals. "My sister was right—you probably have enough biscuits for breakfast. Just make some gravy."

"Gravy?" Piper let the word leak out without thinking.

"I'll make it if you want," Nick said. "You're probably used to a fancier setup, I know."

His warm gaze meeting hers without guile made her throat thicken. Why had she thought she could pull off this charade? What if Nick and all his words about changing, about fighting for justice and his family, had been spoken from the heart?

What if she was the real outlaw here?

Piper climbed to her feet. She couldn't look at him, not at the lazy way he balanced his arms on his knees, his cowboy hat pushed back on his head, revealing that curly black hair. She fought the memory of riding behind him, her hands around his waist, the occasional brush against his sturdy back, and tried to keep his particular aroma of soap and leather and hard work from weaving through her pores.

She needed to leave—now—if she hoped to survive this assignment.

"Turning in?" he asked, rising like a true cowboy gentleman.

Piper managed a nod and stumbled past him toward her tent. Tomorrow. She'd leave tomorrow right before dawn, right after the rest of the hands rode out.

She had enough information to concoct a story ... even if it wasn't the right one.

Unzipping her tent, she climbed in, toed off her boots, and left them inside the door. Then she crawled into the sleeping bag, fully clothed, and zipped it up to her chin. Tomorrow she'd be back in civilization, with a chai, the Discovery Channel, and decent cell-phone reception. And soon her demo tape for *Wanted: Justice*.

She closed her eyes, forcing Nick from her thoughts, and felt tears slide down her cheeks into her ears.

⁂

Cole saw the light go on in the barn as CJ banged into the house. He'd heard Maggy and CJ drive in and looked up from the book on his lap. He'd probably read three pages all night, imagining instead the scene at the roundup, Maggy laughing with Nick, a twinkle in her eyes. He well remembered when he used to be able to draw that smile from her. But he'd always wondered if it was a true smile or simply a resigned one.

"Hey, Dad," CJ said, coming into the darkened room after pulling off his boots and coat. He plopped onto the sofa. "You missed a great roundup." His hair was matted to his head and dirt smeared his shirt and chin, but his face glowed. "I even got to practice roping—worked as a header for Miss Noble."

"Good job, Son." Cole ached with the words. How he longed to see CJ rope, see him take the reins of the ranch. "Your mom says Dutch has been teaching you some new techniques."

CJ stood up, demonstrating his words. "And Miss Noble's brother was there. He told me to angle my rope down and to work on my rhythm. I'm getting better."

Cole felt as if he'd been sat upon by a bull. "That's great, CJ," he managed without sounding like all the air had been sucked out of his lungs. "Nick's got a great technique. He and I won first place in the high school rodeo finals our senior year."

"He told me. That's who won the other buckle, right?" He pointed to the framed silver buckle hanging over the sofa.

Cole nodded. He'd never had the hankering to wear it. Besides, Nick wore his, and everyone who mattered had already seen Cole's. It only felt like more competition.

"I was the heeler—Nick was the header. We were a good team." *Once upon a time.* Cole had the urge to grab CJ and pull him close, to pin him and tickle him, to hear him giggle and shout with joy and yell, "Uncle!" He wanted to stop the flow of time and hold on to everything he held dear. Cole's voice thickened. "You'd better get your bath. I'll check on your mother."

"She went in the barn to look after the bums," CJ said. He stood at the door to the hallway, sighing before he turned back to Cole. "Sorry you missed it, Dad. It was a great day."

Cole smiled at him. "Next year."

CJ disappeared into the bathroom, and moments later Cole heard the shower running. He eased his leg to the floor, wincing as the blood ran to his toes. It ached ferociously tonight—probably because he'd been doing exactly the opposite of the doctor's orders. But he wasn't going to sit by and let the ranch fall to ruin along with his body. He aimed to leave this world with at least most of his to-do list accomplished.

Including making sure Maggy and CJ had a future, even if it took watching the woman he loved in the arms of another man.

He pushed to his feet, stifling a groan, and retrieved his crutches. Jay, their new hired man, had left long ago—Cole figured he'd stopped by the roundup. The front door groaned as Cole closed it behind him.

The rising perfect moon lit the shaggy courtyard of their little ranch—the metal barn, their small two-bedroom rambler. He remembered when they'd ordered the modular home from Sheridan. At the time, he thought he'd built Maggy a castle. Now his thoughts went to Saul Lovell's groomed lawn, the beautiful two-story he'd recently built for his wife. Saul had two grown sons, whom he had hoped would take over the ranching life. But when they'd left for the city, he'd sold off his cattle, throwing his efforts into his law practice. Cole heard recently that he'd also set up some coal-bed methane mines, trying to pump every last resource from his land. Cole wondered if CJ would have followed him into ranch life or been lured away by city dreams.

Light puddled from under the barn doors. Cole hobbled out on his crutches and eased inside.

Although he didn't see her, he could hear Maggy's gut-wrenching sobs. Anger welled within him, the old fury of watching Nick destroy lives returning.

He'd sent his beautiful wife out to the wolf, and he felt sick.

The same kind of sick he'd felt ten years ago, tasting the tinny flavor of his own blood on his lips as he'd lain in the dirt, watching Nick drive away. Maggy had sobbed then also. Deep, wrenching sobs that had torn his heart out as he got to his feet. She'd come into his embrace easily, and he held her, watching Bishop shake his head as he climbed into his pickup to chase after Nick.

In that moment, at least for Cole, Maggy had become his—the one with whom she shared her dreams, her fears, her burdens. Although he knew that somehow Nick would always claim a piece of her, she bore Cole's name and a son.

He should have held on to her tonight too. Should have begged her to stay with him. But how could he, knowing that she might finally have the chance to have everything she always wanted?

He stood in the open doorway, searching the sky. *I can't do this, Lord. I can't let her go.*

But what if he'd never really had her at all? What if she was mourning her lost dreams? He'd never been able to shake the feeling that somehow he'd gotten her by default. That in the end he claimed only second place in her heart.

Cole muscled through his grief to the truth. He had to make this easier for her, for CJ. And if Nick wanted her back, well, he could give her a life and a future. Especially if Bishop's will didn't take.

Cole shuffled over to the stall and found Maggy curled in the hay, a bum's head in her lap, holding a bottle of milk in one hand, tears streaming down her face. Escaping wisps of hair framed her face, made her appear breakable.

"Oh, Mags, what happened?" Nick's name was on his lips, but he couldn't voice his questions. *Does he have your heart? Or do I?*

Startled, she looked up at Cole.

He leaned the crutches on the stall and crawled over to her as she put down the bottle and wiped her face.

She forced a smile, one he'd come to expect. "Nothing. I'm . . . I'm just worried about this little bum here."

*Liar.* But that's what their marriage had become. Polite lies to keep each other away from the pain, the disappointment. He laid a hand on the bum's head. "He's breathing."

"He won't drink. I'm afraid we're losing him."

Cole checked the calf's eyes, felt his chest.

"He's so little," Maggy continued, her voice breaking. "It's like he's fading right before my eyes. I don't know how to help him." She urged the bottle into the calf's mouth. The long tongue curled around it, made a feeble effort, and gave up. "I don't know what I did wrong."

Cole took the bottle from her hand, pushed her hair back from her face. It was wet on the ends from her tears. "You didn't do anything wrong. Sometimes things just go bad."

Maggy stared at him, her eyes puffy, her cheeks red. "I refuse to believe that. I know we can save this little guy. He's my responsibility."

"No, he's not, Mags." He touched her chin. "God's in charge of this bum, and He's going to do what's right."

"I'm not letting him die."

"You might not have a choice. You're always trying to take care of everyone, trying to make sure no one gets hurt. It's time to let it go, honey."

"I can't let go." She reached up and laced her fingers into his. She swallowed. "I can't do this alone, Cole."

He ran the back of his finger down her cheek, then moved in beside her and put his arm around her. "Yes, you can, Maggy. You always could. From the first moment, I knew you didn't need me. You're not alone. God is with you, every breath you take. He's given you a way with animals and a strength you don't even know you have."

She closed her eyes and snuggled into his embrace. She put a hand on his chest, and he felt her take a long, tremulous breath. "You're wrong. I've always needed you. And you've always been there." She wrapped her arm around him. She smelled of campfire smoke and the faintest essence of the conditioner she put in her hair. He drank it in, emotion in his throat.

"I love you, Cole," she whispered.

Cole pressed a kiss on her head and pulled her tight against him. Soon her breaths became deeper, and he felt her sleep. "I love you too, Mags."

Nick followed the sound of the harmonica drifting over the horde of black cattle grazing in the stunted cheatgrass, knowing he'd find Dutch on the other side of the melodies. How many times had he wandered out here after roundup to sit beside the trail boss, sometimes in silence, other times hoping to receive praise for his hard day's work?

Dutch sat on his bedroll, serenading the cows. His actions hadn't changed from Nick's youth.

Nick sat beside him, listening to the music, watching the movement of the cattle. They seemed restless, still working out the stress of the day. Tomorrow they'd settle down in the field, enjoying the wide space and ample water supply.

Dutch finished his song and tucked the harmonica into his shirt pocket. He said nothing as he leaned back on his saddle, pulling his hat low over his face.

"Do you think they'll ever forgive me?" Nick's voice sounded thin, weak.

Dutch breathed deeply beside him, as if mulling over his words.

"I didn't expect Maggy to be so angry. I knew that I hurt her by leaving her like I did, but it wasn't as if we were married. Besides, she found Cole pretty quick." He cast a look at Dutch, who made no reaction outside his deep breathing.

"Cole probably deserves her anyway. He always had a thing for her. I thought they were just good friends, but I guess I was wrong." Nick sighed, pulled off his hat, ran his hand over the rim.

"I really did love her, you know. But sometimes you can love someone and not be ready for it. I think that's how it was with Maggy. She was good and decent, and I took that for granted. I didn't treat her right; I know that." He thought of the night he left, the broken look on Maggy's face when he'd accused her of cheating. No, Maggy would have never cheated on him. "I didn't deserve her."

Dutch grunted beside him, shifted his hat.

"The thing is, Piper reminds me of Maggy in a way. I realize that she isn't a cowgirl by any stretch of the imagination." He chuckled, thinking of Piper's reaction to the Rocky Mountain oysters. But she'd held her own with the ribs and biscuits today. Impressed him even. And the way she'd looked tonight sitting on that boulder–her hair like a halo around her face, her blue eyes bright as she studied the heavens, her look of delight at the shooting star–well, he'd never seen anything quite so beautiful in his life. Sitting beside the warmth of the campfire with her, he'd felt something come to life inside him, an old hope that he'd long ago buried. "But she's patient and she listens. And the fact that she's out here, trying new things even though she's so clearly in over her head makes me . . . like her, I guess. She's strong in a different way than Maggy, but still I see it in her."

Nick picked up a rock, tossed it in his hand. "I haven't . . . uh . . . dated anyone since Maggy. There were a few women along the way that I thought might . . . take her place. But it wasn't so much about her but me. I wasn't ready to let someone that close. Thought if they got a good look at the real Nick Noble, it would run 'em off." He thought of the way Piper had listened to his story without flinching.

Dutch's chest rose and fell in deep slumberous breaths.

"I guess you don't know what I'm talking about–it's not like you've had a string of ladies or anything. But I thought it would be easier. I mean, how do you go about letting them close without scaring them off with your secrets?"

Come to think of it, he'd told Piper his worst, and she hadn't run, had she?

Maybe he didn't deserve her either. But hopefully he wasn't the same man he'd been ten years ago. And Piper seemed to like the ranch. He loved to watch her drink in the beauty, enjoyed even her most probing questions. Maybe after a summer together . . .

"I used to be part of this land, Dutch. Now I don't even know if I belong here. Stef says that God brought me back, but I haven't really been on speaking terms with Him for a while. . . . I guess I just wonder if I deserve to come back. That maybe I shouldn't have the right to fix things if I ever could." Nick pressed the rock into the ground, then lay back beside Dutch and drew his hat over his face.

"'He has removed our sins as far from us as the east is from the west.'" Dutch's voice was barely a murmur. "Out here, you should have a pretty good view of just how wide that is, Son."

Nick recognized the quote from his father's favorite Scripture. Of all the Bible passages his father had memorized—and it was his favorite fence-riding pastime—Psalm 103 had been on his lips most often. Enough for Nick to commit it to memory and to hear his father's voice in his thoughts. *The love of the Lord remains forever with those who fear him. His salvation extends to the children's children of those who are faithful to his covenant, of those who obey his commandments!*

Nick clenched his jaw against a rise of regret. He certainly hadn't been faithful to the covenant or obeyed any commandments.

As if reading his thoughts, Dutch spoke again, this time louder. "God finishes what He starts. And I have a feelin' He ain't done with you yet."

Dutch's words zeroed in on Nick's open wounds and salved them. But as much as he wanted to—

A gunshot cracked the night.

Nick sat up, his chest pounding.

Beside him, Dutch was nearly to his feet.

Another shot. And in its wake the piercing wail of a woman's scream.

# CHAPTER 13

NICK RAN TOWARD CAMP and the sound of the scream while Dutch and Pete scrambled to their horses to calm the cattle.

Whoever was being attacked in camp was putting up a stellar defense judging from the screaming and the words punctuated between bursts of terror–"No! Leave me alone!"

Nick's blood turned hot when he saw Stefanie tumble out of her tent. *Thank You, God.* She stood up, pale, in her stocking feet. "What's going on?"

"I don't know!" Nick reached Piper's tent and fumbled with the zipper. "Piper!" If someone was in there with her–Quint?–he was going to tear him limb from limb.

He wrestled the zipper open, peered into the darkness. The moon turned the interior an eerie orange, and in the darkness he saw only Piper, thrashing in her sleeping bag. "No! Get away!"

"Piper!" He climbed in and gripped her shoulders. "Piper, you're having a nightmare!"

Her eyes flew open, and the expression on her face turned to pure horror. As if she didn't recognize him, she jerked and screamed again. Then, to his shock, she twisted her body in the sleeping bag and managed to kick him.

He sprawled backward, tasting blood on his lip. "Piper, it's me, Nick!"

She untangled herself from the sleeping bag in seconds and stood, banging her head on the tent, staring at him with wild eyes. With her hair plastered to her face, her breaths coming fast on top of each other, and her hands balled, Nick recognized the residue of a nightmare. A bad one.

Nick put his hands up in surrender. "Remember me? Nick? The guy on horseback? I cook sometimes?"

She continued to stare at him, but he finally saw recognition flash through her eyes. Crumpling to her knees, she put her hands over her face and began to sob.

"I see you have everything under control in here," Stefanie said, peering into the tent. "I'll go check on the cattle."

Nick climbed to his knees, feeling helpless. He held out his hands, not sure if he should touch her but rattled by her tears. When she put her hands over her head, he gave in to his protective instincts and pulled her toward him. To his surprise, she let him. He tightened his embrace, his cheek on the top of her head as her body trembled. "Shh, Piper, it was only a nightmare."

Her breath came out in a shudder, and she shook her head as she pushed away from him. "No, it wasn't."

"Yeah, it was. I know because I'm the only one who's bloody here."

Her face reddened, tears heavy on her lashes. "Sorry." She breathed out a tremulous breath. "And no . . . it wasn't."

Her expression scared him. He swallowed, not sure he wanted to hear more. "What do you mean?"

She looked away. "It's nothing."

"Apparently it's *not* nothing because I thought the James gang was attacking you. I was ready to seriously hurt someone."

She closed her eyes, as if to hold back her pain. "I'll be fine."

"I won't. I'll never sleep again after hearing you scream like that. And if I remember correctly, you kung-fued me, which means that you thought I was attacking you. If it wasn't a nightmare, then it was a memory, and I'm going to kill the person who left you with that."

Piper turned, her mouth open, her eyes roaming over him.

*Uh-oh, not the right thing to say.*

Or was it? She leaned toward him, and he found his arms around her as she clung to him. She still smelled of the campfire, and he pressed his lips against her hair, gently, softly, wishing he knew how to take away this thing that made her tremble. "What is it, Piper?"

She shook her head again, but this time it felt more feeble, less vehement. "I can't . . . you don't . . ."

"Piper, you can trust me."

She drew away, searching his face, his eyes, his mouth.

The look on her face made him ache right through to his soul, and he couldn't let her go. "Piper—"

She lifted her face and kissed him, sweetly pressing her lips to his. But he felt fear in her touch.

He closed his eyes, not sure what to do, not sure why she was kissing him, but not wanting to push her away. The feeling of her swept over him, through him, and touched emotions that he'd held in check for so long that he'd nearly forgotten them. He brushed a strand of hair from her cheek, rested his hand behind her neck, and kissed her back, drinking her in.

Her kiss turned more desperate, more intense, and he matched her emotions, pulling her closer, both arms around her as if he might lose everything if he let go. She had her arms around his waist, and his hands were in her hair, and he kissed her as if he'd never kissed another woman. Tasting and needing and forgetting who he was in her embrace.

When she disentangled herself from his arms, she didn't look at him.

He swallowed, afraid of how she'd overwhelmed him, invaded his senses, his hopes. His heart thundered, and he thought he heard a roar in his ears. He even had a slight sweat along his neck. "Piper, I ah ... whoa, I ..." He licked his lips. His mouth had turned to dust. "Are you okay?"

She nodded. "I'm sorry. I don't know why–"

"You were crying, and I shouldn't have taken advantage–"

Piper looked at him sharply, an awfulness in her eyes that stopped him cold. "You didn't." She closed her mouth, breathing fast, as if on the edge of another round of tears. "That's the problem."

"What?" The roar in his ears became louder.

"Why can't you be a jerk?" she whispered in a broken voice.

He barely stifled an incredulous huff. Had she heard nothing of what he'd said earlier tonight? He was the king of jerks.

She backed out of the tent, wiping her cheeks.

The roaring became even louder, a thundering that rushed right through him, as if she'd stolen his heart right out of his chest and left a gaping hole.

Or ...

His breath jerked, and he barreled out of the tent, a quiet dread turning him toward the sound.

*Oh no!*

At that moment, Dutch's voice rose over the chaos. "Stampede!"

⚜

Piper had heard about stampedes in movies. Huge, thunderous affairs where the frantic cows trampled everything as they ran to safer ground. According to her calculations, as the black mass swept toward her, she would be among the trampled.

Piper didn't have time to think about the way she'd thrown herself at Nick, how she'd clearly lost every scrap of sense. No time to consider his response or finally how in his arms she'd not only felt safe and alive but protected from all the demons that roamed in her past and often in her nightmares.

She still tingled from head to toe.

"Run!" Nick grabbed her arm, propelling her across the camp toward the pickups.

Hooves pounded the ground, and she heard tearing as first one tent, then another, ripped to smithereens. Nick sprinted full out, pulling her along with him. She barely felt the ground.

Hot breath grazed her neck as a cow closed in behind her. She cried out, tripping. Nick hauled her up and practically carried her to Stef's pickup. He opened the door and shoved her inside, crawling in beside her.

The stampede hurtled by, rocking the pickup in a violent wave. Without thinking, she clung to Nick, breathing hard.

He held her tight, his arms a cocoon of safety, his own chest sawing air. "Are you okay?"

She nodded over and over, but she wasn't sure of her answer. And not because she'd nearly become hamburger. Now that she could think, she realized that back in the tent she'd forgotten everything she'd come to the Silver Buckle to find, everything she'd planned on doing to Nick Noble, and let herself be in his arms. He'd kissed her as if he needed her as desperately as she needed him, and she couldn't stop herself—especially when he told her that he wanted to kill the person who had left her with her nightmares.

What was she thinking? She knew Nick's games. Knew that trusting him could only lead to disaster. And hadn't he confirmed that he had shattered several lives?

Shaking, she moved away from him, feeling cold and weak. He let her go as she wrapped her arms around herself. She couldn't look at him.

He ducked his head, searching for her eyes. "Piper?"

"I said yes." Her tone emerged sharper than she wanted. She closed her eyes, hearing him blow out a deep breath, as if she'd punched him. Well, his hurt feelings were the best thing for both of them.

"It'll be over soon," he said, his voice hard. Then it softened. "You could have been killed."

His kindness, his worry for her only made her feel ashamed. Worse, more than anything she wanted to turn to him, feel his arms around her, as if she were really Piper Sullivan, resident chef and not transient liar. She felt on the edge of telling him everything, of begging him to start over, and the sharp-edged, objective journalist in her might be the only thing to save her now.

"How'd it start?" she asked, glancing at him.

His his hair was tousled and dirty, and he had one hand braced on the dash, as if to hold the truck together. Outside, animals bellowed, and bodies still slammed the truck.

"I don't know," he said just as a cow leaped into the bed and skidded against the cab. The glass shattered.

Piper screamed.

Nick launched himself at her, protecting her with his body. The cow bellowed as it thrashed, finding its footing. The truck nearly turned over as it jumped out.

"We're going to get killed," Piper said, shaking, her hands over her face.

Nick pulled her to his chest. She savored his smell, the feeling of him close, his whiskers rough against her cheek, his strong arms around her as he kept her safe.

"No, we're not. I promise I won't let anything happen to you, Piper."

It was no use. She wrapped her hands around his arms and held on, knowing that somewhere down the road she'd find herself right in the middle of heartbreak.

⚜

As she awoke, Maggy smelled the sweet pungency of the barn. When she opened her eyes, she realized why she'd slept so well last night.

Cole held her close against his chest in one arm, while his other draped the little bum she'd been crying over. He'd managed to get some food into the calf because Maggy found it sleeping soundly.

He was a miracle worker, her man. Maggy lifted her head to watch him sleep. He was always moving, and when he finally sat it seemed such a gift to just be quiet with him. He had long eyelashes—she used to call him Pretty Eyes—and a smattering of reddish brown whiskers along his chin. But this morning he looked jaundiced—something that hitched her breath even as she ran her fingers through his hair. He shouldn't have spent the night out here with her, not in his condition.

But wasn't he supposed to be getting better? She closed her eyes, laying her head on his chest, listening to his heartbeat. He had lied to her. She knew it. Cole wasn't getting better.

She felt him jerk, and then his arm around her tightened. She raised her head and saw that he was looking at her.

A slow smile crept up his face. "Have I ever told you how beautiful you look with hay in your hair?"

"I smell like the barn."

"I love the barn." He kissed the top of her head. "Your bum made it."

*For today.* She petted the animal's hide, which twitched under her touch. "Remember the first year we were ranching? We spent nearly every night for a month in the barn." She waggled her eyebrows, remembering more than that.

He rolled his eyes, but they twinkled. "I also remember Dutch finding us more than once."

Dutch had also found her with Nick. But the stoic cow boss had never said a word. The man knew way too many Noble family secrets. But he'd kept them all. Someday she'd thank him for that.

"You didn't have to sleep out here, Cole."

He made to sit up. "I wanted to. You shouldn't be out here by yourself."

She pushed herself off him without comment. They both knew how much she did alone. "Did CJ get settled in?"

"I assume so. He's a big kid. Told me last night that he's been roping with Nick."

She stiffened, trying to read Cole's expression.

He blew out a breath, and she recognized a forced smile. "If anyone can teach him to rope, it's Nick."

"I was going to tell you, Cole, but I didn't want you to get upset."

He shook his head even before she finished. "I'm not upset, Mags. If CJ wants to win, Nick can help him. I was never the roper Nick was."

She knew what he was really saying: *I was never the man Nick was.*

Her throat tightened. "That's not true. You were every bit as good as Nick. You won together as I remember. I was so proud of you."

His eyes didn't meet hers. "You were there for Nick."

"I was there for *both* of you. Besides, Nick didn't even notice me." She cupped Cole's face, turning it toward her. "But I remember when you rode around the ring. You looked for me in the stands and waved right at me. Don't you remember that?"

Cole gave a slight nod. "I didn't think *you* remembered."

"Cole, don't you know that I always noticed what you did? You made a point of seeing me. Of listening to me. Of making me feel as if I alone made you smile."

Her words didn't seem to penetrate. Reaching out for the stall wall, Cole wrestled himself to his feet. She swallowed the pain of seeing him struggle, wanting to cry.

"Did you see Nick last night?" he asked, breathing hard.

"He was there. Acted like he didn't know a thing about the baby."

Cole looked at her, and she couldn't bear the concern on his face. "Maybe he doesn't know."

"How could he not? You were there. You helped me leave the note."

"He was angry. Maybe he never saw it." Cole hung on the walls as he dragged himself to his crutches. He walked like an eighty-year-old cowboy. "We need to find out if he knows."

"No, we don't. You're my husband. You're the father of my son. That's all I care about. It doesn't matter if Nick ever finds out—"

"It does matter, Mags." His voice had softened almost to a groan. "Especially now."

Maggy felt his words like a brand on her soul. "What are you talking about?"

He leaned on his crutches, turned to her. "I think you need to give Nick a chance to apologize."

She stared at him, horrified. "Who are you? Don't you remember the feel of his fist on your face? remember what he did to your mother?"

"Nick isn't to blame for Mom's death. We all knew she wasn't well." He didn't look at Maggy as he spoke. "And Nick's back for better or worse. We have to accept it and let him back into our lives."

Her voice lowered. "Do you remember what I said to you the night CJ was born?"

Cole swallowed and looked away.

"I told you that God loved me because He gave me a husband who wouldn't leave me. Who loved me better than himself. And that I didn't deserve you. I didn't want Nick then . . . and I don't want him now."

"You deserve better than me." He turned to leave. "You deserve a man who can take care of you."

"No, I don't!" She ran to intercept him, grabbing his crutch. "Yes, I need you here on the ranch, making it work. But I need you for more than that. You alone know the mistakes I made, and you loved me in spite of them."

Cole met her eyes, and she saw in them their past, that night when she'd realized not only that Nick wasn't coming back but that Cole had found his way into her heart.

The night she'd accepted his marriage proposal. He'd looked at her the same way then—with the suspicion that her words were born from desperation.

He broke her gaze. "I loved you with your mistakes, Mags."

"I know, Cole." She stepped close and grasped his jean jacket, pulling his lapels. He still felt strong and capable. She wrapped her hands around his waist and put her head on his chest.

One arm came around her, and for a long while, he just held her. She listened to his heartbeat and wished that once more Dutch might find them in the hay.

Finally, he lifted his head and touched her chin, raising her face to his. "Mags, I want you to promise me something."

She frowned, his expression scaring her.

"If something happens to me, I want you to sell the ranch. Go south to Arizona and be with your parents. Send CJ to a great college. And remarry."

She felt as if he'd reached down and scooped all her insides out.

Then his eyes darkened, and his expression turned hard. "Or if you want, you should marry Nick."

# CHAPTER 14

EARLY DAWN REVEALED the carnage of the stampede. With the sunrise spilling over the prairie, lighting it nearly afire, Nick and Stefanie totaled their losses. The Buckle had lost at least eight calves and four cows. Nick waved his lariat, whistling as he dogged the stray cattle back toward the camp. They'd scattered in the draws and gullies, many of them wounded, some caught in brush.

After spending part of the night with Piper in his arms, Nick also felt disoriented, tangled in unfamiliar feelings. She hadn't kissed him again—and he wasn't about to try after the horrified look on her face—but she had let him hold her and had finally fallen asleep. That felt strange. Not because his arm had fallen asleep, but because he well remembered the last time he'd held a sleeping woman. All he'd been thinking then was what if his father found them, if his mother could see him from heaven, and how guilty he felt for talking Maggy into something they both knew was wrong.

But sitting in the cab of the truck last night, cradling Piper, none of those feelings had assaulted him. In fact, as he'd smoothed her hair and tried not to jostle her, he felt as if maybe–finally–he'd done something right.

When light crept over the horizon, he'd settled her onto the seat and climbed out of the mangled truck. Dutch caught up with him, and they'd spent the next three hours rounding up the horses and taking a head count of the cattle. Thankfully, all the hands were accounted for–Pete and Quint and Andy and the three from the other ranch who had stayed to help them today. Nick felt nearly hollow with relief that Maggy and CJ had gone home. The kid had gotten inside him just a little–perhaps in CJ's eagerness, Nick had seen a smidgen of his own youthful zeal.

"C'mon, doggie," Nick hollered as he drove a handful of cows and calves toward the rest of the herd, not penned but grazing happily and monitored by the few hands on horseback. Stefanie or Old Pete had rebuilt the fire pit, and he smelled coffee brewing. Whistles and calls, the sounds of a dog barking, laced the air.

The chuck wagon had taken a hit–its wheel had cracked in two places, and Nick would have to unload it and transport the wagon on a flatbed to get it home. Dishes and utensils littered the ground, Piper's delicious biscuits trampled into the grass.

He spied Piper collecting the debris as he rode closer. Herding the cattle toward the others, he turned his horse toward camp, dismounted, and tied the bay to the chuck wagon.

Piper didn't look at him while she loaded tin plates and cups into her apron, then dumped them into the washbasin.

He picked up a runaway pot and tossed it into the wagon. "You in one piece this morning, Piper?" He walked over to her and helped her gather silverware.

She nodded but still didn't look at him.

"Everything okay, George?" He reached for her, but she skittered away. "What's the matter?"

"Nothing." Only her voice didn't sound like nothing. It was sharp and nasty.

He caught up with her, touched her elbow.

This time, she turned and looked at him. She'd been crying. But this wasn't the sad, nearly frantic grief of last night. Piper gave him a look of pure fury.

*Ouch*. He dropped her elbow and stepped back. "Please tell me that you're not mad at me."

She looked momentarily shocked, then shook her head. "Dutch said that someone started this stampede on purpose."

Nick raised an eyebrow. Since when did Dutch turn chatty?

"He said gunshots scared the cattle into running. I'll bet that if we look around, we'll find hoofprints of the culprit at the far edge of the field."

"Hoofprints? You are cognizant of the fact that cows have hooves, right?"

She glared at him, hands on her hips. She had a smudge of dirt across her cheek, and her hair had been blown by the wind. He couldn't help a sudden burst of affection for her.

"Don't patronize me. You yourself said that Cole wanted this ranch. And didn't Stefanie say that a bunch of cattle had mysteriously died in Hatcher's field? Is it outside the realm of possibility that someone might try and make you lose more cattle? Look at this!" She spread her hands, and he saw her emotions flash across her face at the destruction. "It's wrong."

"I think you're jumping to conclusions, Lois Lane. Yes, I was there, and they sounded like shots, but sometimes cowboys shoot their guns as a warning."

"And how many of the hands had guns on them last night? Excuse me for noticing, but this isn't the OK Corral. People don't walk around with guns at their hips anymore."

Nick hid a smirk. "No, but an occasional cowboy carries a rifle. More do now that we've had wolves and coyotes in the area."

"I thought you're not allowed to shoot wolves."

What was with this woman? "No one stampeded the cattle. It was an accident, and while I do believe Cole wants this property, I highly doubt he'd try and kill us to get it."

In fact, he was sure of it. His own words shook him. He'd been so sure that Cole had hornswoggled his father out of the land. But was that the Cole he'd known, had grown up with?

He took off his glove and lifted his hand to wipe off the smudge on Piper's cheek. She stood there, her lips pursed, looking so sure of herself he had to laugh.

"I appreciate the indignation, but really, Piper, I think this was just an accident. Let's not round up the lynch mob yet."

She regarded him with narrowed eyes.

"I think you need a hat. Help cool you off."

She harrumphed and shook her head.

Nick looked up, hearing hooves.

Andy rode in, towing a horse behind him. A paint, an overo with white legs and body, and a splash of black across his back.

Nick felt paralyzed watching the animal, everything inside him burning. No, it couldn't be . . . "Andy, where did you get that horse?" He heard the catch in his voice and cleared his throat.

"Found him back behind the herd. Must have broken away from the cavvy during the ruckus."

Nick moved toward the animal, his hands out so the horse could watch him approach. As he drew closer, he thought he saw recognition flicker in the animal's blue eyes. His throat constricted. "This horse wasn't in the cavvy."

He touched the horse's neck, ran his hand down his jaw, then rubbed his nose.

The horse blew out, as if in recognition.

"Pecos?" he whispered.

"Do you know this horse?" Piper asked. She'd followed Nick and now reached out to touch the horse's face.

Pecos jerked his head.

"Shh," Nick soothed, his pulse rushing. How . . . ? Stepping closer, he put his arms around the animal's neck, unable to push through any more words. He inhaled the familiar smell, traced the shape of an animal that had been as close as a brother. No, closer.

"It's my roping horse," he said in a voice that didn't sound like his at all. "I . . . I thought he'd died."

Piper touched his shoulder. "Where did he come from?"

"Back behind the herd," Andy said again.

Nick drew a deep breath, stepped away from Pecos, grabbing his halter. The horse wasn't bridled, but Pecos didn't need a bit to respond to the commands of his master. Nick stroked the horse's white face. "Where did you come from, old friend?"

"The St. John place." Stefanie's voice sounded tight behind him.

Nick turned to see Stefanie sitting on her own horse. She pushed her hat up so he could see her eyes. Dark, even disturbed. "Dad gave Pecos to Maggy shortly before he died."

"I don't think Cole told me the truth, Doctor, and I need to know what's going on."

Cole heard Maggy in the next room, pacing the kitchen floor, and knew he'd better brace himself. The fact that she'd tracked down Doctor Lowe on a Sunday meant Maggy wasn't going to be deterred from the truth. But Cole had a feeling that bigger things might be coming down the pike because as he stared at the road, he saw Bishop Noble's old pickup pulling a horse trailer and headed their direction. So Nick Noble was paying him a visit.

Cole rose and snatched his crutches, maneuvering out the front door and onto the porch. The cherry red pickup churned up gravel, while Cole felt the same churning in his stomach. *Lord, give me wisdom.* Although he'd forgiven Nick years ago, thankful for the blessings the nightmare had wrought, he'd still wrestled the dread that coiled inside him. That he could lose everything he loved to a man who despised him.

The truck pulled into the courtyard, and again Cole wished he had a bigger house, something like Saul's, to make Nick take a breath. Cole reminded himself of Bishop's advice to him: a boy didn't become a man through his fists but by facing his fears.

Cole's foot throbbed in tune to his heartbeat as Nick stopped and got out of the truck. He slammed the door and went straight to the horse trailer.

Nick had changed. Cole saw it in his face as he worked the lock. A hardness in his expression had replaced the laughter of a boy who loved trouble. Maybe Nick, too, had learned the wisdom of measuring his words. He wondered if perhaps that only made him more dangerous.

The trailer door swung open, and Nick disappeared inside to back out a horse. Cole tightened his jaw. Pecos. How had he gotten out?

Cole supposed that Nick would eventually discover Bishop's gift to Maggy. Cole hadn't been surprised—the animal hadn't been ridden since Nick's temper tantrum/escape, and Maggy's history of helping her father train Pecos when he was a colt at the Big K gave her a special bond with the animal. Not only that, but Bishop knew how Nick had hurt Maggy. The gesture contained the fragments of guilt, the hope of forgiveness. The fact that he'd made it legal in the will said that Nick couldn't take the horse back. But ever since the day Dutch delivered the animal, Cole knew that Nick would come calling for it anyhow.

In many ways, Cole understood that his having Pecos was as terrible as his marrying Maggy.

Nick said nothing as he led the horse to the corral. The other two horses nickered in greeting. Nick opened the corral gate and let the horse inside. Then he turned and stared at Cole. Nick's dark eyes edged on rage as he took a long breath.

Cole could hardly believe it when Nick simply marched back toward the truck. He heard the door behind him squeak, and Maggy stepped out onto the porch. She came to stand beside him.

Nick stopped when he reached the truck. He stood there, saying nothing, his face granite, but his gaze ran over Cole, then Maggy.

It shouldn't be like this. They'd been more than friends—they'd been like brothers. Cole knew more about Nick than he did about himself, had a scar on his hand to prove his loyalties.

All at once he longed for things to be right between them for Maggy's sake.

For CJ's sake.

The urge to step forward and hold out his hand nearly overpowered him. *I forgive you, Nick.*

But even as his thoughts screamed it, his pride locked it inside. So he lifted his chin.

Maggy put her hand on Cole's shoulder.

Nick gave a tiny shake of his head. "You always wanted what I had, Cole. My father, my girl, my horse, and now my land. For some reason you won't rest until you've taken everything from me."

Cole kept his voice cool, detached, afraid he might betray how close that accusation hit. "You lost Maggy on your own, pal. As for your father, I don't know what you're talking about. But I promise you, I'm not trying to steal anything. Your father's decisions were his own. I had nothing to do with it."

Nick glared at them. Finally, "I'm not sure what to think, Cole. But I promise this isn't the end of it."

"Let it go, Nick."

He ignored Cole and got into the truck.

Cole stood there, his stomach in his knees. In his peripheral vision, he saw a tear streak down Maggy's cheek.

They watched Nick pull away, his truck kicking up a wake of debris and fury. A wake of destruction.

Just as it had so many years ago.

❧❧❧

"See if you can get me the editor at *Montana Monthly*. Tell her I have a great feature for her. Besides, she owes me a favor." Piper shifted so the cell signal could clear the mountains. This morning the blue sky touched the far corners of the earth, with only the slightest wisps of clouds streaked high above. The smell of cows and grass and even woodsmoke tinged the air. Piper drank deeply, amazed at how a week on the range had awakened her soul. Made her feel clean. Almost.

"You're going to owe *me* favors if you don't get back here soon," Carter said. "Our editor asked me yesterday when you were coming back from your vacation. I told her you were incommunicado." Behind his voice, Piper could hear the sounds of the newsroom.

A wave of familiarity swept through her, tugging her back to her real life—deadlines, endless pots of coffee, the tick of computer keys. It felt as if she'd been gone for a decade rather than a week. She could barely remember when she hadn't woken every day with the smell of the land permeating her thoughts, her dreams. Or the image of Nick Noble loving this land. When he'd embraced Pecos, the look on his face had made her nearly cry.

She would never again ridicule the love between a man and his horse. But she did wonder what it might feel like to love something that purely, that freely.

She'd never let herself love anyone but her mother and Jimmy. Letting someone that close meant they were within hitting distance then, weren't they? She had enough scars from the first go-around to last her a lifetime.

"Remind her that I have at least three more weeks of vacation coming. Besides, after I put together my audition tape, I won't need the bit salary she pays me."

"Countin' your chickens a little early, aren't you, Piper?" But

Carter's voice held tease. "Or have you finally got the goods on Noble?"

The view from here overlooked the valleys and bluffs for miles. Piper saw Nick working on the new wheel for the chuck wagon, recognized Dutch coming from the barn, leading his roan. Andy, Quint, and Old Pete had left earlier to check on the herd.

After they'd counted their losses, the hands had driven the herd into the spring pasture while Piper and Nick unloaded the chuck-wagon supplies into the truck. She'd watched as Nick led his roping horse into a trailer, and the look on his face had raised the hairs on her arms. Betrayal? Anger?

Whatever the case, it was just enough to remind her exactly why she'd come to the Silver Buckle Ranch.

He'd said little as they drove back to the ranch. Piper unloaded the supplies while he hitched up the trailer to the red pickup and took off.

When he returned, the horse trailer was empty. He'd headed back to the field to help dispose of the dead cattle while Piper stayed back in camp, feeling helpless. She hated that they'd all worked so hard to get the cattle branded only to have so many die. She'd taken those thoughts to bed with her and stared at the ceiling, conjuring up scenarios.

"I think someone is trying to sabotage the ranch," she said to Carter. "A few days ago they found two of their bulls dead, and this weekend someone started a stampede."

Carter's voice changed. "Do you have enough for your article on Noble?"

"Yeah, I guess. I mean, I didn't prove anything really–"

"Come home, Piper. I mean it. If Nick is the man we think he is, he probably has a list of enemies larger than the population of Montana. I know that you think you're safe . . . but I want you to come home before you get hurt. There's only so much a guy can do trying to protect you from afar."

His concern touched her. He'd always been a sort of fill-in brother for her . . . someone she counted on to pick her up from the airport or eat dinner with on a lonely Saturday night. But she never considered that he might also feel the same brotherly affection. "I'm okay. You don't need to protect me."

She heard Carter sigh, as if holding back a retort.

Piper watched the black bodies of the remaining cattle grazing in the winter pasture. She wasn't sure why they'd left the cattle there. She had a sinking feeling that they might soon be headed to their dark fate. "Besides, I have Nick."

"What?"

She winced at his tone and even the lunacy of the statement. "Nick saved my life."

He'd done more than that. He'd kissed her and held her and let her see inside his heart. And what she'd seen only made her long for more.

Worse, in his arms, she'd slept better than she had in years. That alone should send her running for the border.

"He saved your life?" She could picture Carter taking his feet off his desk and leaning over it. "How?"

"In the stampede. I was nearly killed. He dragged me to a pickup for protection. As it was, a cow came through the glass."

"Okay, really, that's it. You're leaving today."

Piper shook her head. "I can't. I—they need help. The Silver Buckle is going under and with these cows lost—that's why I want you to call the editor at *Montana Monthly*. And you're going to have to teach me to cook."

She heard him groan, imagined him closing his eyes, rubbing his face. "I think all that fresh air has gone to your head, Piper. You can't cook, remember?"

"Yes, I can. I will. I'll read these cookbooks, and you'll tell me what to do."

"You can't learn to cook over the phone."

"I can—it's just beans and biscuits."

His pause told her how much he cared about her. "Listen to me carefully. Don't fool yourself. You can't cook. You can't even reheat well. And if Noble finds out you're stringing them along, he'll kill you with his bare hands. If you have what you need, then you should leave. Now."

"I *can* cook. My mother cooked for years—how hard can it be?"

"Even if you learn to cook—and, yes, you're smart so you can probably do anything—you *can't* stay there all summer! You have a job, and if you don't come back to it, you'll lose it. I never liked this idea anyway. Don't make me come down there and throw you over my shoulder and drag you home."

"You could teach me to cook while you're here then."

She pictured Carter shaking his head, and she smiled when his voice lowered. "Listen to me. You're not a cowgirl. You're not a cook. You're a reporter. A good one whose career could be sliding through her fingers if she doesn't get ahold of her senses."

In her mind's eye, she saw the devastated expression on Stefanie Noble's face. "I can't leave them in the lurch."

"Piper, you *are* the lurch."

Her mouth opened in a long, exaggerated gasp. "I cooked a great meal for roundup."

"You had it catered!"

"I warmed it well. Nick liked it."

"Oh, Piper," Carter said, "you're falling for him."

"I am not." Piper flinched at her tone. "I'm not. It's just that they're so close to losing everything, and you know what a sap I am for the underdog."

"Not Nick Noble. Have you forgotten that you went there to find dirt on him so you could even the scales of justice?"

How she wanted to pace. "Okay, listen, I'm starting to wonder if—"

"What? That your brother was really guilty?"

"No, of course not!" But, well, Piper hadn't talked to her brother in years before his murder conviction. And he had lived all that time with their father; maybe Russell's ways had infected his son more than she wanted to admit.

No. "Jimmy didn't do anything. But maybe Nick didn't either."

"We did research on Nick, if you remember. He was the last one to see the victim, besides your brother. And we only know about your brother because he confessed. You and I both came to the same conclusion—Nick framed him."

Piper dug her boot into the ground, not quite sure what to say. Yes, the facts pointed to fishy circumstances. But after spending a week with Nick, her instincts practically screamed Nick's innocence. Or perhaps that was her heart. At the moment she didn't know the difference between truth and wishful thinking.

Some ace reporter she'd turned out to be.

"I think I can still get a confession from him." Her words felt hollow, but she had nothing else, no other reason to stay at the Silver Buckle.

At least not one she'd admit to herself.

"Are you sure?"

"Yes. Yes. But I need to stay here and . . . cook. However, I don't know the first thing—"

"Okay, fine. If you can boil water, you can cook. Piper, you're one of the smartest women I know. And what you don't accomplish in smarts, you make up for in charm. So go open a cookbook and start reading. Call me tonight with questions."

"You're the greatest. Thank you. Thank you! Meanwhile, could you send me a bag of yogurt pretzels and a current edition of the *Gazette* and—"

"Promise me that you'll take me with you when you go to *Wanted: Justice*?"

"Carter, I couldn't live without you—you know that."

"The words I love to hear." She heard his smile on the other end of the line. "I'll keep my phone with me, Chef Pierre."

Piper closed her phone, slipping it into her jeans pocket. Right next to her tape recorder.

# CHAPTER 15

"Okay, CJ, ANTICIPATE, take a breath–" Nick opened the chute, and the calf sprang out, terrified, running for the end of the corral–"now!"

CJ spurred his horse, and the bay shot forward, breaking through the barrier toward the calf. He had already swung his lasso once . . . twice. Then he let it fly. Even as the rope hung in the air, CJ yanked on the reins, bringing the calf to a stop. The rope landed around the calf's neck, and a second later it broke off from the flimsy string attached to the saddle horn.

"That was 9.24 seconds," Nick said, looking at his stopwatch. "You're getting faster every day, kid."

He remembered his and Cole's practice sessions, from sunup to nightfall before the big events. He'd break out first, aiming for the head, and a split second later Cole would be aiming for the back feet. They made a synchronic pair–Nick leading, Cole following.

It hadn't been Cole the Follower who had stood on the St. Johns' porch a few days ago when Nick had returned Pecos. No, his eyes had flashed with ownership, his face resolute and unforgiving. And when Maggy joined him on the porch, her hand on his shoulder in a united front against the enemy—*him*—Nick knew exactly who'd been left behind.

Cole had become a rancher, followed his dream.

Nick had simply drifted.

He had to admit, however, that seeing Maggy and Cole on the porch . . . somehow it looked . . . well, right. As if they belonged together.

It made him wonder if they always had. *"You lost Maggy on your own, pal."* Cole's words had speared right through him, hitting the mark.

He *had* lost Maggy on his own. Which meant that Cole hadn't stolen her, not really. Truth be told, seeing Maggy didn't stir up the old feelings like he thought it might. He could honestly say that he wanted her to be happy.

Nick stepped into the corral, working with CJ as they drove the calf back into the pen. He locked the pen and leaned against the corral as CJ went at it again.

He couldn't help but like the boy for his energy and enthusiasm. And helping him took his mind off what Piper was up to in the kitchen. He'd probably stopped by the dining hall more often than necessary. Of course, Piper looked adorable in her chef's coat, with flour on her face, her hair in a ponytail.

"Nick, get out!" He remembered her startled expression yesterday as he'd burst in, smelling smoke yet again. The woman had a knack for setting the kitchen on fire. And her wretched expression as she held a blackened pan of—were those supposed to be biscuits?—only made him laugh.

"Too many irons in the fire, George?"

She'd smiled at him meekly as he approached, then wiped the flour from her nose with his finger. It took everything in him not to bend over and kiss her.

"You're not supposed to be bothering the cook," she said, tossing the pan onto the counter and using a metal spatula to work off the biscuits. "I don't get it. I followed the recipe. . . ."

"Are you trying something new?" He glanced at the open page in the *Joy of Cooking*.

"Uh . . . yeah," she said, but her smile didn't reach her eyes.

For the first time in over a week, again he felt the niggling sense that something wasn't right. The ingredients she'd left on the counter only confirmed it—flour, lard, salt, and baking soda. "You know that this is soda . . . not powder, right?"

She frowned and took in the container in his hand. "Oh, wow. Yeah. I'm just tired."

"You've been holed up in here for two days, like some sort of outlaw. What's going on?"

She'd pushed her bangs back with her forearm, leaving a fresh trail of flour. She didn't comment as she went back to prying the flattened disks from the pan. Three broke off with a whoosh, and one hit him in the chest. She looked up, wide eyed.

"Hey, look out. Those things are lethal."

Her expression darkened.

*Uh-oh*, he'd made George mad. Hiding a grin, he scooped one off the floor and winged it back at her.

She ducked, but a small smile creased her face. Before Nick knew it, she'd gathered the pile of black bullets into her arms, shielded herself behind the counter, and begun to pick him off.

He held his arms over his face and took cover behind the other end of the counter. "Piper!"

"Get out of my kitchen, Nick!"

"Okay, okay!" He hit his knees, slinking out, then ran out the door. But he wore a silly grin on his face all day.

Now, as CJ lit out after another calf, Nick couldn't help but let his thoughts roam. Like . . . what if he had a son, one with chocolate brown eyes and unruly blond hair, with Piper's freckles and her devastating smile? Or a little girl, who would climb into his lap to hear his stories and learn to cook like her mother?

The thought so took him, he didn't notice as CJ roped the calf. "What did you think of that, Nick?"

Nick rounded up his thoughts, tried to find his footing in reality. "Uh, great."

CJ grinned as he rewound his rope.

"CJ, I have to ask you—your horse is great, but he's still a little scared of the rope. Why haven't you tried Pecos?" He kept his voice light, but seeing Pecos had shaken him, and his insides burned every time he thought of his father giving his paint away. If his father had been trying to hurt him, he'd done a stellar job.

"Well, I'm not supposed to ride Pecos," CJ said, bringing his horse around and backing him into the chute. "Mom told me I couldn't. The day Uncle Dutch brought him over, she sat on the porch and cried. I don't know why, but she doesn't want anyone to ride him."

"Then why did Bishop give him to her?"

CJ straightened the coils in his rope. "She said it was a gift of love."

*Oh.* Nick let that thought simmer. Bishop had always liked

Maggy, but the gift seemed extreme for a caretaker. He had a feeling Bishop was trying to apologize in his stead.

What if, in fact, the gift wasn't meant to hurt so much as to heal?

Nick locked the calf into the gate, got her straightened around while CJ measured out the loop of his rope and fixed it in his grip. "Try and send it on the second loop this time," he instructed.

The kid would nail the prize at the Custer County rodeo. But Nick suddenly wanted more for him. He wanted the championship. He wanted to see the hard-earned smile of victory in CJ's dark brown eyes.

CJ absorbed Nick's instruction, determination on his suntanned face. *Thata boy.*

"Ready?"

The boy leaned forward in his saddle, watching the gate.

Nick popped it open, and the calf shot out. A second later, CJ followed. He threw on his second go-round and tagged the calf dead-on. The rope broke at 8.25 seconds.

"Good job, kid."

CJ grinned at him, again winding up his rope. "I gotta get home. Mom needs help. The bulls dug up a hose, and it's draining the water tanks. We don't want any more cows dying."

"You had a cow die?"

CJ worked to move the calf into a holding corral. "Five of them near the south end. My dad rented the land this winter, and when we went for roundup, we found them and the tank mostly dry."

"That land bumps up to Hatcher's Table on Silver Buckle land," Nick said, mostly to himself.

CJ closed the cattle gate. "I cut through there sometimes on my way to Mr. Lovell's land. He lets me do some hand work."

Like mother, like son, apparently. How did this kid find time to practice, homeschool, help his mother, and do odd jobs? Nick wondered if CJ's workload had anything to do with Cole's cast and the comments he'd picked up from Stefanie alluding to Cole's health problems.

To see Cole hurting had bothered Nick more than he wanted to admit. Cole had always worked ten times harder than Nick, and Nick knew it must be sheer torture for Cole to watch Maggy and CJ run the ranch on their own. Cole had set the bar when it came to cowboying.

*"Let it go, Nick."* Cole's words had latched on, dogged him like a hungry coyote. *"Let it go."*

And then what? Nick had returned to make sure the Silver Buckle stayed in Noble hands. Letting go would mean giving up. It might even mean selling out. Perhaps to that buyer Saul had rustled up.

No. He'd never surrender the family legacy.

"You and your mom need any help?" Nick wasn't sure why he asked, but suddenly he couldn't stop himself. Maybe helping Maggy would give him a peek at their side of the fence. He'd discover why Cole had been so important to Bishop.

"Thanks, Mr. Noble, but we just hired on a man—Jay. He's working with my mom."

An old flare of protectiveness—probably left over from his cop days—burst to life inside him. "Jay who?"

"He's just Jay. He answered an ad my mom put up in Lolly's. He said he'd been in Wyoming, rodeoing." CJ climbed down from his horse, led the animal through the fence as Nick closed it.

Nick stood there, rolling that information through his head. Hiring temporary hands was a way of life out here. Still, his past experience with drifters in Wellesley had his instincts buzzing. "You watch over your mom, okay?"

CJ gave him a curious look, then nodded. "You comin' to the rodeo on Saturday?"

"Wild horses couldn't keep me away." He grinned at CJ, then slapped the horse's hindquarters. "Remember to angle your rope!"

CJ lifted his hat without looking back as he trotted across the field toward the St. John spread.

Nick chuckled, remembering the days when he rode the Silver Buckle as if he already owned it—cocky, young, brash.

Stupid.

*"The Lord is compassionate and merciful, slow to get angry and filled with unfailing love. He will not constantly accuse us, nor remain angry forever. He does not punish us for all our sins; he does not deal harshly with us, as we deserve."* The words from Psalm 103 filled his thoughts, a replay from what he'd read last night. Since the roundup and Dutch's comments, he'd dug out his father's old, marked-up Bible. Seeing Bishop's comments written in the margins stirred up memories of his father's voice: *"The love of the Lord remains forever with those who fear him. His salvation extends to the children's children of those who are faithful to his covenant, of those who obey his commandments!"*

Nick hadn't exactly kept God's precepts. He'd thrown them out like every other remnant of his upbringing. But without a compass to guide him, he had been left lonely and wandering. And harboring an anger that only festered.

Certainly not the future his father had hoped for him.

His father probably hadn't hoped for a future in which his children lost the Silver Buckle either. Nick had spent the better part of three days clearing the last of the carcasses from the field and meeting with the Custer County sheriff again over the circumstances of the stampede. He bristled when the sheriff asked if he thought anyone might be out to cause trouble for the Silver Buckle. Neither he nor Stefanie had mentioned Cole or Pecos.

Stefanie didn't out of loyalty. Nick didn't because he wanted to solve this on his own terms.

Everything inside him said Cole wouldn't start a stampede. And certainly Cole wasn't responsible for the sick, dehydrated cattle out at Hatcher's Table. Yes, Cole most likely hated Nick, but could a man change that much? Cole had always been the peacemaker.

Pecos had probably escaped his corral and set out for the home he'd known all his life—the Silver Buckle. An instinct Nick should have followed long ago.

Last night, long after the sun slid behind the Bighorns, Nick had sat in darkness on the porch, watching the light from Piper's window and wondering how long forgiveness took to incubate and what it might look like when it was birthed.

He was starting to believe that Cole would get everything Bishop had promised him.

And Nick couldn't do a thing about it.

———※———

To Piper, the smell of baking bread—without the added scent of char—felt like the applause of thousands. She sat on the stainless-steel counter, her attention on the little brown-stained oven window.

Carter would be so impressed. *She* was so impressed. Four days of devouring the how-to sections in Chet's cookbooks, experimenting with ingredients, learning the difference between biscuit batter and bread dough, and she'd finally managed to cook something that might have Nick's mouth watering.

She no longer tried to dodge the truth–Nick had camped out at the edge of her heart and was fast sneaking his way inside. She felt the fool for how often she listened for his boots, hoping he'd call her George in that deep, husky voice.

To say that she'd fully immersed herself in this alias seemed a bit understated. She *was* Piper Sullivan, cookie of the Silver Buckle. The thought made her smile.

The screen door whined, and footsteps crossed the planks of the dining hall.

She jumped off the counter as Nick entered.

"I am under your command, O Bread Queen," he said as he pulled off his hat.

Piper quirked an eyebrow at him.

"The smell. It's not part of your magical powers?"

She smirked. "As a matter of fact, it is. . . ." Only, what would she command him to do first? The timer dinged before she could finish her thought, and she grabbed a set of pot holders. Nick opened the oven, and Piper nearly cheered at the two light brown loaves of white bread. She took them out of the oven as if they were freshly blown glass.

She set the bread on the counter, then flipped the loaves onto a baking rack to cool. "I think that's going to turn out."

He smiled. "Of course it will."

She tossed the hot pads onto the counter, put her hands on her hips, and stared at her creation, satisfaction full and deep within her. *Take that, Carter.*

She looked at Nick. He was staring at her with an odd look.

"What?"

He shrugged. "It's just nice to see you taking such pride in your work. Like it's a new creation every day. Makes me rethink the simple tasks that seem so mundane."

*Oh. Right.* She nodded, unable to contain her emotions. "This is going to work out, Nick."

He looked at her so sweetly, so oddly delighted, that something burst inside her. She liked the Piper she saw in his eyes—capable, nurturing, even a part of this project to turn the Noble ranch into a getaway for families. A place where she might find a family too.

That thought swept through her, wiping the smile right off her face. She turned away before he saw regret cut through her expression.

"Cookie," he said shaking his head, "you make anything taste great."

She did? Wow, did she have him fooled.

"Hey . . . while we wait for the bread to cool . . . you wanna go for a ride?"

She turned back, considering what that might mean in her state of mind. Perhaps some fresh air to cool off the longing that seemed to burn through her. "All right." She took off her apron as she followed him out of the dining hall.

He ran his hands through his hair just before he put his hat back on. The gesture made her want to do the same—twirl her fingers around his curls.

So maybe Carter had been right. She was falling—just a little—for a cowboy. The sudden memory of being in Nick's arms broadsided her—his strength, his response to her kiss . . . he hadn't even hinted at kissing her again, a gesture that, up until now, she'd pegged as gentlemanly. Now she wondered if she should suggest they ride together, like they had on the first day.

*No, bad idea.* Instead, "When does the first guest arrive?"

"Next week, after Memorial Day."

"I'll be ready," she said, realizing that she meant it. *Pull yourself together, Piper!* She gazed out across the range, smelling the wild-flowers, the loamy smell of earth and animal. It seemed such a natural, even fragrant part of the ranch.

"I know you will, George. You're going to be a hit."

A strange joy engulfed her as they entered the barn.

He saddled a horse for her, then swung up on his own.

The late-afternoon sun warmed her neck as they headed out of the driveway and across the winter pasture. Piper felt comfortable in the saddle, especially with Nick close enough to grab the reins should her horse startle. The squeak of the saddle, the smell of leather, the sound of cattle. It almost felt like a date.

A date. She hadn't had a date since . . . well, she couldn't remember the last time she'd let a man near enough to know her. But Nick didn't really know her, did he? He knew Piper Sullivan, the chef with a Curious George streak. He hadn't the foggiest idea that she might be an ace—or *former* ace—reporter with an agenda.

What exactly was that agenda again?

They climbed a rocky bluff littered with limestone and boulders, cut with jack pine and scrub brush. The wind stirred the leaves, and the horses snorted.

"Go easy here," Nick shouted over his shoulder. "It's not a hard climb." He glanced behind him to ensure she followed him.

How sweet, her protector. She smiled at him.

Nick reined in his horse at the top of the hill. Climbing off, he tethered the animal to a downed log, held Piper's reins as she dismounted, then tied her horse with his.

"This place is called the Cathedral," he said, starting up the rocky incline.

She followed him along a dirt path dissecting the rocky hillside. A grove of trees shaded a fire pit flanked by two rough-hewn benches. In every direction, the land rolled out over bluff and wash, covered by a carpet of white yarrow and purple kittentail. The Bighorn Mountains, hazy and magenta on the horizon, rimmed the western view. To the east, only hills and endless blue sky.

"Wow," Piper said when they entered the clearing. A fresh feeling of awe washed through her, taking with it her breath.

"'He has removed our sins as far from us as the east is from the west.'" The words emerged from Nick in a mumble.

But she felt them like a warm breath, drawing through her, invading her pores. Nudging something that felt hidden and barren. Her soul perhaps. "What is that?"

"It's a verse from Psalms. My dad quoted it sometimes when we'd come here. We'd come on the Sundays when we didn't make it to church. He'd open his Bible, which he almost always carried with him, and read Psalm 103."

Nick seemed to be back in time, listening to his father, as he quoted: "'The Lord is like a father to his children, tender and compassionate to those who fear him. For he knows how weak we are; he remembers we are only dust.'"

Father . . . *compassionate*? Piper issued an involuntary harrumph, and she instantly wanted to take it back. The last thing she wanted to do was let Nick close enough to see her scars. To pity her.

Nick obviously heard it, however, because he frowned. "What's the matter?"

*What was the matter?* She had one formerly broken bone and a scar on her arm to illustrate what a *father's* compassion meant to her. She yanked her shirtsleeves down over her thumbs, crossed her arms over her chest.

"Piper?"

*No, Nick* . . . Only, her mouth wasn't listening to the warning sound her brain emitted. "I don't like thinking about God in terms of *father*. Not all fathers have compassion on their children."

As expected, a sick look came over him. She replayed his reaction to her nightmare: *"If it wasn't a nightmare, then it was a memory, and I'm going to kill the person who left you with that."*

Nick also seemed to remember that moment because he said, "Were your nightmares about your dad?"

She didn't mean to, but she reacted as if he'd hit her. Cringing and turning so he couldn't see her.

"Oh no." The softness in his tone made Piper close her eyes. Sometimes he reminded her so much of Jimmy. Jimmy, who hadn't hesitated when he'd stepped between her and Russell over and over . . . until it had nearly gotten him killed.

She almost jumped from her skin when Nick put a hand on her shoulder. "I'm sorry, Piper. I . . . shouldn't have asked."

She closed her eyes, horrified that she'd let him inside but burning with the sudden need to tell him. To let him care, and, if only for a moment, not face her demons alone.

"My mother always said she shouldn't have married him. She was young and stupid, and he was a dashing cowboy with devastating charm. He'd been married before—his wife had died in childbirth, and he needed a mom for his five-year-old son."

Piper stepped away from Nick, her back stiff, and took a deep breath. "Mom said that he didn't start hitting her—hitting *us*—until he broke his leg rodeoing one winter. After that, they fell on hard times, and he started drinking. My earliest memory is hiding under the bed while he tore the trailer apart. He even broke my arm once."

She felt Nick's presence beside her, felt the way he held his breath, felt even the anger that radiated from him. She couldn't look at him. Instead, she faced the breathtaking scenery. "My mother was a Christian. Whenever she prayed, I remember wondering why God, if He loved me or my mother, would let those things happen. I mean, weren't fathers supposed to protect their children? Instead, Russell . . . well, most of the time, I wished he were dead."

"Oh, Piper."

There it was, the pity. She clenched her jaw, despising the tears that welled in her eyes. She hadn't cried over Russell McPhee for nearly ten years. She wouldn't start—

"I'd give anything to have been there to protect you," Nick said softly, almost desperately.

"Don't say that, Nick." Her voice sounded distant, and she felt herself starting to crumble. She'd erected a nice, sturdy wall around herself for the better part of a lifetime, and suddenly, in a little over a week, she'd let some man inside to chip it away. Not only that, but he was a man she'd so recently believed was a bully like her father. She wanted to scream or even run.

Run away.

She turned, pushing past him, but he stopped her, grabbing her arm. "Don't . . . Piper. Don't leave."

"Why? I don't—"

"I ran away. From my anger and from everyone who loved me. And . . . I regret it. I should have stayed, should have never let my grief keep out the people who cared about me."

She saw the pain on his face and heard herself speaking words that she had rarely spoken even to herself. "My brother . . . tried to protect me, and he nearly got killed."

Nick's face darkened.

"When my mother and I escaped, we left him behind." Tears blurred her eyes, and she swiped at them. "I've never been able to . . . to forget him."

"What happened to him?"

She just about told him. Felt the words in her throat, felt almost as if . . . as if he might forgive her.

Or . . . be furious. She took a breath. "Nothing good."

She saw sadness on his face, the kind that only made her want to weep more. And that would turn her into a sodden mess. Swell.

He slid his hand down her arm and took her hand. "Piper, my sister said that God brought me back here. I'm thinking she's right. I've been walking around with a ball of fury inside me—first at my dad, then at Cole. I'm wondering . . . well, mostly I'm just tired of feeding that hate."

Piper knew the feeling. Waking up each morning, dodging the cloud of despair that crowded her.

Nick released her hand and touched her face. "Maybe God did bring me here . . . and I think He brought you here too."

Piper went still. *Nick, you couldn't be more wrong.* But her voice had deserted her.

"'He redeems me from death and crowns me with love and tender mercies.'"

"What?"

"My dad wrote it in his journal. I read it last night. Made me think of Joseph in the pit after his brothers had attacked and stripped him. In the end, God made him a ruler over a nation to save his people. It's a lot easier to see God at work in hindsight than when we're in the pit, with barely a hint of light."

Piper stepped away from him, rubbing her hands over her arms. "Maybe God isn't even there in those dark moments. Maybe He doesn't care."

"No, Piper, I think God does care. In fact, I think He's at work even when we're in over our heads, even when there seems to be no hope."

Piper said nothing.

He blew out another long breath, sounding of frustration. "I have this overpowering desire to reach back in time and get my hands on the man who left you with such deep wounds."

His words staggered her. He appeared so wounded, so angry, that for a moment Piper felt as if she might be looking at herself. But when he reached out to take her in his arms, her reflexes moved her away.

Nick's voice turned ragged. "George, please come here. . . . I don't know what else to do."

She studied him a long time; then she felt herself crumple. She hated this place inside her that couldn't push through her glass walls into his arms. Couldn't trust, couldn't love. She covered her mouth with her hands, shook her head.

He took a half step toward her.

*Please, Nick.* Only she wasn't sure what she was pleading for.

However, a moment later when he drew her close, she knew the answer. She needed Nick to shatter those walls and let himself into her life. To love her. To protect her. Maybe even to help her find . . . peace.

Because obviously she couldn't do it herself. Even if suddenly it was the one thing she wanted even more than justice.

❧

"My husband's dying, and I think you know that." Maggy sat in the leather chair of Saul Lovell's office, her hands folded on her lap. "Our doctor told me the basics . . . and Cole confirmed it. I know what's going on."

Saul leaned back in his chair, his gaunt face solemn as he regarded her. He probably saw her as everyone else did—the girl who had loved and lost. She often felt branded that way—Nick Noble's former love. But what they didn't know was that she'd been the winner. She'd loved . . . and loved again. And having loved Nick only made her realize the precious gift of Cole's love. She learned what real love felt like, what it looked like, the day she married Cole St. John. He was her real hero, and even now he sought to protect her.

"Tell me the disposition of Bishop's bequest to us. I know it has to go through probate before we get the land. Can you tell me when that will be?" Maggy despised the tremor in her voice. But she heard the clock ticking every night Cole lay beside her, in his shallow breathing, his groans in the morning as fatigue assaulted him, as if he hadn't had hours of sleep. She hadn't needed to talk to the doctor to confirm it, but Dr. Lowe's words had felt like hot tar seeping through her, blanketing her days with blackness.

Saul sighed. "It could be as soon as a month, especially if Nick makes no move to contest the will. If he does, it might take a year or more—"

"A year!" Maggy schooled her voice. "We need it settled soon. Now. I . . . I need the money for Cole's operation."

Saul lifted an eyebrow. "Cole told me that there was no cure."

"He has to have a liver transplant. We don't have insurance . . . but if I sell the land, I'll have the money."

"What's the status on finding a donor?" Saul's expression contained compassion, tempering the harsh question.

"We . . . don't have one yet." She looked away, not wanting him to see the pain on her face. "But we will." *Please, Lord, please* . . . She'd spent hours on her knees or looking to the sky over the past few days, praying, hoping. . . . She had to believe that God would save Cole.

Or everything inside her would simply shrivel up and die.

Saul sighed, then rubbed his hand over his mouth. "Do you have a buyer for the land?"

Maggy shook her head. "I was thinking that . . . well, maybe the Nobles would buy us out." It was a long shot, but after Nick's caustic words last week on the ranch, the idea had begun to incubate. He wanted the land to stay in the family.

"That's a fine idea, Maggy. But the land isn't yours to sell."

"It's Cole's once the bequest goes through."

"But it's *Cole's* land, not yours. You're only the secondary beneficiary. If Cole dies, then it passes to you."

Maggy stared at him, confused. "So? Once we have the land, I'll sell it off and use the money to help Cole."

"Cole made me power of attorney over the land. He told me that he didn't want you to sell it, even if he became incapacitated."

Maggy felt her breath whoosh away, as if someone had wrapped a noose around her neck and left her to dangle, kicking air. For a moment, she simply tried to comprehend Saul's words. "What?"

Saul picked up a pen and rolled it between his fingers. "You can't sell the land until . . . unless . . . well, after it passes to your name. Yes, Bishop left it to you as a secondary beneficiary, but ultimately, if the will passes through probate before . . . while Cole is still with us, the land is his. And you can't do anything with it."

"But I was there when we made our wills. And he made me power of attorney. I remember."

"Yes, over your *jointly* held property. Your stock, your home, and your current land—you have joint ownership. When—*if*—he becomes incapacitated, you can do what you want with that. But because the Noble land is in Cole's name alone and it is an inherited gift, it falls under a different category. He had to create a codicil to the will without your presence to give it to you."

"I don't understand." Mostly she didn't want to understand. She wanted the nightmare fixed. She wanted Cole back, healthy. Riding beside her on their land. Holding her at night.

"If a direct beneficiary of a *non*jointly held property is in attendance during the signing of a will, then, if there is a dispute, there are grounds for the will to be set aside."

"I still don't understand what you're saying. I was there when Cole signed his first will—"

"Again, of your jointly held property. But when he made his codicil for the new property, you couldn't be present at the signing. If you were, anyone contesting the will could say that you pressured him into signing. And the will could be set aside."

Maggy churned his words through her mind. "So, you're saying that if Cole had been in the room when Bishop signed his will, then Nick could claim that Cole pressured Bishop into signing and challenge the bequest?"

Saul nodded. "Good thing Cole wasn't around."

*Good thing.*

"That's why we asked Stefanie to leave. Remember?"

"Yes, I remember." A cold tremor started inside Maggy. Remembering the day Saul had shown up at the Silver Buckle with John Kincaid to finalize Bishop's will. Remembering how she'd fixed them tea and stood outside the room, listening to their secrets.

"If anyone who had benefited from Bishop's will had been present during the signing, then Nick Noble would have a reason to contest it and grounds to demand that it be set aside."

"And Cole wouldn't get his land."

Saul shrugged. "Probably not."

Maggy stared at her whitened hands in her lap. "Cole knew he was dying when he gave you power of attorney, didn't he?"

Saul put down the pen but didn't look at her. "I believe so."

She closed her eyes, her emotions clogging her throat. Why would he do that? Why would he sacrifice his life so she could have the land?

Tears filmed her eyes. Because Cole was that kind of husband. He cared more for her than he ever had himself. Cared more for CJ. "Did he tell you what he wanted me to do with it . . . I mean, if he . . . ?" Maggy finished her sentence by shaking her head, covering her mouth with her hand.

"I think he wants you to sell out."

She wiped an errant tear from her cheek. "I *won't* sell. I'll stay and work the ranch that we—"

"Maggy—" Saul's voice was gentle—"you can't run a ranch alone. And CJ's too young. . . ." He sighed. "I might be willing to buy it."

Maggy looked up, and the expression on her face must have startled Saul, for he frowned. "I'm not selling, Saul. And I'm not giving up on Cole."

But for the first time Maggy realized how close Cole's fears could be to coming true . . . and how she might lose the most of all.

# CHAPTER 16

PIPER HAD SEEN RODEOS up close and smelly while researching the Professional Bull Riders circuit. But sitting here in the stands next to Nick, sipping a soda from a soggy paper cup while he explained the points systems and the rules, gave her an entirely new appreciation for the sport as well as for the cowboys and cowgirls who pitted themselves against the animals.

Or maybe her newfound interest could be linked to the fact that Nick sat close to her, his presence powerful and way too intoxicating. He wore a jean jacket over a denim shirt, jeans, cowboy boots, and a black Stetson that only accentuated his dark eyes. The gleam of appreciation she'd seen in those eyes at her T-shirt, the petticoat skirt in calico colors that she'd found at a Western store, boots, and short red jean jacket had turned this outing into a bona fide date.

A date. With Nick Noble. Carter would be beside himself, although he'd take some solace in the fact that even now she carried her tape recorder in her jacket. She didn't plan on using it, but from habit she had slid it into her pocket with her cell phone.

Fans packed the Phillips rodeo stands. Wrangler, Carhartt, and Ford banners stretched along the corral fences. The smells of popcorn and hot dogs added ambience to the air, along with the scents of dirt and animal sweat. Horse and cattle trailers from the four corners of the county and beyond crowded the fields outside the stands. Piper had watched with her investigator's eyes the worried mothers and fathers helping dress and calm the contestants.

This Memorial Day weekend had begun with national-anthem tryouts for Phillips residents on the public stage set up in the community park. Past rodeo queens and clowns gathered in a tent afterward for autographs. Nick had settled his hand on the small of Piper's back, more comforting than proprietary, and led her around the tent, whispering into her ear, identifying children of fellow ranchers as well as the new rodeo queen, who had been selected the day before.

In a way, Piper felt like the queen.

A parade along Main Street reminded her of bygone days in hometown America, complete with the town's fire truck, a color guard from the VFW, the high school marching band, and a cavalry of contestants on prettied-up horses.

Now this was the Old West charm she'd hoped to discover. She'd dived after candy, just like the kids, and laughed when Nick scooped her up a bubble gum. After the parade, they'd found Stefanie setting up for dinner in the back of her pickup. Old Pete had a grill going, and Piper finagled a husk-roasted ear of corn—and avoided the hot dog. The sun was beginning to sink by the time they found their seats in the stands. The announcer called everyone to their feet for the national anthem—sung by the winner of the contest. Piper felt a surge of unfamiliar patriotism as a little buckaroo from the Double B squealed out "The Star-Spangled Banner."

The rodeo events started with barrel racing. Piper found herself leaning into the turns, cheering. She caught Nick grinning at her more times than she wanted to count.

Of course, she managed a few sly glances his way also.

Oh, boy, she was going to leave Montana with her heart in pieces. Because ever since Nick had taken her into his arms at the Cathedral, silently asking for nothing but to try and calm her nightmares, she had spent too many hours thinking what it would be like to stay here, help him run the ranch, learn to ride a horse properly.

After all, she *could* cook.

She couldn't believe that this man she'd nearly hated a month ago had splintered the walls she'd put between herself and men. At least men who might have the power to hurt her. And Nick had serious potential to leave deep wounds.

Not only that, but she felt as if he'd peeled back the layers of her soul and looked inside with his words about being trapped in a pit. It felt like a fair description of her life. No matter how she tried, she couldn't climb out. Couldn't free herself from the darkness that pinned her in on every side.

Except, out here in this beautiful country, for the first time she felt as if the light at the top of her prison had brightened, begun to warm her. Perhaps it was the open spaces, the beauty of the land. They seemed to seep inside her and allowed her to breathe deeply.

Even her nightmares seemed less . . . potent. She woke each morning with a vague recollection . . . only to pour herself into

making porridge or biscuits or even a batch of chocolate-chip cookies. And she was getting pretty good at not burning them.

Carter was right. She'd completely forgotten who she was. And
had not a clue how to disentangle herself from this charade.

She wasn't sure she wanted to.

Ever.

Because being with Nick felt as if she'd stepped out of the realities of being Piper Sullivan and instead become someone else.
Cookie. Something sweet. A treat.

No–George. Curious George, the endearing monkey who got
in trouble, well loved by the man in the yellow hat.

Nick had a hat . . . even if it wasn't yellow.

*Oh, brother.*

The crowd cheered when the champion barrel racer loped
around the ring, waving.

"I went to school with her mother," Nick said, lifting a hand to
someone in the stands. "I'm shocked she has a daughter old enough
for the junior events."

"Why? CJ's old enough–"

Nick frowned.

She watched as something entered his eyes. Regret? Envy? It
struck her then that CJ could have been *his* son. His son with
Maggy, if he'd stuck around. A ball formed in her throat, and she
stared into the arena, her mood deflating.

Nick leaned over to her. "I'm going to find CJ and give him a
few last-minute pointers."

She nodded.

"I'll be right back. And I'll bring cotton candy with me." He
winked, and she realized he'd noticed her recent proclivity toward

sweets. Well, what was a vegetarian to do when surrounded by beef?

He stepped over people and excused himself out of the row while the announcer named the next event.

Piper felt a tap on her shoulder and turned. Lolly sat above her, looking very cowgirl in a pair of jeans, a turquoise hat, and a matching leather jacket. "I thought that was you. Remember me?" She stuck out her hand. "I was expecting a food order from you."

Piper took her grip, managed a smile. *Oh yeah, a food order.* She'd given Stefanie a basic list, but hadn't thought about the groups she was supposed to be preparing for. All her time had been spent trying to learn how to *cook.* "Hi, Lolly. I know; I'm still working on menus."

Lolly held her cup with both hands and took a sip of her drink, one eye on the rodeo ring. "You could ask Nick to help you. He used to work for me as a cook."

"He said he lasted one day."

Lolly winked at her. "He could flip a mean burger. I hated to see him go. But even I knew that he and Bishop were in the middle of an argument. The man came to the café and nearly dragged the kid home by his ear."

"Why did you hire him?" Piper slid her hand into her pocket and out of habit flipped on her tape recorder.

"Just to annoy Bishop, I reckon. He was always digging at me to marry John, as if it were any of his business. It irked me. Bishop always acted like some paragon of virtue." Lolly huffed and rolled her eyes. "Like the entire town didn't know about his wild days."

"His wild days?"

Lolly had her full attention now, and she knew it. She bent close to Piper's ear. "Wild days and wild nights." She paused, letting that information sink in. Then, "Nick comes by his reputation honestly. Bishop grew up here, and if Nick thought he raised a scandal when he left, he should have been around when Bishop ran off with Elizabeth Hatcher. Saul was furious—he'd been dating Elizabeth for a year. Come to find out that Bishop had been courting her on the sly."

"Saul?" Piper had heard the name but couldn't place it.

"He's a lawyer. After Elizabeth married Bishop, Saul settled for her younger sister, Loretta. *And* the family's good graces. When Beau Hatcher passed on, he left everything to his two daughters."

Piper remembered Nick referring to Hatcher's Table. Now it clicked into place. Two dead bulls.

"I have to tell you, after what Bishop did to catch Elizabeth, you would have thought he'd have stuck around home."

A streak of heat went through Piper, igniting her curiosity like tinder. She quirked an eyebrow at Lolly, who leaned closer yet, spoke in a stage whisper. "Elizabeth was in the hospital for a long time while she was pregnant with Nick. And Bishop wasn't exactly spending every weekend in Sheridan."

Piper stopped short of letting her mouth gape open.

Lolly nodded slowly, her face solemn.

"Who was he–?"

"Let's just say that no one was surprised when Nick found Bishop in Irene St. John's arms after Elizabeth died."

Piper was wordless.

Lolly lifted a shoulder. "It's just talk. But I think there is a reason Cole and Nick were closer than brothers. If you know what I mean."

The crowd around them cheered. Lolly rose, apparently impressed with the action in the ring.

Piper heard nothing but ringing in her ears. Could Cole and Nick be brothers? Did Bishop leave the land to Cole because he was trying to atone for his sins? She stood up, clapping, but leaned back to Lolly. "What about Elizabeth—did she ever find out?"

Lolly shrugged, but an enigmatic smile played across her face. "Phillips is a small town, even for the discreet."

Piper stared ahead but saw nothing, wondering if Nick knew he was an uncle.

⁂

Cole worked his way down the metal steps of the grandstands, moving in slow motion. He felt punky today, as if his insides might be made of cornmeal mush, his brain unable to climb out of the sludge that bogged his thoughts. He heard the roar of the crowd, smelled the hot dogs and popcorn, and instead of being able to focus on CJ and the day that should belong to him, Cole's thoughts were mired in memories.

As if time were playing tricks on him, over and over in his thoughts, he found himself behind the stands with Nick, practicing their roping. Maggy sat on the truck, her legs crossed, the sun in her hair. She giggled, encouraging them, clapping when they both managed to land their coils around the dummy steer they'd set up in the lot.

Or maybe those memories were conjured up by the sound of Maggy cheering on CJ this morning as he'd practiced his technique one last time in the yard. The way she'd sat on the top rail, clapping, grinning, pride on her beautiful face, she seemed eighteen again.

Cole had forced himself to limp outside and lean against the fence, a smile on his face, but all he saw was Nick's technique in CJ's form, the snap of his wrist, the angle of his throw, the grin of his victory. The hours CJ spent with Nick this past week, honing his throw, perfecting his timing, would pay off today.

He should have been the one helping CJ instead of lying on the sofa, but he felt drunk, weighted by an unfamiliar exhaustion. Crushed by the sense that perhaps the end might be near.

A kid holding a box of popcorn in one hand and a Coke in the other slammed into him, knocking him into the handrail. "Sorry, mister."

Cole tried to right himself, to respond, but the kid had vanished by the time he caught his breath. He heard the announcer sum up the scores and proclaim the winner of the goat-tying round. Breakaway roping was next.

Cole moved around the bleachers toward the stock area where CJ would be lining up. He and Maggy had come here early to affix his number, calm his horse, and warm up. Cole should have left with them, but he'd made the mistake of wanting to watch the opening of the rodeo one last time, and he had been caught in the press of the crowd.

A cheer went up as the first rider clocked a time of 9.47. Cole couldn't help but smile—CJ had better times. But if he broke the barrier that held his horse back and gave the calf a split-second lead too soon, it would add ten seconds.

It struck him that Nick had been notorious for breaking the barrier—in rodeo, in life. Cole had learned to take a breath as the steer broke out, and on the outtake, let the horse free. He should remind CJ—

Cole stopped. CJ stood beside his horse, looking every inch the champion, with his number pinned to his black snap-button shirt, and wearing a matching hat and boots. He held the reins, his rope coiled over the horn of his saddle.

Crouching before him, giving him a pep talk . . . was Nick. He had his hands clamped on CJ's shoulders, and even from here, Cole recognized Nick's game face. The one that put 100 percent into being a champion.

Beside him, looking down upon her son and the man she'd first loved, stood Maggy. She had her arms folded but was nodding to Nick's sage words. And wearing a smile. As if this might be the moment she'd always hoped for.

Cole gasped for breath, sure that his body was reacting to the truth he saw before him. Maggy might be married to him, but she would always love Nick.

He turned away, moving stiffly back to the ring, leaning against it as he forced himself to breathe. This was what he wanted, wasn't it? For Maggy to be happy? For CJ to have a father? a home?

He white-fisted the rail, hanging on. Apparently God had answered his prayers for provision for his family.

But He could have at least waited until Cole didn't have to watch.

※

"Are you listening to me, CJ?" Nick watched CJ's attention flicker away from him toward the stands as if he were searching for someone.

CJ looked back at Nick. "Yeah. Take a breath as the calf breaks away. I remember."

Nick patted the boy's shoulder. "Good. Your dad told me that more than once." In fact, Cole had probably been the reason they'd won the championship. Cole had always had the clear head, the right timing.

"Mom, is he coming?" CJ glanced up at Maggy.

Nick glanced at her too. She looked like a rodeo mom today, dressed in a jean jacket, her hair in braids under her hat, her face somber as she helped CJ with his number. She'd seemed only momentarily surprised when Nick showed up to offer CJ his go-for-it speech. But he saw a chip in her icy demeanor when she stood back to let Nick have his say.

Now in answer to CJ's question, she frowned, first at her son, then at Nick.

Nick shrugged, as if to say, *I didn't see him.* Not that he'd been looking, per se. He'd actually been hoping he didn't have to see Cole today . . . not after the last words Nick had said to him: *"You won't rest until you've taken everything."*

After the last couple weeks on the ranch and his most recent talk with Piper, he'd begun to wonder if God had something more for him. Something that he wouldn't have had with Maggy. He'd searched his emotions for any remnant of feelings he might have for Maggy and realized that the old ache had healed. Instead, he only felt a kind of peace. Yes, Maggy would always occupy a part of his heart, along with the memory of her smile, her friendship, but he hadn't been able to love her like she deserved. Cole, however, had. But somehow *saying* that seemed . . . well, it might be easier to ride the two-ton Brahma bull they'd shipped in for the final round of excitement tonight.

Nick straightened. "I don't know where Cole is."

Worry flashed across Maggy's face, but she hid it in a second. "I'm sure he's in the stands, watching. It's just that he promised he'd be here."

CJ nodded, and Nick wondered at the air of tension between mother and son. Worry suddenly pricked him also. "Should I . . . ah, go look for him?"

Maggy smiled at him—a real smile. "Thanks, Nick. But no. He's fine." She blew out a breath that indicated the opposite and turned to CJ. "You'd better line up."

The boy's eyes shone. He cast a look at Nick.

"You're ready, bucko. Go get that calf."

CJ swung into the saddle and urged his horse into line. He worked the coil into the loop, fitted it into his grip.

"Thanks, Nick." Maggy's tone made him turn. "You really gave CJ confidence this week. Even if he doesn't win, he's learned so much."

"He's got natural talent."

Maggy's smile slipped. "Yeah. His dad was a great roper." She looked away, and again he saw worry flash across her face.

Nick couldn't take it. "Maggy, what's wrong with Cole? He didn't look well last time I saw him."

Maggy's smile disappeared. Then she shook her head. "Let's go watch CJ."

He followed her, freshly hating himself and all he'd done to destroy the friendships in his life.

They wove their way through the crowd pressed against the rail, then climbed the stairs to the stands and stood in the aisle. Feeling Maggy next to him, he had the strangest feeling of contentment, of peace. He searched the stands for Piper, but she wasn't in their seats. He frowned, seeing the empty place. Maybe she went after that cotton candy herself.

CJ's name bellowed from the speakers.

*C'mon, CJ.* Nick located him in the shoot, watched him fix his loop, noticed the look of concentration on his boyish face. Nick held his breath, every muscle coiled.

The calf broke free, and half a second later, CJ broke the barrier, his loop already spinning above his head. Once, twice—he threw on the second go-round. A perfect loop, a perfect angle, and the horse was already planting his back end before the rope snagged the calf. The breakaway rope snapped off.

Nick looked at the bank of judges and watched as the announcer said, "Wow! That was a record-breaking 7.24 seconds, folks!"

Nick let out a breath as Maggy erupted beside him. She cheered, shooting her hands above her head.

Nick waved his hat in the air, trying to catch CJ's eye. The boy gathered in his rope, and Nick saw him search the crowd. But when his eyes caught on something, it wasn't Nick. CJ grinned, and Nick cheered for Cole, who had seen his boy triumph.

Maggy's expression glowed. "He did it!"

Nick high-fived her. "You got some boy there, Mags. Cole should be so proud of his son."

She closed her mouth, and he saw tears in her eyes. "I need to find Cole."

Nick felt strangely close to tears himself. "Congratulate him for me."

Maggy took off toward the pens, and Nick turned to pick his way back to his seat. Piper had reappeared and was clapping wildly.

He wound his way through the crowd as the next contestant fed into the shoot.

"Hey!" he said as he plunked down beside her. "Did you get cotton candy?"

"No, it was all gone," she said, her face pink, alive. "Didn't CJ do great?"

Piper's smile added to his swell of pride. "He did everything I told him. And, of course, his dad was a champion roper."

Piper's eyes sparkled. "Apparently it runs in the family."

Nick reached out and took her hand, and when she laced her fingers through his, he wondered what he'd done to deserve such a perfect day.

CJ's time won him first place. He ran his horse around the ring in his victory lap, waving his hat just like Cole had done when he'd won. Like father, like son. Nick searched for Maggy and Cole but didn't spot them in the cheering crowd.

No matter. His heart nearly burst for Cole's son, and he hoped that somehow it might be the beginning of healing for them all.

The rodeo continued with team roping, steer wrestling, and bronc riding and ended with three brave cowboys riding the Brahmas under a star-speckled sky. Piper sat beside him, occasionally meeting his gaze with a mysterious smile as if she were harboring a secret. He hoped it had something to do with the way she held his hand. As if not wanting to let it go.

Fireworks and the grand parade of winners closed the rodeo. Nick's smile dimmed when CJ didn't show in the lineup. Then again, neither did the goat wrestler, and he wondered if CJ might be fast asleep in the cab of the truck. He himself had missed a few finales, having been wiped out from the adrenaline rush.

He and Piper worked their way out of the bleachers and toward his truck. Their joined hands swung between them. He waved to Stefanie, who was packing up their dinner. She turned, and he couldn't read her expression as she stared at the couple.

Nick knew Stefanie liked Piper, but her pensive look soured his joy. Well, Piper was sorta his employee. He'd have to talk to Stefanie and assure her that his relationship with Piper wouldn't affect the Silver Buckle's ability to serve their guests.

He hadn't exactly warmed to the idea of guests on the land, but without a reason to contest Bishop's will and with their recent losses, it looked like he'd have to put on his happy face and pitch in.

Unless, of course, he wanted to throw in the towel and see if he could land a job in the police department in Sheridan. The thought tasted bitter. He hadn't exactly been a stellar detective. At best, he'd jailed a few drunk cowboys, found some wandering cows. At worst, he'd put the wrong man in jail.

No, he had horrible instincts when it came to law enforcement. He'd even suspected Piper of having a secret agenda when she'd first arrived. He glanced at her now, at the way the moonlight lit her face, turned her hair to gold, and he felt like a class-A jerk for suspecting her.

Ranching had been the only thing he'd ever been good at. And for the first time in years, Nick felt as if he might be right where he belonged.

He opened the door for Piper, and she slid into the seat, clasping her hands between her knees. "Let's go to the Cathedral," she said, wearing that mysterious look again.

Nick closed the door, feeling a burst of long-tamped feelings. He got into the truck, feeling her eyes on him, wondering what she might be thinking.

He hoped her thoughts matched his own feelings—his own unspoken, unnamed hopes.

They drove out of Phillips in silence, following one pickup after another until they came to Buckle property. Instead of turning onto the road under the Buckle sign, he continued and turned in west of the property, driving over the grassy fields, bumping along until they came to the hill. "We'll have to climb."

Piper got out without a word. Nick followed her up the bluff, hearing her breath puff out as the climb grew steeper. Finally, they topped the hill, and Piper walked out to the edge, standing with her hands in her pockets. Nick joined her.

The moon and stars threw light against the bluffs and draws, turning patches of grass to silver. The vault of brilliance stretched as far as the eye could see, streaked only with the Milky Way. He saw it anew as they stood in silence.

"It feels so close. As if I could touch it," Piper said quietly.

Nick wanted to touch her, to draw her close, but she suddenly seemed far away, as if in her own galaxy. "Yeah. I came here a lot after my mom died. I felt closer to her in a way. Like she might be right out of sight but watching."

Piper stared at her feet. "My mother died a couple years ago. Lung cancer. My father smoked, and she was a victim. It gave me another reason to hate him."

No wonder Piper had such a hard time feeling God's love for her, seeing Him at work in her life. He reached out to embrace her.

She stepped away. "I like it here, Nick. Probably too much."

He felt a crazy spurt of panic at her words. "That's a good thing, right?"

She shrugged. "I don't know. I guess it scares me."

Nick swallowed, feeling her words as his own. "We have time, Piper. And I'm not going anywhere."

Her expression seemed troubled. "You're sticking around to make sure Cole doesn't get your land, right?"

He said nothing, her words stinging. Put like that, his actions sounded—no, *felt*—vindictive. Like revenge. For the first time, he saw himself in Stefanie's words: *"I can't believe this! You didn't come back to help. You came back out of revenge."*

He didn't want to be that man. "I don't know. I still haven't figured out why Bishop gave the land to Cole. But it's looking like I can't do anything about it." He reached for her hand.

Piper let him take it, then stared at her hand in his. "I think you should let it go. What if your sister's right? What if God brought you here but not to get the land?"

"Then why?" He gave her a little tug, wanting her closer, wanting to smell her, to wrap his arms around her. To kiss her.

"To find something Bishop left behind?"

"I've searched his journals. His Bible. He didn't leave any clues."

Piper's expression seemed troubled. "Maybe he did."

Nick shook his head, bracketed her face with his hands. "I'm starting to think that God sent me back here to find you."

Her mouth opened slightly, and before she could protest, he kissed her. Closing his eyes, he gently brushed his lips against hers, testing, hoping. She seemed surprised, for she didn't immediately respond. But as he held her and kissed her cheek, her forehead, trailing his way back to her lips, she closed her eyes and found his mouth to kiss him back. She tasted of salty popcorn, but he relished the feel of her touch. He held her without rushing, lingering, and when he drew away, he saw tears in her eyes.

"That was nice," she said with a soft smile.

Nice was good. Nice, for a woman who probably had a plethora of not-nice memories, seemed breathtaking.

He pressed his forehead to hers. "George, you should know that I haven't even tried to have a relationship with someone since . . . well, since Maggy. And I blew that one good, as you know."

Piper fisted her hands into his shirt. "I'm not so good at this either. In fact . . . I don't do relationships."

He cupped her face with his hand. "Like I said, we have time."

She turned back to the view, entwining her hands into his. "I'll bet you missed this."

"Yeah, I did. I should have returned sooner. Regret is a powerful thing. It begets itself and changes a person, not always for good."

She leaned her head back against his chest.

"I kept thinking I had to prove something before I came back. I wasn't sure that I deserved the Noble name, the Noble legacy."

"Is that why you became a cop?"

He didn't remember telling her that, but perhaps he had. He'd told her a lot of things. "I wasn't very good at that either, however."

"Why do you say that?"

Nick hated this part about himself. But now could be the time to finally let go. "I was a cop in a little town in northern Montana. My second year there, a girl came to town. Her name was Jenny Butler. She worked as a rodeo instructor at the nearby school. She was . . .

let's just say that the way she filled out her jeans caught the eye of every cowhand north of Miles City. And she had a sweet smile."

"Sounds like you and she hit it off." Piper's tone didn't change, but he felt a subtle shift in her demeanor. She let go of his hands, slid hers into her pockets. But she didn't move away.

"We were friends, but I was worried about her more than anything. I guess I saw Stefanie in her, and in a way I felt responsible for her well-being . . . particularly since I knew the reputations of most of the cowboys in the area. I didn't want anything to happen. . . ." His voice felt tight, and he looked off into the distance, seeing again Jenny's broken body lying at the bottom of the quarry.

Piper turned in his arms, a frown on her pretty face.

He looked at her, unable to tear his eyes away from the kind gesture. He forced his voice from his chest. "She was murdered. The thing was, I had asked her out a couple times, and people around town thought we were an item. One night when I was on shift, she went to a local bar, and the bartender said he saw her leave with a guy named Jimmy McPhee. His friends said that she told him she had a flat tire. We found her car about a quarter mile away, but we found her body at the bottom of a quarry in the opposite direction, along with tire tracks that matched McPhee's truck. He claimed he went out into the parking lot with her, and someone attacked him, but we found him sleeping off a hangover in the bed of his truck not far from the quarry. A jury convicted him of murder."

"So he was guilty." Her voice sounded cold, even angry.

"I don't know now. At the time it was all I had, and I might have pushed too hard." He blew out a breath, looking over her head. "McPhee was recently set free. A drifter convicted in Wyoming for a stretch of serial murders confessed to Jenny's murder."

"What do you think? Who was the real murderer?"

Nick's voice fell. "Me."

She blinked, and in the moonlight, he thought he actually saw her pale.

He had to wrestle his next words out. "For a long time I blamed myself. I believed the prosecution when they argued that McPhee wanted revenge for the times I'd arrested him on DUI, that he'd wanted to scare her—and thereby me—and things got out of hand. The defense clung to his story of being ambushed."

"So he could have been trying to be a hero." Her eyes glistened, as if feeling Nick's anguish.

Her response felt nearly overpowering, and for a second he didn't know what to say. He stepped away from her, took off his hat, tapped it against his leg. "Either way, I felt to blame."

Piper touched his arm. "You weren't to blame, Nick. It wasn't your fault."

"It was a small town, and I was a cop. I should have spotted a killer. I should have been there to protect her."

A tear trickled down Piper's cheek. He watched it and reached out to wipe it from her chin. It was quite possible he was falling hard for this woman who knew how to listen, how to care. She covered his hand with hers.

"At the least, I owe McPhee an apology." Nick put his hat back on and flashed her a smile, desperate to control the emotions running maverick through him. "I just hope he can start over."

Piper stared at Nick a long time before she gave him a small smile. "Me too."

The sound of a truck, then the slamming of a door jerked his attention from her.

"Nick?" Stefanie came into view, flashing a light before her as she ran up the path.

"What is it?" He hurried toward the light, heard Piper right behind him.

"It's Cole. He collapsed at the rodeo." Stefanie looked frantic, tears chapping her cheeks. "They're flying him to Sheridan right now."

Nick felt Piper's hand in his and squeezed. "What's wrong with him?"

Stefanie shook her head. "Maggy called. She says she needs you, Nick."

# CHAPTER 17

OF *COURSE* MAGGY needed Nick.

Piper tried to not let those words or Nick's reaction sting as she watched him sprint down the hill toward the truck. Thankfully, he waited for Piper to climb into the cab before he started the truck and floored it across the prairie. She belted herself in and braced her hands on the dashboard, knowing a request to slow down probably wouldn't do any good.

Because Maggy *needed* him.

Piper swallowed the pain in her throat, hating herself for believing him, for shutting off her tape recorder, and for wanting him to love *her*, not Maggy.

Like it or not, she was beginning to love him. She wanted to bang her head against the dashboard—although the way Nick was driving, it would probably happen anyway—and jostle her common sense out of hiding. Nick didn't love her. He loved Maggy. Always had, probably always would. Hadn't Piper seen them together at the rodeo?

Stupid woman! Carter would strangle her with her apron strings. And to think she'd spent the last few weeks trying to learn how to cook! She hated cooking. Hated chopping vegetables, having to follow directions. But she'd hated the idea of Stefanie and Nick losing this ranch even more. No, she'd just been *duped* into hating it. Well, wasn't that what she wanted? For Nick to suffer loss, like Jimmy had?

"Piper, you okay?"

She took in Nick, the way he gripped the steering wheel, muscling the truck over the ruts and onto the dirt road. "Fine," she snapped.

"You look white as a sheet."

"I'm fine . . . just don't kill us."

He shot her a frown, and she felt like a jerk. And scolded herself for that. *He* was the jerk here, the way he got inside her heart with his charming, deceptive cowboy ways. Like mother, like daughter, apparently.

"I won't kill us; I promise." He sounded hurt.

"Sorry. I'm just worried about Cole." She looked out the window, trying to decide if that was a lie.

Nick said nothing the entire way to the Silver Buckle. He parked in a cloud of dust, followed seconds later by Dutch and Stefanie.

"Take the plane!" Stefanie hollered as she sprang out of her truck and ran up the porch steps and into the house.

Piper stood there, caught in the drama of watching Nick race across the courtyard and fling open the doors of a wide barn.

Sure enough, tied inside sat a white-and-red airplane. Someone could have pushed her over with a coneflower. "Does Nick have his pilot's license?" she asked nobody.

Stefanie banged out of the house, holding a briefcase. "C'mon, Piper. I know he'll want you to go with him."

*He will?* Piper's legs moved toward the garage even as her good sense told her to hop in her Jeep Liberty and head north by northwest.

Nick and Dutch were pushing the plane out of the hangar, then pulling it toward the driveway. Nick opened the door and climbed inside as Stefanie handed him the briefcase.

"Piper, get in."

*Get in?* "What is happening here? Someone please tell me that Nick knows how to fly this thing–Get *in?*"

Stefanie was walking around the plane, checking for something. Like gas or wheels or wings, maybe? Shouldn't a plane be at an airstrip?

"Where is he planning on taking-off?"

"From the driveway," Stefanie said without looking up. She opened the door, speaking to Nick. "Maggy's at the hospital–Lolly called and said she'd meet you at the strip." Stefanie held the door open, looking in anticipation at Piper. "Well, c'mon."

Piper put her hands to her head. "I . . . are you sure . . . I . . ."

Emotion flashed across Stefanie's face. Worry? No, more than that. Piper saw in Stefanie's expression hope that Piper meant something to Nick. That he might need her. And because of that, Stefanie might need her too.

For a sweeping moment, Piper felt like part of the family.

As if to confirm her thoughts, Stefanie let the door close and ran toward her. She took Piper's hands, pierced her with her dark eyes. "Please, Piper. I'll be right behind you in the truck. Nick is a great pilot. Or at least he was."

That was comforting.

Stefanie smiled through the tears gleaming on her cheeks. "I know you care about Nick. And he might need you."

Piper swallowed hard and made herself nod. Made herself let go of Stefanie and climb into the plane. Made herself strap in, hang on, and keep her eyes open as Nick fired up the propeller and floored the two-seater down the patch of dirt driveway before soaring into the sky.

As the propeller buzzed and her ears clogged, Piper thought she heard another shattering of the walls that kept her safe and pain free. The walls around her heart that, before she'd come to the Silver Buckle, she hadn't even known existed.

Maggy had never felt so brittle. For the last hour, she'd stood with her head pressed to the cool pane of the window, trying to calm the shaking that emanated from inside. At least here in the waiting room, she didn't have to watch Cole die.

She'd lingered far too long outside the hanging curtain walls of the ER, watching as Doctor Lowe, who had met them in the emergency room, started intravenous lines, dripping fluids into her pale, weak husband. Everything inside her had wanted to scream, to let go and fall apart right there.

CJ had stayed in the waiting room with Big John Kincaid, who'd flown them both to Sheridan after Maggy had found Cole slumped in the bed of their pickup. Her sweet husband had hung on long enough to see CJ's performance—that much she knew from his mumbled words and the way he'd taken CJ's hand.

*Please, God.* She couldn't do this. Couldn't raise CJ alone. She wrapped her arms around herself, repulsed by the smells of anti-septic that clung to her, the memory of the respirator, the beeping of the EKG monitor still boring into her mind. Cole's chest had barely moved, and if it weren't for the faintest flickering of his eyes when she watched Doctor Lowe close the curtain as he came out to talk to her, she'd think Cole might be already gone.

Even now, she felt as if she might be choking. She covered her mouth with her hand, fighting back the sobs. She wouldn't cry in front of CJ.

Maggy still felt Lowe's firm grip on her arm as he'd led her from Cole's curtained room, past other closed curtains, and out into the hall. Her heart had turned more leaden with each step.

The prognosis felt fresh and raw, her own desperation pain-ful as she ran it over in her mind. "You said we had weeks, even months."

Lowe had worn a stony expression. "I said you *could* have weeks. But Cole's condition has obviously plummeted." He shook his head. "I checked the transplant list on the way over here. Even if we bump him up because of his condition, he's in bad enough shape that there's . . . well, he might not get a donor."

Maggy had closed her eyes and reached out to brace her arm on the wall, her knees feeling as if they'd give out at any moment.

"I have to ask again—how about testing CJ?"

Maggy stared at him, horrified. "CJ? I don't understand. CJ . . . is *alive*. What do you mean?"

Doctor Lowe frowned, pursed his lips, sighed. "I see. Cole didn't tell you."

What hadn't Cole told her? A thread of anger entwined her fraying emotions. "Tell me what?"

"That a liver donor can be a *live* donor. The liver is the one organ that grows back."

"A live donor?" Her breath gusted fast and hard from her chest. "A *live* donor?"

"Yes, which is why I suggested that CJ get tested. It's not always sure that a family member is a match, but at this point it's worth a try. CJ is young, but he might be strong enough."

Maggy's mind had reeled. She pressed her hand to her forehead, finding it cool and clammy. "Uh . . . no . . . no, that won't work. But I have an idea . . . okay . . ." She took a deep breath, feeling herself shake as the truth formed, took shape. "I can do this."

Doctor Lowe had touched her arm. "Are you okay, Maggy?"

She'd closed her eyes. No, she wasn't okay. After Cole realized what she was about to do, he'd probably never forgive her.

But he'd be *alive* to never forgive her. When she nodded, a fierceness had come over her, taken possession of her body, her tone. "You keep him alive, Doc, and I'll deliver a donor." She'd rushed past him to the front desk and called Nick Noble.

Now, with her thoughts churning over what she was about to do, she thumped her head against the glass of the window. *Nick, where are you?* She'd called nearly two hours ago, and Stefanie had promised to send him. But what if Stefanie knew? What if she'd already told Nick everything? *What if he'd said no?*

She glanced at CJ, her heart breaking. How could he? Especially after today? *"You got some boy there, Mags. Cole should be so proud of his son."* If that wasn't Nick's way of forgiving Cole, what was?

Maggy stilled, a gasp tunneling through her. Was it possible that Cole had been right—that Nick didn't know? That he'd left without . . .

She put her palm to her chest. If he didn't know . . . well, then he couldn't find out. Ever.

If Nick discovered that CJ was his son after all these years, would he risk his life to save the man who had replaced him?

Even as she thought it, she caught sight of Nick running up to the emergency-room entrance and flinging open the door. He strode into the waiting room. When he saw her, the look he gave her left her feeling as if she'd been broadsided by a bull, her emotions completely scattered.

And he didn't stop at hello. He crossed the room and hauled her into his arms, tight and hard and desperate. "Maggy, are you hurt? What's wrong with Cole?"

She closed her eyes, hating the fact that she needed—oh, so much—this man she'd long ago loved and who had deeply hurt her to come to her rescue.

⁂

Nick loosened his hold on Maggy and stepped back, realizing that he'd probably scared her. But he wasn't going to act like he didn't care—for her or CJ or even Cole. He'd been fending off his emotions since taking off in the plane, and during the entire hour-long flight to Sheridan he had only barely managed to keep his focus on the instrument panel.

If Piper hadn't been sitting beside him, he might have flipped out and landed on the side of a mountain. He wasn't sure why Stefanie insisted she accompany him, but as usual his sister had excellent instincts. Thinking about Piper sitting beside him, trusting him—as if he didn't notice the way she gripped the straps—made him slow down and breathe.

He spotted Piper and Lolly coming through the door, even as he focused on Maggy. She looked like she might pass out. "What's going on? Where's Cole?"

Maggy touched his hand lightly, and he felt her tremble. "I'll take you to him, Nick. But I need to talk to you." Her voice seemed small, even breakable, not Maggy at all.

He caught Piper watching him, worry on her beautiful face. For a second, he wished he could explain to her exactly how he felt—how Maggy would always be a part of the fabric of his past, but now he knew she belonged to Cole. And how he hoped that Piper might someday belong to him.

Instead, he let Maggy lead him toward the emergency exam rooms. Every time he'd been in a hospital, he'd felt nauseous and light-headed. It didn't help his stomach when she opened Cole's curtain and he saw him lying there, chalky and barely breathing, wires and tubes hooked up to him, oxygen hissing through the mask that covered his face. "What's wrong with him?"

Maggy touched Cole's leg, anguish on her face. Her braids hung in a disheveled mess, and in the fluorescent lights she looked ashen.

He took her by the shoulders and lowered her onto a nearby chair, crouched before her. "What is it?"

She took a deep breath.

"You're really scaring me, Mags." He couldn't look at Cole.

"Nick . . . Cole's dying."

Words sucked out of him, his mouth dry.

Her eyes filled, and she didn't bother to wipe away her tears. "He's got liver failure."

"What?" He gasped, as if he'd been hit, but he couldn't wrap his mind around her words. He stood, backing away from her, suddenly aware of the sound of Cole's breathing machine, the beep of the monitors. The roaring in his head. "Cole hasn't had a drink in his life."

"It's not cirrhosis. They don't know why. They've done dozens of tests, but they don't know what's causing it. All we know is that if he doesn't get a new liver he'll die. Soon."

Maggy faced him, and only her steady, almost clinical voice made Nick hear her. How could she be so calm? "I don't under-stand. How long have you known?"

"Only a short while. And CJ doesn't know at all. Cole's been having symptoms for a couple years now. Weakness, brittle bones, bleeding, depression, jaundice."

"You should have told me."

The look on her face made him want to crawl into a hole. He cringed, loathing himself. "I should have been here," he amended. He crouched before her again, feeling very, very close to erupting, want-ing desperately to hit something. "Maggy, I am so, so sorry for what I did. I'm sorry for hurting you. I feel sick about it. Please forgive me."

Maggy covered her mouth with her hands. Then she nodded. Her voice dropped to just above a whisper. "Of course, Nick. Cole and I forgave you years ago."

He simply stared at her.

She touched his cheek. "Cole loved you like a . . . a brother. And you were . . . well, you knew I loved you." Her face twitched, and she managed the saddest of smiles.

"I don't deserve friends like you," Nick said, barely able to dredge up his voice.

Maggy's smile fell, and she bowed her head, looking at her hands. "Actually, Nick, I need to ask you something."

"Anything."

She swallowed, but no words came.

"Maggy, what is it?" He touched her chin, tipping up her face.

"Cole needs a liver donor."

Nick nodded.

"And . . . well, a liver donor can be a live donor."

"What about CJ?" Nick got to his feet, hope filling him. "Is he a match?"

Maggy licked her lips, and if it were possible, she went even more pale. "No . . . CJ's not a match. But . . . you could be."

Nick felt like the floor had opened up or moved beneath him. He had to steady himself on the end of Cole's bed as he asked, "What do you . . . mean?"

Maggy sucked in a breath and smiled. "Cole is your brother."

"What . . . are you . . . talking about?" He knew his voice was louder than it should be in a hospital. "What are you talking about, Maggy!" He felt a remnant of anger begin to surface, something ugly and hard and overpowering.

Maggy's smile vanished, and a look of pleading came over her as she stood up. "Please, Nick, hear me out."

He clenched his jaw, forcing himself to stand there.

She licked her lips, put her hand to her chest, and glanced down at Cole. "Your dad told me."

"*What?*"

"Yes. Well . . . sorta. Actually, he told Saul. And I was there. I heard him."

"What exactly did you hear?" Nick recognized his tone from his cop days but didn't retract it.

Maggy's voice shook. "The day Saul and John came over to

finalize the will, I was there, taking care of your dad. I went out to get your father some tea, like he asked. When I came back, he was talking to Saul. He told him that he wanted to give Cole in death what he couldn't in life—a part of the Noble legacy. He told Saul that Cole was his son, that while your mom was in the hospital during the early days of her pregnancy, he'd had an affair—"

"That is *not true!*" Nick thundered.

Maggy jerked, but she recovered fast, catching him before he could turn and stalk away. He tried to shrug her away, but she held on like a bulldogger. "It *is* true. Think about it. He was always including Cole in everything you all did. And he supported Cole and his mother for years. I found deposits in Irene's account after I took over the books."

Nick turned, casting a look at Cole. "Why didn't Cole tell me?"

"I don't think he knows. Bishop said he hadn't told anyone, and Irene had promised to keep it quiet for Elizabeth's sake too. Irene's brother worked at the Buckle, and he was the only family she had. She didn't want to leave . . . so she stayed, and Bishop took care of her, of Cole. But Cole has never said a word, so . . ."

Nick narrowed his eyes, unable to fathom the depths of Maggy's duplicity. "You've known all this time, and you didn't tell anyone? What else are you keeping from me?" He gestured to Cole. "From us?"

Maggy let go of him and wrapped her arms around herself, as if trying to hold herself together. "Nick, you're Cole's brother. And his only hope for a liver match. Please, please will you get tested? To save his life?"

Nick's attention went from Cole to Maggy and back as he turned her words over in his mind. Cole was his brother? He sighed as the emotions caught up to him. "Did my mother know?"

Maggy shook her head. "I don't know. But this mistake changed Bishop. He became the father you knew because he felt sick about his sins and asked God to make him a new man. He told Saul all of this and how he longed for years to tell you, how he hoped that someday you and Cole could share the land you both loved so much."

Nick wanted to close his ears, but even as she spoke, he saw himself and Cole, riding side by side, the opposite ends of one pole. Cole, dependable, patient; Nick, passionate, reckless. Both of them loving cowboying. Loving the Silver Buckle. Hoping to be the men Bishop challenged them to be.

Not only that, but as he looked at Maggy, he remembered the grief he'd felt over Cole as he'd taken her into his arms in the waiting room. Because of that moment, perhaps he might understand, however briefly, how his father had felt after Elizabeth died. Alone. Needing someone to bear it with him.

Someone he'd once loved.

Nick looked at Maggy, pleading through those beautiful eyes that had always believed in him, even when he didn't deserve it. "He *is* my brother, isn't he?" he said softly.

Maggy's face tore with emotion, and she nodded.

"I've been a fool."

Maggy shook her head and shrugged, apparently not sure what to say.

Nick blew out a breath, clinging to the barest grip on his emotions. "How could I have not seen this? My brother." He stared at Cole, seeing the solid, nearly stubborn chin. And if it weren't written on his face, the Noble character filled Cole's veins. Cole had turned out more like Bishop than Nick had ever been.

Finally, Nick could make Bishop proud of him. Be the Noble he should be. "Okay, I'll do it. Find the doctor."

"Oh, Nick, thank you!"

Before he could brace himself, she launched herself into his arms, burying her face into his neck, sobbing.

He pulled her tight. "It's going to be okay, Maggy. It's going to be okay."

Piper stood at the end of the hallway, calling herself stupid as she watched Nick hold Maggy. Tears slicked her eyes, and she blinked them away, hating herself for getting this far in over her head. She hated hospitals—the smells and textures and noises of people gasping for air. Including herself.

She beelined back to the waiting room, where Lolly and John waited with CJ. Lolly smoothed CJ's hair as he slept on her lap. John had his arm around her.

"How is he?" Lolly asked.

"Fine. They're all fine."

Lolly quirked a penciled eyebrow.

Piper didn't elaborate. She sat in a vinyl chair, incredulous at how she'd been roped into flying to Sheridan. Clearly, Stefanie didn't know her brother nor his true feelings about the women in his life. Piper should have listened to her instincts and packed her bags.

After all, she had the evidence she needed right here on digital recording. "What do you think? Who was the real murderer?" she'd asked.

"Me," Nick had answered. *Me.*

Her chest burned, and she pushed the feeling away. She couldn't wait to put her piece together and submit it. *Wanted: Justice* relished this type of story—a cop gone over the edge. She'd gotten what she'd come looking for—Nick's confession.

So it wasn't *exactly* a confession. And was it really what she'd come to the Silver Buckle to find?

It didn't matter. She'd land her new job, move to Seattle, and forget everything about Nick Noble and his deceptions.

She winced, rubbing her eyes. She needed coffee before someone else got hurt. She pushed to her feet. "I'm going to find the cafeteria. Need anything?"

Lolly frowned at her tone. "Nope."

Piper said nothing as she marched down the hall. She'd get a coffee, a salad, then call Carter and get on the next flight out of Dodge.

# CHAPTER 18

COLE FULLY EXPECTED to wake up in heaven. So when he opened his eyes to the sun turning the bedsheets flaxen, the sound of a respirator, and Maggy asleep near the foot of his bed, he wasn't sure whether to rejoice or cry.

He reached down and touched her head, twining her auburn hair through his fingers. She stirred, and he wondered how he'd gotten so lucky as to spend the last ten years with her. Her eyes fluttered open, and he watched her scramble to place her surroundings.

Apparently last night had also caught her by surprise. Why couldn't he have peacefully gone to sleep while staring at the stars from the bed of his truck? His mother had gone in her sleep, and now he saw what a blessing it had been for them all. At least he'd seen CJ win—God had answered that prayer. After seeing Maggy and Nick together while watching CJ win his event, Cole knew he was ready. Nick would watch over them. When Maggy got the land from Bishop's will, she'd at least have choices. She could marry

Nick or move. And that's all Cole had wished for her. Choices. A future.

Now, as Maggy raised her head, gave him a smile, he didn't know what to think. She sat up and twined her fingers through his, setting their hands on the soft cotton sheets. "Everything's going to be okay, Cole."

He nodded. Yes, it was. "I'll always love you, you know."

"Me too." She scooted her chair closer. The sheets had left lines on her beautiful face, and her hair had abandoned her braids and curled deliciously around her head. She'd cried away any makeup, leaving only the sun's color on her cheeks.

He'd miss her, and that thought nearly made him groan aloud. Instead he squeezed her hand. "Where's CJ?"

She stretched her neck from side to side. "Last I saw him, he was asleep in the waiting room with Lolly and John and the others." Maggy reached over to the table next to his bed. "Do you want some water?"

He caught her arm as she brought it to him. "Mags, is Nick here? I thought I heard him last night after they brought me in."

Fear flashed across her face. "Did you hear what we were talking about?"

He'd been just below the surface of consciousness, but, yes, he'd heard Nick when he said, "It'll be okay." Cole knew instinctively what Nick meant. As in, "I'm here. I promise to stay by you."

Cole ignored the pain and forced a smile. "It's fine, Maggy. I want you to be happy." His mouth felt dry. He reached for the water, but she jerked it away.

"What are you talking about?" Her voice sounded harsher than he thought it might—after all, her husband had just given her permission to marry the man she loved. Seemed like she might be . . . well, *sensitive* to that situation.

"You and Nick. I understand. I give you my . . . my blessing." He tried not to sound jaded, but it came out as he'd feared. Filled with hurt.

To his confusion, anger filled Maggy's face. When she set down the cup, water splashed onto the table. "I can't believe you. You think I want to be with Nick?"

Cole said nothing.

She shook her head and touched her fingers to her temples. "This is more serious than I thought. Apparently you need a brain transplant too!" She stood up, knocking the chair against the wall. "No, wait—you were *serious* the other day in the barn?" Her face twisted in disbelief. "You want me to marry Nick? Why? I don't love Nick. I love you!"

"You've always loved Nick. He's—"

"You don't get it, do you? Love is an investment. It's a lifetime of giving and sharing and . . . struggling. Yes, Nick was the man who introduced me to charm and passion and adventure, but you, Cole, taught me about patience and kindness and gentleness. You taught me that love is spending the night in the barn nursing a sick calf, riding out together in the quiet of a snowy morning, or sitting at home together under an afghan, rustling the pages of a good book. You taught me that it's loving someone despite their mistakes and rushing them to the hospital and holding their hand as their life changes forever. And shouldering that responsibility, even though it isn't yours. Yeah, I might have loved Nick once, but he was just a *shadow* of my love for you. A glimpse of what was waiting for me. I would never, *ever* marry Nick after being with you." She whisked tears from her cheeks and glared at her husband.

*Oh.* Cole licked his lips, his mouth prairie dry. To his dismay, his eyes began to burn. He looked down, refusing the rush of emotions.

Maggy sat on the bed. "I know you think I settled for you, Cole. But you're my gift from God. You're the proof that God loves me so very much."

Cole ducked his head, closing his eyes, feeling her words seep into the parched places of his spirit. "I just wanted to give you what you deserved, Mags. This life is so hard—"

"This life is what I love. But I'd chuck it all for one more day with you. I love our land. But I love you more. I don't care if we have to sell everything we have and I have to wait tables at Lolly's—we're going to have our happily ever after."

He looked at her, a streak of cold rushing through him. "What are you talking about?"

She wore a tremulous smile. "I found you a donor."

He heard the words but couldn't feel them, couldn't let them touch him for fear they'd vanish. "I don't . . . how? I thought I was so far down on the list—"

"It's Nick."

Cole blinked at her, unable to take a full breath. "What? . . . I . . . I don't understand."

Maggy patted his chest. "I have to tell you something." She took a breath; she looked as rattled as he did. "Nick is your brother, Cole. The day Bishop signed his will, I was there. And I overheard him talking to Saul. He told him everything—that when Elizabeth was here in Sheridan during her hospitalization, Bishop had a brief affair with your mother, who'd come to visit her brother—"

"Dutch."

She nodded. "Well, Bishop felt sickened by what he'd done, and evidently it caused him to reach out for salvation, but Irene got pregnant. I know you always wondered why you never had a father, why your mother never told you. It's because she promised to keep it quiet. I don't know if Nick's mom ever knew, but the last thing Bishop did was make you a part of the family. He left you that land so you could be the Noble you should have been."

Maggy took his hand, her face softening, her eyes wet. "But you didn't need the land or the name to prove that you're a man of noble character."

Cole took this in without speaking. He'd always known that Dutch was his uncle, and he'd filled in the gap for a father in so many ways. Cole's face tightened into a frown as he replayed his past, all those mysterious Christmas presents, the money to buy his horse, Suds, the home and land his mother certainly couldn't afford, the pickup that appeared on his eighteenth birthday after Nick had left for school.

He thought of the sporting events Bishop had always attended, how he'd treated both Nick and Cole to pizza, and the time he'd been in the audience during Cole's band concert, even though Nick didn't play an instrument. Nick had been right when he'd accused Cole of wanting Bishop to be his father too. Truthfully, the day Nick had found Bishop with his mother, Cole had hoped—more than he should have—that that dream might finally come true. As Cole's mother's health faded more each day—despite Bishop's attention and the visits to doctors in Sheridan—Bishop became more than a boss to Cole. He'd wept at her bedside when she died. And he'd put his arms around Cole at the graveside. Just like a father might do to his son.

"Bishop was my father?"

"And Nick is your brother. He was tested last night to see if he is a liver match for you."

"Nick did that for me?" Cole shook his head. "But . . . did you tell him about Bishop? I guess you had to . . . but doesn't he hate me?"

"I think, like you, he might have known all along. And, no. In fact, I think he's relieved."

Cole blew out a breath, squeezing her hand. "You can't let him do this, Mags. It's dangerous. He could die."

"He's cowboy enough for this. He knows what he's doing."

Cole looked at her hand, feeling the calluses, the hard work etched into her palms. "At least we have the land. We can sell it, pay for this." A swell of gratitude for Bishop's gift, even if it had been given in guilt, swept over him.

Maggy gave a feeble smile and looked down, tracing the IV taped to his hand. "Yeah . . ."

"This isn't how I had it worked out. You were supposed to get the land and sell it—"

"Or marry Nick," she said, her voice hard.

Cole shrugged. "He is CJ's father."

She shook her head. "No, you are."

"Has Nick told CJ what he's doing? CJ needs to know about Nick. I know we always said we'd tell him when the time was right. I think that's now. . . . What is it?"

Maggy looked stricken, the blood draining from her face. "I don't think Nick knows about him. He . . . he asked me if CJ would be a match for you."

Cole went cold. "All these years he hasn't known? But you wrote him that letter–you told him." He cradled his head in his hands. "How could he not know?" All those lost years . . . "Maggy, I feel sick. We have to tell him. Nick has to know about CJ before he goes into surgery. What if something happens to him? He has to know–"

Maggy looked as if he'd struck her.

Cole lowered his voice. "I'm not doing this unless Nick knows about CJ. Unless he's given the choice. He might not want to go through with it if he knows he has a son."

A knock came at the door, but Maggy didn't move.

Cole stared at her, willing her to agree.

She tightened her jaw as a nurse entered and said, "It's time, Mr. St. John."

"What? No–wait. I'm not ready."

Doctor Lowe appeared one step behind the nurse. He was dressed in surgical scrubs, scuffies on his feet. "Good morning, Cole." He wore a smile that Cole didn't feel. "You are a lucky man today. Normally I wouldn't recommend a live-donor transplant without the donor having sufficient time to consider the situation. But your brother is not only a perfect match–with six out of six HLA proteins–he's in excellent physical condition. And he's persuasive."

Cole knew how persuasive Nick could be. Gratitude washed over him, wrecking his voice. But he couldn't let go of Maggy's hand. "Maggy and I have some unfinished business."

The nurse moved over to lower his bed, put down the rails.

Panic filled Cole's grip. "Wait–I want to see CJ."

Maggy came close, brushed her lips across his forehead. "I'll get him."

He didn't let her go. "Mags, you have to tell him—"

"Shh." She pressed her lips to his, gently, sweetly, conjuring up so many memories. "Nick isn't going to change his mind. Not when his brother needs him." She pulled away, stepped back while two attendants wheeled in a gurney.

"Maggy, promise me that if anything happens—"

"Nothing's going to happen."

"—you'll tell Nick everything." He grimaced as the attendants moved him to the gurney.

Maggy sighed. "Be strong, Cole. I need you. CJ needs you. And we love you."

He gazed at her, frustration turning him inside out as they rolled him away.

❦

Nick had had a chest X-ray, an EKG, an ultrasound, a CT scan, been poked, sucked of blood, starved, and this last humiliation made him want to hit something.

"Okay, Mr. Noble, you're all set for surgery." The nurse coiled up the tube and did the favor of not looking at him as she lowered his sheets and patted his leg.

His face felt ten shades of red, and he didn't roll over until she exited. No one ever said the E-word when he'd agreed to this last night.

Then again, last night he'd been overwrought with emotion, not thinking clearly. But even in the light of day, he wouldn't change his mind. Not after he spent half the night pleading his case to Doctor Lowe. How he'd probably been ready for this his entire life, how God had brought him back, maybe for this reason alone.

Nick had another *brother*. It made him think of Rafe, of losing him, and he'd asked Stefanie to call him. Just . . . in case.

Nick rolled over, adjusting himself on the hospital bed. They'd given him a single room, probably wanting to keep him free from infection before surgery. Outside, clouds streaked a beautiful blue sky, and he made out the Bighorn Mountains.

He wished he'd had time to donate blood for himself. Instead, Stefanie had rolled up her sleeve shortly after he'd broken the news to her.

That had been an interesting conversation. And an even more interesting reaction from his sister, who barely blinked. After a pause, she'd simply touched his hand, given him a cryptic smile, and said, "I wondered about that."

Was he the only one who'd lived nearly thirty years in the dark? Well, according to Maggy, Cole didn't know either. Attesting to the fact that they were probably related. Only a couple of dunces from the same gene pool could miss the fact that they were half brothers.

Nick traced the scar on his palm with his thumb, thinking about the day he and Cole, in their boyish games, had cut their palms and pressed them together, pledging loyalty and friendship.

He wanted to see Cole before surgery.

*"God brought you here for a reason, Nick."* Stefanie's words replayed in his head, and he felt a rush of emotion at the immensity of God's plan. His eyes misted, and he decided he could blame that on the surgery and the thought that they were going to cut into him, take out a piece, and give it to his best friend. No, his brother.

*Bishop, why didn't you tell me or at least tell Cole?* It seemed to him that a kid had a right to know about his father, regardless of the repercussions. But Bishop had probably been trying to protect Elizabeth. And he could hardly blame his father for that.

He rubbed his forehead, wincing at the pinch of the IV tube in his hand. A knock came at the door, and he adjusted his blankets, hoping it might be Piper. "Enter."

He hadn't seen Piper since last night and had carried her worried expression in his mind through all his tests and the dark hours as he'd waited for the results. He would like to have had her near him while he waited to hear whether or not he might be used by God to help save Cole's life.

*Thank You, God.*

The door opened, and Stefanie popped her head in. "Hey there, Spare Parts, how're you doing?"

Nick gave her a mock glare. "Wishing I was back home on my horse."

Stefanie came in, closed the door behind her. "I think that outfit might be a bit breezy for a ride on the range."

"Oh, ha-ha." He did feel a little . . . exposed. Even with the covers tucked around him. It reminded him—too well—of the times he'd visited his mother in the hospital. She always acted so strong, always assured him that everything would be all right.

Kind of like he'd done last night to Maggy. For the first time, he realized that his mother's words had been as much for herself as for him. "Have you seen Cole?"

"Nope." She pointed to the crease inside her elbow, where a lump of cotton raised her shirt. "Pouring out my life for you took up all my time."

"You could give me a break here."

She grinned. "I like the fact that I can help. A little." She patted his leg, and he saw her eyes glisten. "You're the hero I always thought you were, Nick."

*Oh.* He felt another hot rush of emotion. For pete's sake, he was turning into a blubbering mess. "Took me a while."

"You're right on time." Her smile dimmed. "CJ's out there, though. Wanna see him before you go into surgery?"

Nick shrugged, not sure what he'd say to the kid–his *nephew*! A smile came easily. "How's he taking his dad's illness?"

Stefanie sat down on his bed. "I don't think he knows much. Just that Cole is sick, and you're helping him get well." She crossed her arms over her chest. "I think you need to . . . ah . . . tell him that you're proud of him, winning the breakaway roping."

He'd forgotten that he hadn't talked to CJ since before the event. "Yeah, send him in. And Piper too. How is she? Did you tell her?"

Stefanie frowned.

"What?"

"Well, I haven't seen Piper. I got here late, and I thought she'd gone to a hotel or something. But no one has seen her. All night."

"Not at all?"

Stefanie shook her head.

"Can you please find her for me?" He hated the desperation in his voice, but it matched his pitiful attire, and frankly he should probably scuttle any attempts at pride.

Especially after the E-word.

Stefanie touched his hand. "You like her, don't you?"

Nick turned his gaze toward the window. "I might be falling in love with her, Stef. I always thought I'd never get over Maggy. And I did love Maggy, but my feelings for Piper are so much bigger. Or maybe it's just the right timing, but she's . . . she's—"

"She fits you. Anyone can see that. She's patient and—"

"Beautiful and sweet and a great listener and funny, and I can't stop thinking about her. She gets to me."

"I was going to say she likes the ranch."

He smiled. "She told me she doesn't want to leave the ranch." He was sorta hoping she meant that she didn't want to leave him either.

"Well, that's good, because we need her. But more importantly, I think she feels the same about you. At least that's what it looked like last night when I asked her to go with you."

"Why did you do that?"

Stefanie gave a sly grin. "Women's intuition and the hope that what I saw at the rodeo might be the start of something . . . permanent."

Nick wasn't quite sure what to say to that.

Stefanie got to her feet and gave his hand a final squeeze. "I'll find her. And I'll send in CJ." She leaned over, pressing a kiss to his cheek. "I love you, Brother. And I'm so proud of you."

Nick couldn't speak as she turned and walked away.

Piper heard voices when she opened her eyes. She pushed herself into a sitting position, trying to get a fix on her surroundings. Low light, a quietness that filled the air, padded red velvet pews, a crucifix hanging above the altar. She turned to see a young couple huddled in the back pew, praying.

She remembered discovering the cafeteria closed and settling for trying to find a place to sleep. Apparently the third pew of the hospital chapel had seemed suitable at three in the morning.

Checking her watch, she realized she'd been out for six hours. Her mouth tasted gummy, and her body felt as if it had gone about ten rounds with one of those Brahma bulls. She'd definitely cross out pews as appropriate sleeping berths.

She needed to eat, shower, and gather what little common sense she still possessed. She checked her cell phone to see if Carter had returned any of her messages. Nothing. And her battery was low.

She stood, combed her fingers through her snarled hair, and tiptoed past the couple holding each other. They looked so . . . together. The man had his arm around his wife, and her hands were wound in his as they prayed in low tones. The sight of them made Piper ache.

She wanted that. Wanted someone to cling to when life felt overwhelming.

No, she didn't simply want *someone*; she wanted Nick. She closed her eyes, thinking of the way she'd seen him hugging Maggy, both arms around her as if he would never let go. She knew how that felt—he'd held her exactly the same way the night of the stampede. And in so many just as heartbreaking ways since then.

She felt barren thinking about how much she'd misjudged him. First, believing he had framed her brother and now considering he might love her. Some reporter she'd turned out to be. She shoved her hand into her pocket, curling her fingers around the tape re-corder containing Nick's incriminating words, running her fingers along its cool, smooth edges.

Her cell phone vibrated, and she fumbled for it, hurrying out the door and into the hall. "Hello?"

"Tell me you're okay." Carter's voice betrayed the fact that he'd picked up the five frantic messages she'd left overnight.

"Did you get the information I asked you to find?"

"Let's see, I've had roughly zero working hours between eight o'clock last night and nine this morning. Not only that, but the public-records office in Miles City isn't open until Tuesday, this being Memorial Day weekend. So, you must think I'm some sort of Internet whiz–"

"What did you find out?"

"Testy. Did you sleep in your clothes again?"

She slunk down the hall toward the bathroom. Maybe she didn't want to see the results of her night on a pew. . . . "Please, Carter–"

"Okay, calm down. Get a chai." She heard his keyboard clicking. "You're lucky I miss you and spend every free hour at my computer."

"It's just because you're in between girlfriends."

"Speaking of romance, how is that cowboy of yours?"

Piper pushed into the bathroom, lowering her voice, and stared at the damage in the mirror. She'd aged about ninety years in one night, with bags under her eyes and sleep wrinkles on her face. Her makeup had smeared, and her hair hung in stringy tangles. Her T-shirt matched her skirt wrinkle for wrinkle, and she probably smelled. Lovely. "He's moving on to greener pastures, and I'm coming home."

The pause on the other end told her that her tone held a hint of bitterness. "Piper, I'm sorry."

She hated how Carter's gentle words pushed tears into her eyes. She ground her teeth, getting a fix on the essentials. "I got my confession. That's what I came to do."

"But you and I both know that's not what really happened."

She'd clearly made a mistake babbling on to Carter about Nick and the Silver Buckle and her worries and especially trying a little too hard to learn how to make biscuits. "It's over; that's all that matters. I need you to get me a flight out of Sheridan today."

He said nothing.

"What?"

"Nothing. I hear and obey, master."

She wet a paper towel and began to wipe the mascara from around her eyes. "So, what did the records turn up?"

"I couldn't find anything under Saul, but I found the probate records of a Beau Hatcher, daughters Loretta and Elizabeth."

"And?"

"I faxed the file numbers to the clerk. I'll call her tomorrow on the off chance someone is in the office, but we probably won't hear anything until Tuesday. Why is this important?"

"Just a hunch . . . it's probably nothing." She wadded the paper and threw it in the trash, then ran the water hot to wash her face. "I just think there's more story here."

"Go get 'em, Ace."

*My name's George.* The nickname and Nick's voice filled her mind. "I gotta run, Carter. And my phone is dying, so I'm turning it off. I'll check for messages later, but get me a flight out of here ASAP." She congratulated herself on holding her voice steady as she said it. Now if she could sneak out of the hospital without running into Nick or Stefanie.

"Aye, aye, Captain."

"You can be replaced, you know."

He laughed loudly, then hung up.

Piper closed the phone and set it on the counter, pressing her hand against her stomach. It didn't ache, and for the first time she realized how long she'd been off her daily diet of antacids.

In fact, it seemed a decade since her stomach had writhed in pain. She bent to wash her face. At least she'd feel awake, even if she looked like death warmed over.

She heard the door open as another woman entered the room. Closing her eyes, she splashed water over her face again, then reached for another paper towel.

Someone placed it in her hand, and she pressed it to her face. "Thanks."

"I'm glad I found you."

Piper opened her eyes to find Stefanie Noble standing there, her face dark, worried. "I've been looking all over for you."

Piper studied her through the mirror. Stefanie looked like she did—as if she'd spent the night curled on a bench or worse. Her face seemed drawn, her dark hair recklessly pulled back from her face, her eyes pensive. "What's the matter?"

"It's Nick. He needs you."

Piper debated her response, looking at her hands as she wiped them. "Stefanie, you should probably know something about me."

"What, that you're in love with Nick?"

Hardly. Piper gave a bitter huff and shook her head. "No . . . I'm not able to work at the ranch this summer."

Stefanie stood, unblinking, and in that instant Piper felt shame climb through her. But she straightened her spine and tossed her hair from her face. "Sorry. It's just not working out."

Stefanie frowned, as if trying to sort through the information.

Piper crumpled up the paper towel and tossed it into the trash. "I'll be leaving as soon as I can get a flight out."

She expected anger. Instead, Stefanie nodded. "Okay, well, I don't know what Nick did to hurt you, but that's not important right now."

Did the woman not hear what she said? Piper picked up her phone, slipped it into her pocket. "Again, I'm sor–"

Stefanie grabbed her arm and, to her surprise, hauled her from the bathroom.

"Excuse me?" Piper jerked from Stefanie's grasp. "I told you, I'm leaving."

"No, you're not. Nick needs you."

"Nick doesn't need me. He has *Maggy*."

"You're kidding, right?" Stefanie's expression matched her angry tone.

Piper took a step back. "Not in the least. He loves her–"

"Loved . . . *loved*. Past tense. And, yes, he probably still cares about her, but he wasn't asking for Maggy." Stefanie's voice broke. "He wants you."

"Stefanie, are you all right?" Piper barely resisted touching her on the shoulder. But the woman had recently arm locked her. She wasn't taking any chances.

"No, I'm not all right." Stefanie covered her face with her hands, and Piper wondered if she might fall apart right there in the hall. Maybe they should go back to the chapel.

"What's the matter? You're scaring me. Is it Cole?"

Stefanie gave her the most mournful look she'd ever seen. "He needs a liver transplant. And Nick is the one giving it to him."

Piper absorbed that information. Nick would do that because he was a hero, right down to his bones. "Of course he is. He's his brother. He's not going to let Cole die."

Stefanie stared at her as if she'd grown an extra ear. "How did you know that?"

*Hmm. Good question.* "It's a long story." Piper rubbed her tired eyes. "When is it scheduled?"

"They're already in surgery."

"What?" Piper reached out to brace herself against the wall.

"Nick had me running around the hospital searching for you, but I couldn't find you before they took him away." She touched Piper's arm. "He wants you there when he wakes up."

Piper leaned her head back against the wall. *Oh, Nick.*

Stefanie breathed out a long sigh of pent-up worry. "My brother is falling in love with you, Piper. And I don't know how you feel about him, but please stay until he gets out of surgery."

Stefanie looked at her with such pleading, Piper couldn't speak. So, she did the only thing she could . . . she nodded.

# CHAPTER 19

MAGGY STOOD in the empty hospital room, hearing the quiet beating of her heart tapping a rhythm of hope. She didn't know what to do, where to go. It felt almost . . . disrespectful to sit with Stefanie Noble as she worried about her brother. Yes, they were in this together, but Maggy felt that in a way she'd stolen something from them—not once, but twice.

Starting with Nick's son.

She couldn't tell him about CJ. Not now. She could forgive him for not returning for her ten years ago—honestly, a colossal part of her had been relieved. Nick embodied her girlhood fantasies, but he was pure adrenaline, pure passion. She needed faithfulness. Someone to stand beside her.

She needed Cole.

She walked over to the hospital bed, still warm from his body, and found herself climbing in, laying her head on his pillow, hoping to catch his scent. She drew up her knees and wrapped her arms around herself, feeling frail and alone.

*Lord, please, please save Cole.* The prayer felt like a moan. How would she live without him? The thought left her breathless, empty.

*"The love of the Lord remains forever with those who fear him. His salvation extends to the children's children of those who are faithful to his covenant, of those who obey his commandments!"* The words from Bishop's favorite psalm filled her mind. How many times had he asked her to read it to him, as he'd savored the words? She remembered wondering how God's salvation, His righteousness could be passed from Bishop to Nick, scoffing at that thought.

Regret burned inside her. She should have trusted Nick. Should have known that he had the character of Bishop. The character of Cole. Like father, like sons.

CJ bore the character of both his fathers–his biological father and his adoptive father. She was so proud of him–she felt as if she might burst with love.

She closed her eyes at the sudden dread welling inside her. What would Nick do when–*if*–he found out about CJ? Would he try and take him from her? Would he enact vengeance, stripping from Cole the land Bishop left him?

Nick could contest the will. And win. Although Bishop hadn't left her the land, he'd given her something else. Pecos.

Nick's favorite horse. And if she thought Nick had been angry when he found out about Pecos . . .

*"The love of the Lord remains forever with those who fear him."*

Maggy pressed her hand against her chest, hearing her own words the day she and Cole had tended the sick calf.

*"He's my responsibility."*

*"No, he's not, Mags. God's in charge of this bum, and He's going to do what's right."*

*"I'm not letting him die."*

*"You might not have a choice. You're always trying to take care of everyone to make sure no one gets hurt. It's time to let it go, honey."*

Cole was right. She couldn't let go. She spent every waking moment trying to keep the ranch running, her son warm and fed, her husband safe. And why?

She closed her eyes again, breathing hard as the truth broadsided her. Because, deep inside, she couldn't believe that God was on her side. That He would protect her, would bless her if she didn't create those blessings for herself. After all, she was just a ranch hand's daughter, who'd gotten herself pregnant before marriage.

*"His unfailing love toward those who fear him is as great as the height of the heavens above the earth. He has removed our sins as far from us as the east is from the west."*

As the words filled her head, Maggy had an odd thought—what if all those times Bishop asked her to read were not for his benefit . . . but for hers?

*"As far from us as the east is from the west . . ."* Including the land from Bishop's bequest, it took her an entire day to ride from one end of their property to another. She couldn't even see the two edges of it.

*" . . . as the height of the heavens above the earth . . ."* There were days when she lay on her back, surrounded by alfalfa, and the sky appeared close enough to touch. Other times, at night, with the stars scattered like dandelions tossed to the wind, they seemed so far away they went on forever. She loved the land, and suddenly she realized why.

Because the land gave her a glimpse of God. Showed her the creativity, the power, the intricacies of her heavenly Father. The depth and breadth of His love. Being a rancher had taught her that her entire life sat squarely in God's hands. So far, the Almighty had given her more than she could have asked for or dreamed of. A healthy son. A devoted husband.

And now a fresh start.

*Lord, help me to trust You. I've been afraid to do that. To trust You with CJ. I'm afraid of losing him to Nick, afraid that Nick will hurt him. But I'm also afraid that he will love Nick more than he loves Cole.*

Her breath caught on her thoughts. She'd been afraid that *she'd* love Nick more than Cole. But loving Nick had only made her love for Cole richer. More precious. And by having two Noble men in his life, CJ would be even more the man of character.

*Lord, You've given me so much. I'm giving it all back to You. Your will be done.*

"Mom?" The door to the room opened, and Maggy turned as CJ came in.

Maggy rolled over, patting the space next to her on the bed. "Climb in, buckaroo. We'll wait for Daddy together."

He snuggled in beside her. She curled a hand around his waist. He sighed. "Is it true that Nick is my uncle?"

Maggy pressed a kiss to the top of his head. "He's definitely family, CJ. In fact, you could probably say that after today, he and your father share more than blood."

CJ wove his fingers through hers. "That's cool," he said softly.

"Yes," Maggy murmured. "Very, very cool."

Piper sat in the waiting room with Stefanie, Dutch, Lolly, John, and Saul Lovell, who'd had the kindness to visit his clients, waiting for

Cole and Nick to return from surgery. She felt like one of the family. She also felt like the world's greatest liar, her hand clutched around her cell phone in one pocket, her tape recorder in the other, her death grips on reality.

Outside, the sky matched their moods—it had turned to bullet silver and began pelting the ground with rain. The plinks on the windows were the only sounds to accompany their vigil in the tiny surgical waiting room.

Piper wanted to run far and fast and never return. But the fact that Nick had asked for her had kept her tethered, and she couldn't break free. Not yet at least.

She dreaded the pain if Stefanie was right—that he was falling in love with her. Because, well, she loved him right back. Deep and strong and full of all the fairy-tale dreams she knew she could never have.

She wasn't the sort of girl who could stay home and cook dinner and round up cattle. As Carter had tried to drill into her head over and over—she was simply playing a part.

She might be able to cook a few biscuits, learn to ride a horse, even figure out the hot spots for cell-phone reception, but she had no real future at the Silver Buckle. Especially when Nick discovered that everything she'd said and done had been to support a massive lie in order to hurt him.

Piper pressed her hand to her churning stomach.

She'd wait until he was out of surgery; then she'd disappear. He'd never have to know how much she had despised him.

Or how much she'd come to care for him.

Maggy and CJ came down the hall, looking rumpled and tired. She wondered where they'd gone and watched as CJ sat next to

Dutch. Maggy walked to the window, rubbing her hands over her arms. Still dressed in the clothes from the rodeo, her hair curling in strings around her shoulders, she looked fragile. Yet she gazed out the window without tears.

Piper's heart twisted—it couldn't be easy to have both men one loved in the operating room at the same time. Piper got up, went to her. "I'm sorry about Cole," she said softly.

Maggy glanced at her. "They'll be okay." She nodded, as if agreeing with herself. "I'm trusting that God has plans for both of them."

Piper stared out the window, watching cars splash through puddles on the street and people cover their heads as they ran inside. An ambulance pulled up, lights off. "My mother died a couple years ago. Lung cancer. I hated the hospital—the smells, the sounds. The suffering felt suffocating."

Maggy's voice was gentle. "I'm sorry about your mother. I guess I always saw hospitals as a source of hope. But every time we came here over the past two years, Cole got a little worse. So I can see your point. So much suffering. It does invade a person's soul."

Piper leaned her forehead against the glass. It cooled her, jolted her awake. After sitting for four hours, she felt punky and fuzzy around the edges.

"I remember when Cole's mom passed on. At first, the doctors were baffled by her disease. In the end, she had liver failure and died at home. She was never a healthy woman, but she was a trooper. We really never knew until the end how sick she was." Maggy sighed. "The secrets we hold on to, the suffering we endure so others won't have to." She shook her head, lost in her thoughts.

Piper watched a woman open an umbrella and dash across the

parking lot. "My mother left my father on a day like this. She endured a lot of suffering from him too." Her voice felt distant even as she spoke, mired in the memory. "He was a horrible man, abusive and an alcoholic. The day she left him was the day my life started. I didn't know until later that every day she lived in fear that he'd find us. He died when I was fifteen. We got a funeral notice from his sister. My mother didn't attend. I think she always bled a little from what he'd done to her."

"I'm sorry, Piper." Maggy gave her a sympathetic smile. "I think we always carry the wounds the people we love inflict on us. The best we can hope for is to find someone who helps heal them, who loves us scars and all."

Piper didn't have scars; she had soul-deep wounds that sometimes felt as fresh as the day they'd been inflicted. "Once Cole has this transplant, will he be okay?"

Maggy shrugged. "Yes . . . well, if they can find out what is causing his liver damage. But it'll give him a good chance. It should make him stronger, give us an opportunity to find a future for him."

"A new start."

Maggy wore a strange expression. "Thank you, Piper, for being here, for being with Nick. I think you gave him a reason to want to stick around the Silver Buckle. And if he weren't here, then Cole wouldn't be either."

Piper frowned at that. Of course Maggy didn't know about her investigation.

Maggy smiled. "He's some cowboy, isn't he?" She touched her arm. "I hope it works out between you two. I'd love to have you in the family."

Piper stared after her as Maggy sat and put her arm around CJ. She leaned against Dutch and closed her eyes.

Piper felt nearly ill as she walked past them. What had she done? She longed for this—a family who cared and sacrificed for each other. But as usual, it felt just beyond her reach, as if she were looking at everything she ever wanted through a window, her nose pressed up against the glass. The longing was so alive that it felt like fire inside her.

She took off down the hall. She kept walking, past the nurses' station, past the bank of elevators, down the back stairs. She needed air. But as she passed the chapel, music slowed her steps and drew her to the door.

A man stood in the front, singing a hymn. She hadn't heard it before, but his deep and twangy voice reminded her of Nick's. Tears burned her eyes, and as she wiped them away, she snuck in and sat in the back row, listening. A dozen or so people sat scattered in the pews.

The man finished the song, parked his guitar on a stand, and approached the podium. He was good-looking with a gaunt face, sandy brown hair, and an angular jaw, and he wore a denim shirt, jeans, and boots—not the usual attire of a pastor, but then again this was the West.

Piper leaned back in the pew, too tired to get up. She wondered if anyone would notice if she simply leaned over and fell asleep on the cushions again.

"I know that most of you are here because you have a loved one who is sick or dying. Today I'd like to give you hope from the book of Mark chapter 5."

Piper's eyes began to close as the pastor opened his Bible. She'd never been a person who relied on the whims of God. Her mother had believed that God watched over them, but Piper always felt her mom must have some sort of brain damage. After all, Piper had been there when her dad returned home in drunken rages. She'd felt the rage, heard her mother's screams. Where was God then? *Watching?*

The thought made her want to retch.

The few times she'd attended church with her mother, anger had seeped into her as she listened to the sermons, and she'd found herself arguing with the pastor in her head. God simply didn't notice the hurting, the wounded, as the pastor had indicated.

The pastor began to read: "'A woman in the crowd had suffered for twelve years with constant bleeding. She had suffered a great deal from many doctors, and over the years . . .'"

Preachers were a lot like the counselors her mother had sent her to in those early years. The counselors might have meant well, but Piper had emerged from those sessions more angry, more bitter. More wounded.

*See, I can't go to church without having these sores opened.* Piper rolled her eyes, looking for an opportunity to escape from the chapel.

"'. . . she had spent everything she had to pay them, but she had gotten no better. In fact, she had gotten worse,'" the pastor continued.

*Of course she had.*

"'She had heard about Jesus, so she came up behind him through the crowd and touched his robe. For she thought to herself, "If I can just touch his robe, I will be healed."'"

Unexpected tears pricked Piper's eyes at the woman's desperation.

She took a deep breath. So the woman was hopeless. So she'd tried everything. That wasn't Piper—Piper had a successful life. A life that made a difference. She could heal herself, thank you.

"'Immediately the bleeding stopped, and she could feel in her body that she had been healed of her terrible condition.'"

Piper's eyes narrowed, angry that she still sat in the pew yet suddenly riveted on the story.

The preacher scanned the small audience. "It's important for you to know that this woman was not only suffering in body but in soul. By Old Testament law, she was deemed unclean. She wasn't allowed to go to the temple to sacrifice, wasn't able to enjoy forgiveness, redemption, or a relationship with God. She'd been walking around with unredeemed sin and guilt, feeling dry and untouchable for twelve years. She wasn't even supposed to be around people, yet here she was, touching a rabbi, a holy man."

Piper heard her pulse in her ears. She knew how that might feel, to walk around with a ball of dirt and sickness inside, hoping to hide her illness, wanting so badly to reach out and not only be healed but be made whole.

*Like Cole.*

Instead, she hid behind her words, her reputation as a cutting-edge investigative reporter. When all along, she left the marks of her wounds on every life she touched. She recalled her editor's words: *"Piper, your work is good but jaded. Someday you're going to go too far and fabricate what isn't there. And then this paper is going to pay the price."*

Or Nick would pay the price.

Piper thought of him, risking his life for Cole, and she wanted to cry at her stupidity.

She didn't want to bleed anymore. She didn't want the bitterness,

the anger, the fear that not only filled her body but stained everything she did—her work, her feelings about herself, even her ability
to love Nick. Even if she could learn to trust him, he'd never trust
her. She was dirty. Wounded.

Unlovable.

But, oh, how she longed to be clean.

The pastor read on: "'Jesus realized at once that healing power
had gone out from him, so he turned around in the crowd and
asked, "Who touched my robe?"'"

*See, that's just like God to accuse. To blame the woman for wanting
to be healed and free.*

Piper's mother had lived for years with guilt about leaving her
husband—perpetuated by the women at her church who hadn't the
foggiest idea what it felt like to lie in bed in terror, dreading what
the night might bring.

Piper scooted to the edge of the pew, poised to make a break
for it.

"'Then the frightened woman, trembling at the realization of
what had happened to her, came and fell at his feet and told him
what she had done. And he said to her, "Daughter, your faith has
made you well. Go in peace. Your suffering is over."'"

Piper stared at the preacher. No condemnation? No blame? No
"You brought this on yourself"? Just "Go in peace; you have been
healed"?

The pastor put his Bible aside before he spoke. "Jesus reached
out to a woman who'd been ostracized from society, from Himself,
and healed her from the inside out. All it took was her faith in God,
her surrender to His healing power. Her willingness to reach out
and touch Him."

Piper clasped her hands between her knees, glad she sat in the back of the chapel. She closed her eyes, willing herself to be like the woman who had touched Jesus, to simply reach out. But where was Jesus when her dad was hitting her? when he'd thrown her across the tiny hotel room after their trailer caught fire and broken her arm? She traced the old scar, remembering her terror, remembering how Jimmy had tackled him and taken the rest of her beating on himself.

No, Jesus hadn't been there then. And she certainly couldn't count on Him to heal her now.

Besides, even if she fell at Nick's feet and told him everything, peace would be the last thing he'd offer her.

*But wait.* He'd harbored a ten-year grudge against Cole and right now was offering him a piece of himself to save his life.

*But Cole was his brother.*

*And Cole was dying.*

She couldn't exactly claim mortal wounds or a deadly disease. Not really.

Even if he had held her. Had asked her to stay . . .

Every cell within her wanted to scream *yes!* To start over and be the person she saw reflected in Nick's eyes. To be healed. Made whole.

*"He redeems me from death and crowns me with love and tender mercies."* Nick's voice, a gentle recollection of their time at the Cathedral, filled her mind. She brushed it away, hurting.

Piper snuck from the chapel and closed the door gently behind her, her throat tight.

She stood outside the chapel, wrestling the urge to leave, to walk outside and never return. Certainly that would be best for everyone.

She nearly jumped out of her tired skin when a hand pressed her shoulder. She turned and met Dutch's grim look.

"Cole and Nick are out of surgery."

❦

Cole had entertained a few dreams about heaven. None of them, however, resembled this one: the eastern Montana landscape, the lime-colored grass, the roll of the land over hills and draws, the blue sky as far as he could see. Nor did he expect Suds inside the pearly gates, yet here he was, along with the squeak of saddle leather as Cole rode him across the field toward home.

The warm day told him it must be mid-June, and the sprinkling of coneflower and larkspur evidenced a good season. In the distance, he heard contented cows lowing, and something warm curled in his stomach. His ranch. His land.

His woman. The thought sent a spike of panic through him. Maggy always rode out with him, had spent so many hours working the ranch with him that she felt like an extension of his thoughts. He heard himself calling, but his voice seemed feeble.

Maybe she was in the house with CJ. He urged his horse toward the yard and hopped off, heading toward the back door in long strides. He stepped into the entryway, and voices in the nearby room—the kitchen—stopped him.

Bishop and Maggy.

This wasn't a dream but a memory. He let the memory free from the places he'd hidden it for so many years.

"I know that is Nick's child you're carrying, Maggy."

Cole took the news with a wince. He longed to see Maggy's expression. Relief? Shock? Regret?

"The night Nick left, Stefanie found the note and gave it to me."

"All this time, you've known?" Maggy's voice, Cole's question. How could Bishop have known and not said a word? Every day Bishop drove over here to sit with Irene, and yet he hadn't mentioned anything to Cole.

"I'm prepared to make it right," Bishop said. "I want to build you a home on Noble property. Give you and your baby a piece of the Noble legacy. When Nick comes to his senses—which I know he will—you'll be there, waiting for him. This child can grow up running a ranch right beside his father."

Maggy's voice sounded tight, even angry. "He—or *she*—will run the ranch with their father—Cole. I love Cole, Bishop. Nick might have given me a taste of what love might be, but Cole showed me what real love is. I know you mean well, but I don't want Nick back. I want Cole. And if Nick wants to be in his son's life, he can be. But if Cole will have me, I want this child to bear his name. His character. His legacy. Even if Nick comes back, Cole will always be my choice."

Cole stepped out of the entryway, his heart thundering. Maggy loved him?

He hadn't tried to make her love him, although deep inside he'd longed to hear those words. Honor and guilt had pushed the desires back, buried them.

Even now, he felt shame, feeling as if he'd stolen her somehow.

*"Cole will always be my choice."*

In his memory he saw himself push open the door, but it wouldn't give. Instead, he saw Maggy again, standing in a stream of light. Stoic as someone hurtled words at her.

"What were you thinking, telling Nick about Cole being his brother?"

Cole struggled to place the voice. Bishop? Dutch? He saw Maggy, her hair in two braids, her eyes fierce. This was the Maggy he'd married, the Maggy who hung on to life with both hands. The Maggy he adored. "I was thinking about saving his life. I was thinking that I didn't want Cole to die."

"This isn't what Cole wanted."

"That's because Cole is living under the warped illusion that I don't really want him. That I don't love him. But he's wrong. I would do anything to save his life."

*No, Maggy* . . .

"Nick will figure it out. He'll argue that you influenced Bishop. That he signed the will under duress."

"I know." Maggy rubbed her hands over her arms, but her chin tightened. "But I don't care."

"You'll lose the land, Maggy. And then everything else after the hospital bills."

Maggy only stared at him.

"You'll even lose CJ."

Maggy's voice had dropped to a whisper. "How do you know about CJ?"

The voice paused, and Cole found his own breath choked in this chest. "Bishop told me. He told me that by giving Cole the land, he was also standing in Nick's stead."

Maggy's tone sharpened, as if regrouping. "Nick would never take CJ from me."

"He would if he could provide for him, and you and Cole

couldn't. I suggest you keep CJ's paternity quiet. I'm the only one besides you and Cole who knows, and I'm not telling a soul."

Maggy said nothing. Then she looked over at Cole, seeing him through the cracked door. Without a word, she walked over and shut it.

Cole stood in the entryway, feeling the wind kicking up, shivering.

"His pressure is dropping. I think we have an internal bleed. We may have to go back into surgery."

Cole's eyes flickered open, and he tried to place the images through the haze of sleep. Tubes and Maggy, dressed in a gown, her nose and mouth covered with a mask, standing at the foot of a metal bed. Her eyes were wide and laced with worry, and the words she'd spoken before he went into surgery assaulted him now, clicking suddenly into place with stinging clarity.

*"But I'd chuck it all for one more day with you. I love our land. But I love you more. And I don't care if we have to sell everything we have and I have to wait tables at Lolly's—we're going to have our happily ever after."*

She'd given up their land to save him. The truth made him weak with grief.

Her gaze found his. *Don't die,* it said.

And his replied, *Oh, Maggy, what have you done?*

❧❧❧

He'd spent two days pacing, waiting for the opening he needed to end this. But he saw someone with Nick nearly every moment, and he wasn't really considered one of the family.

Instead, he'd watched from the shadows as Maggy hovered over

Cole in ICU. He didn't want to wish ill upon them, but when Cole had been rushed back into surgery twice, he felt a surge of hope. Maybe Nick would be next.

But after a day, it seemed Nick would live. With Piper and Stefanie playing nurse, he hadn't had a second to get near him, and time was running out. He leaned against the wall, holding a paper cup, sipping the acrid hospital coffee. He had to get Nick alone, just for a moment. He knew what he would do . . . had planned it out in the wee hours of the night. All he needed was a second to realize his revenge. A second to turn the nightmare back into the American dream.

Just one second.

# ᔕ CHAPTER 20

NICK FELT AS IF he'd been hit by a semi going fifty miles an hour. Everything ached, and his back felt as if it had been bludgeoned.

He opened his eyes, stifling a groan. His emotions overtook him when he saw Piper seated next to him, her head nestled on the side of his bed, her blonde hair cascading over her face, her eyes gently closed.

*Whoa, she is beautiful.* He'd dreamed of her as he'd drifted in and out of consciousness, dreamed that she would be sitting right here, waiting for him.

Waiting for him to tell her he loved her. That feeling welled in his chest, so alive, so rich that it fed his healing more than any of the drugs pumped into him. He reached down, wanting only to twine his finger around her silky hair, but the bed moved and nudged her awake.

She opened her eyes, and a soft smile creased her face.

"Hi," he said.

She lifted her head. "Hi." Her makeup had worn off, leaving only her blue eyes and freckles. That and her rumpled clothes—the same ones she'd worn to the rodeo.

"What time is it?"

"What day is it, you mean?" Piper grinned. "You've been out for two days. Well, in and out. You had a complication—some extra bleeding. Evidently you have a condition called von Willebrand's disease. Your blood doesn't clot well. They had to give you two pints of blood."

No wonder he felt as if he could melt into the bed and sleep for another decade.

Piper cupped his face with her hand. "But if it weren't for your bleeding, they would have never caught it in Cole."

He took her hand, wincing at the pinch of an IV. "How is he?"

She met his eyes. "He's still in ICU, but they think he'll pull through."

Nick leaned back into the pillow. "Thank God."

"Yes," Piper said softly. She clasped his hand, brought it to her lips. "You scared me."

"Sorry."

She gave him a mock glare. She rose and levered the bed tray toward him. He noticed a pink water jug as well as a soggy cup of coffee and the remains of a salad. An empty Caesar dressing packet lay on the tray atop a napkin. "Are you hungry?"

Nick shook his head. "But I could use a glass of water."

Piper poured the glass, handed it to him with a straw.

He drank deeply, the moisture soothing his parched throat.

When Piper sat back down, he noticed that tension lined her face. "I didn't get a chance to talk to you before the surgery," she began. "And . . . well, there's something I have to tell you."

He felt the same way, had regretted that he hadn't been able to pull her close and explain to her that she'd become precious to him. A fresh breeze in his life. A gift.

"I . . . I'm not the person you think I am, Nick." She looked away as she said it.

"Piper, you already told me about your past. It's not your fault—"

"Shh." She touched his mouth with her fingers. "I gotta get this out."

An icy dread trickled through him. He tightened his grip on her hand. "What is it?"

"I can't cook, Nick."

He snorted in laughter at her confession. "Don't be so hard on yourself, George. Your ribs were great. Although, yes, there were a few biscuits I thought we might be able to patent for use in the war on terror."

She narrowed one eye at him. "What happened to 'Cookie, you make anything taste great'?"

He laughed at her mimic of him, then grimaced. "Don't make me laugh. It hurts."

Her smile dimmed.

"So, if you don't cook—which I don't believe—then why did you come to the Silver Buckle?"

She turned his hand over, tracing the place where the IV entered, as if contemplating his words. "Listen, I came because I was searching for something."

*A husband perhaps?* Because Phillips was full of women searching for the right cowboy. Look at Lolly. "What?" he asked, wanting to ask if she had found it.

Her forlorn expression hinted at no.

Something didn't feel right again. Then she swallowed, as if fortifying herself for her answer, and he knew that he wasn't going to like her next words. . . .

Instead, he heard the theme from *Scooby Doo.*

He raised his eyebrows as she reached into her pocket. "That's my cell."

She had a cell phone that played *Scooby Doo?*

She flipped open the phone. "Hello?" Her face tightened into a frown. "Just a second." She covered the phone with her hand. "I'll be right back." Then she got up and exited into the hallway.

Leaving his hard, cold questions to roil through his head.

Outside, the sun had begun to shine against the Bighorns. Nick leaned back into the pillow, sifting through the little information she'd given him. What was Piper searching for that would make her lie about being a cook?

A fist tightened in his gut as he stared at the remains of her salad.

The door swung open. "Piper . . . ah, I have to ask you something kinda crazy. . . ."

"What's that, Nick?" The voice didn't belong to Piper. Saul Lovell walked over to the far side of his bed, scanned his monitors, surveying his morphine pack. "How're you feeling?"

"I'm . . . okay. What are you doing here?"

Saul stared at him, his face dark. "You should have signed over the land, Nick. You brought this on yourself."

Nick's mind reeled. In the dim morning light, Saul looked old, even weary, bags under his eyes.

"I'm sorry, Nick. I never thought it would turn out like this. But I don't have a choice. I promise I'll take care of Stefanie as if she were my own." He leaned over Nick, pressed his hand against Nick's mouth.

Nick roared, but beneath Saul's grip, it came out as a moan. Saul pressed his arm into the bed and dodged as Nick took a swipe at him. He felt his energy drain as his arm flopped onto the bed. Then he went weak as he watched Saul Lovell, his father's best friend and lawyer, open his morphine drip to full.

The cold liquid poured into Nick's veins.

⁂

"Back up, Carter. Say that again?" Piper moved close to the window at the end of the hall, where her cell had full reception.

"Elizabeth Hatcher inherited half of the Hatcher estate when her father died."

"You mean Elizabeth Noble—"

"Yes. But it's important to know that she had a sister—Loretta."

"I know about Loretta."

"Loretta got half the estate also."

Piper pressed her hand over her forehead. Her face felt hot, her pulse skipping. She wasn't sure how she felt about Carter interrupting her confession to Nick. She'd been winding herself up for it for two days, each beep of the heart monitor strengthening her resolve to come clean, each hour spent memorizing Nick's face solidifying her feelings for him.

She loved him. He'd gotten inside the wall of her defenses and tended the wounded soil inside. He'd loved her with his patience, his protection, his laughter. His gentleness. And by his sacrifice for Cole, he'd made her believe that if she threw herself at his feet or in his arms, he'd forgive her.

She hoped she wasn't lying to herself.

Then again, that would make the circle complete, wouldn't it? She'd been lying in one form or another for years. Seemed only right that she would finally be her own worst enemy.

But Carter's call had hiccupped her momentum, her stride toward reaching out, finding healing. "Get to the point, Carter."

"You know, someone who ate the cost of your plane ticket yesterday deserves a little respect."

She schooled her tone. "Sorry. Listen, Nick just woke up so—"

"Elizabeth Noble knew about her husband's indiscretion."

Piper's breath caught. "What? How do you know?"

"Probate records. Upon her death, she left her property—her half of the Hatcher ranch—to her eldest son."

"I don't understand. Wasn't the property owned jointly?"

"Nope. According to Beau Hatcher's will, the property passed to Elizabeth. Then she passed it to Nick, making a specific request that it not go to Bishop. In case of Nick's death without a surviving heir, the land was to pass back to the Hatcher estate, aka Saul and Loretta Lovell."

"How much land are we talking about?"

"About half their current holdings."

"Losing the Hatcher property would decrease the Buckle land by half?"

"Yep."

"That means, with Cole's bequest, the Nobles would be left with nearly nothing. They'd never be able to run their cattle on such a small section of land."

"There's more. I looked into the coal-bed mining like you asked. They mine for methane—a source of natural gas found in coal-bed seams. The thing is, one of the byproducts is sulfur. It can contaminate the underground water and turn it into liquid death. Anything that drinks it only becomes more thirsty, which then sucks all the moisture out of them."

"Dying of dehydration right next to a water source." Piper glanced toward Nick's room.

"Not only that, but do you want to know who has the biggest contract for drilling in eastern Montana?"

"Who?" She turned back to the window.

"Saul Lovell."

Piper's breath whooshed out of her, and she lowered her voice. "Saul Lovell's been here the entire time, making sure Nick and Cole made it out of surgery. He's their lawyer."

"And the only one who would benefit if Nick died."

"I'll call you back, Carter." She closed the phone, hurried to Nick's room, her investigator's mind churning.

If Saul was drilling for methane on his property, then the underground streams could easily seep into the Noble land. And poison the cattle.

Saul had been at the roundup, at least until sunset.

If Nick died, Saul would get the land . . . so why was he here, acting like he cared?

She winced . . . the question hitting too close. Only, she *did* care. She couldn't get close to the Nobles without wanting to be part of the Silver Buckle family. Her longing had become a growing ache inside her.

She pushed open the door, cell phone in her grip, hand around the recorder in her pocket.

Saul Lovell looked up at her, one hand over Nick's mouth, the other holding Nick's arm.

Nick's eyes found hers. Angry yet drooping.

"What is going on in here?" Piper demanded, moving to the foot of Nick's bed.

Saul moved so fast that even Piper's karate classes didn't have a chance to kick in. He slammed Piper against the wall, his hand around her neck.

She let out the tiniest of screams before he pinched her throat tight. She gasped against his grip, dropping the cell, raking his arm. She . . . couldn't . . . breathe.

Saul held her there, his face tight, squeezing.

She tried to kick, but Saul dodged her. She twisted, fighting. Fear turned her muscles to lead.

His face swam before her, morphed, and became her father. Piper's fear boiled out of her in a silent scream.

No, no, *no*! She punched at him, aiming for his face, catching his nose. Blood spurted out, and he caught her arm at the wrist and flattened it to the wall.

Black dotted Piper's vision, and she felt her knees weaken. *Please, God.* She heard her pleading in her head, a five-year-old's voice. *Don't let him hurt me!*

A bang sounded. "Leave her alone!"

Saul jerked in surprise.

Piper's knees buckled as his grip loosened.

The voice sounded too familiar, too easy. Footsteps, then someone lunged at Lovell. His fingers peeled off skin as they ripped from her neck.

Piper slumped down against the wall, gasping in hot razors of air. She battled the gray blurring her vision. She heard scuffling, groans. Bone meeting bone.

"Don't you touch her!"

Another crunching blow.

Her breaths sawed in her chest. But as her vision cleared, she wondered for a second if perhaps she *had* died.

Her brother, Jimmy, sprawled over Saul Lovell, both hands wrapped around his neck. Jimmy, filled out and strong, his dark hair scruffy, wearing cowboy boots and a canvas jacket.

Jimmy, coming to her rescue . . . again.

"Jimmy?" she said, her voice unrecognizable.

He looked at her, and suddenly she was back in that ramshackle trailer, watching as their father dragged Jimmy away to give him the beating he was about to hand out to her.

Jimmy had always been there for her. He had always thrown himself between her and her father, an answer to her prayers.

*An answer to her prayers.*

As if God might have heard her all along. As if He *had* been there, even in her darkest moments.

She gulped in that thought as she gripped the bed and stumbled to her feet.

Nick lay fighting the press of sleep, his hand tugging at the morphine drip coursing into his arm.

Piper launched herself onto the bed and in one swift move ripped the IV from his arm, causing Nick to cry out. She pressed her hand over the wound and yelled, "Help! Help!" She looked at her brother, at the hot twist of fury on his face. "Jimmy, let him go."

He didn't move, and in his angry, hurting expression, Piper saw herself. Wanting revenge. Wanting to hurt others because she'd been hurt. "Jimmy, let him go."

Jimmy shook his head—fast, hard. "He tried to kill you."

Piper leaned over and pushed the Call button. *Please, God, send someone!* But she couldn't leave, not with Jimmy squeezing the life out of Saul. "You'll end up back in jail."

"Maybe I deserve jail."

His words felt like a slap, but behind them she heard the guilt, even his worst nightmares—that he'd turn out just like their father. "You're not Russell, Jimmy. You're not that kind of man."

Jimmy flinched. Saul had given up trying to pry him off, his hands flopping at his sides.

"Jimmy, let him go! I know you aren't a killer. I'm sorry—I know I should have believed in you. But I believe in you now. Don't do this."

For the first time, he looked up at her. He looked gaunt and tired, but at her words his anger crumbled.

The door banged open. Dutch and Stefanie barreled in, followed by a nurse. "What happened here?" the nurse demanded.

Jimmy rolled off Saul, breathing hard.

Dutch took one look at Jimmy and hauled him up by the shirt, fury in his eyes.

"No—he's my brother!" Piper screamed. "Saul tried to kill me. And he hurt Nick!"

"What's wrong with Nick?" Stefanie said, grabbing Nick's hand.

Piper climbed off the bed, still keeping pressure on Nick's wound, blood all over her hands. "I think Saul tried to overdose him on morphine."

The nurse leaned over Nick. "Stay with me, Nick."

*Stay with me, Nick.* Piper pressed her lips together, fighting tears.

Nick regained consciousness. He looked at Piper with a question in his eyes. And in them she saw the words he couldn't say, cutting through her heart like a sharp-edged knife: *who are you?*

Piper felt everything inside her begin to shatter. "I'm sorry, Nick. I'm so sorry."

Nick closed his eyes.

The door opened again, and two more nurses entered. "Everyone out. Now!"

Piper backed away, right behind Jimmy and Dutch, who muscled Saul from the floor and dragged him out into the hall.

Dutch cornered all three of them, zeroing in on Piper. "Start explaining."

Piper wrapped her hands around her neck, felt the abrasions from Saul's grip, not sure where to begin. Footsteps echoed down the hall, and all the air went out of her at Maggy's white face and CJ's frightened expression.

"Is Nick okay? What's going on?" She skidded to a stop, seeing Jimmy.

But CJ ran right up to him with a high five. "What are you doing here?"

Confusion rendered Piper nearly speechless. "You know this man?"

CJ looked from Piper to Jimmy and back. "Sure I do. This is Jay. Our hired man."

<hr>

"Nick, wake up! Nick, can you hear me?"

Nick felt buried in the darkness, thick and heavy upon him, suffocating him.

"Nick, squeeze my hand if you can hear me."

He strained to channel his strength to his hand. Was he squeezing? Or was he dreaming that he was squeezing?

"C'mon, Nick, come back to us."

Like a swimmer kicking his way to the surface with his last lungful of air, Nick tunneled through the layers of shadow and confusion and forced his eyes open.

The room swam with colors, vibrant lights that made him blink. He felt sluggish as he turned his head.

"Oh, thank You, Lord." Stefanie stood beside his bed, holding his hand, worry etched in her dark eyes. "I was really scared. You've been out for hours. They flushed your system with IV fluid, but a trace might still remain."

Nick tried to sort through the pieces of his memory, fragments of images. Saul Lovell. Piper. And, oddly, a face from his past. He frowned at Stefanie, not sure how to word his question.

She must have sensed it because she nodded. "Saul Lovell tried to kill you."

He couldn't speak.

"Because of Mom's will. If you die without an heir, all her property reverts back to the Hatchers." She smoothed her hand over his, lightly touching the tape that held his IV in place. His skin felt itchy, and he nearly recoiled. But she was holding on pretty tight, and for some reason he needed that right now. "Saul's been after me for months to sell the Buckle. Piper caught him trying to kill you, and then he tried to kill her too."

Nick found his voice. "I saw a man—"

"Jay Mullins—Piper's brother. He's been working for the St. Johns for the last month. He came in to check on Cole—or rather, Piper—and heard the ruckus."

Nick said nothing, putting together that information. He shook his head. "I think that was Jimmy McPhee. I sent him away for murder a few years ago."

Stefanie's mouth opened a fraction. "Are you sure?"

As the memory crystallized, became sharper, Nick nodded. "Yeah, I'm sure. Believe me when I say I'll never forget his face."

Nick replayed the last several weeks: Piper's abysmal biscuits, her tenacious questions, her quiet posture when he told her about Jenny's death. He went back further to the day Saul Lovell appeared at the café and again saw the woman who'd ordered the salad. Who'd wiped the table with a wet wipe. Who'd covered her wrist with a Band-Aid from a wound . . . or perhaps a scar?

Piper.

Sickness roiled through him. Had she been stalking him? What about Jimmy? Had they been at the helm of the attacks on the ranch?

"Get her," Nick growled.

Stefanie looked ashen. "What is it, Nick? You're scaring me a little."

"Piper and Jimmy were working in cahoots to destroy us."

Stefanie blinked at him, then frowned. "I don't think so. She looked pretty shocked to see him and even more so when CJ called him their hired man. Besides, the cops already have Saul's confession. He's been mining for methane gas, but his land is nearly pumped dry. That's how our cattle died—sulfur poisoned the underground spring that ran into Hatcher's Table. Saul also started the stampede."

Stefanie tucked his hand into his sheets. "Piper's been outside giving a statement for the last couple hours. She's the one who figured out Saul's scheme. He wanted you out of the way to get the Hatcher land, and when Cole died, he planned on buying the St. John place too. Eventually, with so much land gone, the Silver Buckle would have gone under. We would have been forced to sell the rest."

"But what about Pecos? He was at the stampede."

Stefanie shook her head. "CJ tried to ride him, and the horse bucked him off. Pecos ran back to the Silver Buckle. CJ was afraid to tell his parents, but it came out when Dutch accused Jay—Jimmy—of starting the stampede."

"Then why did Piper come to the ranch? It certainly wasn't to cook."

"I don't know. Maybe God brought her here, just like He did you."

He had no words for that. God *had* brought him back. Had given him a chance not only to start over but to be a man of honor. Of grace. To be the son he should have been.

Nick closed his eyes, unable to dislodge the gut feeling that there was more to Piper's story than he could wrap his mind around. He longed to believe the Piper he'd let into his heart, the Piper who had made him laugh, who had shown him his land through new eyes, who had given him the strength to forgive and surrender. But his detective instincts roared to life. "Please go get her, Stef."

He opened his eyes just as she nodded and left the room.

Outside, the sun left a shimmering rim of light over the Bighorns. He wondered how Cole was doing, and for a moment he lifted his gaze to the heavens beyond. *Lord, I don't know what You're doing, but thank You for letting me be here. For not giving up on me. Help me to hear Piper out and to listen. Help me see the truth. Help me give to her what she's given to me.*

The door opened, and Stefanie returned, a grim look on her face. "She's not here, Nick. Piper left."

***

"Jimmy, I still can't believe you've been spying on me." Piper sat in the bench seat of Jimmy's beat-up Ford truck as he drove north toward the Silver Buckle. Her mind was still reeling. She'd listened to his story as he told to the police—how he'd cajoled Carter into telling him Piper's location and how he'd secured a job with the St. Johns to give him proximity to the Buckle ranch. How he'd feared for his sister's safety.

"I wasn't going to let anyone hurt you. Or you hurt anyone else." Jimmy looked thinner than the pictures from the trial. Hard work had turned him lean and muscled. As had prison, she supposed.

"What did you think I'd do to Nick?" Piper kept her voice steady, hoping not to betray her true agenda. It felt surreal to sit next to her big brother, who had saved her on so many occasions. She'd ached with missing him when she and her mother left, and even now she wondered at the man he'd become.

"It wasn't so much what you'd do to Nick as what kind of trouble you'd get into. I read your exposés in the newspaper while I was in prison—Mom sent them to me until she passed—and I saw how you put yourself in dangerous situations. When Carter told me you'd gone to work for the Nobles, I knew you were up to something." He glanced at her, his face betraying the stress over the past years. "I didn't want you to get in over your head."

"Do you think Nick tried to frame you?" Piper weighed Jimmy's expression for signs of hatred.

His expression turned solemn. "Nick was doing his job. I was rattled, and I'd been drunk the night I went out to help Jenny. To be frank, I wasn't sure what happened, and I was scared. A part of me *was* afraid that I had done something to her."

"You'd never kill someone, Jimmy."

"I could have killed Saul." He swallowed. "And I wanted to kill my dad a few times."

Piper sat with her hands in her lap, her eyes filling. "Jimmy, I never thanked you for what you did . . . today and . . . back then. For all those times you . . . you stood in the way when–"

Jimmy reached across the seat, taking her hand. "I remember the day you were born. I was six, and Dad brought me into the room. I hadn't ever had a mom, and your mom loved me like I was her own. She read me stories and drove me to school, and I adored her. So, when you were born and she put you in my arms and said, 'Here's your baby sister,' I knew I had a job to do. I had to protect you. And that feeling's never gone away."

Piper wiped her cheek, flicking away the tear that slid down her face. "We should have taken you with us when we left. Mom was so scared that Dad would come after her. She thought that you'd be fine with him–that it was us that he hated, not you.  But I was afraid for you. I'm so sorry, Jimmy."

He squeezed her hand. "I missed you too, Sis."

Piper looked at his fingers, woven through hers, and her throat filled. "I'm sorry that I didn't come and visit you in prison."

He shrugged, but his face jerked.

Piper stared out the windshield, replaying her conversation with the police. After her and Jimmy's statements and a conversation with Carter, the Sheridan police had arrested Saul on charges of attempted murder.

Which left only Nick's unanswered questions. Piper knew then that she couldn't face him. Couldn't watch the disappointment, even hatred appear on his face. Besides, she had a job to get back to. A report to put together.

She let out a sigh.

"Piper, Carter told me you went to the ranch for some article you were writing. Did you get what you were looking for?"

Had she been looking for Nick to shatter all her preconceptions about men? to find emotions she'd thought forever buried? for God to break her heart enough to let Him inside? Nick wasn't the bully, the abuser she'd pegged him to be, and that had rattled her enough to loosen her grip on everything she had believed—about love, about friendship, about God. But more than that, being with Nick only made her long for something more. A family. A home. She remembered her thoughts the day she'd driven to the Silver Buckle, a prayer that she'd assumed had been merely a thought, an empty wish.

She had pleaded that God would help her find justice. Even a measure of peace. Seeing Nick surrender his life for Cole had made her believe that people could change. Be healed from their pasts, their hurts. Made her believe she could be healed. At least it made her realize she *wanted* to be healed.

Piper continued to stare out at the sagebrush, the rocky hills, the sky that stretched to eternity. Perhaps she *had* found what she was after at the Silver Buckle without even knowing it. Maybe, in fact, it was a God thing.

*"He heals all your diseases . . . and crowns you with love and compassion."* What might it feel like to let go of the anger, the bitterness? to fall at Jesus' hem and beg for healing? to be shown compassion and granted peace?

*Heal me, Lord. Please make me whole. Give me peace.*

"You're in love with him, aren't you?"

Piper looked at Jimmy.

He smirked as he put his hand back on the wheel. "It seemed that the way you were hovering over him the last few days, you'd given out too much of yourself on this assignment. Let him in under your skin."

Was Nick under her skin? Yes. And in her pores and her mind and her heart. "It doesn't matter anymore."

She leaned back into the seat, closing her eyes. As the truck droned, eating the miles, she fell into a dreamless sleep.

# ~ CHAPTER 21

"YOU CLEAN UP WELL, Mr. St. John." Maggy came up behind Cole, putting her hands on his shoulders, and beamed at him through the mirror.

Cole raised an eyebrow. At best, he looked like he'd spent the winter in Siberia—he was pale and gaunt; his hair was thinning. The suit and coat only gave the illusion of being robust and capable. Inside, he felt as if he might be waking from a long hibernation. And if having a defective liver hadn't nearly killed him, lying around the house all summer as CJ, Maggy, and their new hired man had worked the ranch nearly had. By next spring he'd be strong and healthy and riding Suds again. Working whatever land they still had after today's meeting in court.

He could hardly believe the grace the hospital had given them—writing off half their expenses and allowing them to pay the rest over time. However, even if they received Bishop's land, it would take them two lifetimes to pay it off—his and Maggy's as they worked together.

Cole touched his hands to hers. "You're the eye candy here, Mrs. St. John."

Maggy nearly glowed. The summer sun had touched her skin with a magical kiss and streaked her hair in tones of copper. He'd always loved her green cardigan, black skirt, and boots, but it was the anticipation in her eyes that set Maggy apart today. A new chapter in their lives, starting this afternoon in Sheridan.

"Are you nervous?" He turned, wrapped his arms around her waist.

Maggy cupped his face in her work-worn hands. They smelled faintly of lotion and a fresh coat of nail polish. "A little." She ducked her head.

He caught her chin, raised it to look in her eyes. "It'll be okay. I promise. I'll be there. And Nick . . . well, after all he's done, he deserves this day."

"I'm not worried about CJ—well, a little, I guess. But not as much as Bishop's will. Nick could do it, Cole—he could have it set aside. And then—"

"Shh, Mags. We'll trust God. He's taken us this far. I think we can trust Him for the rest." He leaned his forehead against hers.

Maggy forced a small smile.

Leaning down, Cole kissed her ever so gently. She closed her eyes, and he felt her relax, lean into his embrace.

Maggy. How could he have ever wished for her to return to Nick? He tightened his arms around her, deepening his kiss, feeling something awaken inside him. Something new and alive.

A fresh start.

He leaned back, feeling a curl of warmth that he'd ignored for far too long. "Mags, I'm sorry for ever doubting your love for me."

He saw in her eyes what his words meant. How they dug deep and found tender soil. "It's oka–"

"No, hear me out. I've always felt like a thief. Like I stole you from Nick. Like I stole CJ from Nick."

He watched her frown and put his finger over her lips. "I couldn't help it. You were such a gift to me–I felt shame all the time because I knew Nick wouldn't ever know that. And those feelings of shame turned into hatred for him. It made me angry at Nick, made me even despise him."

"But you forgave him. You said you did."

"I did forgive him. But I never got over the shame, the feeling that I got away with something I didn't deserve–like the thief hanging on the cross next to Jesus getting heaven. Until the surgery. Nick might have given me a part of himself out of guilt, but I saw it as a gift of grace. I didn't deserve that gift, but neither did I deserve you or CJ, and God gave me both of you."

He heard his voice begin to crack and swallowed the emotions in his throat, continuing. "More than that, He gave me a father and a heritage, even if I never have the land." He took her hands. "I'm so ashamed that I ever asked you to marry Nick, honey. I know it felt like I was scorning the love you've given me since the day we were married. Lying there in that hospital bed and every day after, I realized that not believing in your love would be like me ripping out the organ Nick gave me and handing it back to him. I'll never be able to earn your love or Nick's gift. But if I could, it wouldn't be a gift. It wouldn't be an act of love. My only choice is to accept the grace."

He ran his hands down her arms, caught her hands. "Nick's sacrifice deserves my respect. Your love deserves my respect, and

I promise to be the best husband and father I can be." He added new warmth to his gaze. "I know I've also held back from you what you really wanted. A family."

Her eyes glistened.

"Lord willing, we'll have another child, Maggy." He brushed his fingers through her soft hair. "A girl with a love of horses."

She smiled despite her tears.

"I hate the fact that Nick doesn't know CJ is his son. He's such an incredible kid. I look at him and long for Nick to know he's a part of that." Cole wiped one of her tears with a thumb. "Things *will* change when Nick finds out. But we have to trust that God will continue the work He started in our lives, through the good times and the bad, whatever may come." His gaze traced her face, landed on her mouth. "And today, my Maggy, will be one of those very, very good times."

He kissed her again, this time molding her body to his.

For the first time in what seemed like years, she wrapped her arms around him and really kissed him back, reminding him of everything he'd missed. Everything he still had.

Everything his brother had given him.

The judge peered down at Nick. Thick necked and white haired, he had the voice of a man who brooked no argument. Sorta reminded Nick of his father, and as if sucked back in time, he felt sixteen and about to be dressed down.

Nick felt the silence and the smell of polished wood in the tiny paneled room settle upon him; a sweat broke out across the back of his neck. Last time he'd been in a courtroom, he'd been testifying against Jimmy McPhee. And now, like then, he'd been wrong. He managed a tight nod.

Why hadn't he withdrawn his petition to keep Cole from inheriting Noble land? Well, when he filed it, he'd been a different person, an angry person. A prodigal looking for redemption.

Who knew that he'd find a sort of redemption in giving away a huge chunk of himself? That by sacrificing and letting go of his birthright, he might earn what he'd always hoped for: his fathers' smiles–Bishop's . . . and his heavenly Father's. The past three months–and recuperation time on the sofa–had given him ample time to read Bishop's Bible. To follow the scribbled notes in the margins, to learn exactly how his father had worked out his faith.

He'd learned what it meant to be a Noble. And while he certainly couldn't claim to be the finished product, he at least felt as if he'd finally figured out what it meant to walk the path carved out for him.

He'd taken the first step today. He placed his hands on the oak table and pushed to his feet. "Your Honor, could I–?"

"Sit down, son. We'll get to arguments in a moment."

"But I–"

"Sit."

Nick pursed his lips, cast a glance at Maggy. She had her arms crossed over her chest, her face solemn. But her posture had lost that defiant, angry edge. In fact, the few times she'd been to the Silver Buckle, delivering casseroles or bringing CJ to visit, she'd been . . . kind. It made him see her as he should have–a woman of strength and humor. He admired how she encouraged CJ as he went on to win two more roping events at local rodeos. And the day she unloaded Pecos and ushered him back into the corral, Nick hadn't been able to speak.

Seeing her, however, had only made him miss Piper more. Miss her laughter, her listening ear. Miss her smile. By the time he'd returned to the ranch, she'd cleaned out her gear and vanished. Leaving him with only fragments of pain.

Cole looked at him.

Nick gave him a wry smile, which Cole returned.

"I've reviewed the materials with respect to the petition regarding the bequest of Bishop A. Noble. Frankly, this case is a mess. I see the primary personal representative is currently in custody, indicted for attempted murder?"

Nick nodded, quelling the flash of anger Lovell's name ignited. "But I–"

"Quiet, Mr. Noble." The judge shuffled the papers before him. "And the secondary personal representative is Dutch Johnson?"

"That's me, Your Honor." Dutch's voice came from right behind Nick.

"Okay, Mr. Noble, I'm ready to hear your submissions."

Nick found his feet. Cleared his throat. Smiled at the judge. "I'm withdrawing my petition."

The judge gave him a look that made Nick feel about three feet tall. "Why didn't you do so before now? This is a waste of the court's time and resources."

"Because he had surgery, Your Honor," Cole said from his side of the room.

"Quiet." The judge sent Cole a dark look before turning back to Nick. "Do you have a stipulation?

"Uh . . . a stipulation?"

"The document that sets out the terms on which you have settled the matter?"

"Settled? We haven't settled anything, have we?" Nick glanced at Maggy, at Cole. Well, maybe they had.

"Do you have a stipulation?" the judge repeated.

"No . . . I just made a mistake," Nick said. *Too many mistakes.*

The judge gave a long sigh. "If you don't have a stipulation, I will have to hear the matter. Proceed with your submission."

Nick stared at the judge. "I'm sorry, Your Honor. I'm not prepared to make any submissions. I want to withdraw. The bequest should be distributed as Bishop wanted."

Maggy stood up. "That's not entirely true, Your Honor. Bishop wanted the land to stay in the Noble family."

"Order! You'll get your chance, young lady."

Maggy sat down.

The judge turned back to Nick. "Continue."

"I have no other submissions, Your Honor." Nick shook his head.

The judge turned to Maggy and Cole. "Now you may speak."

Maggy stood up and smiled. "Okay, good. We'd like you to set aside the will."

"Maggy!" Nick said.

"Maggy?" Cole repeated.

"Order!" The judge banged his gavel. He turned to Maggy. "What?"

Maggy crossed her arms. "On the basis that I was present when the will was signed. And it's the right thing to do." She turned to Cole. "I don't want you to get this land because I was quiet. That's lying and wrong." Then she looked at Nick. "But Cole is a Noble too . . . and I was thinking that . . . well, instead of splitting the land, we'd–"

"–combine it." Nick said the words softly, reading her expression, the idea growing like a fire in his chest. "Combine it." He looked at Cole. "Double the size of the Silver Buckle. Your land, mine, and Bishop's land . . . with all of us Nobles working the ranch."

"I'll have some order here!"

A smile creeped up Cole's face. "You have to promise to actually do some work, Nick."

Nick grinned. "This coming from a guy who used to sneak out on Sundays to watch a certain redhead train her horses?"

Maggy blushed, looking at Cole.

He shrugged. "Nick thought it was his idea."

"Listen!" the judge growled. "Order, all of you. If you interrupt again, I'll have you removed from the courtroom." He shook his head, rolling his eyes. "There is a reason people hire attorneys to represent them." He looked at Nick, then at Cole. "Are you sure you're sitting on the right sides of the room?"

Nick smiled at Cole.

Clearly, they were making the judge crazy. Now the judge zeroed in on Maggy. "Are you listed as a beneficiary to the land in the will, Mrs. St. John?"

"No. But Bishop gave me a horse." She flicked a glance at Nick. "Sorta."

"Then why aren't you a beneficiary?"

"He gave me the horse *before* he died, but he wrote it into the will."

"Did he actually give you the horse, or were you just using the horse?"

She glanced at Nick, and he saw her redden. "He gave it to me. I never rode it."

"But if he gave it before he drafted the will, then you had no reason to exert undue influence on him." The judge put down the paper. "Is there any other basis on which the will should be set aside?"

Maggy shook her head.

"Mr. Noble, do you have anything to add?"

Nick glanced at Cole, his brother. The son who had earned the Noble name. "No, Your Honor."

The judge nodded. "Okay. I'm going to deny Mr. Noble's petition. The will stands. Your personal representative will assure the assets are divided and . . . recombined if you so wish."

"Dandy," Dutch muttered from behind them.

The judge gathered his papers as Nick turned to Maggy. "You didn't have to do that."

"This is Noble land. It belongs to the Noble men." She looped her arm around Cole, beaming at him. "I want to see them working it together."

"Me too," Nick said, holding out his hand to Cole.

Cole shook his head and wrapped him in a one-armed embrace.

Maggy turned away, glancing at Dutch.

Nick saw her wipe away moisture under her eyes.

"By the way, Nick, we, ah, have something to tell you. Will you let us take you out for lunch?" Cole asked, releasing him.

"Lunch sounds good. Now that we're both back on solid food."

Cole grinned, and Nick followed them out of the courtroom.

They found Stefanie and CJ in the courtyard, throwing pennies into the fountain.

Stefanie raised her eyebrows in silent question. He'd told her of his intent to withdraw the petition on the drive to Sheridan, and she'd responded with a hug and another you're-my-hero speech. He could get used to that.

"Get everything settled?" she asked.

"Yes," Nick said.

"Mostly," Maggy answered. "Would you and Auntie Stefanie like to get some lunch? Daddy and I are going to talk to Uncle Nick."

*Uncle Nick.* How he loved the sound of that.

Evidently, by Stefanie's grin, she had also embraced the auntie moniker. She took CJ's hand. "I hear a pizza calling our name." She winked at Maggy.

Nick sensed a conspiracy as Dutch left with them. "What's going on?"

Maggy's gaze had lingered on her son, her eyes still misty. Oh no—what if CJ had the same disease Cole had? After Cole's surgery—and getting a complete medical history from Nick—they'd narrowed his disease to a genetic disorder passed on through Irene—Wilson's disease—a condition that collected copper in his system, shutting down his organs one by one. A condition Cole's mother had most likely died from in the form of liver failure.

A condition Nick couldn't have possibly caused. The relief at that news, along with Cole's forgiveness, felt overpowering. But now what if CJ–? "What's wrong with CJ?"

Maggy gave him a sharp look. "Nothing. Why?"

"It's just . . . you're scaring me." He ran a hand behind his neck, feeling his tension. "He doesn't have the same condition as his dad, does he?"

"You mean smart but cocky, with a tendency to think he rules the world?"

Nick stared at her, his mouth open. "I don't think Cole's that cocky."

Cole grinned. "Yeah, but you are, pal. Like father, like son."

Nick chuckled.

But Cole and Maggy didn't.

After a second, something clicked in Nick's brain—a realization that fit into place with a whoosh. His breath felt hot, heavy in his chest. He opened his mouth but couldn't breathe, couldn't speak—*son?*

"Nick, are you okay?" Maggy grabbed his arm.

He looked at her. Saw again that horrible day when he'd accused Cole and Maggy of . . . of . . . *"I would never betray you."* Her words nearly one-two punched him. "I think I need to sit." His legs turned to rubber as he reached out for the edge of the fountain. He sat hard.

"Do you need to put your head between your knees?" This from Cole, who didn't sound in the least concerned.

He took in the grin on his brother's face and felt a sweat break out along his spine. "You're not . . . I don't . . . *how* . . . ?"

Maggy gave him a sad shake of her head. "How do you think?"

"But we only . . . that once . . . oh, Mags, I didn't know. I'm sorry. . . ." He swallowed as memory shook him. "You tried to tell me in the note, didn't you?"

Maggy sank down before him. "You got the note?"

Nick raked his hands through his hair, remembering. "I thought you were writing me a Dear John letter. I mean, I'd just seen you arrive with Cole . . . and I was angry. I crumpled it up and threw it in the trash." He leaned forward. "Yeah, maybe I do need to put my head between my knees."

He felt Cole's hand on his shoulder. "Congratulations, man. You're a dad."

*A dad.*

Nick studied his best friend. The man who had raised CJ to be the boy he was . . . the man he would be. *The father to his son.* "You are too."

Maggy took Cole's hand. "For years I thought you were angry. That you didn't want CJ. But you should be a part of his life, Nick. He's so much like you in so many ways."

Nick scrubbed his face and shook his head. "Does CJ know?"

Cole slipped his arm around Maggy. "We thought we'd all tell him together. Both his dads."

Nick felt a smile fill him, through every cell in his body. Him, a dad. CJ, his son. They had two-thirds of a family.

A family that needed a wife. A mother.

"I have to find Piper."

Cole raised an eyebrow. "Not the response I expected, but . . . well . . ."

Maggy grinned. "Guess what I picked up today while we were waiting for our hearing?" She reached into her satchel and tugged out a copy of *Montana Monthly.*

On the cover he recognized a sunrise climbing the eastern horizon. A picture that looked very much like it might have been taken from the Cathedral. "What's this?"

Maggy leaned over him and flipped the pages until she came to a dog-earred article called "Everyday Heroes." At the top of the page was the picture of him and Cole, holding their silver-buckle prizes for their championship roping win. "When she called to ask for the picture, I told her I'd get your permission." Her eyes gleamed. "Whoops." She released the magazine. "Interesting reading, if I do say so myself."

"She's a journalist?"

Maggy lifted a shoulder. "Or a cook. Depends on you, I think."

❧

"When I said take me with you, I was thinking that I'd end up some place warmer, with an ocean view and excellent coffee, not across town with a view of the railroad." Carter stood on the stoop of the two-story Victorian, holding his Styrofoam cup close to his face, blowing on it as he shivered. "If you're going to rope me into volunteering, at least you could give me off-street parking."

"You're late." Piper opened the door wider for him to step inside.

"I had a deadline—I know that means nothing to you now. Traitor."

Piper grinned. "I'll give you a parka, the picture of Puget Sound that used to hang over my desk, and a gift card to Montana Coffee Traders if you carry in that box of clothes that just came in." Piper pushed past him and picked up one of the boxes left on the porch. The smell of cookies baking escaped behind her.

"Oh, Piper, you didn't—"

"Come inside before we heat the entire city."

She lugged the box into the family room. Marci and her daughter, Amelia, sat together, watching *Scooby Doo*. At seventeen, Marci had the reflexes of a streetwise forty-year-old. Still, sitting with her four-year-old daughter curled in her lap and purposely using her blonde hair to curtain her battered face, her blue eyes glued to the television screen, she looked about thirteen years old.

The sight skewered Piper's heart anew. So many girls starting life way too early. She sat beside them on the donated, fraying sectional.

"Miss Piper!" Amelia crawled over to her, her blonde ringlets wild around her head. She plunked herself in Piper's lap without apology. "Can I have a cookie?"

Piper popped a kiss on the little girl's forehead. "After they cool." She looked past her at Marci. "You two doing okay today?" Marci's face had begun to heal, the purple bruise that had swelled half her cheek fading to a greenish yellow. With her arm set, her body had mustered its white cells and begun healing. Her psyche and emotions might take longer. Much longer. But Hope House offered time and a safe haven. Piper wished the shelter had been around when she and her mother had been sleeping in their car, living hand to mouth.

She still couldn't believe how much her life had changed over the past three months. How God had taken her feeble prayer—no, her feeble *moan*—and turned it into a fresh start. Who knew that surrendering her time, her writing to God's work might help her wounds heal? might give her the purpose she'd been searching for her entire life? might make her whole?

"I read your article in *Montana Monthly*," Marci said. "It's a true story?"

Piper nodded, putting Amelia down and opening the box in front of her. Toddler clothes, donated from a local church.

"I can't believe that guy would ever give his liver to someone he'd hated."

Piper didn't look at her. She smoothed a pair of light blue overalls. Her throat felt thick as she drove Nick's face from her thoughts. Sometimes missing him nearly doubled her over with pain. Other times she found a smile, remembering his teasing. His laughter. The way he'd held her.

Most of the time, however, she only remembered the expression on his face when he'd asked, "Was that Jimmy McPhee?"

Apparently they weren't going to ride into the sunset together. Not that she'd expected him to chase after her, but his silence only confirmed that some things couldn't be forgiven.

"He's pretty hot too." Marci made a sound of appreciation.

Piper rolled her eyes. She tossed the overalls back into the box. "I need a cookie." Rising, she saw that Carter had finished lugging the rest of the boxes inside and was shucking off his jacket. "Thanks, Carter."

His brown eyes twinkled. He hadn't suffered too much by her recent change in careers. Her absence left a void he easily filled at the *Kalispell Gazette*. So long, food critic—hello, features editor. The day she'd returned to the *Gazette*, cleaned out her desk, and hung out her shingle as a freelance writer had been the day her life truly began. And who knew that inside her inquisitive mind she had a storehouse of ideas and stories she could use to raise support for Hope House? Her newsletter and features in the local papers had actually doubled Hope House's summer revenue.

Most of all, she'd found a way to reach out and find healing. For herself. For other women who still bled. A way to reach out that didn't endanger her life.

"Want a cookie?" she asked Carter as she headed to the kitchen.

"Are you doing the baking?"

"Oh, ha-ha," she said, hiding a smile. Just because a girl burned a few biscuits . . . and she was getting better. Much better.

She found Jodie, the housemother, bending over the oven, retrieving another batch of snickerdoodles. The widowed grand-mother made them all feel like kids at Christmas with her pamper-ing. Precisely what a group of hurting women needed. Piper snuck behind her and snatched a cooling cookie just as Jodie turned. She made to slap Piper's hand.

Piper waggled her eyebrows. "I think we should print your recipe in the next newsletter. Mmm."

"Flattery won't get you another cookie." Jodie set the tray on a hot pad and loaded another into the oven.

Piper leaned her hip against the counter. "A few more tries and I might get this figured out."

"Piper, I'm sure that someday soon you'll make excellent cook-ies," Jodie said. "You've got the touch."

"I couldn't agree more." The voice came from the doorway. Slow and drawled out, with a hint of arrogance in the tone.

Piper's breath caught, and she turned, shock turning her mouth dry.

*Nick?*

Carter stood behind him, giving her a sly grin.

*What–?* Her mind reeled, trying to sort fact from fantasy. Sure, she'd dreamed this, but–

"Hi, George." Nick entered the kitchen, his smile and devastating good looks sucking every thought from her.

She stared at him, mouth agape. Cookie half eaten.

He tipped his hat to Jodie. "Ma'am, can I have a moment, please?"

Jodie glanced from Piper to Nick, then back to Piper. "I'll be right outside if you need me, honey." She gave Nick a grandmother glare on her way out.

Piper let herself smirk.

Three months of recuperation had revived Nick's rugged cowboy looks, and in a leather jacket, a pair of jeans, boots, and his familiar black Stetson—well, she just might swoon.

He swept his hat off, looking suddenly sheepish. "You're hard to find."

She wanted to leap at him, to let her feelings and everything inside spill out. But it all came back to her in a whoosh—the deception, the game she'd played, hoping to hurt him. She put her cookie down, her stomach roiling, and wiped her hands on her jeans. "How did you find me?"

He harrumphed. "I was a detective, remember?"

"He called the newspaper," Carter piped up from the other room.

Piper shook her head. "Apparently I need to pay my sources better."

Nick lifted a shoulder in a shrug. "I called the magazine first. They gave me your old number."

And she suspected that Carter had answered.

Nick held his hat in his hands and didn't make another move toward her. Except, of course, for having traveled over three hundred miles to Kalispell.

"What are you doing here?" She didn't mean for her tone to be so sharp. Nick had never been anything but kind to her. But a good defense is a strong offense, and right now she didn't know what else to say to keep her heart from springing right out of her chest and into his arms.

Nick didn't flinch. Simply fastened his dark eyes on her, probing, paralyzing. "Why did you leave, Piper?"

She gave a cry of disbelief. "Why do you think? Because . . . I . . ." She turned away, unable to say the words. *Because I was ashamed of myself. Because I loved you, and I couldn't watch you hate me.* She shook her head. "Because I was sorry, but I didn't know how to say that."

She heard him put his hat on the counter. Felt his hands on her shoulders. She stiffened.

"You said it now."

She shrugged.

"Did you come to the Silver Buckle to spy on me, Piper? to get me to say that I framed your brother?"

Piper closed her eyes.

"Oh, George." Nick turned her around, lifted her chin, but she couldn't look at him. She stared instead at his chin. At the smattering of dark whiskers. "I wish you'd trusted me. Given me the benefit of the doubt." He blew out a breath. "I learned the hard way that jumping to conclusions only leads to pain. I would have listened."

"Would you have forgiven me?" She hated how feeble her voice sounded.

"I would have. And I have."

Her eyes flickered up to his. She frowned, trying to comprehend his words.

He cupped his hand to her cheek, running his thumb down it. "Don't you get it, Piper? God used you to help me see what He had for me. All that I could have, all that I'd missed out on. The ranch, a life. A family. I fell in love with you."

She felt her emotions flicker across her face, her resolve start to shatter. She touched his chest, flattening both palms against it, knowing she should push him away but longing with everything in her to curl inside his protective embrace. "Nick . . ."

"You probably think I don't know the real you, Piper, but I do. I know that you're tenderhearted, and you fight for what you believe in. I know that you have wounds, but you're reaching past them to help others. I know that you're a hard worker, you're so stubborn I'd like to strangle you, and you have a wallop of a roundhouse kick."

She smirked.

"I know that you are afraid of getting hurt, but you put yourself at risk for other people . . . otherwise you wouldn't have stuck around the hospital for three days just because I asked you to–"

"They had real food–"

"I know that you have a wicked throw, and you're willing to learn new things even if you're afraid, like riding a horse or cooking. I also know that you love the Buckle. I saw it in your face, in your eyes. And most of all, I know you love me too."

His words had tangled her emotions in knots. Now she felt a spurt of panic. "How–?"

"I read your article. I've had a lot of names thrown at me over the years . . . but *hero* has never been among them. Thank you."

"Nick, you *are* a hero. You're brave and kind, and you do the right thing. You made me believe that a man could be honorable. Noble." Her mouth tweaked up at her words. "There's something else too.

Remember when you said that you thought God had brought you to the Buckle to find me?" She felt herself begin to tremble, but she had to get the words out. "I think He wanted me to find you, too, and to learn that He'd been looking out for me all along. That He could heal me and give me a fresh start."

She shrugged, trying to deny the impact of her words, but his eyes misted, and it curled a wave of warmth inside her. Yes, God had sent her to find Nick. And so much more.

Nick's gaze traced her eyes, a look filled with amazement, with hope, with desire. Then he cradled her face in both hands and kissed her. Sweetly, gently, the essence of the man she'd come to know.

She closed her eyes and kissed him back. *Nick*. He tasted of sweet coffee, of sunshine, and of strength and hope.

Nick pulled away, just enough to lean his forehead to hers. "I love you, Piper. And I know this is a lot to ask, but please, will you come back to the Silver Buckle with me?"

Piper backed away, a slight frown on her face. "As a cook?"

He broke into a grin. "No! For an investigative reporter, you have trouble putting the facts together." He caught her hands, then knelt on one knee before her.

Every muscle inside Piper stiffened, caught in shock.

"Piper George Cookie Sullivan, will you marry me?"

Silence trickled out as she stared at him, her mouth falling open.

"Yes! Say yes!" Carter yelled from the other room.

A smile slid up Nick's face.

Heat filled Piper's cheeks, but tears pricked her eyes. Marry Nick? The arrogant, swaggering outlaw who'd broken through her defenses, roped her heart, and stolen it clean out of her chest? Could she be his wife, let him be her hero?

*"Your faith has made you well. Go in peace."* A wave of heat, of realization, of something that tasted like joy swept through her. God had redeemed her, healed her . . . and now crowned her with love. He'd sent her to the wide spaces of the Silver Buckle to break through the pain and fears that had held her prisoner for so long, to a new life. A life of love, a life of healing. A big sky kind of life.

Piper's nod started small, her smile peeking through the layers of fear to emerge full out and whole. "Yes, Nick. Yes, I'll marry you."

Nick's expression left her breathless. He stood and swept her up, holding her tight. He smelled like his own brand of cologne—leather and hard work and sunshine and laugher and passion. "You are the proof that God is compassionate and abounding in love." He buried his head into her neck. "I love you, Curious George."

"I love you too, Nick." Piper leaned back, catching his face in her hands, and kissed him. Thoroughly. Freely.

Without fear.

When she released him, his eyes twinkled. "But you have to make me one promise."

She raised her eyebrows, one eye tightening. "What?"

"Please, please let me do the cooking."

# ≈ A NOTE FROM THE AUTHOR ≈

I have two friends. Let's call them Jim and John. Both are great guys, men I grew up with. They're friends. One day Jim gets sick. He's sick for a long time until the doctors discover he has liver failure. He has a beautiful wife and four sweet children. Jim is dying, and without a liver transplant, he won't live to see his children grow up. His entire family (and it's a large one) is tested. No one is a match. A prayer request goes out to churches far and wide. For two years nothing happens.

Then one day John, who has been praying for Jim, decides to go to the doctor and get tested to see if he's a match. Miraculously, though they are unrelated, he matches. Although he has a wife and three little boys, John decides to give part of his liver to Jim. John spends the next year preparing for this surgery, taking care of himself, eating right. And then one day he risks his life to save the life of his friend.

Jim lives. John lives. And it makes me ponder the gift of grace—what it means to give—and receive.

Meanwhile, I am studying Philippians—especially verse 1:6: "I am certain that God, who began the good work within you, will continue his work until it is finally finished on the day when Christ Jesus returns." I'm overjoyed with a God who is constantly at work in my life, through all times and circumstances, and I wonder what that might look like from the view of a person with a tainted past, whatever that might be.

For a year, God kept bringing these two events to my mind, tangling them with the love I have of all things cowboys (trucks, horses, country music). Then one day . . . I went fishing. While I was trying to land a walleye, I told my fishing pals (Dan, Bob, and Andrew—yeah, I see the oddball in the group) about my story. I discovered that Bob just so happened to live on a ranch.

A year later I found myself on a ranch outside a little town called Otter, Montana. I fell in love with the big sky, the quiet wind, the wide-open spaces, and the passage I was studying at the time—Psalm 103—came to life for me. As I stood on the bluffs, I got a glimpse of what it might mean for God to separate us from our sins so much that we can no longer even see them! And loving us beyond even the heavens. Right there, Nick's story took life.

*Reclaiming Nick* is about God drawing a man back to the person he could be, helping him reclaim the legacy he'd lost, and then giving that blessing to others. It's a story for all of us really. The truth is that God throws out our mistakes "as far from us as the east is from the west" and allows us to start over. Again and again, if necessary. It is possible to be healed in our spirits, like the woman who touched Jesus' robe. Or like Cole, with new life inside.

God is at work in our lives. This is both a hope and a promise. And most importantly a gift of grace. I pray that you are able to get a view of His love for you, through all circumstances, all times.

Thank you for reading *Reclaiming Nick*. I hope you'll join me for the next installment of the Noble Legacy—Rafe's story. In the meantime, "Praise the Lord, everything he has created, everything in all his kingdom." As for me—I too will praise the Lord!

God bless you!

In His grace,
*Susan May Warren*

# ABOUT THE AUTHOR

SUSAN MAY WARREN recently returned home after serving eight years with her husband and four children as missionaries in Khabarovsk, Far East Russia. Now writing full-time as her husband runs a lodge on Lake Superior in northern Minnesota, she and her family enjoy hiking and canoeing and being involved in their local church.

Susan holds a BA in mass communications from the University of Minnesota and is a multipublished author of novellas and novels with Tyndale, including *Happily Ever After*, the American Christian Romance Writers' 2003 Book of the Year and a 2003 Christy Award finalist. Other books in the series include *Tying the Knot* and *The Perfect Match*, the 2004 American Christian Fiction Writers' Book of the Year. *Flee the Night, Escape to Morning,* and *Expect the Sunrise* comprise her romantic-adventure, search-and-rescue series.

*Reclaiming Nick* is the first book in Susan's new romantic series.

Susan invites you to visit her Web site at
**www.susanmaywarren.com.**
She also welcomes letters by e-mail at
**susan@susanmaywarren.com.**

# 🌿TAMING RAFE

RAFE NOBLE, TWO-TIME world champion bull rider and current king of the gold buckle, had never met a bull he feared. Oh, sure, he'd been afraid before, that sort of nervous tension before a ride that buzzed every nerve ending and slicked his hand inside his taped-tight leather glove. But normally he shook it off the second he wound the bull rope, sticky with rosin, around the animal's chest and wedged it around his grip. Then the adrenaline, the heat, took over.

And for eight long, harrowing seconds, it was just man against beast.

With rare exception, man won.

However, as Rafe now straddled the champion bull known as Doc, coldness rushed through him. Something foreign and overwhelming ignited a tremble from deep within his bones.

For the first time since he was thirteen he felt . . . terror.

Maybe it was just the residual agony of watching one of his fellow bull riders being carried out on a stretcher only minutes earlier. Maybe it was the roar of the crowd hammering at the raging headache he'd nursed most of the day. It could be the fact that he rode in pain, that he'd had to tape his hand, wear his knee brace, and the sports medicine doctor had reminded him that one more fracture to his neck would land him in a wheelchair permanently.

Or perhaps it was just the eerie feeling that hung in the air tonight, along with the smells of animal sweat and popcorn and leather and dirt, a surreal sense that tragedy hovered right outside the ring of spectators.

Whatever the reason, as Rafe worked his rope around his hand, through his index finger, then hit his grip with his fist to tighten it, he couldn't shake the bone-deep feeling that tonight someone would die.

Even the bullfighters, the brave men who distracted the bull as the thrown or triumphant riders scrambled to safety, seemed jumpy. Rafe caught eyes with his pal Manuel. Dressed in his blue-and-red vest, a black cowboy hat, and long shorts and cleats, the man had agility that kept him ahead of horns and made the crowd gasp. And he'd saved Rafe's hide on more than a few occasions.

Manuel nodded, and despite the distance between them, the roar of the crowd, the announcer, and the advice from fellow cowboys as Rafe settled into his mount, he could hear Manuel's mouthed words: "Get 'er done."

Rafe returned the slightest nod and refrained from searching for Manuel's six-year-old son and pretty wife, Lucia, in the audience. Rafe had arranged their tickets and trip up from New Mexico to see Manuel perform under the big lights of the PBR World Championship in Las Vegas.

"You're my favorite bull rider," little Manny had said as he handed Rafe his hat to sign at the pre-event celebrity showcase.

Behind Manny, a leggy blonde cowgirl with a black T-shirt emblazoned with the Professional Bull Riding logo gave him a loaded smile.

Rafe winked at her and returned his attention to Manny. "Are you going to be a bullfighter like your daddy when you get big?" he asked, signing the brim.

"Oh no. I wanna be just like you," Manny had said.

Rafe gave a half chuckle and plopped the hat back on Manny's head, but the kid's words and his shiny, dark, hero-worshiping gaze made his gut twist. The feeling came too often these days.

"Our next bull rider, two-time world champion and overall leader going into the short round . . ."

The announcer brought Rafe's attention back to the snorting animal he straddled. He blew out several short breaths and banged his protective vest with his free hand. His biceps tightened against the sleeve of his rolled-up shirt, and he set his feet into the spur position under his fringed black chaps, scooting up tight against his grip.

*"Don't ride tonight, Rafe."*

He heard the voice deep inside. Soft yet clear. Clenching his teeth, he refused to listen to Fear's whispers. Besides, he had no choice. He'd never had a choice really, but tonight his title was on the line.

"All the way from eastern Montana, riding the champion bull Doc Holiday . . . ," the announcer droned on.

Some men prayed before they got on a bull. Rafe had known plenty of cowboys to pray afterward, stretched out on the ground as a furious animal tried to trample their brains. But not Rafe. He hadn't prayed since . . . well, what good did it do to pray to a God who had turned His back on those who needed Him? No, worse.

God had responded to Rafe's desperate prayers with breath-stopping brutality. Yes, the Almighty had ripped his life out from under his feet, much like his brother, Nick, had done to the steers in his roping tournaments. Rafe wouldn't waste his breath.

Instead, Rafe found his strength in the anger that always seemed to whir inside him.

He snugged his hat down on his head and wrapped his free hand around the smooth top rail of the metal chute.

His sister, Stefanie, never understood why he rode. Couldn't grasp the fact that sometimes it just needed to be him against animal. That when he rode the bull for those full eight seconds, he felt, just for a fraction of time, alive.

The king of the world.

Invincible.

And he'd never even tried to explain it to Nick. His big brother wouldn't have a clue what it might feel like to always feel . . . less.

*"Don't ride tonight, Rafe."*

The voice crept up his spine as the bull shifted beneath him. He tightened his grip on the rail, took a deep breath, focused on the ride.

*For you, Mom. This is for you.*

Rafe nodded, and the chute opened.

The bull launched into the ring, and everything went silent as the world closed in around him. Heat seared his wrist, his arms, his legs, as the animal twisted. Rafe fought to keep his arm up as the bull threw him forward dangerously close to those killer horns. He barely missed cracking his nose on bone or lowering his hand for protection. The animal threw him again, and Rafe stiffened his arm, realigned his spur position, digging in.

Doc writhed, snorting, throwing back his head. Rafe's grip jarred, and pain spiked up his arm, but he kept his seat. *C'mon, bull, fight me.*

He'd not only have to stay on the bull, but Doc would need to give him a good ride to keep Rafe ahead of a feisty cowboy from Brazil. The two-man judging seemed to be favoring the international riders tonight—Aussies and Brazilians and Mexicans.

The bull seemed to hear him and stretched out into the air, landing with a jerk that rattled Rafe's teeth.

Suddenly, as if washed with cold water, Rafe heard the roar of the crowd.

The bull jerked his head, and his hindquarters changed direction.

Right then Rafe knew.

The bull had won.

Rafe tightened his spurs, but he could feel himself sliding. His bicep spasmed.

The bull bucked again.

And then he was off. Only not quite. Bound up by the bull rope, the rounded cow bell thrashing against him, Rafe flopped like a rag doll, fighting to free his hand as the bull flipped him.

The screams from the crowd branded him, made him wince. A hung-up bull rider terrified a crowd as they watched bones break, their admiration morphing to pity in a split second.

Manuel blurred past Rafe as the bull took him around and around. Something tore, probably his rotator cuff or his shoulder dislocating from the socket, and pain blinded him. For sure he'd broken at least one finger. Hopefully he wouldn't hit his head or snap a c-bone in his neck.

He thrashed again at the rope. *Please.*

He snared it. And just like that he fell free. He landed in the dirt, dazed. He barely managed to cover his head as the bull's lethal hooves landed beside him.

He had to find his feet. But the wind had left him, and darkness edged his sight.

"Rafe!" He heard Manuel's voice, felt hands grab his vest.

He looked up, past Manuel's dark expression, and in that moment everything went quiet, turned black and white. Then the voice. *"Don't ride tonight, Rafe."*

And, as he saw the bull's hooves crashing down over him, he knew Fear had spoken the truth.

Tonight someone would die.